The Reason Why

Elinor Glyn

Contents

CHAPTER I..7
CHAPTER II...13
CHAPTER III..19
CHAPTER IV..26
CHAPTER V..33
CHAPTER VI..40
CHAPTER VII...47
CHAPTER VIII...52
CHAPTER IX..58
CHAPTER X...65
CHAPTER XI..71
CHAPTER XII..77
CHAPTER XIII...86
CHAPTER XIV...91
CHAPTER XV...98
CHAPTER XVI..103
CHAPTER XVII..113
CHAPTER XVIII..119
CHAPTER XIX..126
CHAPTER XX...131
CHAPTER XXI..136
CHAPTER XXII..144
CHAPTER XXIII...152
CHAPTER XXIV...158
CHAPTER XXV...164
CHAPTER XXVI...170
CHAPTER XXVII..178
CHAPTER XXVIII..185
CHAPTER XXIX...191
CHAPTER XXX..199
CHAPTER XXXI...206
CHAPTER XXXII..214
CHAPTER XXXIII...219
CHAPTER XXXIV...225
CHAPTER XXXV..231
CHAPTER XXXVI...238
CHAPTER XXXVII..245
CHAPTER XXXVIII..253
CHAPTER XXXIX...260
CHAPTER XL...264
CHAPTER XLI..270
CHAPTER XLII...276

THE REASON WHY

BY

Elinor Glyn

CHAPTER I

People often wondered what nation the great financier, Francis Markrute, originally sprang from. He was now a naturalized Englishman and he looked English enough. He was slight and fair, and had an immaculately groomed appearance generally--which even the best of valets cannot always produce. He wore his clothes with that quiet, unconscious air which is particularly English. He had no perceptible accent--only a deliberate way of speaking. But Markrute!--such a name might have come from anywhere. No one knew anything about him, except that he was fabulously rich and had descended upon London some ten years previously from Paris, or Berlin, or Vienna, and had immediately become a power in the city, and within a year or so, had grown to be omnipotent in certain circles.

He had a wonderfully appointed house in Park Lane, one of those smaller ones just at the turn out of Grosvenor Street, and there he entertained in a reserved fashion.

It had been remarked by people who had time to think--rare cases in these days--that he had never made a disadvantageous friend, from his very first arrival. If he had to use undesirables for business purposes he used them only for that, in a crisp, hard way, and never went to their houses. Every acquaintance even was selected with care for a definite end. One of his favorite phrases was that "it is only the fool who coins for himself limitations."

At this time, as he sat smoking a fine cigar in his library which looked out on the park, he was perhaps forty-six years old or thereabouts, and but for his eyes--wise as serpents'--he might have been ten years younger.

Opposite to him facing the light a young man lounged in a great leather chair. The visitors in Francis Markrute's library nearly always faced the light, while he himself had his back to it.

There was no doubt about this visitor's nation! He was flamboyantly English. If you had wished to send a prize specimen of the race to a World's Fair you could not have selected anything finer. He was perhaps more Norman than Saxon, for his hair was dark though his eyes were blue, and the marks of breeding in the creature showed as plainly as in a Derby winner. Francis Markrute always smoked his cigars to the end, if he were at leisure and the weed happened to be a good one, but Lord Tancred (Tristram Lorrimer Guiscard Guiscard, 24th Baron Tancred, of Wrayth in the County of Suffolk) flung his into the grate after a few whiffs, and he laughed with a slightly whimsical bitterness as he went on with the conversation.

"Yes, Francis, my friend, the game here is played out; I am thirty, and there is nothing interesting left for me to do but emigrate to Canada, for a while at least, and take up a ranch."

"Wrayth mortgaged heavily, I suppose?" said Mr. Markrute, quietly.

"Pretty well, and the Northern property, too. When my mother's jointure is paid there is not a great deal left this year, it seems. I don't mind much; I had a pretty fair time before these beastly Radicals made things so difficult."

The financier nodded, and the young man went on: "My forbears got rid of what they could; there was not much ready money to come into and one had to live!"

Francis Markrute smoked for a minute thoughtfully.

"Naturally," he said at last. "Only the question is--for how long? I understand a plunge, if you settle its duration; it is the drifting and trusting to chance, and a gradual sinking which seem to me a poor game. Did you ever read de Musset's 'Rolla'?"

"The fellow who had arrived at his last night, and to whom the little girl was so kind? Yes: well?"

"You reminded me of Jacques Rolla, that is all."

"Oh, come! It is not as bad as that!" Lord Tancred exclaimed--and he laughed. "I can collect a few thousands still, even here, and I can go to Canada. I believe there is any quantity of money to be made there with a little capital, and it is a nice, open-air life. I just looked in this afternoon on my way back from Scotland to tell you I should be going out to prospect, about the end of November and could not join you for the pheasants on the 20th, as you were good enough to ask me to do."

The financier half closed his eyes. When he did this there was always something of importance working in his brain.

"You have not any glaring vices, Tancred," he said. "You are no gambler either on the turf or at cards. You are not over addicted to expensive ladies. You are cultivated, for a sportsman, and you have made one or two decent speeches in the House of Lords. You are, in fact, rather a fine specimen of your class. It seems a pity you should have to shut down and go to the Colonies."

"Oh, I don't know! And I have not altogether got to shut down," the young man said, "only the show is growing rather rotten over here. We have let the rabble--the most unfit and ignorant--have the casting vote, and the machine now will crush any man. I have kept out of politics as much as I can and I am glad."

Francis Markrute got up and lowered the blind a few inches--a miserable September sun was trying to shine into the room. If Lord Tancred had not been so preoccupied with his own thoughts he would have remarked this restlessness on the part of his host. He was no fool; but his mind was far away. It almost startled him when the cold, deliberate voice continued:

"I have a proposition to make to you should you care to accept it. I have a niece--a widow--she is rather an attractive lady. If you will marry her I will pay off all your mortgages and settle on her quite a princely dower."

"Good God!" said Lord Tancred.

The financier reddened a little about the temples, and his eyes for an instant gave forth a flash of steel. There had been an infinite variety of meanings hidden in the exclamation, but he demanded suavely:

"What point of the question causes you to exclaim 'Good God'?"

The sang-froid of Lord Tancred never deserted him.

"The whole thing," he said--"to marry at all, to begin with, and to marry an unknown woman, to have one's debts paid, for the rest! It is a tall order."

"A most common occurrence. Think of the number of your peers who have gone to America for their wives, for no other reason."

"And think of the rotters they are--most of them! I mayn't be much catch, financially; but I have one of the oldest names and titles in England--and up to now we have not had any cads nor cowards in the family, and I think a man who marries a woman for money is both. By Jove! Francis, what are you driving at? Confound it, man! I am not starving and can work, if it should ever come to that."

Mr. Markrute smoothed his hands. He was a peculiarly still person generally.

"Yes, it was a blunder, I admit, to put it this way. So I will be frank with you. My family is also, my friend, as old as yours. My niece is all I have left in the world. I would like to see her married to an Englishman. I would like to see her married to you of all Englishmen because I like you and you have qualities about you which count in life. Oh, believe me!"--and he raised a protesting finger to quell an inter-ruption--"I have studied you these years; there is nothing you can say of yourself or your affairs that I do not know."

Lord Tancred laughed.

"My dear old boy," he said, "we have been friends for a long time; and, now we are coming to hometruths, I must say I like your deuced cold-blooded point of view on every subject. I like your knowledge of wines and cigars and pictures, and you are a most entertaining companion. But, 'pon my soul I would not like to have your niece for a wife if she took after you!"

"You think she would be cold-blooded, too?"

"Undoubtedly; but it is all perfectly preposterous. I don't believe you mean a word you are saying--it is some kind of a joke."

"Have you ever known me to make such jokes, Tancred?" Mr. Markrute asked calmly.

"No, I haven't, and that is the odd part of it. What the devil do you mean, re-ally, Francis?"

"I mean what I say: I will pay every debt you have, and give you a charming wife with a fortune."

Lord Tancred got up and walked about the room. He was a perfectly natural creature, stolid and calm as those of his race, disciplined and deliberate in moments of danger or difficulty; yet he never lived under self-conscious control as the finan-cier did. He was rather moved now, and so he walked about. He was with a friend, and it was not the moment to have to bother over disguising his feelings.

"Oh, it is nonsense, Francis; I could not do it. I have knocked about the world as you know and, since you are aware of everything about me, you say, you have probably heard some of my likings--and dislikings. I never go after a woman unless she attracts me, and I would never marry one of them unless I were madly in love with her, whether she had money or no; though I believe I would hate a wife with money, in any case--she'd be saying like the American lady of poor Darrowood: 'It's my motor and you can't have it to-day.'"

"You would marry a woman then--if you were in love, in spite of everything?" Francis Markrute asked.

"Probably, but I have never been really in love; have you? It is all story-book stuff--that almighty passion, I expect. They none of them matter very much after a while, do they, old boy?"

"I have understood it is possible for a woman to matter," the financier said and he drew in his lips.

"Well, up to now I have not," Lord Tancred announced, "and may the day be far off when one does. I feel pretty safe!"

A strange, mysterious smile crept over Mr. Markrute's face.

"By the way, also, how do you know the lady would be willing to marry me, Francis? You spoke as if I only had to be consulted in the affair."

"So you have. I can answer for my niece; she will do as I wish, and, as I said before, you are rather a perfect picture of an English nobleman, Tancred. You have not found women recalcitrant, as a rule--no?"

Lord Tancred was not inordinately vain, though a man, and he had a sense of humor--so he laughed.

"'Pon my word it is amusing, your turning into a sort of matrimonial agent. Can't you see the fun of the thing yourself?"

"It seems quite natural to me. You have every social advantage to offer a woman, and a presentable person; and my niece has youth, and some looks, and a large fortune. But we will say no more about it. I shall be glad to be of any service I can to you, anyway, in regard to your Canadian scheme. Come and dine to-night; I happen to have asked a couple of railway magnates with interests out there, and you can get some information from them."

And so it was arranged, and Lord Tancred got up to go; but just at the door he paused and said with a laugh:

"And shall I see the niece?"

The financier had his back turned, and so he permitted the flicker of a smile to come over his mouth as he answered:

"It might be; but we have dismissed the subject of the niece."

And so they parted.

At the sound of the closing of the door Mr. Markrute pressed the button of a wonderful trifle of Russian enamel and emeralds, which lay on his writing table, and a quiet servant entered the room.

"Tell the Countess Shulski I wish to speak to her here immediately, please," he said. "Ask her to descend at once."

But he had to walk up and down several times, and was growing impatient, before the door opened and a woman came slowly into the room.

CHAPTER II

The financier paused in his restless pacing as he heard the door open and stood perfectly still, with his back to the light. The woman advanced and also stood still, and they looked at one another with no great love in their eyes, though she who had entered was well worth looking at, from a number of points of view. Firstly, she had that arresting, compelling personality which does not depend upon features, or coloring, or form, or beauty. A subtle force of character--a radiating magnetism--breathed from her whole being. When Zara Shulski came into any assemblage of people conversation stopped and speculation began.

She was rather tall and very slender; and yet every voluptuous curve of her lithe body refuted the idea of thinness. Her head was small and her face small, and short, and oval, with no wonderfully chiseled features, only the skin was quite exceptional in its white purity--not the purity of milk, but the purity of rich, white velvet, or a gardenia petal. Her mouth was particularly curved and red and her teeth were very even, and when she smiled, which was rarely, they suggested something of great strength, though they were small and white. And now I am coming to her two wonders, her eyes and her hair. At first you could have sworn the eyes were black; just great pools of ink, or disks of black velvet, set in their broad lids and shaded with jet lashes, but if they chanced to glance up in the full light then you knew they were slate color, not a tinge of brown or green--the whole iris was a uniform shade: strange, slumberous, resentful eyes, under straight, thick, black brows, the expression full of all sorts of meanings, though none of them peaceful or calm. And from some far back Spanish-Jewess ancestress she probably got that glorious head of red hair, the color of a ripe chestnut when it falls from its shell, or a beautifully groomed bright bay horse. The heavy plaits which were wound tightly round her head must have fallen below her knees when they were undone. Her coiffure gave you the impression that she never thought of fashion, nor changed its form of dressing, from year to year. And the exquisite planting of the hair on her forehead, as it waved back in broad waves, added to the perfection of the Greek simplicity of the whole thing. Nothing about her had been aided by conscious art. Her dress, of some black clinging stuff, was rather poor, though she wore it with the air of a traditional empress. Indeed, she looked an empress, from the tips of her perfect fingers to her small arched feet.

And it was with imperial hauteur that she asked in a low, cultivated voice with no accent:

"Well, what is it? Why have you sent for me thus peremptorily?"

The financier surveyed her for a moment; he seemed to be taking in all her points with a fresh eye. It was almost as though he were counting them over to himself--and his thoughts ran: "You astonishingly attractive devil. You have all the pride of my father, the Emperor. How he would have gloried in you! You are enough to drive any man mad: you shall be a pawn in my game for the winning of my lady and gain happiness for yourself, so in the end, Elinka, if she is able to see from where she has gone, will not say I have been cruel to you."

"I asked you to come down--to discuss a matter of great importance: Will you be good enough to be seated, my niece," he said aloud with ceremonious politeness as he drew forward a chair--into which she sank without more ado and there waited, with folded hands, for him to continue. Her stillness was always as intense as his own, but whereas his had a nervous tension of conscious repression, hers had an unconscious, quiet force. Her father had been an Englishman, but both uncle and niece at moments made you feel they were silent panthers, ready to spring.

"So--" was all she said.

And Francis Markrute went on:

"You have a miserable position--hardly enough to eat at times, one understands. You do not suppose I took the trouble to send for you from Paris last week, for nothing, do you? You guessed I had some plan in my head, naturally."

"Naturally," she said, with fine contempt. "I did not mistake it for philanthropy."

"Then it is well, and we can come to the point," he went on. "I am sorry I have had to be away, since your arrival, until yesterday. I trust my servants have made you comfortable?"

"Quite comfortable," she answered coldly.

"Good: now for what I want to know. You have no doubt in your mind that your husband, Count Ladislaus Shulski, is dead? There is no possible mistake in his identity? I believe the face was practically shot away, was it not? I have taken the precaution to inform myself upon every point, from the authorities at Monte Carlo, but I wish for your final testimony."

"Ladislaus Shulski is dead," she said quietly, in a tone as though it gave her pleasure to say it. "The woman Feto caused the fray, Ivan Larski shot him in her arms; he was her lover who paid, and Ladislaus the ***amant du coeur*** for the moment. She wailed over the body like a squealing rabbit. She was there lamenting his fine eyes when they sent for me! They were gone for ever, but no one could mistake his curly hair, nor his cruel, white hands. Ah! it was a scene of disgust! I have witnessed many ugly things but that was of the worst. I do not wish to talk of it; it is passed a year ago. Feto heaped his grave with flowers, and joined the hero, Larski, who was allowed to escape, so all was well."

"And since then you have lived from hand to mouth, with those others." And here Francis Markrute's voice took on a new shade: there was a cold hate in it.

"I have lived with my little brother, Mirko, and Mimo. How could I desert them? And sometimes we have found it hard at the end of the quarter--but it was not always as bad as that, especially when Mimo sold a picture--"

"I will not hear his name!" Francis Markrute said with some excitement. "In the beginning, if I could have found him I would have killed him, as you know, but now the carrion can live, since my sister is dead. He is not worth powder and shot."

The Countess Shulski gave the faintest shrug of her shoulders, while her eyes grew blacker with resentment. She did not speak. Francis Markrute stood by the mantelpiece, and lit a cigar before he continued; he knew he must choose his words as he was dealing with no helpless thing.

"You are twenty-three years old, Zara, and you were married at sixteen," he said at last. "And up to thirteen at least I know you were very highly educated--You understand something of life, I expect."

"Life!" she said--and now there was a concentrated essence of bitterness in her voice. "Mon Dieu! Life--and men!"

"Yes, you probably think you know men."

She lifted her upper lip a little, and showed her even teeth--it was like an animal snarling.

"I know that they are either selfish weaklings, or cruel, hateful brutes like Ladislaus, or clever, successful financiers like you, my uncle. That is enough! Something we women must be always sacrificed to."

"Well, you don't know Englishmen--"

"Yes, I remember my father very well; cold and hard to my darling mother"--and here her voice trembled a little--"he only thought of himself, and to rush to England for sport--and leave her alone for months and months: selfish and vile--all of them!"

"In spite of that I have found you an English husband whom you will be good enough to take, madame," Francis Markrute announced authoritatively.

She gave a little laugh--if anything so mirthless could be called a laugh.

"You have no power over me; I shall do no such thing."

"I think you will," the financier said with quiet assurance, "if I know you. There are terms, of course--"

She glanced at him sharply: the expression in those somber eyes was often alert like a wild animal's, about to be attacked; only she had trained herself generally to keep the lids lowered.

"What are the terms?" she asked.

And as she spoke Francis Markrute thought of the black panther in the Zoo, which he was so fond of going to watch on Sunday mornings, she reminded him so of the beast at the moment.

He had been constrained up to this, but now, the question being one of business, all his natural ease of manner returned, and he sat down opposite her and blew rings of smoke from his cigar.

"The terms are that the boy Mirko, your half-brother, shall be provided for for life. He shall live with decent people, and have his talent properly cultivated--"

He stopped abruptly and remained silent.

Countess Shulski clasped her hands convulsively in her lap, and with all the pride and control of her voice there was a note of anguish, too, which would have touched any heart but one so firmly guarded as Francis Markrute's.

"Ah, God!" she said so low that he could only just hear her, "I have paid the price of my body and soul once for them. It is too much to ask it of me a second time--"

"That is as you please," said the financier.

He seldom made a mistake in his methods with people. He left nothing to chance; he led up the conversation to the right point, fired his bomb, and then showed absolute indifference. To display interest in a move, when one was really interested, was always a point to the adversary. He maintained interest could be simulated when necessary, but must never be shown when real. So he left his niece in silence, while she pondered over his bargain, knowing full well what would be the result. She got up from her chair and leaned upon the back of it, while her face looked white as death in the dying afternoon's light.

"Can you realize what my life was like with Ladislaus?" she hissed. "A plaything for his brutal pleasures, to begin with; a decoy duck to trap the other men, I found afterwards; tortured and insulted from morning to night. I hated him always, but he seemed so kind beforehand--kind to my darling mother, whom you were leaving to die."--Here Francis Markrute winced and a look of pain came into his hard face while he raised a hand in protest and then dropped it again, as his niece went on--"And she was beginning to be ill even at that time and we were so poor--so I married him."

Then she swept toward the door with her empress air, the rather shabby, dark dress making a swirl behind her; and as she got there she turned and spoke again, with her hand on the bronze tracery of the fingerplate, making, unconsciously, a highly dramatic picture, as a sudden last ray of the sinking sun shot out and struck the glory of her hair, turning it to flame above her brow.

"I tell you it is too much," she said, with almost a sob in her voice. "I will not do it." And then she went out and closed the door.

Francis Markrute, left alone, leant back in his chair and puffed his cigar calmly while he mused.

What strange things were women! Any man could manage them if only he reckoned with their temperaments when dealing with them, and paid no heed to their actual words. Francis Markrute was a philosopher. A number of the shelves of this, his library, were filled with works on the subject of philosophy, and a well-thumbed volume of the fragments of Epicurus lay on a table by his side. He picked it up now and read: "He who wastes his youth on high feeding, on wine, on women, forgets that he is like a man who wears out his overcoat in the summer." He had not wasted his youth either on wine or women, only he had studied both, and their effects upon the thing which, until lately, had interested him most in the world-- himself. They could both be used to the greatest advantage and pleasure by a man who apprehended things he knew.

Then he turned to the ***Morning Post*** which was on a low stand near, and he read again a paragraph which had pleased him at breakfast:

"The Duke of Glastonbury and Lady Ethelrida Montfitchet entertained at dinner last night a small party at Glastonbury House, among the guests being--" and here he skipped some high-sounding titles and let his eye feast upon his own name, "Mr. Francis Markrute."

Then he smiled and gazed into the fire, and no one would have recognized his hard, blue eyes, as he said softly:

"Ethelrida! ***belle et blonde!***"

CHAPTER III

While the financier was contentedly musing in his chair beside the fire, his niece was hurrying into the park, wrapped in a dark cloak and thick veil. She had slipped out noiselessly, a few minutes after she left the library. The sun had completely set now and it was damp and cold, with the dead leaves, and the sodden autumn feeling in the air. Zara Shulski shivered, in spite of the big cloak, as she peered into the gloom of the trees, when she got nearly to the Achilles statue. The rendezvous had been for six o'clock; it was now twenty minutes past, and it was so bad for Mirko to wait in the cold. Perhaps they would have gone on. But no; she caught sight of two shabby figures, close up under the statue, when she got sufficiently near.

They came forward eagerly to meet her. And even in the half light it could be seen that the boy was an undersized little cripple of perhaps nine or ten years old but looking much younger; as it could also be seen that even in his worn overcoat and old stained felt hat the man was a gloriously handsome creature.

"What joy to see you, Cherisette!" exclaimed the child. "Papa and I have been longing and longing all the day. It seemed that six would never come. But now that you are here let me eat you--eat you up!" And the thin, little arms, too long for the wizened body, clasped fondly round her neck as she lifted him, and carried him toward a seat where the three sat down to discuss their affairs.

"I know nothing, you see, Mimo," the Countess Shulski said, "beyond that you arrived yesterday. I think it was foolish of you to risk it. At least in Paris Madame Dubois would have let you stay and owe a week's rent. But here--among these strangers--"

"Now do not scold us, Mentor," the man answered, with a charming smile. "Mirko and I felt the sun had fled when you went last Thursday. It rained and rained two--three--days, and the Dubois canary got completely on our nerves; and, heavens above! the Grisoldi insisted upon cooking garlic in his food at every meal!--we had thought to have broken him of the habit, you remember?--and up, up it came from his stove. Body of Bacchus! It killed inspiration. I could not paint, my Cherisette, and Mirko could not play. And so we said: 'At least--at least the sun of the hair of our Cherisette must shine in the dark England; we, too, will go there, away from the garlic and the canary, and the fogs will give us new ideas, and we shall create wonderful things.' Is it not so, Mirko mio?"

"But, of course, Papa," the boy echoed; and then his voice trembled with a pitiful note. "You are not angry with us, darling Cherisette? Say it is not so?"

"My little one! How can you! I could never be angry with my Mirko, no matter what he did!" And the two pools of ink softened from the expression of the black panther into the divine tenderness of the Sistine Madonna, as she pressed the frail, little body to her side and pulled her cloak around it.

"Only I fear it cannot be well for you here in London, and if my uncle should know, all hope of getting anything from him may be over. He expressly said if I would come quite alone, to stay with him for these few weeks, it would be to my advantage; and my advantage means yours, as you know. Otherwise do you think I would have eaten of his hateful bread?"

"You are so good to us, Cherisette," the man Mimo said. "You have, indeed, a sister of the angels, Mirko mio; but soon we shall be all rich and famous. I had a dream last night, and already I have begun a new picture of grays and mists--of these strange fogs!"

Count Mimo Sykypri was a confirmed optimist.

"Meanwhile you are in the one room, in Neville Street, Tottenham Court Road. It is, I fear, a poor neighborhood."

"No worse than Madame Dubois'," Mimo hastened to reassure her, "and London is giving me new ideas."

Mirko coughed harshly with a dry sound. Countess Shulski drew him closer to her and held him tight.

"You got the address from the Grisoldi? He was a kind little old man, in spite of the garlic," she said.

"Yes, he told us of it, as an inexpensive resting place, until our affairs prospered, and we came straight there and wrote to you at once."

"I was greatly surprised to receive the letter. Have you any money at all now, Mimo?"

"Indeed, yes!" And Count Sykypri proudly drew forth eight bits of French gold from his pocket. "We had two hundred francs when we arrived. Our little necessities and a few paints took up two of the twenty-franc pieces, and we have eight of them left! Oh, quite a fortune! It will keep us until I can sell the 'Apache.' I shall take it to a picture dealer's to-morrow."

Countess Shulski's heart sank. She knew so well of old how long eight twenty-franc pieces would be likely to last! In spite of Mirko's care and watching of his father that gentleman was capable of giving one of them to a beggar if the beggar's face and story touched him, and any of the others could go in a present to Mirko or herself--to be pawned later, when necessity called. The case was hopeless as far as money was concerned with Count Sykypri.

Her own meager income, derived from the dead Shulski, was always forestalled for the wants of the family--the little brother whom she had promised her dead and adored mother never to desert.

For when the beautiful wife of Maurice Grey, the misanthropic and eccentric Englishman who lived in a castle near Prague, ran off with Count Mimo Sykypri, her daughter, then aged thirteen, had run with her, and the pair had been wiped off the list of the family. And Maurice Grey, after cursing them both and making a will depriving them of everything, shut himself up in his castle, and steadily drank himself to death in less than a year. And the brother of the beautiful Mrs. Grey, Francis Markrute, never forgave her either. He refused to receive her or hear news of her, even after poor little Mirko was born and she married Count Sykypri.

For on the father's side, the Markrute brother and sister were of very noble lineage; even with his bar sinister the financier could not brook the disgrace of Elinka. He had loved her so--the one soft side of his adamantine character. Her disgrace, it seemed, had frozen all the tenderness in his nature.

Countess Shulski was silent for a few moments, while both Mimo and Mirko watched her face anxiously. She had thrown back her veil.

"And supposing you do not sell the 'Apache,' Mimo? Your own money does not come in until Christmas; mine is all gone until January, and it is the cold winter approaching--and cold is not good for Mirko. What then?"

Count Sykypri moved uneasily. A tragic look grew in his handsome face; his face that was a mirror of all passing emotions; his face that had been able to express love and romance, devotion and tenderness, to wile a bird from off a tree or love from the heart of any woman. And even though Zara Shulski knew of just how little value was anything he said or did yet his astonishing charm always softened her irritation toward his fecklessness. So she repeated more gently:

"What then?"

Mimo got up and flung out his arms in a dramatic way.

"It cannot be!" he said. "I must sell the 'Apache!' Besides, if I don't: I tell you these strange, gray fogs are giving me new, wonderful thoughts--dark, mysterious--two figures meeting in the mist! Oh! but a wonderful combination that will be successful in all cases."

Mirko pressed his arm round his sister's neck and kissed her cheek, while he cooed love words in a soft Slavonic language. Two big tears gathered in Zara Shulski's deep eyes and made them tender as a dove's.

She drew out her purse and counted from it two sovereigns and some shillings which she slipped into Mirko's small hand.

"Keep these, pet, for an emergency," she said. "They are all I have, but I will--I must--find some other way for you soon: and now I shall have to go. If my uncle should suspect I am seeing you I might be powerless to help further."

They walked with her to the Grosvenor Gate, and reluctantly let her leave them; and then they watched her, as she sped across the road between the passing taxi-cabs. When they saw the light from the opening door and her figure disappearing between the tall servants who had come to open it, the two poor, shabby figures walked on with a sigh, to try to find an omnibus which would put them down somewhere near their dingy bedroom in Neville Street, Tottenham Court Road. And as they reached the Marble Arch there came on a sharp shower of icy rain.

Countess Shulski, however poorly dressed, was a person to whom servants were never impertinent; there was something in her bearing which precluded all idea of familiarity. It did not even strike Turner, or James, that her clothes were what none of the housemaids would have considered fit to wear when they went out. The remark the lordly Turner made, as he arranged some letters on the hall table, was:

"A very haughty lady, James--quite a bit of the Master about her, eh?"

But she went on to the lift, slowly, and to her luxurious bedroom, her heart full of pain and rage against fate. Here she sat down before the fire, and, resting her chin on her two hands, gazed steadily into the glowing coals.

What pictures did she see of past miseries there in the flames? Her thoughts wandered right back to the beginning. The stern, peculiar father, and the gloomy castle. The severe governesses--English and German--and her adorable, beautiful mother, descending upon the schoolroom like a fairy of light, always gay and sweet and loving. And then of that journey to a far country, where she saw an old, old, dying gentleman in a royal palace, who kissed her, and told her she would grow as beautiful as her grandmother with the red, red hair. And there in the palace was Mimo, so handsome and kind in his glittering aide-de-camp's uniform, who after that often came to the gloomy castle, and, with the fairy mother, to the schoolroom. Ah! those days were happy days! How they three had shrieked with laughter and played hide-and-seek in the long galleries!

And then the blank, hideous moment when the angel fairy had gone, and the stern father cursed and swore, and Uncle Francis' face looked like a vengeful fiend's. And then a day when she got word to meet her mother in the park of the castle. How she clung to her and cried and sobbed to be taken, too! And they--Mimo and the mother--always so kind and loving and irresponsible, consented. And then the flight; and weeks of happiness in luxurious hotels, until the mother's face grew pinched and white, and no letters but her own--returned--came from Uncle Francis. And ever the fear grew that if Mimo were absent from her for a moment Uncle Francis would kill him. The poor, adored mother! And then of the coming of Mirko and all their joy over it; and then, gradually, the skeleton of poverty, when all the jewels had been sold and all Mimo's uniform and swords; and nothing but his slender income, which could not be taken from him, remained. How he had worked to be a real artist, there in Paris! Oh! poor Mimo. He had tried, but everything was so against a gentleman; and Mirko such a delicate baby, and the mother's lovely face so often sad. And then the time of the mother's first bad illness--how they had watched and prayed, and Mimo had cried tears like a child, and the doctor had said the South was the only thing to help their angel's recovery. So to marry Ladislaus Shulski seemed the only way. He had a villa in the sun at Nice and offered it to them; he was crazy about her--Zara--at that time, though her skirts were not quite long, nor her splendid hair done up.

When her thoughts reached this far, the black panther in the Zoo never looked fiercer when Francis Markrute poked his stick between its bars to stir it up on Sunday mornings.

The hateful, hateful memories! When she came to know what marriage meant, and--a man! But it had saved the sweet mother's life for that winter. And though it was a strain to extract anything from Ladislaus, still, in the years that followed, often she had been able to help until his money, too, was all gone--on gambling and women.

And then the dear mother died--died in cold and poverty, in a poor little studio in Paris--in spite of her daughter's and Mimo's frantic letters to Uncle Francis for help. She knew now that he had been far away, in South Africa, at the time, and had never received them, until too late; but then, it seemed as if God Himself had forsaken them. And now came the memory of her solemn promise. Mirko should never be deserted--the adored mother could die in peace about that. Her last words came back now--out of the glowing coals:

"I have been happy with Mimo, after all, my Cherisette, with you and Mimo and Mirko. It was worth while--" And so she had gasped--and died.

And here the tears gathered and blurred the flaming coals. But Zara's decision had come. There was no other way. To her uncle's bargain she must consent.

She got up abruptly and flung her hat on the bed--her cloak had already fallen from her--and without further hesitation she descended the stairs.

Francis Markrute was still seated in his library; he had taken out his watch and was calculating the time. It was twenty-five minutes to eight; his guests would be coming to dine at eight o'clock and he had not begun to dress. Would his niece have made up her mind by then?

That there could be any doubt about the fact that she would make up her mind as he wished never entered his head. It was only a question of time but it would be better, for every reason, if she arrived at the conclusion at once.

He rose from his chair with a quiet smile as she entered the room. So she had come! He had not relied upon his knowledge of a woman's temperament in vain.

She was very pale. The extra whiteness showed even on her gardenia skin, and her great eyes gleamed sullenly from beneath her lowering brows of ink.

"If the terms are for the certain happiness of Mirko I consent," she said.

CHAPTER IV

The four men--the two railway magnates, Francis Markrute, and Lord Tancred--had all been waiting a quarter of an hour before the drawing-room fire when the Countess Shulski sailed into the room. She wore an evening gown of some thin, black, transparent, woolen stuff, which clung around her with the peculiar grace her poorest clothes acquired. Another woman would have looked pitifully shabby in such a dress, but her distinction made it appear to at least three of the men as the robe of a goddess. Francis Markrute was too annoyed at the delay of her coming to admire anything; but even he, as he presented his guests to her, could not help remarking that he had never seen her look more wonderful, nor more contemptuously regal.

They had had rather a stormy scene in the library, half an hour before. Her words had been few, but their displeasure had been unconcealed. She would agree to the bare bargain, if so be this strange man were willing, but she demanded to know the reason of his willingness.

And when she was told it was a business matter between the two men, and that she would be given a large fortune, she expressed no more surprise than a disdainful curl of the lips.

For her, all men were either brutes--or fools like poor Mimo.

If she had known that Lord Tancred had already refused her hand and that her uncle was merely counting upon his own unerring knowledge of human nature--and Lord Tancred's nature in particular--she might have felt humiliated, instead of full of impotent rage.

The young man, for his part, had arrived exactly on the stroke of eight, a rare effort of punctuality for him. Some underneath excitement to see his friend Markrute's niece had tingled in his veins from the moment he had left the house.

What sort of a woman could it be who would be willing to marry a perfect stranger for the sake of his title and position? The quarter-of-an-hour's wait had not added to his calm. So when the door had eventually opened for her entry he had glanced up with intense interest, and had then drawn in his breath as she advanced up the room. The physical part of the lady at all events was extremely delectable.

But when he was presented and his eyes met hers he was startled by the look of smoldering, somber hate he saw in them.

What could it all mean? Francis must have been romancing. Why should she look at him like that, if she were willing to marry him? He was piqued and interested.

She spoke not a word as they went down to dinner, but he was no raw youth to be snubbed thus into silence. His easy, polished manner soon started a conversation upon the usual everyday things. He received "Yes" and "No" for answers. The railway magnate on her other side was hardly more fortunate, until the entrees were in full swing, then she unfroze a little; the elderly gentleman had said something which interested her.

The part which particularly irritated Lord Tancred was that he felt sure she was not really stupid--who could be stupid with such a face? And he was quite unaccustomed to being ignored by women. A like experience had not occurred to him in the whole of his life.

He watched her narrowly. He had never seen so white a skin; the admirably formed bones of her short, small face caused, even in a side light, no disfiguring shadows to fall beside the mouth and nose, nor on the cheeks; all was velvety smooth and rounded. The remote Jewish touch was invisible--save in the splendor of the eyes and lashes. She filled him with the desire to touch her, to clasp her tightly in his arms, to pull down that glorious hair and bury his face in it. And Lord Tancred was no sensualist, given to instantly appraising the outward charm of women.

When the grouse was being handed, he did get a whole sentence from her; it was in answer to his question whether she liked England.

"How can one say--when one does not know?" she said. "I have only been here once before, when I was quite a child. It seems cold and dark."

"We must persuade you to like it better," he answered, trying to look into her eyes which she had instantly averted. The expression of resentment still smoldered there, he had noticed, during their brief glance.

"Of what consequence whether I like it or no," she said, looking across the table, and this was difficult to answer! It seemed to set him upon his beam-ends. He could not very well say because he had suddenly begun to admire her very much! At this stage he had not decided what he meant to do.

An unusual excitement was permeating his being; he could not account for how or why. He had felt no sensation like it, except on one of his lion hunts in Africa when the news had come into camp that an exceptionally fine beast had been discovered near and might be stalked on the morrow. His sporting instincts seemed to be thoroughly awakened.

Meanwhile Countess Shulski had turned once more to Sir Philip Armstrong, the railway magnate. He was telling her about Canada and she listened with awakening interest: how there were openings for every one and great fortunes could be made there by the industrious and persevering.

"It has not come to a point, then, when artists could have a chance, I suppose?" she asked. Lord Tancred wondered at the keenness in her voice.

"Modern artists?" Sir Philip queried. "Perhaps not, though the rich men are beginning to buy pictures and beautiful things, too; but in a new country it is the man of sinew and determination, not the dreamer, who succeeds."

Her head then drooped a little; her interest now seemed only mechanical, as she answered again, "Yes" and "No."

Lord Tancred wondered and wondered; he saw that her thoughts were far away.

Francis Markrute had been watching things minutely while he kept up his suave small talk with Colonel Macnamara on his right hand. He was well pleased with the turn of events. After all, nothing could have been better than Zara's being late. Circumstance often played into the hand of an experienced manipulator like himself. Now if she only kept up this attitude of indifference, which, indeed, she seemed likely to do--she was no actress, he knew--things might be settled this very night.

Lord Tancred could not get her to have a single continued conversation for the remainder of dinner; he was perfectly raging with annoyance, his fighting blood was up. And when at the first possible moment after the dessert arrived she swept from the room, her eyes met his as he held the door and they were again full of contemptuous hate.

He returned to his seat with his heart actually thumping in his side.

And all through the laborious conversation upon Canada and how best to invest capital, which Francis Markrute with great skill and apparently hearty friendship prolonged to its utmost limits, he felt the attraction and irritation of the woman grow and grow. He no longer took the slightest interest in the pros and cons of his future in the Colony, and when, at last, he heard the distant tones of Tschaikovsky's *Chanson Triste* as they ascended the stairs he came suddenly to a determination. She was sitting at the grand piano in the back part of the room. A huge, softly shaded lamp shed its veiled light upon her white face and rounded throat; her hands and arms, which showed to the elbow, seemed not less pale than the ivory keys, and those disks of black velvet gazed in front of them, a whole world of anguish in their depths.

For this was the tune that her mother had loved, and she was playing it to remind herself of her promise and to keep herself firm in her determination to accept the bargain, for her little brother Mirko's sake.

She glanced at Lord Tancred as he entered. Count Ladislaus Shulski had been a very handsome man, too. She did not know enough of the English type to judge of Lord Tancred morally. She only saw that he was a splendid, physical creature who would be strong--and horrible probably--like the rest.

The whole expression of her face changed as he came and leaned upon the piano. The sorrow died out of her eyes and was replaced by a fierce defiance; and her fingers broke into a tarantella of wild sounds.

"You strange woman!" Lord Tancred said.

"Am I strange?" she answered through her teeth. "It is said by those who know that we are all mad--at some time and at some point. I have, I think, reason to be mad to-night." And with that she crashed a final chord, rose from her seat, and crossed the room.

"I hope, Uncle Francis, your guests will excuse me," she said, with an imperial, aloof politeness, "but I am very tired. I will wish you all a good-night." She bowed to them as they expressed their regrets, and then slowly left the room.

"Goodnight, madame," Lord Tancred said, at the door. "Some day you and I will cross swords."

But he was rewarded by no word, only an annihilating glance from her sullen eyes, and he stood there and gazed at her as she passed up the stairs.

"An extraordinary and beautiful woman--your niece--eh, my dear Markrute?" he heard one of the pompous gentlemen say, as he returned to the group by the fire, and it angered him--he could not have told why.

Francis Markrute, who knew his moments, began now to talk about her, casually; how she was an interesting, mysterious character; beautiful? well, no, not exactly that--a superlative skin, fine eyes and hair, but no special features.

"I will not admit that she is beautiful, my friend," he said. "Beauty suggests gentleness and tenderness. My niece reminds me of the black panther in the Zoo, but one could not say--if she were tamed."

Such remarks were not calculated to allay the growing interest and attraction Lord Tancred was feeling. Francis Markrute knew his audience; he never wasted his words. He abruptly turned the conversation back to Canada again, until even the two magnates on their own ground were bored and said goodnight. The four men came downstairs together. As the two others were being assisted into their coats by Turner and his satellites the host said to Lord Tancred:

"Will you have a cigar with me, Tancred, before you go on to your supper party?" And presently they were both seated in mammoth armchairs in the cozy library.

"I hope, my dear boy, you have all the information you want about Canada," Mr. Markrute said. "You could not find two more influential people than Sir Philip and the Colonel. I asked--" but Lord Tancred interrupted him.

"I don't care a farthing more about Canada!" he flashed out. "I have made up my mind. If you really meant what you said to-day, I will marry your niece, and I don't care whether she has a penny or no."

The financier's plans had indeed culminated with a rush!

But he expressed no surprise, merely raised his eyebrows mildly and puffed some blue rings of smoke, as he answered:

"I always mean what I say, only I do not care for people to do things blindly. Now that you have seen my niece are you sure she would suit you? I thought, after all, perhaps not, to-night: she is certainly a difficult person. It would be no easy task for any man to control her--as a wife."

"I don't care for tame women," Lord Tancred said. "It is that very quality of difficulty which has inspired me. By George! did you ever see such a haughty bearing? It will take a man's whole intelligence to know which bit to use."

"She may close her teeth on whatever bit you use, and bolt with it. Do not say afterwards that I let you take her blindly."

"Why does she look at me with such hate?" Lord Tancred was just going to ask--and then he stopped himself. It was characteristic of him that now he had made up his mind he would not descend to questions or details--he would find all out later for himself--but one thing he must know: had she really consented to marry him? If so, she had her own reasons, of course, and desire for himself was not among them; but, somehow, he felt sure they were not sordid or paltry ones. He had always liked dangerous games--the most unbroken polo ponies to train in the country, the freshest horses, the fiercest beasts to stalk and kill--and why not a difficult wife? It would add an adorable spice to the affair. But as he was very honest with himself he knew, underneath, that it was not wholly even this instinct, but that she had cast some spell over him and that he must have her for his own.

"You might very well ask her history," Francis Markrute said. He could be so gracious when he liked, and he really admired the wholehearted dash with which Lord Tancred had surrendered; there was something big and royal about it--he himself never gambled in small sums either. "So as I expect you won't," he continued, "I will tell you. She is the daughter of Maurice Grey, a brother of old Colonel Grey of Hentingdon, whom everybody knew, and she has been the widow of an unspeakable brute for over a year. She was an immaculate wife, and devoted daughter before that. The possibilities of her temperament are all to come."

Lord Tancred sprang from his chair, the very thought of her and her temperament made him thrill. Was it possible he was already in love, after one evening?

"Now we must really discuss affairs, my dear boy," the financier went on. "Her dower, as I told you, will be princely."

"That I absolutely refuse to do, Francis," Lord Tancred answered. "I tell you I want the woman for my wife. You can settle the other things with my lawyer if you care to, and tie it all up on her. I am not interested in that matter. The only thing I really wish to know is if you are sure she will marry me?"

"I am perfectly sure." The financier narrowed his eyes. "I would not have suggested the affair to-day if I had had any doubt about that."

"Then it is settled, and I shall not ask why. I shall not ask any thing. Only when may I see her again and how soon can we be married?"

"Come and lunch with me in the city to-morrow, and we will talk over everything. I shall have seen her, and can then tell you when to present yourself. And I suppose you can have the ceremony at the beginning of November?"

"Six whole weeks hence!" Lord Tancred said, protestingly. "Must she get such heaps of clothes? Can't it be sooner? I wanted to be here for my Uncle Glastonbury's first shoot on the 2nd of November, and if we are only married then, we shall be off on a honeymoon. You must come to that shoot, by-the-way, old boy, it is the pleasantest of the whole lot he has; one day at the partridges, and a dash at the pheasants; but he only asks the jolliest parties to this early one, for Ethelrida's birthday, and none of the bores."

"It would give me great pleasure to do so," Francis Markrute said. And he looked down so that Lord Tancred should not see the joy in his eyes.

Then they shook hands most heartily, and the newly made fiance said good-night, with the happy assurance in his ears that he might claim his bride in time to be back from a week's honeymoon for the Glastonbury shoot.

When he had gone Francis Markrute's first act was to sit down and write a four-figure check for the Cripple Children's Hospital: he believed in thankofferings. Then he rubbed his hands softly together as he went up to his bed.

CHAPTER V

Then Lord Tancred left the house in Park Lane he did not go on to the supper party at the Savoy he had promised to attend. That sort of affair had bored him, now for several years. Instead, he drove straight back to his rooms in St. James' Street, and, getting comfortably into his pet chair, he steadily set himself to think. He had acted upon a mad impulse; he knew that and did not argue with himself about it, or regret it. Some force stronger than anything he had hitherto known had compelled him to come to the decision. And what would his future life be like with this strange woman? That could not be exactly guessed. That it would contain scenes of the greatest excitement he did not doubt. She would in all cases look the part. His mother herself--the Lady Tancred, daughter of the late and sister of the present Duke of Glastonbury--could not move with more dignity: a thought which reminded him that he had better write to his parent and inform her of his intended step. He thought of all the women he had loved--or imagined he had loved--since he left Eton. The two affairs which had convulsed him during his second year at Oxford were perhaps the most serious; the Laura Highford, his last episode, was fortunately over and had always been rather tiresome. In any case none of those ladies of the world--or other world--had any reasons to reproach him, and he was free and happy. And if he wished to put down a large stake on the card of marriage he was answerable to no one.

During the last eight hundred years, ever since Amaury Guiscard of that house of Hauteville whose daring deeds gave sovereigns to half Europe, had come over with his Duke William, and had been rewarded by the gift of the Wrayth lands-- seized from the Saxons--his descendants had periodically done madly adventurous things. Perhaps the quality was coming out in him!

Then he thought of his lady, personally, and not of the extraordinariness of his action. She was exasperatingly attractive. How delicious it would be when he had persuaded her to talk to him, taught her to love him, because she certainly must love him--some day! It was rather cold-blooded of her to be willing to marry him, a stranger; but he was not going to permit himself to dwell upon that. She could not be really cold-blooded with that face: its every line bespoke capability of exquisite passion. It was not the least cunning, or calculating, either. It was simply adorable. And to kiss! But here he pulled himself together and wrote to his mother a note, short and to the point, which she received by the first post next morning at her small, house in Queen Street, Mayfair; and then he went to bed. The note ran:

"My Dear Mother:

"I am going to be married at last. The lady is a daughter of Maurice Grey (a brother of old Colonel Grey of Hentingdon who died last year), and the widow of a Pole named Shulski, Countess Shulski she is called."

(He had paused here because he had suddenly remembered he did not know her Christian name!)

"She is also the niece of Francis Markrute whom you have such an objection to--or had, last season. She is most beautiful and I hope you will like her. Please go and call to-morrow. I will come and breakfast with you about ten.

"Your affectionate son, Tancred."

And this proud English mother knew here was a serious letter, because he signed it "Tancred." He usually finished his rare communications with just, "love from Tristram."

She leaned back on her pillows and closed her eyes. She adored her son but she was, above all things, a woman of the world and given to making reasonable judgments. Tristram was past the age of a foolish entanglement; there must be some strong motive in this action. He could hardly be in love. She knew him so well, when he was in love! He had shown no signs of it lately--not, really, for several years--for that well conducted--friendship--with Laura Highford could not be called being in love. Then she thought of Francis Markrute. He was so immensely rich, she could not help a relieved sigh. There would be money at all events. But she knew that could not be the reason. She was aware of her son's views about rich wives. She was aware, too, that with all his sporting tastes and modern irreverence of tradition, underneath he was of a proud, reserved nature, intensely proud of the honor of his ancient name. What then could be the reason for this engagement? Well, she would soon know. It was half-past eight in the morning, and Tristram's "about ten" would not mean later than, half-past, or a quarter to eleven. She rang the bell for her maid, and told her to ask the young ladies to put on dressing-gowns and come to her.

Soon Lord Tancred's two sisters entered the room.

They were nice, fresh English girls, and stood a good deal in awe of their mother. They kissed her and sat down on the bed. They felt it was a momentous moment, because Lady Tancred never saw any one until her hair was arranged--not even her own daughters.

"Your brother Tristram is going to be married," she said and referred to the letter lying on the coverlet, "to a Countess Shulski, a niece of that Mr. Markrute whom one meets about."

"Oh! Mother!" and "Really!" gasped Emily and Mary.

"Have we seen her?"

"Do we know her?"

"No, I think we can none of us have seen her. She certainly was not with Mr. Markrute at Cowes, and no one has been in town, except this last week for Flora's wedding. I suppose Tristram must have met her in Scotland, or possibly abroad. He went to Paris, you remember, at Easter, and again in July."

"I wonder what she is like," said Emily.

"Is she young?" asked Mary.

"Tristram does not say," replied Lady Tancred, "only that she is beautiful."

"We are so surprised," both girls gasped together.

"Yes, it is unexpected, certainly," agreed their mother, "but Tristram has judgment; he is not likely to have chosen any one of whom I should disapprove. You must be ready to call with me, directly after lunch. Tristram is coming to breakfast, so you can have yours now--in your room. I must talk to him."

And the girls, who were dying to ask a hundred thousand questions, felt that they were dismissed, and, kissing their dignified parent, they retired to their own large, back room, which they shared, in common with all their pleasures and little griefs, together.

"Isn't it too wonderful, Em?" Mary said, when they were back there, both curled up in the former's bed waiting for their breakfast. "One can see Mother is very much moved; she was so stern. I thought Tristram was devoted to Laura High-ford, did not you?"

"Oh! he has been sick of that for ages and ages. She nags at him--she is a cat anyway and I never could understand it, could you, Mary?"

"Men have to be like that," said Mary, wisely, "they must have some one, I mean, to play with, and they are afraid of girls."

"How I hope she will like us, don't you?" Emily said. "Mr. Markrute is very rich and perhaps she is, too. How lovely it will be if they are able to live at Wrayth. How lovely to have it opened again--to go and stay there!"

"Yes, indeed," said Mary.

Lady Tancred awaited her son in the small front morning-room. She was quite as much a specimen of an English aristocrat as he was, with her brushed-back, gray hair, and her beautiful, hard, fine-featured face. She was supremely dignified, and dressed well and with care. She had been brought up in the school which taught the repression of all emotion--now, alas! rapidly passing away--so that she did not even tap her foot from the impatience which was devouring her, and it was nearly eleven o'clock before Tristram made his appearance!

He apologized charmingly, and kissed her cheek. His horse, Satan, had been particularly fresh, and he had been obliged to give him an extra canter twice round the Row, before coming in, and was breakfast ready?--as he was extremely hungry! Yes, breakfast was ready, and they went into the dining-room where the old butler awaited them.

"Give me everything, Michelham," said his lordship, "I am ravenous. Then you can go. Her ladyship will pour out the coffee."

The old servant beamed upon him, with a "glad to see your lordship's well!" and, surrounding his plate with hot, covered, silver dishes, quietly made his exit, and so they were alone.

Lady Tancred beamed upon her son, too. She could not help it. He looked so completely what he ought to look, she thought--magnificently healthy and hand-some, and perfectly groomed. No mother could help being proud of him.

"Tristram, dear boy, now tell me all about it," she said.

"There is hardly anything to tell you, Mother, except that I am going to be married about the 25th of October--and--you will be awfully nice to her--to Zara--won't you?" He had taken the precaution to send round a note, early in the morning, to Francis Markrute, asking for his lady's full name, as he wished to tell his family; so the "Zara" came out quite naturally! "She is rather a peculiar person, and--er--has very stiff manners. You may not like her at first."

"No, dear?" said Lady Tancred hesitatingly, "Stiff manners you say? That at least is on the right side. I always deplore the modern free-and-easy-ness."

"Oh, there is nothing free-and-easy about her!" said Tristram, helping himself to a cutlet, while he smiled almost grimly. His sense of humor was highly aroused oven the whole thing; only that overmastering something which drew him was even stronger than this.

Then he felt that there was no use in allowing his mother to drag information from him; he had better tell her what he meant her to know.

"You see, Mother, the whole thing has been arranged rather suddenly. I only settled upon it last night myself, and so told you at once. She will be awfully rich, which is rather a pity in a sense--though I suppose we shall live at Wrayth again, and all that--- but I need not tell you I am not marrying her for such a reason."

"No, I know you," Lady Tancred said, "but I cannot agree with you about its being a pity that she is rich. We live in an age when the oldest and most honored name is useless without money to keep up its traditions, and any woman would find your title and your position well worth all her gold. There are things you will give her in return which only hundreds of years can produce. You must have no feeling that you are accepting anything from her which you do not equalize. Remember, it is a false sentiment."

"Oh, I expect so--and she is well bred, you know, so she won't throw it in my teeth." And Lord Tancred smiled.

"I remember old Colonel Grey," his mother continued; "years ago he drove a coach; but I don't recollect his brother. Did he live abroad, perhaps?"

This was an awkward question. The young fiance was quite ignorant about his prospective bride's late father!

"Yes," he said hurriedly. "Zara married very young, she is quite young now--only about twenty-three. Her husband was a brute, and now she has come to live with Francis Markrute. He is an awfully good fellow, Mother, though you don't like him; extremely cultivated, and so quaintly amusing, with his cynical views on life. You will like him when you know him better. He is a jolly good sportsman, too--for a foreigner."

"And of what nation is Mr. Markrute, Tristram, do you know?" Lady Tancred asked.

Really, all women--even mothers--were tiresome at times with their questions!

"'Pon my word, I don't." And he laughed awkwardly. "Austrian, perhaps, or Russian. I have never thought about it; he speaks English so well, and he is a naturalized Englishman, in any case."

"But as you are marrying into the family, don't you think it would be more prudent, dear, to gather some information on the subject?" Lady Tancred hazarded.

And then she saw the true Tancred spirit come out, which she had often vainly tried to combat in her husband during her first years of married life, and had desisted in the end. Tristram's strong, level eyebrows joined themselves in a frown, and his mouth, clean-shaven and chiseled, shut like a vice.

"I am going to do what I am going to do, Mother," he said. "I am satisfied with my bargain, and I beg of you to accept the situation. I do not demand any information, and I ask you not to trouble yourself either. Nothing any one could say would change me--Give me some more coffee, will you, please."

Lady Tancred's hand trembled a little as she poured it out, but she did not say anything, and there was silence for a minute, while his lordship went on with his breakfast, with appetite unimpaired.

"I will take the girls and call there immediately after lunch," she said presently, "and I am to ask for the Countess Shulski. You pronounce it like that, do you not?"

"Yes. She may not be in, and in any case, perhaps, for to-day only leave cards. To-morrow or next day I'll go with you, Mother. You see, until the announcement comes out in the **Morning Post**, everything is not quite settled--I expect Zara would like it better if you did not meet until after then."

That was probably true, he reflected, since he had not even exchanged personal pledges with her yet himself!

Then, as his mother looked stiffly repulsed, his sense of humor got the better of him, and he burst into a peal of laughter, while he jumped up and kissed her with the delightful, caressing boyishness which made her love him with a love so far beyond what she gave to her other children.

"Darling," she murmured, "if you are so happy as to laugh like that I am happy, too, and will do just what you wish." Her proud eyes filled with mist and she pressed his hand.

"Mum, you are a trump!" he said, and he kissed her again and, holding her arm, he led her back into the morning-room.

"Now I must go and change these things," he announced, as he looked down at his riding clothes. "I am going to lunch with Markrute in the City to discuss all the points. So good-bye for the present. I will probably see you to-night. Call a taxi," he said to Michelham who at that moment came into the room with a note. He had kissed his mother and was preparing to leave, when just as he got to the door he turned and said:

"Don't say a word to any one, to-day, of the news--let it come out in the ***Morning Post***, to-morrow. I ask it--please?"

"Not even to Cyril? You have forgotten that he is coming up from Uncle Charles' to go back to Eton," his mother said, "and the girls already know."

"Oh! Cyril. By Jove! I had forgotten! Yes, tell him; he is a first class chap, he'll understand, and, I say"--and he pulled some sovereigns from his pocket--"do give him these from me for this term."

Then with a smile he went.

And a few minutes afterwards a small, slender boy of fourteen, with only Eton's own inimitable self-confidence and delicious swagger printed upon his every line, drove up to the door, and, paying for the taxi in a lordly way, came into his mother's morning-room. There had been a gap in the family after Tristram's appearance, caused by the death, from diphtheria, of two other boys; then came the two girls of twenty and nineteen respectively and, lastly, Cyril.

His big, blue eyes rounded with astonishment and interest when he heard the important news. All he said was:

"Well, she must be a corker, if Tristram thinks her good enough. But what a beastly nuisance! He won't go to Canada now, I suppose, and we shan't have that ranch."

CHAPTER VI

Francis Markrute also saw his niece at breakfast--or rather--just after it. She was finishing hers in the little upstairs sitting-room which he had allotted to her for her personal use, when he tapped at the door and asked if he might come in.

She said "yes," and then rose, with the ceremonious politeness she always used in her dealings with him--contemptuous, resentful politeness for the most part.

"I have come to settle the details of your marriage," he said, while he waved her to be seated again and took a chair himself. At the word "marriage" her nostrils quivered, but she said nothing. She was always extremely difficult to deal with, on account of these silences of hers. She helped no one out. Francis Markrute knew the method himself and admired it; it always made the other person state his case.

"You saw Lord Tancred last night. You can have no objection to him on the ground of his person, and he is a very great gentleman, my niece, as you will find."

Still silence.

"I have arranged with him for you to be married in October--about the 25th, I suppose. So now comes the question of your trousseau. You must have clothes to fit you for so great a position. You had better get them in Paris." Then he paused, struck by the fact which he had only just noticed, that the garments she had been wearing and those she now wore were shabby enough. He realized the reason he had not before remarked this--her splendid carriage and air of breeding--and it gave him a thrill of pride in her. After all, she was his own niece.

"It will be a very great joy to dress you splendidly," he said. "I would have done so always, if I had not known where the money would go; but we are going to settle all that now, and every one can be happy."

It was not in her nature to beg and try to secure favors for her brother and

Mimo without paying for them. She had agreed upon the price--herself. Now all she had to do was to obtain as much as possible for this.

"Mirko's cough has come back again," she said quietly. "Since I have consented I want him to be able to go into the warmth without delay. They are here in London now--he and his father--in a very poor place."

"I have thought it all out," Francis Markrute answered while he frowned, as he always did, at the mention of Mimo. "There is a wonderfully clever doctor at Bournemouth where the air is perfect for those delicate in the lungs. I have communicated with him; and he will take the child into his own house, where he will be beautifully cared for. There he can have a tutor, and when he is stronger he can return to Paris, or to Vienna, and have his talent for the violin cultivated. I want you to understand," he continued, "that if you agree to my terms your brother will not be stinted in any way."

And her thoughts said, "And Mimo?" but she felt it wiser not to ask anything about him just then. To have Mirko cared for by a really clever doctor, in good air, with some discipline as to bedtime, and not those unwholesome meals, snatched at odd hours at some restaurant, seemed a wonderfully good thing. If the little fellow would only be happy separated from his father; that was the question!

"Are there children in the house?" she asked. Mirko was peculiar, and did not like other little boys.

"The doctor has an only little girl of about your brother's age. He is nine and a half, is it not so? And she is delicate, too, so they could play together."

This sounded more promising.

"I would wish to go down and see the doctor first--and the home," she said.

"You shall do so, of course, when you like. I will set aside a certain sum every year, to be invested for him, so that when he grows up he will have a competence--even a small fortune. I will have a deed drawn out for you to sign; it shall be all *en regle*."

"That is well," she said. "And now give me some money, please, that I may relieve their present necessities until my brother can go to this place. I do not consent to give myself, unless I am certain that I free those I love from anxieties. I should like, immediately, a thousand francs. Forty pounds of your money, isn't it?"

"I will send the notes up in a few minutes," Francis Markrute said. He was in the best of tempers to-day. "Meanwhile, that part of the arrangement being settled, I must ask you to pay some attention to the thought of seeing your fiance."

"I do not wish to see him," she announced.

Her uncle smiled.

"Possibly not, but it is part of the bargain. You can't marry the man without seeing him. He will come and call upon you this afternoon, and, no doubt, will bring you a ring. I trust to your honor not to show so plainly your dislike that no man could carry through his side. Please remember your brother's welfare depends upon your actual marriage. If you cause Lord Tancred to break off the match the bargain between you and me is void."

The black panther's look again appeared in her eyes, and an icy stillness settled upon her. But she began to speak rather fast, with a catch in the breath between the sentences.

"Then, since you wish this so much for your own ends, which I cannot guess, I tell you, arrange for me to go to Paris, alone, away from him, until the wedding day. He must hate the thought as much as I do. We are probably both only marionettes in your hands. Explain to the man that I will not go through the degradation of the pretence of an engagement, especially here in this England, where, **Maman** said, they parade affections, and fiances are lovers. **Mon Dieu!** I will play my part--for the visits of ceremony to his family, which I suppose must take place even here-- but beyond that, after to-day, I will not see him alone nor have any communication with him. Is it understood?"

Francis Markrute looked at her with growing admiration. She was gorgeously attractive in this mood. He obtained endless pleasure out of life by his habit of abstract observation. He was able to watch people in the throes of emotion, like a master seeing his hunters being put through their paces.

"It shall be understood," he said. He knew it was wiser to insist upon no more; her temper would never brook it. He knew he could count upon her honor and her pride to fulfill her part of the bargain if she were not exasperated beyond bearing.

"I will explain everything to Lord Tancred at luncheon," he said, "that you will receive him this afternoon, and that then you are going to Paris, and will not return until the wedding. You will concede the family interviews that are absolutely necessary, I suppose?"

"I have already said so; only let them be few and short."

"Then I will not detain you longer now. You are a beautiful woman, Zara," Francis Markrute said, as he rose and kissed her hand. "None of the royal ladies, your ancestresses, ever looked more like a queen." And he bowed himself out of the room, leaving her in her silence.

When she was alone she clenched her hands and walked up and down for a few moments, and her whole serpentine body writhed with passionate anger and pain.

Yes, she was a beautiful woman, and had a right to her life and joys like another--and now she was to be tied, and bound again to a husband!

"Les Infames!" she hissed aloud. "But for that part, I will not bear it! Until the wedding I will dissemble as best I can--but afterwards--!"

And if Lord Tancred could have seen her then he would have known that all the courage he had used when he faced the big lion would be needed soon again.

But before a servant brought up the envelope with the notes she had calmed herself and was preparing to go out. The good part of the news must be told to the two poor ones in their Tottenham Court Road retreat.

As she sped along in the taxi--her uncle had placed one of his several motors at her disposal, but it was not for such localities--she argued with herself that it would be wiser not to give Mimo all the money at once. She knew that that would mean not only the necessary, instantaneous move to a better lodging, but an expensive dinner at the nearest restaurant as well, and certainly bonbons and small presents for Mirko, and new clothes; twice as much would be spent, if credit could be obtained; and then there would be the worry of the bills and the anxiety. If only Mirko would consent to be parted from his fond and irresponsible parent for a time it would be so much better for his health, and his chance of becoming of some use in the world. Mimo always meant so kindly and behaved so foolishly! With the money she personally would get for her bargain Mimo should, somehow, be made comfortable in some studio in Paris where he could paint those pictures which would not sell, and might see his friends--he had still a few who, when his clothes were in a sufficiently good state, welcomed him and his charming, debonair smile. Mimo could be a delightfully agreeable guest, even though he was changed by years and poverty.

And Mirko would be in healthy surroundings; surely it was worth it, after all!

The taxi drew up in the mean street and she got out, paid the man, and then knocked at the dingy door.

A slatternly, miserable, little general servant opened it. No, the foreign gentleman and the little boy were not in, they said they would be back in a few minutes--would the lady step up and wait? She followed the lumpy, untidy figure upstairs to a large attic at the top. It was always let as a studio, apparently. It had a fine northern light from a big window, and was quite clean, though the wretched furniture spoke of better days.

Cleanliness was one of Count Sykypri's peculiarities; he always kept whatever room he was in tidy and clean. This orderly instinct seemed at variance with all the rest of his easy-going character. It was the fastidiousness of a gentleman, which never deserted him. Now Zara recognized the old traveling rug hung on two easels, to hide the little iron beds where he and Mirko slept. The new wonder, which would be bound to sell, was begun there on a third easel. It did not look extremely promising at its present stage. Mirko's violin and his father's, in their cases, were on a chair beside a small pile of music; the water-jug had in it a bunch of yellow chrysanthemums probably bought off a barrow.

The Countess Shulski had been through many vicissitudes with these two since her husband's death, but seldom--only once perhaps--had they gone down to such poverty-stricken surroundings. Generally it was some small apartment in Paris, or Florence, that they occupied, with rather scanty meals when the end of the quarter came. During Count Shulski's life she had always either lived in some smart villa at Nice, or led a wandering existence in hotels; and for months at a time, in later years, when he disappeared, upon his own pleasures bent, he would leave her in some old Normandy farmhouse, only too thankful to be free from his hateful presence. Here Mimo and Mirko would join her, and while they painted and played, she would read. Her whole inner life was spent with books. Among the shady society her husband had frequented she had been known as "The Stone." She never unbent, and while her beauty and extraordinary type attracted all the men she came across they soon gave up their pursuit. She was quite hopeless, they said--and half-witted, some added! No woman could sit silent like that for hours, otherwise. Zara thought of all these things, as she sat on the rickety chair in the Neville Street lodging. How she had loathed that whole atmosphere! How she loathed bohemians and adventurers, no words could tell.

While her mother had lived there had been none of them about. For all her personal downfall, Elinka, Markrute's sister, and an emperor's daughter, remained an absolute **grande dame**--never mixing or mingling with any people but her own belongings.

But now that she was dead, poor Mimo had sometimes gone for company into a class other than his own.

As yet Zara's thoughts had not turned upon her new existence which was to be. She had drawn a curtain over it in her mind. She knew but vaguely about life in England, she had never had any English friends. One or two gamblers had often come to the Nice villa, but except that they were better looking types and wore well made clothes, she had classed them with the rest of her husband's acquaintances. She had read numbers of English classics but practically no novels, so she could not very well picture a state of things she was ignorant about. Sufficient for the day was the evil thereof.

She was getting slightly impatient when at last the two came in.

They had been told of her arrival; she knew that by their glad, hurried mounting of the stairs and the quick opening of the door.

"Cherisette, Angel! But what joy!" And Mirko hurled himself into her arms, while Mimo kissed her hand. He never forgot his early palace manners.

"I have brought you good news," she said, as she drew out two ten-pound notes. "I have made my uncle see reason. Here is something for the present. He has such a kind and happy scheme for Mirko's health. Listen, and I will tell you about it."

They clustered around her while she explained in the most attractive manner she could the picture of the boy's future, but in spite of all that, his beautiful little face fell as he grasped that he was to leave his father.

"It will only be for a time, darling," Zara said, "just until you get quite well and strong, and learn some lessons. All little boys go to school, and come home for the holidays. You know **Maman** would have wished you to be educated like a gentleman."

"But I hate other boys, and you have taught me so well. Oh! Cherisette, what shall I do? And to whom play my violin, who will understand?"

"Oh, but Mirko mio, it is a splendid offer! Think, dear child, a comfortable home and no anxieties," Mimo said. "Truly your sister is an angel, and you must not be so ungrateful. Your cough will get quite well; perhaps I can come and lodge in the town, and we could walk together."

But Mirko pouted. Zara sighed and clasped her hands.

"If you only knew how hard it has been to obtain this much," she said, with despair in her voice. "Oh, Mirko, if you love me you will accept it! Can't you trust me that I would not ask you to go where they are hard or cruel? I am going down to the place to-morrow, to see it and judge for myself. Won't you be good and try to please me?"

Then the little cripple fell to sobbing and kissing her, nestling in her arms with his curly head against her neck.

But in the end she comforted him, the never varying gentleness toward him which she showed would have soothed the most peevish invalid.

So at last she was able to feel that her sacrifice, of which they must always remain ignorant, would not be all in vain; Mirko appeared reconciled to his fate, and would certainly benefit by more healthy surroundings. Instinct told her there would be no use even suggesting to her uncle that the child should stay with Mimo, the situation would have become an *impasse* if the boy had held out, and between them they would have had only this forty pounds until Christmas--and then very little more--and the life of hand-to-mouth poverty would have gone on and on, while here were comfort and probable health, with a certainty of welfare, and education, and a competence in the future. And who knows but Mirko might grow into a great artist one day!

This possible picture she painted in glowing colors until the child's pathetic, dark eyes glistened with pleasure.

Then she became practical; they must change their lodging and find a better one. But here Mimo interfered. They were really very comfortable where they were, he urged, humble though it looked, and changing was unpleasant. If they were able to buy some linen sheets and a new suit of clothes for each it would be much better to stay for the present, until Mirko's going to Bournemouth should be completely settled. "And even then," Count Sykypri said, "it will do for me. No one cooks garlic here, and there is no canary!"

CHAPTER VII

Neither Lord Tancred nor Francis Markrute was late at the appointment in the city restaurant where they were to lunch, and they were soon seated at a table in a corner where they could talk without being interrupted. They spoke of ordinary things for a moment. Then Lord Tancred's impatience to get at the matter which interested him became too great to wait longer, so he said laconically:

"Well?"

"I saw her this morning and had a talk"--the financier said, as he placed some caviare on his toast. "You must not overlook the fact, which I have already stated to you, that she is a most difficult problem. You will have an interesting time taming her. For a man of nerve, I cannot imagine a more thrilling task. She is a woman who has restricted all her emotion for men, and could lavish it all upon *the* man, I imagine. In any case that is 'up to you,' as our friends, the Americans, say--"

Lord Tancred thrilled as he answered:

"Yes, it shall be 'up to me.' But I want to find out all about her for myself. I just want to know when I may see her, and what is the programme?"

"The programme is that she will receive you this afternoon, about tea-time, I should say; that you must explain to her you realize you are engaged. You need not ask her to marry you; she will not care for details like that--she knows it is already settled. Be as businesslike as you can--and come away. She has made it a condition that she sees you as little as possible until the wedding. The English idea of engaged couples shocks her, for, remember, it is, on her side, not a love-match. If you wish to have the slightest success with her afterwards be careful *now*. She is going to Paris, immediately, for her trousseau. She will return about a week before the wedding, when you can present her to your family."

Tristram smiled grimly and then the two men's eyes met and they both laughed.

"Jove! Francis!" Lord Tancred exclaimed, "isn't it a wonderful affair! A real dramatic romance, here in the twentieth century. Would not every one think I was mad, if they knew!"

"It is that sort of madmen who are often the sanest," Francis Markrute answered. "The world is full of apparently sane fools." Then he passed on to a further subject. "You will re-open Wrayth, of course," he said. "I wish my niece to be a Queen of Society, and to have her whole life arranged with due state. I wish your family to understand that I appreciate the honor of the connection with them, and consider it a privilege, and a perfectly natural thing--since we are foreigners of whom you know nothing--that we should provide the necessary money for what we wish."

Lord Tancred listened; he thought of his mother's similar argument at breakfast.

"You see," the financier went on reflectively, "in life, the wise man always pays willingly for what he really wants, as you are doing, for instance, in your blind taking of my niece. Your old nobility in England is the only one of any consequence left in the world. The other countries' system of the titles descending to all the younger sons, *ad infinitum*, makes the whole thing a farce after a while. A Prince in the Caucasus is as common as a Colonel in Kentucky, and in Austria and Germany there are poor Barons in the streets. There was a time in my life when I could have had a foreign title, but I found it ridiculous, and so refused it. But in England, in spite of your amusing radicalism the real thing still counts. It is a valid asset--a tangible security for one's money--from a business point of view. And Americans or foreigners like myself and my niece, for instance, are securing substantial property and equal return, when we bring large fortunes in our marriage settlements to this country. What satisfaction comparable to the glory of her English position as Marchioness of Darrowood could Miss Clara D. Woggenheimer have got out of her millions, if she had married one of her own countrymen, or an Italian count? Yet she gives herself the airs of a benefactress to poor Darrowood and throws her money in his teeth, whereas Darrowood is the benefactor, if there is a case of it either way. But to me, a sensible business man, the bargain is equal. You don't go to an art dealer's and buy a very valuable Rembrandt for its marketable value, and then, afterwards, jibe at the picture and reproach the art dealer. Money is no good without position, and here in England you have had such hundreds of years of freedom from invasion, that you have had time, which no other country has had, to perfect your social system. Let the Radicals and the uninformed of other lands rail as they will, your English aristocracy is the finest body of thinkers and livers in the world. One hears ever of the black sheep, the few luridly glaring failures, but never of the hundreds of great and noble lives which are England's strength."

"By Jove!" said Lord Tancred, "you ought to be in the House of Lords, Francis! You'd wake them up!"

The financier looked down at his plate; he always lowered his eyes when he felt things. No one must ever read what was really passing in his soul, and when he felt, it was the more difficult to conceal, he reasoned.

"I am not a snob, my friend," he said, after a mouthful of salad. "I have no worship for aristocracy in the abstract; I am a student, a rather careful student of systems and their results, and, incidentally, a breeder of thoroughbred live stock, too, which helps one's conclusions: and above all I am an interested watcher of the progress of evolution."

"You are abominably clever," said Lord Tancred.

"Think of your uncle, the Duke of Glastonbury," the financier went on. "He fulfills his duties in every way, a munificent landlord, and a sound, level-headed politician: what other country or class could produce such as he?"

"Oh, the Duke's all right," his nephew agreed. "He is a bit hard up like a number of us at times, but he keeps the thing going splendidly, and my cousin Ethelrida helps him. She is a brick. But you know her, of course, don't you think so?"

"The Lady Ethelrida seems to me a very perfect young woman," Francis Markrute said, examining his claret through the light. "I wish I knew her better. We have few occasions of meeting; she does not go out very much into general society, as you know."

"Oh, I'll arrange that, if it would interest you. I thought you were perfectly cynical about and even rather bored with women," Lord Tancred said.

"I think I told you--was it only yesterday?--that I understood it might be possible for a woman to count--I have not time for the ordinary parrot-chatterers one meets. There are three classes of the species female: those for the body, those for the brain, and those for both. The last are dangerous. The other two merely occupy certain moods in man. Fortunately for us the double combination is rare."

Lord Tancred longed to ask under which head Francis Markrute placed his niece, but, of course, he restrained himself. He, personally, felt sure she would be of the combination; that was her charm. Yes, as he thought over things, that was the only really dangerous kind, and he had so seldom met it! Then his imagination suddenly pictured Laura Highford with her tiny mouth and pointed teeth. She had a showy little brain, absolutely no heart, and the senses of a cat or a ferret. What part of him had she appealed to? Well, thank God, that was over and done with, and he was perfectly free to make his discoveries in regard to Zara, his future wife!

"I tell you what, Francis," he said presently, after the conversation had drifted from these topics and cigars and liqueurs had come, "I would like my cousin Ethelrida to meet Countess Shulski pretty soon. I don't know why, but I believe the two would get on."

"There is no use suggesting any meetings until my niece returns from Paris," the financier said. "She will be in a different mood by then. She had not, when she came to England, quite put off her mourning; she will then have beautiful clothes, and be more acquiescent in every way. Now she would be antagonistic. See her this afternoon and be sensible; make up your mind to postpone things, until her return. And even then be careful until she is your wife!"

Lord Tancred looked disappointed. "It is a long time," he said.

"Let me arrange to give a dinner at my house, at which perhaps the Duke and Lady Ethelrida would honor me by being present, and your mother and sisters and any other member of your family you wish, let us say, on the night of my niece's return" (he drew a small calendar notebook from his pocket). "That will be Wednesday, the 18th, and we will fix the wedding for Wednesday the 25th, a week later. That gets you back from your honeymoon on the 1st of November; you can stay with me that night, and if your uncle is good enough to include me in the invitation to his shoot we can all three go down to Montfitchet on the following day. Is all this well? If so I will write it down."

"Perfectly well," agreed the prospective bridegroom--and having no notebook or calendar, he scribbled the reminder for himself on his cuff. Higgins, his superb valet, knew a good deal of his lordship's history from his lordship's cuffs!

"I don't think I shall wait for tea-time, Francis," he said, when they got out of the restaurant, into the hall. "I think I'll go now, and get it over, if she will be in. Could I telephone and ask?"

He did so and received the reply from Turner that Countess Shulski was at home, but could not receive his lordship until half-past four o'clock.

"Damn!" said that gentleman as he put the receiver down, and Francis Markrute turned away to hide his smile.

"You had better go and buy an engagement ring, hadn't you?" he said. "It won't do to forget that."

"Good Lord, I had forgotten!" gasped Tristram.

"Well, I have lots of time to do it now, so I'll go to the family jewelers, they are called old-fashioned, but the stones are so good."

So they said good-bye, the young man speeding westwards in a taxi, the lion hunter's excitement thrilling in his veins.

The financier returned to his stately office and passed through his obsequious rows of clerks to his inner sanctum. Then he lit another cigar and gave orders that he was not to be disturbed for a quarter of an hour. He reposed in a comfortable chair and allowed himself to dream. All his plans were working; there must be no rush. Great emergencies required rush, but to build to the summit of one's ambitions, one must use calm and watchful care.

CHAPTER VIII

Countess Shulski was seated in her uncle's drawing-room when Lord Tancred was announced.

It was rather a severe room, purely French, with very little furniture, each piece a priceless work of art. There were no touches of feminine influence, no comfortable sofas as in the morning-room or library, all was stiff, and dignified, and in pure style.

She had chosen to receive him there, on purpose. She wished the meeting to be short and cold. He came forward, a look of determination upon his handsome face.

Zara rose as he advanced, and bowed to him. She did not offer to shake hands, and he let his, which he had half outstretched, drop. She did not help him at all; she remained perfectly silent, as usual. She did not even look at him, but straight out of the window into the pouring rain, and it was then he saw that her eyes were not black but slate.

"You understand why I have come, of course?" he said by way of a beginning.

"Yes," she replied and said nothing more.

"I want to marry you, you know," he went on.

"Really!" she said.

"Yes, I do." And he set his teeth--certainly she was difficult!

"That is fortunate for you, since you are going to do so."

This was not encouraging; it was also unexpected.

"Yes, I am," he answered, "on the 25th of October, with your permission."

"I have already consented." And she clasped her hands.

"May I sit down beside you and talk?" he asked.

She pointed to a Louis XVI. **bergere** which stood opposite, and herself took a small armchair at the other side of the fire.

So they sat down, she gazing into the blazing coals and he gazing at her. She was facing the gloomy afternoon light, though she did not think out these things like her uncle, so he had a clear and wonderful picture of her. "How could so voluptuous looking a creature be so icily cold?" he wondered. Her wonderful hair seemed burnished like dark copper, in the double light of fire and day, and that gardenia skin looked fit to eat. He was thrilled with a mad desire to kiss her; he had never felt so strong an emotion towards a woman in his life.

"Your uncle tells me you are going away to-morrow, and that you will be away until a week before our wedding. I wish you were not going to be, but I suppose you must--for clothes and things."

"Yes, I must."

He got up; he could not sit still, he was too wildly excited; he stood leaning on the mantelpiece, quite close to her, for a moment, his eyes devouring her with the passionate admiration he felt. She glanced up, and when she saw their expression her jet brows met, while a look of infinite disgust crept over her face.

So it had come--so soon! He was just like all men--a hateful, sensual beast. She knew he desired to kiss her--to kiss a person he did not know! Her experience of life had not encouraged her to make the least allowance for the instinct of man. For her, that whole side of human beings was simply revolting. In the far back recesses of her mind she knew and felt that caresses and such things might be good if one loved--passionately loved--but in the abstract, just because of the attraction of sex, they were hideous. No man had ever had the conceded tip of her little finger, although she had been forced to submit to unspeakable exhibitions of passion from Ladislaus, her husband.

For her, Tristram appeared a satyr, but she was no timid nymph, but a fierce panther ready to defend herself!

He saw her look and drew back--cooled.

The thing was going to be much more difficult than he had even thought; he must keep himself under complete control, he knew now. So he turned away to the window and glanced out on the wet park.

"My mother called upon you to-day, I believe," he said. "I asked her not to expect you to be at home. It was only to show you that my family will welcome you with affection."

"It is very good of them."

"The announcement of the engagement will be in the ***Morning Post*** to-morrow. Do you mind?"

"Why should I mind?" (her voice evinced surprise). "Since it is true, the formalities must take place."

"It seems as if it could not be true. You are so frightfully frigid," he said with faint resentment.

"I cannot help how I am," she said in a tone of extreme hauteur. "I have consented to marry you. I will go through with all the necessary ceremonies, the presentations to your family, and such affairs; but I have nothing to say to you: why should we talk when once these things are settled? You must accept me as I am, or leave me alone--that is all"--and then her temper made her add, in spite of her uncle's warning, "for I do not care!"

He turned now; he was a little angry and nearly flared up, but the sight of her standing there, magnificently attractive, stopped him. This was merely one of the phases of the game; he should not allow himself to be worsted by such speeches.

"I expect you don't, but I do," he said. "I am quite willing to take you as you are, or will be."

"Then that is all that need be said," she answered coldly. "Arrange with my uncle when you wish me to see your family on my return; I will carry out what he settles. And now I need not detain you, and will say good-bye." And bowing to him she walked towards the door.

"I am sorry you feel you want to go so soon," he said, as he sprang forward to open it for her, "but good-bye." And he let her pass without shaking hands.

When he was alone in the room he realized that he had not given her the engagement ring, which still reposed in his pocket!

He looked round for a writing table, and finding one, sat down and wrote her a few words.

"I meant to give you this ring. If you don't like sapphires it can be changed. Please wear it, and believe me to be

"Yours,

"Tancred."

He put the note with the little ring-case, inclosed both in a large envelope, and then he rang the bell.

"Send this up to the Countess Shulski," he said to the footman who presently came. "And is my motor at the door?"

It was, so he descended the stairs.

"To Glastonbury House," he ordered his chauffeur. Then he leaned back against the cushions, no look of satisfaction upon his face.

Ethelrida might be having tea, and she was always so soothing and sympathetic.

Yes, her ladyship was at home, and he was shown up into his cousin's own sitting-room.

Lady Ethelrida Montfitchet had kept house for her father, the Duke of Glastonbury, ever since she was sixteen when her mother had died, and she acted as hostess at the ducal parties, with the greatest success. She was about twenty-five now, and one of the sweetest of young women.

She was very tall, rather plain, and very distinguished.

Francis Markrute thought her beautiful. He was fond of analyzing types and breeds, and he said there were those who looked as if they had been poured into more or less fine or clumsy mould, and there were others who were sharply carved as with a knife. He loved a woman's face to look *ciselee*, he said. That is why he did not entirely admire his niece, for although the mould was of the finest in her case, her small nose was not chiseled. Numbers of English and some Austrians were chiseled, he affirmed--showing their race--but very few of other nations.

Now some people would have said the Lady Ethelrida was too chiseled--she might grow peaky, with old age. But no one could deny the extreme refinement of the young woman.

She was strikingly fair, with silvery light hair that had no yellow in it; and kind, wise, gray eyes. Her figure in its slenderness was a thing which dressmakers adored; there was so little of it that any frock could be made to look well on it.

Lady Ethelrida did everything with moderation. She was not mad about any sport or any fad. She loved her father, her aunt, her cousins of the Tancred family, and her friend, Lady Anningford. She was, in short, a fine character and a great lady.

"I have come to tell you such a piece of news, Ethelrida," Tristram said as he sat down beside her on the chintz-covered sofa. Ethelrida's tastes in furniture and decorations were of the simplest in her own room. "Guess what it is!"

"How can I, Tristram? Mary is really going to marry Lord Henry?"

"Not that I know of as yet, but I daresay she will, some day. No, guess again; it is about a marriage."

She poured him out some tea and indicated the bread and butter. Tristram, she knew, loved her stillroom maid's brown bread and butter.

"A man, or a woman?" she asked, meditatively.

"A man--ME!" he said, with reckless grammar.

"You, Tristram!" Ethelrida exclaimed, with as much excitement as she ever permitted herself. "You going to be married! But to whom?"

The thing seemed too preposterous; and her mind had instantly flown to the name, Laura Highford, before her reason said, "How ridiculous--she is married already!"--so she repeated again: "But to whom?"

"I am going to be married to a widow, a niece of Francis Markrute's; you know him." Lady Ethelrida nodded. "She is the most wonderfully attractive creature you ever saw, Ethelrida, a type not like any one else. You'll understand in a minute, when you see her. She has stormy black eyes--no, they are not really black; they are slate color--and red hair, and a white face, and, by Jove! a figure! And do you know, my dear child, I believe I am awfully in love with her!"

"You only 'believe,' Tristram! That sounds odd to be going to be married upon!" Lady Ethelrida could not help smiling.

He sipped his tea and then jumped up. He was singularly restless to-day.

"She is the kind of woman a man would go perfectly mad about when he knew her well. I shall, I know." Then, as he saw his cousin's humorous expression, he laughed boyishly. "It does sound odd, I admit," he said, "the inference is that I don't know her well--and that is just it, Ethelrida, but only to you would I say it. Look here, my dear girl, I have got to be comforted this afternoon. She has just flattened me out. We are going to be married on the 25th of October, and I want you to be awfully nice to her. I am sure she has had a rottenly unhappy life."

"Of course I will, Tristram dear," said Lady Ethelrida, "but remember, I am completely in the dark. When did you meet her? Can't you tell me something more? Then I will be as sympathetic as you please."

So Lord Tancred sat down on the sofa beside her again, and told her the bare facts: that it was rather sudden, but he was convinced it was what he wanted most to do in life; that she was young and beautiful, rich, and very reserved, and rather cold; that she was going away, until a week before the wedding; that he knew it sounded all mad, but his dear Ethelrida was to be a darling, and to understand and not reason with him!

And she did not. She had gathered enough from this rather incoherent recital to make her see that some very deep and unusual current must have touched her cousin's life. She knew the Tancred character, so she said all sorts of nice things to him, asked interested but not indiscreet questions. And soon that irritated and baffled sense left him, and he became calm.

"I want Uncle Glastonbury to ask Francis Markrute to the shoot on the 2nd of November, Ethelrida," he said, "and you will let me bring Zara--she will be my wife by then--although I was asked only as a bachelor?"

"It is my party, not Papa's, you dear old goose, you know that," Lady Ethelrida said. "Of course you shall bring your Zara and I myself will write and ask Mr. Markrute. In spite of Aunt Jane's saying that he is a cynical foreigner I like him!"

CHAPTER IX

Society was absolutely flabbergasted when it read in the ***Morning Post*** the announcement of Lord Tancred's engagement! No one had heard a word about it. There had been talk of his going to Canada, and much chaff upon that subject--so ridiculous, Tancred emigrating! But of a prospective bride the most gossip-loving busybody at White's had never heard! It fell like a bombshell. And Lady Highford, as she read the news, clenched her pointed teeth, and gave a little squeal like a stoat.

So he had drifted beyond her, after all! He had often warned her he would, at the finish of one of those scenes she was so fond of creating. It was true then, when he had told her before Cowes that everything must be over. She had thought his silence since had only been sulking! But who was the creature? "Countess Shulski." Was it a Polish or Hungarian name? "Daughter of the late Maurice Grey." Which Grey was that? "Niece of Francis Markrute, Esquire, of Park Lane." Here was the reason--money! How disgusting men were! They would sell their souls for money. But the woman should suffer for this, and Tristram, too, if she could manage it!

Then she wept some tears of rage. He was so adorably good looking and had been such a feather in her cap, although she had never been really sure of him. It was a mercy her conduct had always been of such an immaculate character--in public--no one could say a word. And now she must act the dear, generous, congratulating friend.

So she had a dose of sal volatile and dressed, with extra care, to lunch at Glastonbury House. There she might hear all the details; only Ethelrida was so superior, and uninterested in news or gossip.

There was a party of only five assembled, when she arrived--she was always a little late. The Duke and Lady Ethelrida, Constance Radcliffe, and two men: an elderly politician, and another cousin of the family. She could certainly chatter about Tristram, and hear all she could.

They were no sooner seated than she began:

"Is not this wonderful news about your nephew, Duke? No one expected it of him just now, though I as one of his best friends have been urging him to marry, for the last two years. Dear Lady Tancred must be so enchanted."

"I am sure you gave him good counsel," said the Duke, screwing his eyeglass which he wore on a long black ribbon into his whimsical old blue eye. "But Tristram's a tender mouth, and a bit of a bolter--got to ride him on the snaffle, not the curb."

Lady Highford looked down at her plate, while she gave an answer quite at variance with her own methods.

"Snaffle or curb, no one would ever try to guide Lord Tancred! And what is the charming lady like? You all know her, of course?"

"Why, no," said His Grace. "The uncle, Mr. Markrute, dined here the other night. He's been very useful to the Party, in a quiet way and seems a capital fellow--but Ethelrida and I have never met the niece. Of course, no one has been in town since the season, and she was not here then. We only came up, like you, for Flora's wedding, and go down to-morrow."

"This is thrilling!" said Lady Highford. "An unknown bride! Have you not even heard what she is like--young or old? A widow always sounds so attractive!"

"I am told that she is perfectly beautiful," said Lady Ethelrida from the other side of the table--there had been a pause--"and Tristram seems so happy. She is quite young, and very rich."

She had always been amiably friendly and indifferent to Laura Highford. It was Ethelrida's way to have no likes and dislikes for the general circle of her friends; her warm attachment was given to so very few, and the rest were just all of a band. Perhaps if she felt anything definite it was a tinge on the side of dislike for Laura. Thinking to please Tristram at the time she had asked her to this, her birthday party, when they had met at Cowes in August, and now she was faced with the problem how to put her off, since Tristram and his bride would be coming. She saw the glint in the light hazel eyes as she described the fiance and her kind heart at once made her determine to turn the conversation. After all, it was perfectly natural for poor

Laura to have been in love with Tristram--no one could be more attractive--and, of course, it must hurt her--this marriage. She would reserve the "putting off," until they left the dining-room and she could speak to her alone. So with her perfect tact and easy grace she diverted the current of conversation to the political situation, and luncheon went on.

But this was not what Lady Highford had come for. She wanted to hear everything she could about her rival, in order to lay her plans; and the moment Ethelrida was engaged with the politician and the Duke had turned to Mrs. Radcliffe, she tackled the cousin, in a lower voice.

He, Jimmy Danvers, had only read what she had, that morning. He had seen Tristram at the Turf on Tuesday after lunch--the day before yesterday--and he had only talked of Canada--and not a word of a lady then. It was a bolt from the blue. "And when I telephoned to the old boy this morning," he said, "and asked him to take me to call upon his damsel to-day, he told me she had gone to Paris and would not be back until a week before the wedding!"

"How very mysterious!" piped Laura. "Tristram is off to Paris, too, then, I suppose?"

"He did not say; he seemed in the deuce of a hurry and put the receiver down."

"He is probably only doing it for money, poor darling boy!" she said sympathetically. "It was quite necessary for him."

"Oh, that's not Tristram's measure," Sir James Danvers interrupted. "He'd never do anything for money. I thought you knew him awfully well," he added, surprised. Apprehension of situations was not one of his strong qualities.

"Of course I do!" Laura snapped out and then laughed. "But you men! Money would tempt any of you!"

"You may bet your last farthing, Lady Highford, Tristram is in love--crazy, if you ask me--he'd not have been so silent about it all otherwise. The Canada affair was probably because she was playing the poor old chap,--and now she's given in; and that, of course, is chucked."

Money, as the motive, Lady Highford could have borne, but, to hear about love drove her wild! Her little pink and white face with its carefully arranged childish setting suddenly looked old and strained, while her eyes grew yellow in the light.

"They won't be happy long, then!" she said. "Tristram could not be faithful to any one."

"I don't think he's ever been in love before, so we can't judge," the blundering cousin continued, now with malice prepense. "He's had lots of little affairs, but they have only been 'come and go.'"

Lady Highford crumbled her bread and then turned to the Duke--there was nothing further to be got out of this quarter. Finally luncheon came to an end, and the three ladies went up to Ethelrida's sitting-room. Mrs. Radcliffe presently took her leave to catch a train, so the two were left alone.

"I am so looking forward to your party, dear Ethelrida," Lady Highford cooed. "I am going back to Hampshire to-morrow, but at the end of the month I come up again and will be with you in Norfolk on the 2nd."

"I was just wondering," said Lady Ethelrida, "if, after all, you would not be bored, Laura? Your particular friends, the Sedgeworths, have had to throw us over--his father being dead. It will be rather a family sort of collection, and not so amusing this year, I am afraid. Em and Mary, Tristram and his new bride,--and Mr. Markrute, the uncle--and the rest as I told you."

"Why, my dear child, it sounds delightful! I shall long to meet the new Lady Tancred! Tristram and I are such dear friends, poor darling boy! I must write and tell him how delighted I am with the news. Do you know where he is at the moment?"

"He is in London, I believe. Then you really will stick to us and not be bored? How sweet of you!" Lady Ethelrida said without a change in her level voice while her thoughts ran: "It is very plucky of Laura; or, she has some plan! In any case I can't prevent her coming now, and perhaps it is best to get it over. But I had better warn Tristram, surprises are so unpleasant."

Then, after a good deal of gush about "dear Lady Tancred's" prospective happiness in having a daughter-in-law, and "dear Tristram," Lady Highford's motor was announced, and she went.

And when she had gone Lady Ethelrida sat down and wrote her cousin a note. Just to tell him in case she did not see him before she went back to the country to-morrow that her list, which she enclosed, was made up for her November party, but if he would like any one else for his bride to meet, he was to say so. She added that some friends had been to luncheon, and among them Laura Highford, who had said the nicest things and wished him every happiness.

Lady Ethelrida was not deceived about these wishes, but she could do no more.

The Duke came into her room, just as she was finishing, and warmed himself by her wood fire.

"The woman is a cat, Ethelrida," he said without any preamble. These two understood each other so well, they often seemed to begin in the middle of a sentence, of which no outsider could grasp the meaning.

"I am afraid she is, Papa. I have just been writing to Tristram, to let him know she still insists upon coming to the shoot. She can't do anything there, and they may as well get it over. She will have to be civil to the new Lady Tancred in our house."

"Whew!" whistled the Duke, "you may have an exciting party. You had better go and leave our cards to-day on the Countess Shulski, and another of mine, as well, for the uncle. We'll have to swallow the whole lot, I suppose."

"I rather like Mr. Markrute, Papa," Ethelrida said. "I talked to him the other night for the first time; he is extremely intelligent. We ought not to be so prejudiced, perhaps, just because he is a foreigner, and in the City. I've asked him on the 2nd, too--you don't mind? I will leave the note to-day; Tristram particularly wished it."

"Then we'll have to make the best of it, pet. I daresay you are right, and one ought not to be prejudiced about anything, in these days."

And then he patted his daughter's smoothly brushed head, and went out again.

Lady Ethelrida drove in the ducal carriage (the Duke insisted upon a carriage, in London), to Park Lane, and was handing her cards to her footman to leave, when Francis Markrute himself came out of the door.

His whole face changed; it seemed to grow younger. He was a fairly tall man, and distinguished looking. He came forward and said: "How do you do," through the brougham window.

Alas! his niece had left that morning ***en route*** for Paris--trousseaux and feminine business, but he was so delighted to have had this chance of a few words with her--Lady Ethelrida.

"I was leaving a note to ask you to come and shoot with my father at Mont-fitchet, Mr. Markrute," she said, "on the 2nd of November. Tristram says he hopes they will be back from the honeymoon in time to join us, too."

"I shall be delighted, and my niece will be delighted at your kindness in calling so soon."

Then they said a few more polite things and the financier finished by:--"I am taking the great liberty of having the book, which I told you about, rebound--it was in such a tattered condition, I was ashamed to send it to you--do not think I had forgotten. I hope you will accept it?"

"I thought you only meant to lend it to me because it is out of print and I cannot buy it. I am so sorry you have had this trouble," Lady Ethelrida said, a little stiffly. "Bring it to the shoot. It will interest me to see it but you must not give it to me." And then she smiled graciously; and he allowed her to say good-bye, and drive on. And as he turned into Grosvenor Street he mused,

"I like her exquisite pride; but she shall take the book--and many other things--presently."

*   *   *   *   *

Meanwhile Zara Shulski had arrived at Bournemouth. She had started early in the morning, and she was making a careful investigation of the house. The doctor appeared all that was kind and clever, and his wife gentle and sweet. Mirko could not have a nicer home, it seemed. Their little girl was away at her grandmother's for the next six weeks, they said, but would be enchanted to have a little boy companion. Everything was arranged satisfactorily. Zara stayed the night, and next day, having wired to Mimo to meet her at the station, she returned to London.

They talked in the Waterloo waiting-room; poor Mimo seemed so glad and happy. He saw her and her small bag into a taxi. She was going back to her uncle's, and was to take Mirko down next day, and, on the following one, start for Paris.

"But I can't go back to Park Lane without seeing Mirko, now," she said. "I did not tell my uncle what train I was returning by. There is plenty of time so I will go and have tea with you at Neville Street. It will be like old times, we will get some cakes and other things on the way, and boil the kettle on the fire."

So Mimo gladly got in with her and they started. He had a new suit of clothes and a new felt hat, and looked a wonderfully handsome foreign gentleman; his manner to women was always courteous and gallant. Zara smiled and looked almost happy, as they arranged the details of their surprise tea party for Mirko.

At that moment there passed them in Whitehall a motorcar going very fast, the occupant of which, a handsome young man, caught the most fleeting glimpse of them--hardly enough to be certain he recognized Zara. But it gave him a great start and a thrill.

"It cannot be she," he said to himself, "she went to Paris yesterday; but if it is--who is the man?"

He altered his plans, went back to his rooms, and sat moodily down in his favorite chair--an unpleasant, gnawing uncertainty in his heart.

CHAPTER X

Mirko, crouched up by the smoldering fire, was playing the ***Chanson Triste*** on his violin when the two reached the studio. He had a wonderful talent--of that there was no doubt--but his health had always been too delicate to stand any continuous study. Nor had the means of the family ever been in a sufficiently prosperous condition, in later years, to procure a really good master. But the touch and soul of the strange little fellow sounded in every wailing note. He always played the ***Chanson Triste*** when he was sad and lonely. He had been nearly seven when his mother died, and he remembered her vividly. She had so loved Tschaikovsky's music, and this piece especially. He had played it to her--from ear then--the afternoon she lay dying, and for him, as for them all, it was indissolubly connected with her memory. The tears were slowly trickling down Mirko's cheeks. He was going to be taken away from his father, his much loved Cherisette would not be near him, and he feared and hated strangers.

He felt he was talking to his mother with his bow. His mother who was in heaven, with all the saints and angels. What could it be like up there? It was perhaps a forest, such as Fontainebleau, only there were sure to be numbers of birds which sang like the nightingales in the Borghese Gardens--there would be no canaries! The sun always shone and ***Maman*** would wear a beautiful dress of blue gauze with wings, and her lovely hair, which was fair, not red like Cherisette's, would be all hanging down. It surely was a very desirable place, and quite different from the Neville Street lodging. Why could he not get there, out of the cold and darkness? Cherisette had always taught him that God was so good and kind to little boys who had crippled backs. He would ask God with all the force of his music, to take him there to ***Maman***.

The sound of the familiar air struck a chill note upon Mimo and Zara, as they came up the stairs; it made them hasten their steps--they knew very well what mood it meant with the child.

He was so far away, in his passionate dream-prayer, that he did not hear them coming until they opened the door; and then he looked up, his beautiful dark eyes all wet with tears which suddenly turned to joy when he saw his sister.

"Cherisette adoree!" he cried, and was soon in her arms, soothed and comforted and caressed. Oh, if he could always be with her, he really, after all, would wish for no other heaven!

"We are going to have such a picnic!" Zara told him. "Papa and I have brought a new tablecloth, and some pretty cups and saucers, and spoons, and knives, and forks--and see! such buns! English buns for you to toast, Mirko mio! You must be the little cook, while I lay the table."

And the child clapped his hands with glee and helped to take the papers off; he stroked the pretty roses on the china with his delicate, little forefinger--he had Mimo's caressing ways with everything he admired and loved. He had never broken his toys, as other children do; accidental catastrophes to them had always caused him pain and weeping. And these bright, new flowery cups should be his special care, to wash, and dry, and guard.

He grew merry as a cricket, and his laughter pealed over the paper cap Mimo made for him and the towel his sister had for an apron. They were to be the servants, and Mimo a lordly guest.

And soon the table was laid, and the buns toasted and buttered; Zara had even bought a vase of the same china, in which she placed a bunch of autumn red roses, to match those painted on it and this was a particular joy.

"The Apache," which had not yet found a purchaser, stood on one easel, and from it the traveling rug hung to the other, concealing all unsightly things, and yesterday Mimo had bought from the Tottenham Court Road a cheap basket armchair with bright cretonne cushions. And really, with the flowers and the blazing fire when they sat down to tea it all looked very cozy and home-like.

What would her uncle or Lord Tancred have thought, could they have seen those tempestuous eyes of Zara's glistening and tender--and soft as a dove's!

After tea she sat in the basket chair, and took Mirko in her arms, and told him all about the delightful, new home he was going to, the kind lady, and the beautiful view of the sea he would get from his bedroom windows; how pretty and fresh it all looked, how there were pine woods to walk in, and how she would--presently-- come down to see him. And as she said this her thoughts flew to her own fate--what would her "presently" be? And she gave a little, unconscious shiver almost of fear.

"What hast thou, Cherisette?" said Mirko. "Where were thy thoughts then?-- not here?"

"No, not here, little one. Thy Cherisette is going also to a new home; some day thou must visit her there."

But when he questioned and implored her to tell him about it she answered vaguely, and tried to divert his thoughts, until he said:

"It is not to **Maman** in heaven, is it, dear Cherisette? Because there, there would be enough place for us both--and surely thou couldst take me too?"

*   *   *   *   *

When she got back to Park Lane, and entered her uncle's library he was sitting at the writing table, the telephone in his hand. He welcomed her with his eyes and went on speaking, while she took a chair.

"Yes, do come and dine.--May you see her if by chance she did not go to Paris?" He looked up at Zara, who frowned. "No--she is very tired and has gone to her room for the evening.--She has been in the country to-day, seeing some friends.--No--not to-morrow--she goes to the country again, and to Paris the following night--To the station? I will ask her, but perhaps she is like me, and dislikes being seen off," then a laugh,--and then, "All right--well, come and dine at eight--good-bye." The finan- cier put the receiver down and looked at his niece, a whimsical smile in his eyes.

"Well," he said, "your fiance is very anxious to see you, it seems. What do you say?"

"Certainly not!" she flashed. "I thought it was understood; he shall not come to the train. I will go by another if he insists."

"He won't insist; tell me of your day?"

She calmed herself--her face had grown stormy.

"I am quite satisfied with the home you have chosen for Mirko and will take him there to-morrow. All the clothes have come that you said I might order for him, and I hope and think he will be comfortable and happy. He has a very beautiful, tender nature, and a great talent. If he could only grow strong, and more balanced! Perhaps he will, in this calm, English air."

Francis Markrute's face changed, as it always did with the mention and discussion of Mirko--whose presence in the world was an ever-rankling proof of his loved sister's disgrace. All his sense of justice--and he was in general a just man--could never reconcile him to the idea of ever seeing or recognizing the child. "The sins of the fathers"--was his creed and he never forgot the dying Emperor's words. He had lost sight of his niece for nearly two years after his sister's death. She had wished for no communication with him, believing then that he had left her mother to die without forgiveness, and it was not until he happened to read in a foreign paper the casual mention of Count Shulski's murder, and so guessed at Zara's whereabouts, that a correspondence had been opened again, and he was able to explain that he had been absent in Africa and had not received any letters.

He then offered her his protection and a home, if she would sever all connection with the two, Mimo and Mirko, and she had indignantly refused. And it was only when they were in dire poverty, and he had again written asking his niece to come and stay with him for a few weeks, this time with no conditions attached, that she had consented, thinking that perhaps she would be able in some way to benefit them.

But now that she looked at him she felt keenly how he had trapped her, all the same.

"We will not discuss your brother's nature," he said, coldly. "I will keep my side of the bargain scrupulously, for all material things; that is all you can expect of me. Now let us talk of yourself. I have ventured to send some sables for your inspection up to your sitting room; it will be cold traveling. I hope you will select what you wish. And remember, I desire you to order the most complete trousseau in Paris, everything that a great lady could possibly want for visits and entertainments; and you must secure a good maid there, and return with all the *apanages* of your position."

She bowed, as at the reception of an order. She did not thank him.

"I will not give you any advice what to get," he went on. "Your own admirable taste will direct you. I understand that in the days of your late husband you were a beautifully dressed woman, so you will know all the best places to go to. But please to remember, while I give you unlimited resources for you to do what I wish, I trust to your honor that you will bestow none of them upon the--man Sykypri. The bargain is about the child; the father is barred from it in every way."

Zara did not answer, she had guessed this, but Mirko's welfare was of first importance. With strict economy Mimo could live upon what he possessed, if alone and if he chose to curtail his irresponsible generosities.

"Do I understand I have your word of honor about this?" her uncle demanded.

Her empress' air showed plainly now. She arose from the chair and stood haughtily drawn up:

"You know me and whether my spoken word 'is required or no," she said, "but if it will be any satisfaction to you to have it I give it!"

"Good--Then things are settled, and, I hope, to the happiness of all parties."

"Happiness!" she answered bitterly. "Who is ever happy?" Then she turned to go, but he arrested her.

"In two or three years' time you will admit to me that you know of four human beings who are ideally happy." And with this enigmatic announcement ringing in her ears, she went on up the stairs to her sitting-room.

Who were the *four* people? Herself and himself and Mimo and Mirko? Was it possible that after all his hardness towards them he meant to be eventually kind? Or was the fourth person not Mimo, but her future husband? Then she smiled grimly. It was not very likely *he* would be happy--a beast, like the rest of men, who, marrying her only for her uncle's money, having been ready to marry her for that when he had never even seen her--was yet full enough of the revolting quality of his sex to be desirous now to kiss her and clasp her in his arms!

As far as she was concerned he would have no happiness!

And she herself--what would the new life mean? It appeared a blank--an abyss. A dark curtain seemed to overhang and cover it. All she could feel was that Mirko was being cared for, that she was keeping her word to her adored mother. She would fulfill to the letter her uncle's wishes as to her suitable equipments, but beyond that she refused to think.

All the evening, when she had finished her short, solitary dinner, she played the piano in her sitting-room, her white fingers passing from one divine air to another, until at last she unconsciously drifted to the **Chanson Triste**, and Mirko's words came back to her:

"There, there would be enough place for us both"--Who knows--that might be the end of it!

And the two men heard the distant wail of the last notes as they came out of the dining-room, and, while it made the financier uncomfortable, it caused Tristram a sharp stab of pain.

CHAPTER XI

The next three weeks passed for Lord Tancred in continuously growing excitement. He had much business to see to for the reopening of Wrayth which had been closed for the past two years. He had decided to let Zara choose her own rooms, and decorate them as she pleased, when she should get there. But the big state apartments, with their tapestry and pictures, would remain untouched.

It gave him infinite pleasure--the thought of living at his old house once again--and it touched him to see the joy of the village and all the old keepers and gardeners who had been pensioned off! He found himself wondering all sorts of things--if he would have a son some day soon, to inherit it all. Each wood and broad meadow seemed to take on new interest and significance from this thought.

His home was so very dear to him though he had drilled himself into a seeming indifference. The great, round tower of the original Norman keep was still there, connected with the walls of the later house, a large, wandering edifice built at all periods from that epoch upwards, and culminating in a shocking early-Victorian Gothic wing and porch.

"I think we shall pull that wretched bit down some time," he said to himself. "Zara must have good taste--she could not look so well in her clothes, if she had not."

His thoughts were continually for her, and what she would be likely to wish; and, in the evening, when he sat alone in his own sanctum after a hard day with electricians and work-people, he would gaze into the blazing logs and dream.

The new electric light was not installed yet, and only the big, old lamps lit the shadowy oak panelling. There in a niche beside the fireplace was the suit of armor which another Tristram Guiscard had worn at Agincourt. What little chaps they had been in those days in comparison with himself and his six feet two inches! But they had been great lords, his ancestors, and he, too, would be worthy of the race. There were no wars just now to go to and fight for his country--but he would fight for his order, with his uncle, the Duke, that splendid, old specimen of the hereditary legislator. Francis Markrute who was a good judge had said that he had made some decent speeches in the House of Lords already, and he would go on and do his best, and Zara would help him. He wondered if she liked reading and poetry. He was such a magnificently healthy sportsman he had always been a little shy of letting people know his inner and gentler tastes. He hoped so much she would care for the books he did. There was a deep strain of romance in his nature, undreamed of by such women as Laura Highford, and these evenings--alone, musing and growing in love with a phantom--drew it forth.

His plan was to go to Paris--to the Ritz--for the honeymoon. Zara who did not know England would probably hate the solemn servants staring at her in those early days if he took her to Orton, one of the Duke's places which he had offered him for the blissful week. Paris was much better--they could go to the theater there--because he knew it would not all be plain sailing by any means! And every time he thought of that aspect, his keen, blue eyes sparkled with the instinct of the chase and he looked the image of the Baron Tancred who, carved in stone, with his Crusader's crossed feet, reposed in state in the church of Wrayth.

A lissom, wiry, splendid English aristocrat, in perfect condition and health, was Tristram Guiscard, twenty-fourth Baron Tancred, as he lounged in his chair before the fire and dreamed of his lady and his fate.

And when they were used to one another--at the end of the week--there would be the party at Montfitchet where he would have the joy and pride of showing his beautiful wife--and Laura would be there;--he suddenly thought of her. Poor old Laura! she had been awfully nice about it and had written him the sweetest letter. He would not have believed her capable of it--and he felt so kindly disposed towards her--little as she deserved it if he had only known!

Then when these gayeties were over, he and Zara would come here to Wrayth! And he could not help picturing how he would make love to her in this romantic setting; and perhaps soon she, too, would love him. When he got thus far in his picturings he would shut his eyes, stretch out his long limbs, and call to Jake, his solemn bulldog, and pat his wrinkled head.

And Zara, in Paris, was more tranquil in mind than was her wont. Mirko had not made much difficulty about going to Bournemouth. Everything was so pretty, the day she took him there, the sun shining gayly and the sea almost as blue as the Mediterranean, and Mrs. Morley, the doctor's wife, had been so gentle and sweet, and had drawn him to her heart at once, and petted him, and talked of his violin. The doctor had examined his lungs and said they certainly might improve with plenty of the fine air if he were very carefully fed and tended, and not allowed to catch cold.

The parting with poor Mimo had been very moving. They had said good-bye to him in the Neville Street lodging, as Zara thought it was wiser not to risk a scene at the station. The father and son had kissed and clasped one another and both wept, and Mimo had promised to come to see him soon, soon!

Then there had been another painful wrench when she herself left Bournemouth. She had put off her departure until the afternoon of the following day. Mirko had tried to be as brave as he could; but the memory of the pathetic little figure, as she saw it waving a hand to her from the window, made those rare tears brim up and splash on her glove, as she sat in the train.

In her short life with its many moments of deep anguish she had seldom been able to cry; there were always others to be thought of first, and an iron self-control was one of her inheritances from her grandfather, the Emperor, just as that voluptuous, undulating grace, and the red, lustrous hair, came from the beautiful opera dancer and great artiste, her grandmother.

She had cautioned Mrs. Morley, if she should often hear Mirko playing the **Chanson Triste**, to let her know, and she would come to him. It was a sure indication of his state of mind. And Mrs. Morley, who had read in the **Morning Post** the announcement of her approaching marriage, asked her where she could be found, and Zara had stiffened suddenly and said--at her uncle's house in Park Lane, the letters to be marked "To be forwarded immediately."

And when she had gone, Mrs. Morley had told her sister who had come in to tea how beautiful Countess Shulski was and how very regal looking, "but she had on such plain, almost shabby, black clothes, Minnie dear, and a small black toque, and then the most splendid sable wrap--those very grand people do have funny tastes, don't they? I should have liked a pretty autumn costume of green velveteen, and a hat with a wing or a bird."

The financier had insisted upon his niece wearing the sable wrap--and somehow, in spite of all things, the beautiful, dark, soft fur had given her pleasure.

And now, three weeks later, she was just returning from Paris, her beauty enriched by all that money and taste could procure. It was the eighteenth of October, exactly a week before her wedding.

She had written to Mimo from Paris, and told him she was going to be married; that she was doing so because she thought it was best for them all; and he had written back enchanted exclamations of surprise and joy, and had told her she should have his new picture, the London fog--so dramatic with its two meeting figures--for his wedding gift. Poor Mimo, so generous, always, with all he had!

Mirko was not to be told until she was actually married.

She had written to her uncle and asked him as a great favor that she might only arrive the very day of the family dinner party, he could plead for her excess of trousseau business, or what he liked. She would come by the nine o'clock morning train, so as to be in ample time for dinner; and it would be so much easier for every one, if they could get the meeting over, the whole family together, rather than have the ordeal of private presentations.

And Francis Markrute had agreed, while Lord Tancred had chafed.

"I **shall** meet her at the station, whatever you say, Francis!" he had exclaimed. "I am longing to see her."

And as the train drew up at Victoria, Zara caught sight of him there on the platform, and in spite of her dislike and resentment she could not help seeing that her fiance was a wonderfully good-looking man.

She herself appeared to him as the loveliest thing he had ever seen in his life, with her perfect Paris clothes, and air of distinction. If he had thought her attractive before he felt ecstatic in his admiration now.

Francis Markrute hurried up the platform and Tristram frowned, but the financier knew it might not be safe to leave them to a tete-a-tete drive to the house! Zara's temper might not brook it, and he had rushed back from the city, though he hated rushing, in order to be on the spot to make a third.

"Welcome, my niece!" he said, before Lord Tancred could speak. "You see, we have both come to greet you."

She thanked them politely, and turned to give an order to her new French maid--and some of the expectant, boyish joy died out of Tristram's face, as he walked beside her to the waiting motor.

They said the usual things about the crossing--it had been smooth and pleasant--so fortunate for that time of the year--and she had stayed on deck and enjoyed it. Yes, Paris had been charming; it was always a delightful spot to find oneself in.

Then Tristram said he was glad she thought that, because, if she would consent, he would arrange to go there for the honeymoon directly after the wedding. She inclined her head in acquiescence but did not speak. The matter appeared one of complete indifference to her.

In spite of his knowledge that this would be her attitude and he need not expect anything different Tristram's heart began to sink down into his boots, by the time they reached the house, and Francis Markrute whispered to his niece as they came up the steps:

"I beg of you to be a little more gracious--the man has some spirit, you know!"

So when they got into the library, and she began to pour out the tea for them, she made conversation. But Tristram's teeth were set, and a steely light began to grow in his blue eyes.

She looked so astonishingly alluring there in her well-fitting, blue serge, traveling dress, yet he might not even kiss her white, slender hand! And there was a whole week before the wedding! And after it?--would she keep up this icy barrier between them? If so--but he refused to think of it!

He noticed that she wore his engagement ring only, on her left hand, and that the right one was ringless, nor had she a brooch or any other jewel. He felt glad--he would be able to give her everything. His mother had been so splendid about the family jewels, insisting upon handing them over, and even in the short time one or two pieces had been reset, the better to please the presumably modern taste of the new bride of the Tancreds. These, and the wonderful pearls, her uncle's gift, were waiting for her, up in her sitting-room.

"I think I will go and rest now until dinner," she said, and forced a smile as she moved towards the door.

It was the first time Tristram had ever seen her smile, and it thrilled him. He had the most frantic longing to take her in his arms and kiss her, and tell her he was madly in love with her, and wanted her never to be out of his sight.

But he let her pass out, and, turning round, he found Francis Markrute pouring out some liqueur brandy from a wonderful, old, gold-chased bottle, which stood on a side-table with its glasses. He filled two, and handed one to Tristram, while he quoted Doctor Johnson with an understanding smile:

"'Claret for boys, port for men, but brandy for heroes!' By Jove! my dear boy," he said, "you are a hero!"

CHAPTER XII

Lady Tancred unfortunately had one of her very bad headaches, and an hour before dinner, in fact before her son had left the Park Lane house, a telephone message came to say she was dreadfully sorry, it would be impossible for her to come. It was Emily who spoke to Francis Markrute, himself.

"Mother is so disappointed," she said, "but she really suffers so dreadfully. I am sure Countess Shulski will forgive her, and you, too. She wants to know if Countess Shulski will let Tristram bring her to-morrow morning, without any more ceremony, to see her and stay to luncheon."

Thus it was settled and this necessitated a change in the table arrangements.

Lady Ethelrida would now sit on the host's right hand, and Lady Coltshurst, an aunt on the Tancred side, at his left, while Zara would be between the Duke and her fiance, as originally arranged. Emily Guiscard would have Sir James Danvers and Lord Coltshurst as neighbors, and Mary her uncle, the Duke's brother, a widower, Lord Charles Montfitchet, and his son, "Young Billy," the Glastonbury heir--Lady Ethelrida was the Duke's only child.

At a quarter before eight Francis Markrute went up to his niece's sitting-room. She was already dressed in a sapphire-blue velvet masterpiece of simplicity. The Tancred presents of sapphires and diamonds lay in their open cases on the table with the splendid Markrute yards of pearls. She was standing looking down at them, the strangest expression of cynical resignation upon her face.

"Your gift is magnificent, Uncle Francis," she said, without thanking him. "Which do you wish me to wear? Yours--or his?"

"Lord Tancred's, he has specially asked that you put his on to-night," the financier replied. "These are only his first small ones; the other jewels are being reset for you. Nothing can be kinder or more generous than the whole family has been. You see this brooch, with the large drop sapphire and diamond, is from the Duke."

She inclined her head without enthusiasm, and took her own small pearls from her ears, and replaced them by the big sapphire and diamond earrings; a riviere of alternate solitaire sapphires and diamonds she clasped round her snowy throat.

"You look absolutely beautiful," her uncle exclaimed with admiration. "I knew I could perfectly trust to your taste--the dress is perfection."

"Then I suppose we shall have to go down," she said quietly.

She was perfectly calm, her face expressionless; if there was a tempestuous suggestion in her somber eyes she generally kept the lids lowered. Inwardly, she felt a raging rebellion. This was the first ceremony of the sacrifice, and although in the abstract her fine senses appreciated the jewels and all her new and beautiful clothes and *apanages*, they in no way counterbalanced the hateful degradation.

To her it was a hideous mockery--the whole thing; she was just a chattel, a part of a business bargain. She could not guess her uncle's motive for the transaction (he had a deep one, of course), but Lord Tancred's was plain and purely contemptible. Money! For had not the whole degrading thing been settled before he had ever seen her? He was worse than Ladislaus who, at all events, had been passionately in love, in his revolting, animal way.

She knew nothing of the English customs, nor how such a thing as the arrangement of this marriage, as she thought it was, was a perfectly unknown impossibility, as an idea. She supposed that the entire family were aware of the circumstances, and were willing to accept her only for her uncle's wealth--she already hated and despised them all. Her idea was, "noblesse oblige," and that a great and ancient house should never stoop to such depths.

Francis Markrute looked at her when she said, "I suppose we shall have to go down," with that icy calm. He felt faintly uneasy.

"Zara, it is understood you will be gracious? and *brusquer* no one?"

But all the reply he received was a glance of scorn. She had given her word and refused to discuss that matter.

And so they descended the stairs just in time to be standing ready to receive Lord and Lady Coltshurst who were the first to be announced. He was a spare, unintelligent, henpecked, elderly man, and she, a stout, forbidding-looking lady. She had prominent, shortsighted eyes, and she used longhandled glasses; she had also three chins, and did not resemble the Guiscards in any way, except for her mouth and her haughty bearing.

Zara's manner was that of an empress graciously receiving foreigners in a private audience!

The guests now arrived in quick succession. Lord Charles and his son, "Young Billy," then Tristram and his sisters, and Jimmy Danvers, and, lastly, the Duke and Lady Ethelrida.

They were all such citizens of the world there was no awkwardness, and the old Duke had kissed his fair, prospective niece's hand when he had been presented, and had said that some day he should claim the privilege of an old man and kiss her cheek. And Zara had smiled for an instant, overcome by his charm, and so she had put her fingers on his arm, and they had gone down to dinner; and now they were talking suavely.

Francis Markrute had a theory that certain human beings are born with moral antennae--a sort of extra combination beyond the natural of the senses of sight, smell, hearing and understanding--which made them apprehend situations and people even when these chanced to be of a hitherto unknown race or habit. Zara was among those whose antennae were highly developed. She had apprehended almost instantaneously that whatever their motives were underneath, her future husband's family were going to act the part of receiving her for herself. It was a little ridiculous, but very well bred, and she must fall in with it when with them collectively like this.

Before they had finished the soup the Duke was saying to himself that she was the most attractive creature he had ever met in his life, and no wonder Tristram was mad about her; for Tristram's passionate admiration to-night could not have been mistaken by a child!

And yet Zara had never smiled, but that once--in the drawing-room.

Lady Ethelrida from where she sat could see her face through a gap in the flowers. The financier had ordered a tall arrangement on purpose: if Zara by chance should look haughtily indifferent it were better that her expression should escape the observation of all but her nearest neighbors. However, Lady Ethelrida just caught the picture of her through an oblique angle, against a background of French panelling.

And with her quiet, calm judgment of people she was wondering what was the cause of that strange look in her eyes? Was it of a stag at bay? Was it temper, or resentment, or only just pain? And Tristram had said their color was slate gray; for her part she saw nothing but pools of jet ink!

"There is some tragic story hidden here," she thought, "and Tristram is too much in love to see it." But she felt rather drawn to her new prospective cousin, all the same.

Francis Markrute seemed perfectly happy--his manner as a host left nothing to be desired; he did not neglect the uninteresting aunt, who formed golden opinions of him; but he contrived to make Lady Ethelrida feel that he wished only to talk to her; not because she was an attractive, young woman, but because he was impressed with her intelligence, in the abstract. It made things very easy.

The Duke asked Zara if she knew anything about English politics.

"You will have to keep Tristram up to the mark," he said, "he has done very well now and then, but he is a rather lazy fellow." And he smiled.

"'Tristram,'" she thought. "So his name is 'Tristram'!" She had actually never heard it before, nor troubled herself to inquire about it. It seemed incredible, it aroused in her a grim sense of humor, and she looked into the old Duke's face for a second and wondered what he would say if she announced this fact, and he caught the smile, cynical though it was, and continued:

"I see you have noticed his laziness! Now it will really be your duty to make him a first-rate fighter for our cause. The Radicals will begin to attack our very existence presently, and we must all come up to the scratch."

"I know nothing as yet of your politics," Zara said. "I do not understand which party is which, though my uncle says one consists of gentlemen, and the other of the common people. I suppose it is like in other countries, every one wanting to secure what some one above him has got, without being fitted for the administration of what he desires to snatch."

"That is about it," smiled the Duke.

"It would be reasonable, if they were all oppressed here, as in France before the great revolution, but are they?"

"Oh! dear, no!" interrupted Tristram. "All the laws are made for the lower classes. They have compensations for everything, and they have openings to rise to the top of the tree if they wish to. It is wretched landlords like my uncle and myself who are oppressed!" and he smiled delightedly, he was so happy to hear her talk.

"When I shall know I shall perhaps find it all interesting," she continued to the Duke.

"Between us we shall have to instruct you thoroughly, eh, Tristram, my boy? And then you must be a great leader, and have a salon, as the ladies of the eighteenth century did: we want a beautiful young woman to draw us all together."

"Well, don't you think I have found you a perfect specimen, Uncle!" Tristram exclaimed; and he raised his glass and kissed the brim, while he whispered:

"Darling, my sweet lady--I drink to your health."

But this was too much for Zara--he was overdoing the part--and she turned and flashed upon him a glance of resentment and contempt.

Beyond the Duke sat Jimmy Danvers, and then Emily Guiscard and Lord Coltshurst, and the two young people exchanged confidences in a low voice.

"I say, Emily, isn't she a corker?" Sir James said. "She don't look a bit English, though, she reminds me of a--oh, well, I'm not good at history or dates, but some one in the old Florentine time. She looks as if she could put a dagger into one or give a fellow a cup of poison, without turning a hair."

"Oh, Jimmy! how horrid," exclaimed Emily. "She does not seem to me to have a cruel face, she only looks peculiar and mysterious, and--and--unsmiling. Do you think she loves Tristram? Perhaps that is the foreign way--to appear so cold."

At that moment Sir James Danvers caught the glance which Zara gave her fiance for his toast.

"Je-hoshaphat!" he exclaimed! But he realized that Emily had not seen, so he stopped abruptly.

"Yes--one can never be sure of things with foreigners," he said, and he looked down at his plate. That poor devil of a Tristram was going to have a thorny time in the future, he thought, and he was to be best man at the wedding; it would be like giving the old chap over to a tigress! But, by Jove!--such a beautiful one would be worth being eaten by--he added to himself.

And during one of Francis Markrute's turnings to his left-hand neighbor Lord Coltshurst said to Lady Ethelrida:

"I think Tristram's choice peculiarly felicitous, Ethelrida, do not you? But I fear her ladyship"--and he glanced timidly at his wife--"will not take this view. She has a most unreasonable dislike for young women with red hair. 'Ungovernable temperaments,' she affirms. I trust she won't prejudice your Aunt Jane."

"Aunt Jane always thinks for herself," said Lady Ethelrida. She announced no personal opinion about Tristram's fiance, nor could Lord Coltshurst extort one from her.

As the dinner went on she felt a growing sense that they were all on the edge of a volcano.

Lady Ethelrida never meddled in other people's affairs, but she loved Tristram as a brother and she felt a little afraid. She could not see his face, from where she sat--the table was a long one with oval ends--but she, too, had seen the flash from Zara which had caused Jimmy Danvers to exclaim: "Jehoshaphat!"

The host soon turned back from duty to pleasure, leaving Lady Coltshurst to Lord Charles Montfitchet. The conversation turned upon types.

Types were not things of chance, Francis Markrute affirmed; if one could look back far enough there was always a reason for them.

"People are so extremely unthinking about such a number of interesting things, Lady Ethelrida," he said, "their speculative faculties seem only to be able to roam into cut and dried channels. We have had great scientists like Darwin investigating our origin, and among the Germans there are several who study the atavism of races, but in general even educated people are perfectly ignorant upon the subject, and they expect little Tommy Jones and Katie Robinson, or Jacques Dubois and Marie Blanc, to have the same instincts as your cousin, Lord Tancred, and you, for instance. Whatever individual you are dealing with, you should endeavor to understand his original group. In moments of great excitement when all acquired control is in abeyance the individual always returns to the natural action of his group."

"How interesting!" said Lady Ethelrida. "Let us look round the table and decide to what particular group each one of us belongs."

"Most of you are from the same group," he said meditatively. "Eliminating myself and my niece, Sir James Danvers has perhaps had the most intermixtures."

"Yes," said Lady Ethelrida, and she laughed. "Jimmy's grandmother was the daughter of a very rich Manchester cotton spinner; that is what gives him his sound common sense. I am afraid Tristram and the rest of us except Lord Coltshurst have not had anything sensible like that in us for hundreds of years, so what would be your speculation as to the action of our group?"

"That you would have high courage and fine senses, and highly-strung, nervous force, and chivalry and good taste, and broad and noble aims in the higher half and that in the lower portion you would run to the decadence of all those things-- the fine turned to vices--yet even so I would not look for vulgarity, or bad taste, or cowardice in any of you."

"No," said Lady Ethelrida--"I hope not. Then, according to your reasoning it is very unjust of us when we say, as perhaps you have heard it said, that Lady Darrowood is to blame when she is noisy and assertive and treats Lord Darrowood with bad taste?"

"Certainly--she only does those things when she is excited and has gone back to her group. When she is under her proper control she plays the part of an English marchioness very well. It is the prerogative of a new race to be able to play a part; the result of the cunning and strength which have been required of the immediate forbears in order to live at all under unfavorable conditions. Now, had her father been a Deptford ox-slaughterer instead of a Chicago pig-sticker she could never have risen to the role of a marchioness at all. This is no new country; it does not need nor comprehend bluff, and so produces no such type as Lady Darrowood."

At this moment Lady Ethelrida again caught sight of Zara. She was silent at the instant, and a look of superb pride and disdain was on her face. Almost before she was aware of it Ethelrida had exclaimed:

"Your niece looks like an empress, a wonderful, Byzantine, Roman empress!"

Francis Markrute glanced at her, sideways, with his clever eyes; had she ever heard anything of Zara's parentage, he wondered for a second, and then he smiled at himself for the thought. Lady Ethelrida was not likely to have spoken so in that case--she would not be acting up to her group.

"There are certain reasons why she should," he said. "I cannot answer for the part of her which comes from her father, Maurice Grey, a very old English family, I believe, but on her mother's side she could have the passions of an artist and the pride of a Caesar: she is a very interesting case."

"May I know something of her?" Ethelrida said, "I do so want them to be happy. Tristram is one of the simplest and finest characters I have ever met. He will love her very much, I fear."

"Why do you say you *fear?*"

Lady Ethelrida reddened a little; a soft, warm flush came into her delicate face and made it look beautiful: she never spoke of love--to men.

"Because a great love is a very powerful and sometimes a terrible thing, if it is not returned in like measure. And, oh, forgive me for saying so, but the Countess Shulski does not look as if--she loved Tristram--much."

Francis Markrute did not speak for an instant, then he turned and gazed straight into her eyes gravely, as he said:

"Believe me, I would not allow your cousin to marry my niece if I were not truly convinced that it will be for the eventual great happiness of them both. Will you promise me something, Lady Ethelrida? Will you help me not to permit any one to interfere between them for some time, no matter how things may appear? Give them the chance of settling everything themselves."

Ethelrida looked back at him, with a seriousness equal to his own as she answered, "I promise." And inwardly the sense of some unknown undercurrent that might grow into a rushing torrent made itself felt, stronger than before.

Meanwhile Lady Coltshurst, who could just see Zara's profile all the time when she put up those irritating, longhandled glasses of hers, now gave her opinion of the bride-elect to Lord Charles Montfitchet, her neighbor on the left hand.

"I strongly disapprove of her, Charles. Either her hair is dyed or her eyes are blackened; that mixture is not natural, and if, indeed, it should be in this case then I consider it uncanny and not what one would wish for in the family."

"Oh, I say, my lady!" objected Lord Charles, "I think she is the most stunning-looking young woman I've seen in a month of Sundays!"

Lady Coltshurst put up her glasses again and glared:

"I cannot bear your modern slang, Charles, but 'stunning,' used literally, is quite appropriate. She does stun one; that is exactly it. I fear poor Tristram with such a type can look forward to very little happiness, or poor Jane to any likelihood that the Tancred name will remain free from scandal."

Lord Charles grew exasperated and retaliated.

"By George! A demure mouse can cause scandal to a name, with probably more certainty than this beauty!"

There was a member of Lady Coltshurst's husband's family whom she herself, having no children, had brought out, and who had been perilously near the Divorce Court this very season: and she was a dull, colorless little thing.

Her ladyship turned the conversation abruptly, with an annihilating glance. And fortunately, just then Zara rose, and the ladies filed out of the room: and so this trying dinner was over.

CHAPTER XIII

Nothing could exceed Zara's dignity, when they reached the drawing-room above. They at first stood in a group by the fire in the larger room, and Emily and Mary tried to get a word in and say something nice in their frank girlish way. They admired their future sister-in-law so immensely, and if Zara had not thought they were all acting a part, as she herself was, she would have been touched at their sweetness. As it was she inwardly froze more and more, while she answered with politeness; and Lady Ethelrida, watching quietly for a while, grew further puzzled.

It was certainly a mask this extraordinary and beautiful young woman was wearing, she felt, and presently, when Lady Coltshurst who had remained rather silently aloof, only fixing them all in turn with her long eyeglasses, drew the girls aside to talk to her by asking for news of their mother's headache, Ethelrida indicated she and Zara might sit down upon the nearest, stiff, French sofa; and as she clasped her thin, fine hands together, holding her pale gray gloves which she did not attempt to put on again, she said gently:

"I hope we shall all make you feel you are so welcome, Zara--may I call you Zara? It is such a beautiful name I think."

The Countess Shulski's strange eyes seemed to become blacker than ever--a startled, suspicious look grew in them, just such as had come into the black panther's on a day when Francis Markrute whistled a softly caressing note outside its bars: what did this mean?

"I shall be very pleased if you will," she said coldly.

Lady Ethelrida determined not to be snubbed. She must overcome this barrier if she could, for Tristram's sake.

"England and our customs must seem so strange to you," she went on. "But we are not at all disagreeable people when you know us!" And she smiled encouragingly.

"It is easy to be agreeable when one is happy," Zara said. "And you all seem very happy here--sans souci. It is good."

And Ethelrida wondered. "What can make you so unhappy, you beautiful thing, with Tristram to love you, and youth and health and riches?"

And Zara thought, "This appears a sweet and most frank lady, but how can I tell? I know not the English. It is perhaps because she is so well bred that she is enabled to act so nicely."

"You have not yet seen Wrayth, have you?" Ethelrida went on. "I am sure you will be interested in it, it is so old."

"Wr--ayth--?" Zara faltered. She had never heard of it! What was Wrayth?

"Perhaps I do not pronounce it as you are accustomed to think of it," Ethelrida said kindly. She was absolutely startled at the other's ignorance. "Tristram's place, I mean. The Guiscards have owned it ever since the Conqueror gave it to them after the Battle of Hastings, you know. It is the rarest case of a thing being so long in one family, even here in England, and the title has only gone in the male line, too, as yet. But Tristram and Cyril are the very last. If anything happened to them it would be the end. Oh! we are all so glad Tristram is going to be married!"

Zara's eyes now suddenly blazed at the unconscious insinuation in this speech. Any one who has ever watched a caged creature of the cat tribe and seen how the whole gamut of emotions--sullen endurance, suspicion, resentment, hate and rage, as well as contentment and happiness--can appear in its orbs without the slightest aid from lids or eyebrows, without the smallest alteration in mouth or chin, will understand how Zara's pools of ink spoke while their owner remained icily still.

She understood perfectly the meaning of Ethelrida's speech. The line of the Tancreds should go on through her! But never, never! That should never be! If they were counting upon that they were counting in vain. The marriage was never intended to be anything but an empty ceremony, for mercenary reasons. There must be no mistake about this. What if Lord Tancred had such ideas, too? And she quivered suddenly and caught in her breath with the horror of this thought.

And who was Cyril? Zara had no knowledge of Cyril, any more than of Wrayth! But she did not ask.

If Francis Markrute had heard this conversation he would have been very much annoyed with himself, and would have blamed himself for stupidity. He, of course, should have seen that his niece was sufficiently well coached, in all the details that she should know, not to be led into these pitfalls.

Ethelrida felt a sensation of a sort of petrified astonishment. There is a French word, ***ahuri***, which expresses her emotion exactly, but there is no English equivalent. Tristram's fiance was evidently quite ignorant of the simplest facts about him, or his family, or his home! Her eyes had blazed at Ethelrida's last speech, with a look of self-defence and defiance. And yet Tristram was evidently passionately in love with her. How could such things be? It was a great mystery. Ethelrida was thrilled and interested.

Francis Markrute guessed the ladies' lonely moments would be most difficult to pass, so he had curtailed the enjoyment of the port and old brandy and cigars to the shortest possible dimensions, Tristram aiding him. His one desire was to be near his fiance.

The overmastering magnetic current which seemed to have drawn him from the very first moment he had seen her now had augmented into almost pain. She had been cruelly cold and disdainful at dinner whenever she had spoken to him, her contempt showing plainly in her eyes, and it had maddened and excited him; and when the other men had all drunk the fiances' health and wished them happiness he had gulped down the old brandy, and vowed to himself, "Before a year is out I will make her love me as I love her, so help me God!"

And then they all had trooped up into the drawing-room just as Ethelrida was saying,

"The northern property, Morndale, is not half so pretty as Wrayth--"

But when she saw them enter she rose and ceded her place to Tristram who gladly sank into the sofa beside his lady.

He was to have no tete-a-tete, however, for Jimmy Danvers who felt it was his turn to say something to the coming bride came now, and leant upon the mantelpiece beside them.

"I am going to be the most severe 'best man' next Wednesday, Countess," he said. "I shall see that Tristram is at St. George's a good half-hour before the time, and that he does not drop the ring; you trust to me!" And he laughed nervously,

Zara's face was so unresponsive.

"Countess Shulski does not know the English ceremony, Jimmy," Tristram interrupted quickly, "nor what is a 'best man.' Now, if we were only across the water we would have a rehearsal of the whole show as we did for Darrowood's wedding."

"That must have been a joke," said Jimmy.

"It was very sensible there; there was such a lot of fuss, and bridesmaids, and things; but we are going to be quite quiet, aren't we, Zara? I hate shows; don't you?"

"Immensely," was all she answered.

Then Sir James, who felt thoroughly crushed, after one or two more fatuous remarks moved away, and Zara arose in her character of hostess, and spoke to Lady Coltshurst.

Tristram crossed over to the Duke and rapidly began a political discussion, but while his uncle appeared to notice nothing unusual, and entered into it with interest, his kind, old heart was wrung with the pain he saw his favorite nephew was suffering.

"Mr. Markrute, I am troubled," Lady Ethelrida said, as she walked with the host to look at an exquisite Vigee le Brun across the room. "Your niece is the most interesting personality I have ever met; but, underneath, something is making her unhappy, I am sure. Please, what does it mean? Oh, I know I have promised what I did at dinner, but are you certain it is all right? And can they ever be really at peace together?"

Francis Markrute bent over, apparently to point to a *bibelot* which lay on a table under the picture, and he said in a low, vibrating tone.

"I give you my word there is some one, who is dead--whom I loved--who would come back and curse me now, if I should let this thing be, with a doubt in my heart as to their eventual happiness."

And Lady Ethelrida looked full at him and saw that the man's cold face was deeply moved and softened.

"If that is so then I will speculate no more," she said. "Listen! I will trust you!"

"You dear, noble English lady," the financier replied, "how truly I thank you!" And he let some of the emotion which he felt, gleam from his eyes, while he changed the conversation.

A few minutes after this, Lady Coltshurst announced it was time to go, and she would take the girls home. And the Duke's carriage was also waiting, and good nights were said, and the host whispered to Jimmy Danvers,

"Take Tancred along with you, too, please. My niece is overtired with the strain of this evening and I want her to go to bed at once." And to Tristram he said,

"Do not even say good night, like a dear fellow. Don't you see she is almost ready to faint? Just go quietly with the rest, and come for her to-morrow morning to take her to your mother."

So they all left as he wished, and he himself went back upstairs to the big drawing-room and there saw Zara standing like a marble statue, exactly as they had left her, and he went forward, and, bending, kissed her hand.

"Most beautifully endured, my queenly niece!" he said; and then he led her to the door and up to her room. She was perfectly mute.

But a little while afterwards, as he came to bed himself, he was startled and chilled by hearing the **Chanson Triste** being played in her sitting-room, with a wailing, passionate pathos, as of a soul in anguish.

And if he could have seen her face he would have seen her great eyes streaming with tears, while she prayed:

"Maman, ask God to give me courage to get through all of this, since it is for your Mirko."

CHAPTER XIV

Satan was particularly fresh next morning when Tristram took him for a canter round the Park. He was glad of it: he required something to work off steam upon. He was in a mood of restless excitement. During the three weeks of Zara's absence he had allowed himself to dream into a state of romantic love for her. He had glossed over in his mind her distant coldness, her frigid adherence to the bare proposition, so that to return to that state of things had come to him as a shock.

But, this morning, he knew he was a fool to have expected anything else. He was probably a great fool altogether, but he never changed his mind, and was prepared to pay the price of his folly. After all, there would be plenty of time afterwards to melt her dislike, so he could afford to wait now. He would not permit himself to suffer again as he had done last night. Then he came in and had his bath, and made himself into a very perfect-looking lover, to present himself to his lady at about half-past twelve o'clock, to take her to his mother.

Zara was, if anything, whiter than usual when she came into the library where he was waiting for her alone. The financier had gone to the City. She had heavy, bluish shadows under her eyes, and he saw quite plainly that, the night before, she must have been weeping bitterly.

A great tenderness came over him. What was this sorrow of hers? Why might he not comfort her? He put out both hands and then, as she remained stonily unresponsive, he dropped them, and only said quietly that he hoped she was well, and his motor was waiting outside, and that his mother, Lady Tancred, would be expecting them.

"I am ready," said Zara. And they went.

He told her as they flew along, that he had been riding in the Park that morn-

ing, and had looked up at the house and wondered which was her window; and
then he asked her if she liked riding, and she said she had never tried for ten years-
-the opportunity to ride had not been in her life--but she used to like it when she
was a child.

"I must get you a really well-mannered hack," he said joyously. Here was a
subject she had not snubbed him over! "And you will let me teach you again when
we go down to Wrayth, won't you?"

But before she could answer they had arrived at the house in Queen Street.

Michelham, with a subdued beam on his old face, stood inside the door with
his footmen, and Tristram said gayly,

"Michelham, this is to be her new ladyship; Countess Shulski"--and he turned
to Zara. "Michelham is a very old friend of mine, Zara. We used to do a bit of poach-
ing together, when I was a boy and came home from Eton."

Michelham was only a servant and could not know of her degradation, so Zara
allowed herself to smile and looked wonderfully lovely, as the old man said,

"I am sure I wish your ladyship every happiness, and his lordship, too; and, if I
may say so, with such a gentleman your ladyship is sure to have it."

And Tristram chaffed him, and they went upstairs.

Lady Tancred had rigidly refrained from questioning her daughters, on their
return from the dinnerparty; she had not even seen them until the morning, and
when they had both burst out with descriptions of their future sister-in-law's beauty and strangeness their mother had stopped them.

"Do not tell me anything about her, dear children," she had said. "I wish to
judge for myself without prejudice."

But Lady Coltshurst could not be so easily repressed. She had called early, on
purpose to give her views, with the ostensible excuse of an inquiry about her sister-
in-law's health.

"I am afraid you will be rather unfavorably impressed with Tristram's choice,
when you have seen her, Jane," she announced. "I confess I was. She treated us all
as though *she* were conferring the honor, not receiving it, and she is by no means a
type that promises domestic tranquillity for Tristram."

"Really, Julia!" Lady Tancred protested. "I must beg of you to say no more. I
have perfect confidence in my son, and wish to receive his future wife with every

mark of affection."

"Your efforts will be quite wasted, then, Jane," her sister-in-law snapped. "She is most forbidding, and never once unbent nor became genial, the whole evening. And besides, for a lady, she is much too striking looking."

"She cannot help being beautiful," Lady Tancred said. "I am sure I shall admire her very much, from what the girls tell me. But we will not discuss her. It was so kind of you to come, and my head is much better."

"Then I will be off!" Lady Coltshurst sniffed in a slightly offended tone. Really, relations were so tiresome! They never would accept a word of advice or warning in the spirit it was given, and Jane in particular was unpleasantly difficult.

So she got into her electric brougham, and was rolled away, happily before Tristram and his lady appeared upon the scene; but the jar of her words still lingered with Lady Tancred, in spite of all her efforts to forget it.

Zara's heart beat when they got to the door, and she felt extremely antagonistic. Francis Markrute had left her in entire ignorance of the English customs, for a reason of his own. He calculated if he informed her that on Tristram's side it was purely a love match, she, with her strange temperament, and sense of honor, would never have accepted it. He knew she would have turned upon him and said she could be no party to such a cheat. He with his calm, calculating brain had weighed the pros and cons of the whole matter: to get her to consent, for her brother's sake in the beginning, under the impression that it was a dry business arrangement, equally distasteful personally to both parties--to leave her with this impression and keep the pair as much as possible apart, until the actual wedding; and then to leave her awakening to Tristram--was his plan. A woman would be impossibly difficult to please, if, in the end, she failed to respond to such a lover as Tristram! He counted upon what he had called her moral antennae to make no mistakes. It would not eventually prejudice matters if the family did find her a little stiff, as long as she did not actually show her contempt for their apparent willingness to support the bargain. But her look of scorn, the night before, when he had shown some uneasiness on this score, had reassured him. He would leave things alone and let her make her own discoveries.

So now she entered her future mother-in-law's room, with a haughty mien and no friendly feelings in her heart. She was well acquainted with the foreign

examples of mother-in-law. They interfered with everything and had their sons
under their thumbs. They seemed always mercenary, and were the chief agents
in promoting a match, if it were for their own family's advantage. No doubt Uncle
Francis had arranged the whole affair with this Lady Tancred in the first instance,
and she, Zara, would not be required to keep up the comedy, as with the uncle and
cousins. She decided she would be quite frank with her if the occasion required,
and if she should, by chance, make the same insinuation of the continuance of the
Tancred race as Lady Ethelrida had innocently done, she would have plainly to say
that was not in the transaction. For her own ends she must be Lord Tancred's wife
and let her uncle have what glory he pleased from the position; if that were his
reason, and as for Lord Trancred's ends, he was to receive money. That was all: it
was quite simple.

The two women were mutually surprised when they looked at one another.
Lady Tancred's first impression was, "It is true she is a very disturbing type, but how
well bred and how beautiful!" And Zara thought, "It is possible that, after all, I may
be wrong. She looks too proud to have stooped to plan this thing. It may be only
Lord Tancred's doing--men are more horrible than women."

"This is Zara, Mother," Tristram said.

And Lady Tancred held out her hands, and then drew her new daughter--that
was to be--nearer and kissed her.

And over Zara there crept a thrill. She saw that the elder lady was greatly
moved, and no woman had kissed her since her mother's death. Why, if it were all
a bargain, should she tenderly kiss her?

"I am so glad to welcome you, dear," Lady Tancred said, determining to be very
gracious. "I am almost pleased not to have been able to go last night. Now I can have
you all to myself for this, our first little meeting."

And they sat down on a sofa, and Zara asked about her head; and Lady Tancred
told her the pain was almost gone, and this broke the ice and started a conversation.

"I want you to tell me of yourself," Lady Tancred said. "Do you think you will
like this old England of ours, with its damp and its gloom in the autumn, and its
beautiful fresh spring? I want you to--and to love your future home."

"Everything is very strange to me, but I will try," Zara answered.

"Tristram has been making great arrangements to please you at Wrayth," Lady Tancred went on. "But, of course, he has told you all about it."

"I have had to be away all the time," Zara felt she had better say--and Tristram interrupted.

"They are all to be surprises, Mother; everything is to be new to Zara, from beginning to end. You must not tell her anything of it."

Then Lady Tancred spoke of gardens. She hoped Zara liked gardens; she herself was a great gardener, and had taken much pride in her herbaceous borders and her roses at Wrayth.

And when they had got to this stage of the conversation Tristram felt he could safely leave them to one another, so, saying he wanted to talk to his sisters, he went out of the room.

"It will be such happiness to think of your living in the old home," the proud lady said. "It was a great grief to us all when we had to shut it up, two years ago; but you will, indeed, adorn it for its reopening."

Zara did not know what to reply. She vaguely understood that one might love a home, though she had never had one but the gloomy castle near Prague; and that made her sigh when she thought of it.

But a garden she knew she should love. And Mirko was so fond of flowers. Oh! if they would let her have a beautiful country home in peace, and Mirko to come sometimes, and play there, and chase butterflies, with his excited, poor little face, she would indeed be grateful to them. Her thoughts went on in a dream of this, while Lady Tancred talked of many things, and she answered, "Yes," and "No," with gentle respect. Her future mother-in-law's great dignity pleased her sense of the fitness of things; she so disliked gush of any sort herself, and she felt now that she knew where she was and there need be no explanations. The family, one and all, evidently intended to play the same part, and she would, too. When the awakening came it would be between herself and Tristram. Yes, she must think of him now as "Tristram!"

Her thoughts had wandered again when she heard Lady Tancred's voice, saying,

"I wanted to give you this myself," and she drew a small case from a table near and opened it, and there lay a very beautiful diamond ring. "It is my own little personal present to you, my new, dear daughter. Will you wear it sometimes, Zara, in remembrance of this day and in remembrance that I give into your hands the happiness of my son, who is dearer to me than any one on earth?"

And the two proud pairs of eyes met, and Zara could not answer, and there was a strange silence between them for a second. And then Tristram came back into the room, which created a diversion, and she was enabled to say some ordinary conventional things about the beauty of the stones, and express her thanks for the gift. Only, in her heart, she determined never to wear it. It would burn her hand, she thought, and she could never be a hypocrite.

Luncheon was then announced, and they went into the dining-room.

Here she saw Tristram in a new light, with only "Young Billy" and Jimmy Danvers who had dropped in, and his mother and sisters.

He was gay as a schoolboy, telling Billy who had not spoken a word to Zara the night before that now he should sit beside her, and that he was at liberty to make love to his new cousin! And Billy, aged nineteen--a perfectly stolid and amiable youth--proceeded to start a laborious conversation, while the rest of the table chaffed about things which were Greek to Zara, but she was grateful not to have to talk, and so passed off the difficulties of the situation.

And the moment the meal was over Tristram took her back to Park Lane. He, too, was thankful the affair had been got through; he hardly spoke as they went along, and in silence followed her into the house and into the library, and there waited for her commands.

Whenever they were alone the disguises of the part fell from Zara, and she resumed the icy mien.

"Good-bye," she said coldly. "I am going into the country to-morrow for two or three days. I shall not see you until Monday. Have you anything more it is necessary to say?"

"You are going into the country!" Tristram exclaimed, aghast. "But I will not--" and then he paused, for her eyes had flashed ominously. "I mean," he went on, "must you go? So soon before our wedding?"

She drew herself up and spoke in a scathing voice.

"Why must I repeat again what I said when you gave me your ring?--I do not wish to see or speak with you. You will have all you bargained for. Can you not leave my company out of the question?"

The Tancred stern, obstinate spirit was thoroughly roused. He walked up and down the room rapidly for a moment, fuming with hurt rage. Then reason told him to wait. He had no intention of breaking off the match now, no matter what she should do; and this was Thursday; there were only five more days to get through, and when once she should be his wife--and then he looked at her, as she stood in her dark, perfect dress, with the great, sable wrap slipping from her shoulders and making a regal background, and her beauty fired his senses and made his eyes swim; and he bent forward and took her hand.

"Very well, you beautiful, unkind thing," he said. "But if you do not want to marry me you had better say so at once, and I will release you from your promise. Because when the moment comes afterwards for our crossing of swords there will be no question as to who is to be master--I tell you that now."

And Zara dragged her hand from him, and, with the black panther's glance in her eyes, she turned to the window and stood looking out.

Then after a second she said in a strangled voice,

"I wish that the marriage shall take place.--And now, please go."

And without further words he went.

CHAPTER XV

On her way to Bournemouth next day, to see Mirko, Zara met Mimo in the British Museum. They walked along the galleries on the ground floor until they found a bench near the mausoleum of Halicarnassus. To look at it gave them both infinite pleasure; they knew so well the masterpieces of all the old Greeks. Mimo, it seemed, had been down to see his son ten days before. They had met secretly. Mirko had stolen out, and with the cunning of his little brain fully on the alert he had dodged Mrs. Morley in the garden, and had fled to the near pine woods with his violin; and there had met his father and had a blissful time. He was certainly better, Mimo said, a little fatter and with much less cough, and he seemed fairly happy and quite resigned. The Morleys were so kind and good, but, poor souls! it was not their fault if they could not understand! It was not given to every one to have the understanding of his Cherisette and his own papa, Mirko had said, but so soon he would be well; then he would be able to come back to them, and in the meantime he was going to learn lessons, learn the tiresome things that his Cherisette alone knew how to teach him with comprehension. The new tutor who came each day from the town was of a reasonableness, but no wit! "Body of Bacchus!" the father said, "the poor child had not been able to make the tutor laugh once--in a week--when we met."

And then after a while it seemed that there was some slight care upon Mimo's mind. It had rained, it appeared, before the end of their stolen meeting. It had rained all the morning and then had cleared up gloriously fine, and they had sat down on a bank under the trees, and Mirko had played divinely all sorts of gay airs. But when he got up he had shivered a little, and Mimo could see that his clothes were wet, and then the rain had come on immediately again, and he had made him run back. He feared he must have got thoroughly soaked, and he had had nothing since but one postcard, which said that Mirko had been in bed, though he was now much better and longing--longing to see his Cherisette!

"Oh, Mimo! how could you let him sit on the grass!" Zara exclaimed reproachfully, when he got thus far. "And why was I not told? It may have made him seriously ill. Oh, the poor angel! And I must stay so short a while--and then this wedding--" She stopped abruptly and her eyes became black. For she knew there was no asking for respite. To obtain her brother's possible life she must be ready and resigned, at the altar at St. George's, Hanover Square, on Wednesday the 25th of October, at 2 o'clock, and, once made a wife, she must go with Lord Tancred to the Lord Warren Hotel at Dover, to spend the night.

She rose with a convulsive quiver, and looked with blank, sightless eyes at an Amazon in the frieze hard by. The Amazon--she saw, when vision came back to her--was hurling a spear at a splendid young Greek. That is how she felt she would like to behave to her future husband. Men and their greed of money, and their revolting passions!--and her poor little Mirko ill, perhaps, from his father's carelessness--How could she leave him? And if she did not his welfare would be at an end and life an abyss.

There was no use scolding Mimo; she knew of old no one was sorrier than he for his mistakes, for which those he loved best always had to suffer. It had taken the heart out of him, the anxious thought, he said, but, knowing that Cherisette must be so busy arranging to get married, he had not troubled her, since she could do nothing until her return to England, and then he knew she would arrange to go to Mirko at once, in any case.

He, Mimo, had been too depressed to work, and the picture of the London fog was not much further advanced, and he feared it would not be ready for her wedding gift.

"Oh, never mind!" said Zara. "I know you will think of me kindly, and I shall like that as well as any present."

And then she drove to the Waterloo station alone, a gnawing anxiety in her heart. And all the journey to Bournemouth her spirits sank lower and lower until, when she got there, it seemed as if the old cab-horse were a cow in its slowness, to get to the doctor's trim house.

"Yes," Mrs. Morley said as soon as she arrived, "your little brother has had a very sharp attack."

He escaped from the garden about ten days before, she explained, and was gone at least two hours, and then returned wet through, and was a little light-headed that night, and had talked of "Maman and the angels," and "Papa and Cherisette," but they could obtain no information from him as to why he went, nor whom he had seen. He had so rapidly recovered that the doctor had not thought it necessary to let any one know, and she, Mrs. Morley--guessing how busy one must be ordering a trousseau--when there was no danger had refrained from sending a letter, to be forwarded from the given address.

Here Zara's eyes had flashed, and she had said sternly,

"The trousseau was not of the slightest consequence in comparison to my brother's health."

Mirko was upstairs in his pretty bedroom, playing with a puzzle and the nurse; he had not been told of his sister's proposed coming, but some sixth sense seemed to inform him it was she, when her footfall sounded on the lower stairs, for they heard an excited voice shouting:

"I tell you I will go--I will go to her, my Cherisette!" And Zara hastened the last part, to avoid his rushing, as she feared he would do, out of his warm room into the cold passage.

The passionate joy he showed at the sight of her made a tightness round her heart. He did not look ill, only, in some unaccountable way, he seemed to have grown smaller. There was, too, even an extra pink flush in his cheeks.

He must sit on her lap and touch all her pretty things. She had put on her uncle's big pearl earrings and one string of big pearls, on purpose to show him; he so loved what was beautiful and refined.

"Thou art like a queen, Cherisette," he told her. "Much more beautiful than when we had our tea party, and I wore Papa's paper cap. And everything new! The uncle, then, is very rich," he went on, while he stroked the velvet on her dress.

And she kissed and soothed him to sleep in her arms, when he was ready for his bed. It was getting quite late, and she sang a soft, Slavonic cradle song, in a low cooing voice, and, every now and then, before the poor little fellow sank entirely to rest, he would open his beautiful, pathetic eyes, and they would swim with love and happiness, while he murmured, "Adored Cherisette!"

The next day--Saturday--she never left him. They played games together, and puzzles. The nurse was kind, but of a thickness of understanding, like all the rest, he said, and, with his sister there, he could dispense with her services for the moment. He wished, when it grew dusk and they were to have their tea, to play his violin to only her, in the firelight; and there he drew forth divine sounds for more than an hour, tearing at Zara's heart-strings with the exquisite notes until her eyes grew wet. And at last he began something that she did not know, and the weird, little figure moved as in a dance in the firelight, while he played this new air as one inspired, and then stopped suddenly with a crash of joyous chords.

"It is *Maman* who has taught me that!" he whispered. "When I was ill she came often and sang it to me, and when they would give me back my violin I found it at once, and now I am so happy. It talks of the butterflies in the woods, which are where she lives, and there is a little white one which flies up beside her with her radiant blue wings. And she has promised me that the music will take me to her, quite soon. Oh, Cherisette!"

"No, no," said Zara faintly. "I cannot spare you, darling. I shall have a beautiful garden of my own next summer, and you must come and stay with me, Mirko mio, and chase real butterflies with a golden net."

And this thought enchanted the child. He must hear all about his sister's garden. By chance there was an old number of *Country Life* lying on the table, and, the nurse bringing in the tea at the moment, they turned on the electric light and looked at the pictures; and by the strangest coincidence, when they came to the weekly series of those beautiful houses she read at the beginning of the article, "Wrayth--the property of Lord Tancred of Wrayth."

"See, Mirko," she said in a half voice; "our garden will look exactly like this."

And the child examined every picture with intense interest. One of a statue of Pan and his pipe, making the center of a star in the Italian parterre, pleased him most.

"For see, Cherisette, he, too, is not shaped as other people are," he whispered with delight. "Look! And he plays music, also! When you walk there, and I am with *Maman*, you must remember that this is me!"

It was with deep grief and foreboding that Zara left him, on Monday morning, in spite of the doctor's assurance that he was indeed on the turn to get quite well-

-well of this sharp attack--whether he would ever grow to be a man was always a doubt but there was no present anxiety--she could be happy on that score. And with this she was obliged to rest content.

But all the way back in the train she saw the picture of the Italian parterre at Wrayth with the statue of Pan, in the center of the star, playing his pipes.

CHAPTER XVI

The second wedding day of Zara Shulski dawned with a glorious sun. One of those autumn mornings that seem like a return to the spring--so fresh and pure the air. She had not seen her bridegroom since she got back from Bournemouth, nor any of the family; she had said to her uncle that she could not bear it.

"I am at the end of my forces, Uncle Francis. You are so clever--you can invent some good excuse. If I must see Lord Tancred I cannot answer for what I may do."

And the financier had realized that this was the truth. The strings of her soul were strained to breaking point, and he let her pass the whole day of Tuesday in peace.

She signed numbers of legal documents concerning her marriage settlements, without the slightest interest; and then her uncle handed her one which he said she was to read with care. It set forth in the wearisome language of the law the provision for Mirko's life, "in consideration of a certain agreement" come to between her uncle and herself. But should the boy Mirko return at any time to the man Sykypri, his father, or should she, Zara, from the moneys settled upon herself give sums to this man Sykypri the transaction between herself and her uncle regarding the boy's fortune would be null and void. This was the document's sense.

Zara read it over but the legal terms were difficult for her. "If it means exactly what we agreed upon, Uncle Francis, I will sign it," she said, "that is--that Mirko shall be cared for and have plenty of money for life."

And Francis Markrute replied,

"That is what is meant."

And then she had gone to her room, and spent the night before her wedding alone. She had steadily read one of her favorite books: she could not permit herself for a moment to think.

There was a man going to be hanged on the morrow, she had seen in the papers; and she wondered if, this last night in his cell, the condemned wretch was numb, or was he feeling at bay, like herself?

Then, at last she opened the window and glanced out on the moon. It was there above her, over the Park, so she turned out the lights, and, putting her furs around her, she sat for a while and gazed above the treetops, while she repeated her prayers.

And Mimo saw her, as he stood in the shadow on the pavement at the other side of Park Lane. He had come there in his sentimental way, to give her his blessing, and had been standing looking up for some time. It seemed to him a good omen for dear Cherisette's happiness, that she should have opened the window and looked out on the night.

It was quite early--only about half-past ten--and Tristram, after a banquet with his bachelor friends on the Monday night, had devoted this, his last evening, to his mother, and had dined quietly with her alone.

He felt extremely moved, and excited, too, when he left. She had talked to him so tenderly--the proud mother who so seldom unbent. How marriage was a beautiful but serious thing, and he must love and try to understand his wife--and then she spoke of her own great love for him, and her pride in their noble name and descent.

"And I will pray to God that you have strong, beautiful children, Tristram, so that there may in years to come be no lack of the Tancreds of Wrayth."

When he got outside in the street the moonlight flooded the road, so he sent his motor away and decided to walk. He wanted breathing space, he wanted to think, and he turned down into Curzon Street and from, thence across Great Stanhope Street and into the Park.

And to-morrow night, at this time, the beautiful Zara would be his! and they would be dining alone together at Dover, and surely she would not be so icily cold; surely--surely he could get her to melt.

And then further visions came to him, and he walked very fast; and presently he found himself opposite his lady's house.

An impulse just to see her window overcame him, and he crossed the road and went out of the gate. And there on the pavement he saw Mimo, also with face turned, gazing up.

And in a flash he thought he recognized that this was the man he had seen that day in Whitehall, when he was in his motor car, going very fast.

A mad rage of jealousy and suspicion rushed through him. Every devil whispered, "Here is a plot. You know nothing of the woman whom to-morrow you are blindly going to make your wife. Who is this man? What is his connection with her? A lover's--of course. No one but a lover would gaze up at a window on a moonlight night."

And it was at this moment that Zara opened the window and, for a second, both men saw her slender, rounded figure standing out sharply against the ground of the room. Then she turned, and put out the light.

A murderous passion of rage filled Lord Tancred's heart.

He looked at Mimo and saw that the man's lips were muttering a prayer, and that he had drawn a little silver crucifix from his coat pocket, and, also, that he was unconscious of any surroundings, for his face was rapt; and he stepped close to him and heard him murmur, in his well-pronounced English,

"Mary, Mother of God, pray for her, and bring her happiness!"

And his common sense reassured him somewhat. If the man were a lover, he could not pray so, on this, the night before her wedding to another. It was not in human, male nature, he felt, to do such an unselfish thing as that.

Then Mimo raised his soft felt hat in his rather dramatic way to the window, and walked up the street.

And Tristram, a prey to all sorts of conflicting emotions, went back into the Park.

*   *   *   *   *

It seemed to Francis Markrute that more than half the nobility of England had assembled in St. George's, Hanover Square, next day, as, with the beautiful bride on his arm, he walked up the church.

She wore a gown of dead white velvet, and her face looked the same shade, under the shadow of a wonderful picture creation, of black velvet and feathers, in the way of a hat.

The only jewels she had on were the magnificent pearls which were her uncle's gift. There was no color about her except in her red burnished hair and her red, curved mouth.

And the whole company thrilled as she came up the aisle. She looked like the Princess in a fairy tale--but just come to life.

The organ stopped playing, and now, as in a dream she knew that she was kneeling beside Tristram and that the Bishop had joined their hands.

She repeated the vows mechanically, in a low, quiet voice. All the sense of it that came to her brain was Tristram's firm utterance, "I, Tristram Lorrimer Guiscard, take thee, Zara Elinka, to be my wedded wife."

And so, at last, the ceremony was over, and Lord and Lady Tancred walked into the vestry to sign their names. And as Zara slipped her hand from the arm of her newly-made husband he bent down his tall head and kissed her lips; and, fortunately, the train of coming relations and friends were behind them, as yet, and the Bishops were looking elsewhere, or they would have been startled to observe the bride shiver, and to have seen the expression of passionate resentment which crept into her face. But the bridegroom saw it, and it stabbed his heart.

Then it seemed that a number of people kissed her: his mother and sisters, and Lady Ethelrida, and, lastly, the Duke.

"I am claiming my privilege as an old man," this latter said gayly, "and I welcome you to all our hearts, my beautiful niece."

And Zara had answered, but had hardly been able to give even a mechanical smile.

And when they got into the smart, new motor, after passing through the admiring crowds, she had shrunk into her corner, and half closed her eyes. And Tristram, intensely moved and strained with the excitement of it all, had not known what to think.

But pride made his bride play her part when they reached her uncle's house.

She stood with her bridegroom, and bowed graciously to the countless, congratulatory friends of his, who passed and shook hands. And, when soon after they had entered Lady Tancred arrived with Cyril and the girls, she had even smiled sweetly for one moment, when that gallant youth had stood on tiptoe and given her a hearty kiss! He was very small for his age, and full of superb self-possession.

"I think you are a stunner, Zara," he said. "Two of our fellows, cousins of mine, who were in church with me, congratulated me awfully. And now I hope you're soon going to cut the cake?"

And Tristram wondered why her mutinous mouth had quivered and her eyes become full of mist. She was thinking of her own little brother, far away, who did not even know that there would be any cake.

And so, eventually, they had passed through the shower of rice and slippers and were at last alone in the motorcar again; and once more she shrank into her corner and did not speak, and he waited patiently until they should be in the train.

But once there, in the reserved saloon, when the obsequious guard had finally shut the door from waving friends and last hand shakes, and they slowly steamed out of the station, he came over and sat down beside her and tenderly took her little gray-gloved hand.

But she drew it away from him, and moved further off, before he could even speak.

"Zara!" he said pleadingly.

Then she looked intensely fierce.

"Can you not let me be quiet for a moment?" she hissed. "I am tired out."

And he saw that she was trembling, and, though he was very much in love and maddeningly exasperated with everything, he let her rest, and even settled her cushion for her, silently, and took a paper and sat in an armchair near, and pretended to read.

And Zara stared out of the window, her heart beating in her throat. For she knew this was only a delay because, as her uncle had once said, the English nobility as a race were great gentlemen--and this one in particular--and because of that he would not be likely to make a scene in the train; but they would arrive at the hotel presently, and there was dinner to be got through, alone with him, and then--the afterwards. And as she thought of this her very lips grew white.

The hideous, hideous hatefulness of men! Visions of moments of her first wedding journey with Ladislaus came back to her. He had not shown her any consideration for five minutes in his life.

Everything in her nature was up in arms. She could not be just; with her belief in his baseness it seemed to her that here was this man--her husband--whom she had seen but four times in her life, and he was not content with the honest bargain which he perfectly understood; not content with her fortune and her willingness to adorn his house, but he must perforce allow his revolting senses to be aroused, he must desire to caress her, just because she was a woman--and fair--and the law would give him the right because she was his wife.

But she would not submit to it! She would find some way out.

As yet she had not even noticed Tristram's charm, that something which drew all other women to him but had not yet appealed to her. She saw on the rare occasions in which she had looked at him that he was very handsome--but so had been Ladislaus, and so was Mimo; and all men were selfish or brutes.

She was half English herself, of course, and that part of her--the calm, common sense of the nation, would assert itself presently; but for the time, everything was too strained through her resentment at fate.

And Tristram watched her from behind his *Evening Standard*, and was unpleasantly thrilled with the passionate hate and resentment and all the varying; storms of feeling which convulsed her beautiful face.

He was extremely sensitive, in spite of his daring *insouciance* and his pride. It would be perfectly impossible to even address her again while she was in this state.

And so this splendid young bride and bridegroom, not understanding each other in the least, sat silent and constrained, when they should have been in each other's arms; and presently, still in the same moods, they came to Dover, and so to the Lord Warden Hotel.

Here the valet and maid had already arrived, and the sitting-room was full of flowers, and everything was ready for dinner and the night.

"I suppose we dine at eight?" said Zara haughtily, and, hardly waiting for an answer, she went into the room beyond and shut the door.

Here she rang for her maid and asked her to remove her hat.

"A hateful, heavy thing," she said, "and there is a whole hour fortunately, before dinner, Henriette, and I want a lovely bath; and then you can brush my hair, and it will be a rest."

The French maid, full of sympathy and excitement, wondered, while she turned on the taps, how *Miladi* should look so disdainful and calm.

"Mon Dieu! if *Milor* was my Raoul! I would be far otherwise," she thought to herself, as she poured in the scent.

At a quarter to the hour of dinner she was still silently brushing her mistress's long, splendid, red hair, while Zara stared into the glass in front of her, with sightless eyes and face set. She was back in Bournemouth, and listening to "Maman's air." It haunted her and rang in her head; and yet, underneath, a wild excitement coursed in her blood.

A knock then came to the door, and when Henrietta answered it Tristram passed her by and stepped into his lady's room.

Zara turned round like a startled fawn, and then her expression changed to one of anger and hauteur.

He was already dressed for dinner, and held a great bunch of gardenias in his hand. He stopped abruptly when he caught sight of the exquisite picture she made, and he drew in his breath. He had not known hair could be so long; he had not realized she was so beautiful. And she was his wife!

"Darling!" he gasped, oblivious of even the maid, who had the discretion to retire quickly to the bathroom beyond. "Darling, how beautiful you are! You drive me perfectly mad."

Zara held on to the dressing-table and almost crouched, like a panther ready to spring.

"How dare you come into my room like this! Go!" she said.

It was as if she had struck him. He drew back, and flung the flowers down into the grate.

"I only came to tell you dinner was nearly ready," he said haughtily, "and to bring you those. But I will await you in the sitting-room, when you are dressed."

And he turned round and left through the door by which he had come.

And Zara called her maid rather sharply, and had her hair plaited and done, and got quickly into her dress. And when she was ready she went slowly into the sitting-room.

She found Tristram leaning upon the mantelpiece, glaring moodily into the flames. He had stood thus for ten minutes, coming to a decision in his mind.

He had been very angry just now, and he thought was justified; but he knew he was passionately in love, as he had never dreamed nor imagined he could be in the whole of his life.

Should he tell her at once about it? and implore her not to be so cold and hard? But no, that would be degrading. After all, he had already shown her a proof of the most reckless devotion, in asking to marry her, after having seen her only once! And she, what had her reasons been? They were forcible enough or she would not have consented to her uncle's wishes before they had even ever met; and he recalled, when he had asked her only on Thursday last if she would wish to be released, that she had said firmly that she wished the marriage to take place. Surely she must know that no man with any spirit would put up with such treatment as this--to be spoken to as though he had been an impudent stranger bursting into her room!

Then his tempestuous thoughts went back to Mimo, that foreign man whom he had seen under her window. What if, after all, he was her lover and that accounted for the reason she resented his--Tristram's--desire to caress?

And all the proud, obstinate fighting blood of the Guiscards got up in him. He would not be made a cat's-paw. If she exasperated him further he would forget about being a gentleman, and act as a savage man, and seize her in his arms and punish her for her haughtiness!

So it was his blue eyes which were blazing with resentment this time, and not her pools of ink.

Thus they sat down to dinner in silence--much to the waiters' surprise and disgust.

Zara felt almost glad her husband looked angry. He would then of his own accord leave her in peace.

As the soup and fish came and went they exchanged no word, and then that breeding that they both had made them realize the situation was impossible, and they said some ordinary things while the waiters were in the room.

The table was a small round one with the two places set at right angles, and very close.

It was the first occasion upon which Zara had ever been so near Tristram, and every time she looked up she was obliged to see his face. She could not help owning to herself, that he was extraordinarily distinguished looking, and that there were strong, noble lines in his whole shape.

At the end of their repast, for different reasons, neither of the two felt calm. Tristram's anger had died down, likewise his suspicions; after a moment's thought the sane point of view always presented itself to his brain. No, whatever her reasons were for her disdain of him, having another lover was not the cause. And then he grew intoxicated again with her beauty and grace.

She was a terrible temptation to him; she would have been so to any normal man--and they were dining together--and she was his very own!

The waiters, with their cough of warning at the door, brought coffee and liqueurs, and then bodily removed the dinner table, and shut the doors.

And now Zara knew she was practically alone with her lord for the night.

He walked about the room--he did not drink any coffee, nor even a Chartreuse--and she stood perfectly still. Then he came back to her, and suddenly clasped her in his arms, and passionately kissed her mouth.

"Zara!" he murmured hoarsely. "Good God! do you think I am a stone! I tell you I love you--madly. Are you not going to be kind to me and really be my wife?"

Then he saw a look in her eyes that turned him to ice.

"Animal!" she hissed, and hit him across the face.

And as he let her fall from him she drew back panting, and deadly white; while he, mad with rage at the blow, stood with flaming blue eyes, and teeth clenched.

"Animal!" again she hissed, and then her words poured forth in a torrent of hate. "Is it not enough that you were willing to sell yourself for my uncle's money--that you were willing to take as a bargain--a woman whom you had never even seen, without letting your revolting passions exhibit themselves like this? And you dare to tell me you love me! What do such as you know of love? Love is a true and a pure and a beautiful thing, not to be sullied like this. It must come from devotion and knowledge. What sort of a vile passion is it which makes a man feel as you do for me? Only that I am a woman. Love! It is no love--it is a question of sense. Any other would do, provided she were as fair. Remember, my lord! I am not your mistress, and I will not stand any of this! Leave me. I hate you, animal that you are!"

He stiffened and grew rigid with every word that she said, and when she had finished he was as deadly pale as she herself.

"Say not one syllable more to me, Zara!" he commanded. "You will have no cause to reprove me for loving you again. And remember this: things shall be as you wish between us. We will each live our lives and play the game. But before I ask you to be my wife again you can go down upon your knees. Do you hear me? Good night."

And without a word further he strode from the room.

CHAPTER XVII

The moon was shining brightly and a fresh breeze had risen when Tristram left the hotel and walked rapidly towards the pier. He was mad with rage and indignation from his bride's cruel taunts. The knowledge of their injustice did not comfort him, and, though he knew he was innocent of any desire to have made a bargain, and had taken her simply for her beautiful self, still, the accusation hurt and angered his pride. How dared she! How dared her uncle have allowed her to think such things! A Tancred to stoop so low! He clenched his hands and his whole frame shook.

And then as he gazed down into the moonlit waves her last words came back with a fresh lashing sting. "Leave me, I hate you, animal that you are!" An animal, forsooth! And this is how she had looked at his love!

And then a cold feeling came over him--he was so very just--and he questioned himself. Was it true? Had it, indeed, been only that? Had he, indeed, been unbalanced and intoxicated merely from the desire of her exquisite body? Had there been nothing beyond? Were men really brutes?--And here he walked up and down very fast. What did it all mean? What did life mean? What was the truth of this thing, called love?

And so he strode for hours, reasoning things out. But he knew that for his nature there could be no love without desire--and no desire without love. And then his conversation with Francis Markrute came back to him, the day they had lunched in the city, when the financier had given his views about women.

Yes, they were right, those views. A woman, to be dangerous, must appeal to both the body and brain of a man. If his feeling for Zara were only for the body then it was true that it was only lust.

But it was *not* true; and he thought of all his dreams of her at Wrayth, of the pictures he had drawn of their future life together, of the tenderness with which he had longed for this night.

And then his anger died down and was replaced by a passionate grief.

His dream lay in ruins, and there was nothing to look forward to but a blank, soulless life. It did not seem to him then, in the cold moonlight, that things could ever come right. He could not for his pride's sake condescend to any further explanation with her. He would not stoop to defend himself; she must think what she chose, until she should of herself find out the truth.

And then his level mind turned and tried to see her point of view. He must not be unjust. And he realized that if she thought such base things of him she had been more or less right. But, even so, there was some mystery beyond all this--some cruel and oppressing dark shadow in her life.

And his thoughts went back to the night they had first met, and he remembered then that her eyes had been full of hate--resentment and hate--as though he, personally, had caused her some injury.

Francis Markrute was so very clever: what plan had he had in his head? By what scorpion whip had he perhaps forced her to consent to his wishes and become his--Tristram's--wife? And once more the disturbing remembrance of Mimo returned, so that, when at last dawn came and he went back to the hotel, tired out in body and soul, it would not let him rest in his bed. His bed--in the next room his wife!

But one clear decision he had come to. He would treat her with cold courtesy, and they would play the game. To part now, in a dramatic manner, the next day after the wedding, was not in his sense of the fitness of things, was not what was suitable or seemly for the Tancred name.

And when he had left her Zara had stood quite still. Some not understood astonishment caused all her passion to die down. For all the pitifully cruel experiences of her life she was still very young--young and ignorant of any but the vilest of men. Hitherto she had felt when they were kind that it was for some gain, and if a woman relented a second she would be sure to be trapped. For her self-respect and her soul's sake she must go armed at all points. And after her hurling at him all her scorn, instead of her husband turning round and perhaps beating her (as, certainly, Ladislaus would have done), he had answered with dignity and gone out of the room.

And she remembered her father's cold mien. Perhaps there was something else in the English--some other finer quality which she did not yet understand.

The poor, beautiful creature was like some ill-treated animal ready to bite to defend itself at the sight of a man.

It spoke highly for the strength and nobility of her character that, whereas another and weaker woman would have become degraded by the sorrows of such a life, she had remained pure as the snow, and as cold. Her strong will and her pride had kept completely in check every voluptuous instinct which must certainly have always lain dormant in her. Every emotion towards man was frozen to ice.

There are some complete natures which only respond to the highest touch; when the body and soul are evenly balanced they know all that is divine of human love. It is those warped in either of the component parts who bring sorrow--and lust.

The perfect woman gives willingly of herself, body and soul, to the ***one man*** she loves.

But of all these things Zara was ignorant. She only knew she was exhausted, and she crept wearily to bed.

Thus neither bride nor bridegroom, on this their wedding night, knew peace or rest.

They met next day for a late breakfast. They were to go to Paris by the one o'clock boat. They were both very quiet and pale. Zara had gone into the sitting-room first, and was standing looking out on the sea when her husband came into the room, and she did not turn round, until he said "Good morning," coldly, and she realized it was he.

Some strange quiver passed over her at the sound of his voice.

"Breakfast should be ready," he went on calmly. "I ordered it for eleven o'clock. I told your maid to tell you so. I hope that gave you time to dress."

"Yes, thank you," was all she said; and he rang the bell and opened the papers, which the waiters had piled on the table, knowing the delight of young bridal pairs to see news of themselves!

And as Zara glanced at her lord's handsome face she saw a cynical, disdainful smile creep over it, at something he read.

And she guessed it was the account of their wedding; and she, too, took up another paper and looked at the headings.

Yes, there was a flaming description of it all. And as she finished the long paragraphs she raised her head suddenly and their eyes met. And Tristram allowed himself to laugh--bitterly, it was true, but still to laugh.

The lingering fear of the ways of men was still in Zara's heart and not altogether gone; she was not yet quite free from the suspicion that he still might trap her if she unbent. So she frowned slightly and then looked down at the paper again; and the waiters brought in breakfast at that moment and nothing was said.

They did not seem to have much appetite, nor to care what they ate, but, the coffee being in front of her, politeness made Zara ask what sort her husband took, and when he answered--none at all--he wanted tea--she was relieved, and let him pour it out at the side-table himself.

"The wind has got up fiercely, and it will be quite rough," he said presently. "Do you mind the sea?"

And she answered, "No, not a bit."

Then they both continued reading the papers until all pretense of breakfast was over; and he rose, and, asking if she would be ready at about half-past twelve, to go on board, so as to avoid the crowd from the London train, he went quietly out of the room, and from the windows she afterwards saw him taking a walk on the pier.

And for some unexplained psychological reason, although she had now apparently obtained exactly the terms she had decided were the only possible ones on which to live with him, she experienced no sense of satisfaction or peace!

No pair could have looked more adorably attractive and interesting than Lord and Lady Tancred did as they went to their private cabin on the boat an admiring group of Dover young ladies thought, watching from the raised part above where the steamer starts. Every one concerned knew that this thrilling bride and bridegroom would be crossing, and the usual number of the daily spectators was greatly increased.

"What wonderful chinchilla!" "What lovely hair!" and "Oh! isn't he just too splendid!" they said. And the maid and the valet, carrying the jewel case, dressing bags, cushion and sable rug, followed, to the young ladies' extra delight.

The *apanages* of a great position, when augmented by the romance of a wedding journey, are dear to the female heart.

They had the large cabin on the upper deck of the **Queen**, and it was noticed that until the London train could be expected to arrive the bridal pair went outside and sat where they could not be observed, with a view towards Dover Castle. But it could not be seen that they never spoke a word and that each read a book.

When it seemed advisable to avoid the crowd Tristram glanced up and said,

"I suppose we shall have to stay in that beastly cabin now, or some cad will snapshot us. Will you come along?"

And so they went.

"It is going to be really quite rough," he continued, when the door was shut. "Would you like to lie down--or what?"

"I am never the least ill, but I will try and sleep," Zara answered resignedly, as she undid her chinchilla coat.

So he settled the pillows, and she lay down, and he covered her up; and as he did so, in spite of his anger with her and all his hurt pride he had the most maddeningly strong desire to kiss her and let her rest in his arms. So he turned away brusquely and sat down at the farther end, where he opened the window to let in some air, and pulled the curtain over it, and then tried to go on with his book. But every pulse in his body was throbbing, and at last he could not control the overmastering desire to look at her.

She raised herself a little, and began taking the finely-worked, small-stoned, sapphire pins out of her hat. They had been Cyril's gift.

"Can I help you?" he said.

"It is such soft fur I thought I need not take it off to lie down," she answered coldly, "but there is something hurting in the back."

He took the thing with its lace veil from her, and the ruffled waves of her glorious hair as she lay there nearly drove him mad with the longing to caress.

How, in God's name, would they ever be able to live? He must go outside and fight with himself.

And she wondered why his face grew so stern. And when she was settled comfortably again and the boat had started he left her alone.

It was, fortunately, so rough that there were very few people about, and he went far forward and leant on the rail, and let the salt air blow into his face.

What if, in the end, this wild passion for her should conquer him and he should give in, and have to confess that her cruel words did not hinder him from loving her? It would be too ignominious. He must pull himself together and firmly suppress every emotion. He determined to see her as little as possible when they got to Paris, and when the ghastly honeymoon week, that he had been contemplating with so much excitement and joy should be over, then they would go back to England, and he would take up politics in earnest, and try and absorb himself in that.

And Zara, lying in the cabin, was unconscious of any direct current of thought; she was quite unconscious that already this beautiful young husband of hers had made some impression upon her, and that, underneath, for all her absorption in her little brother and her own affairs, she was growing conscious of his presence and that his comings and goings were things to remark about.

And, strengthened in his resolve to be true to the Tancred pride, Tristram came back to her as they got into Calais harbor.

CHAPTER XVIII

The servants at the Ritz, in Paris, so exquisitely drilled, made no apparent difference, when the bride and bridegroom arrived there about half-past seven o'clock, than if they had been an elderly brother and sister; and they were taken to the beautiful Empire suite on the Vendome side of the first floor. Everything was perfection in the way of arrangement, and the flowers were so particularly beautiful that Zara's love for them caused her to cry out,

"Oh! the dear roses! I must just bury my face in them, first."

They had got through the railway journey very well; real, overcoming fatigue had caused them both to sleep, and in the automobile, coming to the hotel, they had exchanged a few stiff words.

"To-morrow night we can dine out at a restaurant," Tristram had said, "but to-night perhaps you are tired and would rather go to bed?"

"Thank you," said Zara. "Yes, I would." For she thought she wanted to write her letters to Mirko and tell him of her new name and place. So she put on a tea-gown, and at about half-past eight joined Tristram in the sitting-room. If they had not both been so strained their sense of humor would not have permitted them to refrain from a laugh. For here they sat in state, and, when the waiters were in the room, exchanged a few remarks. But Zara did notice that her husband never once looked at her with any directness, and he seemed coldly indifferent to anything she said.

"We shall have to stay here for the whole, boring week," he announced when at last coffee was on the table and they were alone. "There are certain obligations one's position obliges one to conform to. You understand, I expect. I will try to make the time as easy to bear for you as I can. Will you tell me what theaters you have not already seen? We can go somewhere every night, and in the daytime you have perhaps shopping to do; and--I know Paris quite well. I can amuse myself."

Zara did not feel enthusiastically grateful, but she said, "Thank you," in a quiet voice, and Tristram, rang the bell and asked for the list of the places of amusement, and in the most stiff, self-contained manner he chose, with her, a different one for every night.

Then he lit a cigar deliberately, and walked towards the door.

"Good-night, Milady," he said nonchalantly, and then went out.

And Zara sat still by the table and unconsciously pulled the petals off an unoffending rose; and when she realized what she had done she was aghast!

It was not until about five o'clock the next day that he came into the sitting-room again.

Milor had gone to the races, and had left a note for *Miladi* in the morning, the maid had said.

And Zara, as she lay back on her pillows, had opened it with a strange thrill.

"You won't be troubled with me to-day," she read. "I am going out with some old friends to Maisons Liafitte. I have said you want to rest from the journey, as one has to say something. I have arranged for us to dine at the Cafe de Paris at 7:30, and go to the Gymnase. Tell Higgins, my valet, if you change the plan." And the note was not even signed!

Well, it appeared she had nothing further to fear from him; she could breathe much relieved. And now for her day of quiet rest.

But when she had had her lonely lunch and her letters to her uncle and Mirko were written, she found herself drumming aimlessly on the window panes, and wondering if she would go out.

She had no friends in Paris whom she wanted to see. Her life there with her family had been entirely devoted to them alone. But it was a fine day and there is always something to do in Paris--though what then, particularly, she had not decided; perhaps she would go to the Louvre.

And then she sank down into the big sofa, opposite the blazing wood fire, and gradually fell fast asleep. She slept, with unbroken deepness, until late in the afternoon, and was, in fact, still asleep there when Tristram came in.

He did not see her at first; the lights were not on and it was almost dark in the streets. The fire, too, had burnt low. He came forward, and then went back again and switched on the lamps; and, with the blaze, Zara sat up and rubbed her eyes. One great plait of her hair had become loosened and fell at the side of her head, and she looked like a rosy, sleepy child.

"I did not see you!" Tristram gasped, and, realizing her adorable attractions, he turned to the fire and vigorously began making it up.

Then, as he felt he could not trust himself for another second, he rang the bell and ordered some tea to be brought, while he went to his room to leave his overcoat. And when he thought the excuse of the repast would be there, he went back.

Zara felt nothing in particular. Even yet she was rather on the defensive, looking out for every possible attack.

So they both sat down quietly, and for a few moments neither spoke.

She had put up her hair during his absence, and now looked wide-awake and quite neat.

"I had a most unlucky day," he said--for something to say. "I could not back a single winner. On the whole I think I am bored with racing."

"It has always seemed boring to me," she said. "If it were to try the mettle of a horse one had bred I could understand that; or to ride it oneself and get the better of an adversary: but just with sharp practices--and for money! It seems so common a thing, I never could take an interest in that."

"Does anything interest you?" he hazarded, and then he felt sorry he had shown enough interest to ask.

"Yes," she said slowly, "but perhaps not many games. My life has always been too ordered by the games of others, to take to them myself." And then she stopped abruptly. She could not suppose her life interested him much.

But, on the contrary, he was intensely interested, if she had known.

He felt inclined to tell her so, and that the whole of the present situation was ridiculous, and that he wanted to know her innermost thoughts. He was beginning to examine her all critically, and to take in every point. Beyond his passionate admiration for her beauty there was something more to analyze.

What was the subtle something of mystery and charm? Why could she not unbend and tell him the meaning in those fathomless, dark eyes?--What could they look like, if filled with love and tenderness? Ah!

And if he had done as he felt inclined at the moment the ice might have been broken, and at the end of the week they would probably have been in each other's arms. But fate ordered otherwise, and an incident that night, at dinner, caused a fresh storm.

Zara was looking so absolutely beautiful in her lovely new clothes that it was not in the nature of gallant foreigners to allow her to dine unmolested by their stares, and although the tete-a-tete dinner was quite early at the Cafe de Paris, there happened to be a large party of men next to them and Zara found herself seated in close proximity to a nondescript Count, whom she recognized as one of her late husband's friends. Every one who knows the Cafe de Paris can realize how this happened. The long velvet seats without divisions and the small tables in front make, when the place is full, the whole side look as if it were one big group. Lord Tancred was quite accustomed to it; he knew Paris well as he had told her, so he ought to have been prepared for what could happen, but he was not.

Perhaps he was not on the alert, because he had never before been there with a woman he loved.

Zara's neighbor was a great, big, fierce-looking creature from some wild quarter of the South, and was perhaps also just a little drunk. She knew a good deal of their language, but, taking for granted that this Englishman and his lovely lady would be quite ignorant of what they said, the party of men were most unreserved in their remarks.

Her neighbor looked at her devouringly, once or twice, when he saw Tristram could not observe him, and then began to murmur immensely *entreprenant* love sentences in his own tongue, as he played with his bread. She knew he had recognized her. And Tristram wondered why his lady's little nostrils should begin to quiver and her eyes to flash.

She was remembering like scenes in the days of Ladislaus, and how he used to grow wild with jealousy, in the beginning when he took her out, and once had dragged her back upstairs by her hair, and flung her into bed. It was always her fault when men looked at her, he assured her. And the horror of the recollection of it all was still vivid enough.

Then Tristram gradually became greatly worried; without being aware that the man was the cause, he yet felt something was going on. He grew jealous and uneasy, and would have liked to have taken her home.

And because of the things she was angrily listening to, and because of her fear of a row, she sat there looking defiant and resentful, and spoke never a word.

And Tristram could not understand it, and he eventually became annoyed. What had he said or done to her again? It was more than he meant to stand, for no reason--to put up with such airs!

For Zara sat frowning, her mouth mutinous and her eyes black as night.

If she had told Tristram what her neighbor was saying there would at once have been a row. She knew this, and so remained in constrained silence, unconscious that her husband was thinking her rude to him, and that he was angry with her. She was so strung up with fury at the foreigner, that she answered Tristram's few remarks at random, and then abruptly rose while he was paying the bill, as if to go out. And as she did so the Count slipped a folded paper into the sleeve of her coat.

Tristram thought he saw something peculiar but was still in doubt, and, with his English self-control and horror of a scene, he followed his wife to the door, as she was walking rapidly ahead, and there helped her into the waiting automobile.

But as she put up her arm, in stepping in, the folded paper fell to the brightly lighted pavement and he picked it up.

He must have some explanation. He was choking with rage. There was some mystery, he was being tricked.

"Why did you not tell me you knew that fellow who sat next to you?" he said in a low, constrained voice.

"Because it would have been a lie," she said haughtily. "I have never seen him but once before in my life."

"Then what business have you to allow him to write notes to you?" Tristram demanded, too overcome with jealousy to control the anger in his tone.

She shrank back in her corner. Here it was beginning again! After all, in spite of his apparent agreement to live on the most frigid terms with her he was now acting like Ladislaus: men were all the same!

"I am not aware the creature wrote me any note," she said. "What do you mean?"

"How can you pretend like this," Tristram exclaimed furiously, "when it fell out of your sleeve? Here it is."

"Take me back to the hotel," she said with a tone of ice. "I refuse to go to the theater to be insulted. How dare you doubt my word? If there is a note you had better read it and see what it says."

So Lord Tancred picked up the speaking-tube and told the chauffeur to go back to the Ritz.

They both sat silent, palpitating with rage, and when they got there he followed her into the lift and up to the sitting-room.

He came in and shut the door and strode over beside her, and then he almost hissed,

"You are asking too much of me. I demand an explanation. Tell me yourself about it. Here is your note."

Zara took it, with infinite disdain, and, touching it as though it were some noisome reptile, she opened it and read aloud,

"Beautiful Comtesse, when can I see you again?"

"The vile wretch!" she said contemptuously. "That is how men insult women!" And she looked up passionately at Tristram. "You are all the same."

"I have not insulted you," he flashed. "It is perfectly natural that I should be angry at such a scene, and if this brute is to be found again to-night he shall know that I will not permit him to write insolent notes to my wife."

She flung the hateful piece of paper into the fire and turned towards her room.

"I beg you to do nothing further about the matter," she said. "This loathsome man was half drunk. It is quite unnecessary to follow it up; it will only make a scandal, and do no good. But you can understand another thing. I will not have my word doubted, nor be treated as an offending domestic--as you have treated me to-night." And without further words she went into her room.

Tristram, left alone, paced up and down; he was wild with rage, furious with her, with himself, and with the man. With her because he had told her once, before the wedding, that when they came to cross swords there would be no doubt as to who would be master! and in the three encounters which already their wills had had she had each time come off the conqueror! He was furious with himself, that he had not leaned forward at dinner to see the man hand the note, and he was frenziedly furious with the stranger, that he had dared to turn his insolent eyes upon his wife.

He would go back to the Cafe de Paris, and, if the man was there, call him to account, and if not, perhaps he could obtain his name. So out he went.

But the waiters vowed they knew nothing of the gentleman; the whole party had been perfect strangers, and they had no idea as to where they had gone on. So this enraged young Englishman spent the third night of his honeymoon in a hunt round the haunts of Paris, but with no success; and at about six o'clock in the morning came back baffled but still raging, and thoroughly wearied out.

And all this while his bride could not sleep, and in spite of her anger was a prey to haunting fears. What if the two had met and there had been bloodshed! A completely possible case! And several times in the night she got out of her bed and went and listened at the communicating doors; but there was no sound of Tristram, and about five o'clock, worn out with the anxiety and injustice of everything, she fell into a restless doze, only to wake again at seven, with a lead weight at her heart. She could not bear it any longer! She must know for certain if he had come in! She slipped on her dressing-gown, and noiselessly stole to the door, and with the greatest caution unlocked it, and, turning the handle, peeped in.

Yes, there he was, sound asleep! His window was wide open, with the curtains pushed back, so the daylight streamed in on his face. He had been too tired to care.

Zara turned round quickly to reenter her room, but in her terror of being discovered she caught the trimming of her dressing-gown on the handle of the door and without her being aware of it a small bunch of worked ribbon roses fell off.

Then she got back into bed, relieved in mind as to him but absolutely quaking at what she had done and at the impossibly embarrassing position she would have placed herself in, if he had awakened and known that she had come!

And the first thing Tristram saw, when some hours later he was aroused by the pouring in of the sun, was the little torn bunch of silk roses lying close to her door.

CHAPTER XIX

He sprang from bed and picked them up. What could they possibly mean? They were her roses, certainly--he remembered she wore the dressing-gown that first evening at Dover, when he had gone to her to give her the gardenias. And they certainly had not been there when at six o'clock he had come in. He would in that case have seen them against the pale carpet.

For one exquisite moment he thought they were a message and then he noticed the ribbon had been wrenched off and was torn.

No, they were no conscious message, but they did mean that she had been in his room while he slept.

Why had she done this thing? He knew she hated him--it was no acting--and she had left him the night' before even unusually incensed. What possible reason could she have, then, for coming into his room? He felt wild with excitement. He would see if, as usual, the door between them was locked. He tried it gently. Yes, it was.

And Zara heard him from her side, and stiffened in her bed with all the expression of a fierce wolfhound putting its hackles up.

Yes, the danger of the ways of men was not over! If she had not unconsciously remembered to lock the door when she had returned from her terrifying adventure he would have come in!

So these two thrilled with different emotions and trembled, and there was the locked harrier between them. And then Tristram rang for his valet and ordered his bath. He would dress quickly, and ask casually if she would breakfast in the sitting-room. It was so late, almost eleven, and they could have it at twelve upstairs--not in the restaurant as he had yesterday intended. He must find out about the roses; he could not endure to pass the whole day in wonder and doubt.

And Zara, too, started dressing. It was better under the circumstances to be armed at all points, and she felt safer and calmer with Henriette in the room.

So a few minutes before twelve they met in the sitting-room.

Her whole expression was on the defensive: he saw that at once.

The waiters would be coming in with the breakfast soon. Would there be time to talk to her, or had he better postpone it until they were certain to be alone? He decided upon this latter course, and just said a cold "Good morning," and turned to the **New York Herald** and looked at the news.

Zara felt more reassured.

So they presently sat down to their breakfast, each ready to play the game.

They spoke of the theaters--the one they had arranged to go to this Saturday night was causing all Paris to laugh.

"It will be a jolly good thing to laugh," Tristram said--and Zara agreed.

He made no allusion to the events of the night before, and she hardly spoke at all. And at last the repast was over, and the waiters had left the room.

Tristram got up, after his coffee and liqueur, but he lit no cigar; he went to one of the great windows which look out on the Colonne Vendome, and then he came back. Zara was sitting upon the heliotrope Empire sofa and had picked up the paper again.

He stood before her, with an expression upon his face which ought to have melted any woman.

"Zara," he said softly, "I want you to tell me, why did you come into my room?"

Her great eyes filled with startled horror and surprise, and her white cheeks grew bright pink with an exquisite flush.

"I?"--and she clenched her hands. How did he know? Had he seen her, then? But he evidently did know, and there was no use to lie. "I was so--frightened--that--"

Tristram took a step nearer and sat down by her side. He saw the confession was being dragged from her, and he gloried in it and would not help her out.

She moved further from him, then, with grudging reluctance, she continued,

"There can be such unpleasant quarrels with those horrible men. It--was so very late--I--I--wished to be sure that you had come safely in."

Then she looked down, and the rose died out of her face, leaving it very white.

And if Tristram's pride in the decision he had come to, on the fatal wedding night, that she must make the first advances before he would again unbend, had not held him, he would certainly have risked everything and clasped her in his arms. As it was, he resisted the intense temptation to do so, and made himself calm, while he answered,

"It mattered to you, then, in some way, that I should not come to harm?"

He was still sitting on the sofa near her, and that magnetic essence which is in propinquity appealed to her; ignorant of all such emotions as she was she only knew something had suddenly made her feel nervous, and that her heart was thumping in her side.

"Yes, of course it mattered," she faltered, and then went on coldly, as he gave a glad start; "scandals are so unpleasant--scenes and all those things are so revolting. I had to endure many of them in my former life."

Oh! so that was it! Just for fear of a scandal and because she had known disagreeable things! Not a jot of feeling for himself! And Tristram got up quickly and walked to the fireplace. He was cut to the heart.

The case was utterly hopeless, he felt. He was frozen and stung each time he even allowed himself to be human and hope for anything. But he was a strong man, and this should be the end of it. He would not be tortured again.

He took the little bunch of flowers out of his pocket and handed it to her quietly, while his face was full of pain.

"Here is the proof you left me of your kind interest," he told her. "Perhaps your maid will miss it and wish to sew it on." And then without another word he went out of the room.

Zara, left alone, sat staring into the fire. What did all this mean? She felt very unhappy, but not angry or alarmed. She did not want to hurt him. Had she been very unkind? After all, he had behaved, in comparison to Ladislaus, with wonderful self-control--and--yes, supposing he were not quite a sensual brute she had been very hard. She knew what pride meant; she had abundance herself, and she realized for the first time how she must have been stinging his.

But there were facts which could not be got over. He had married her for her uncle's money and then shown at once that her person tempted him, when it could not be anything else.

She got up and walked about the room. There was a scent of him somewhere--the scent of a fine cigar. She felt uneasy of she knew not what. Did she wish him to come back? Was she excited? Should she go out? And then, for no reason on earth, she suddenly burst into tears.

*   *   *   *   *

They met for dinner, and she herself had never looked or been more icy cold than Tristram was. They went down into the restaurant and there, of course, he encountered some friends dining, too, in a merry party; and he nodded gayly to them and told her casually who they were, and then went on with his dinner. His manner had lost its constraint, it was just casually indifferent. And soon they started for the theater, and it was he who drew as far away as he could, when they got into the automobile.

They had a box--and the piece had begun. It was one of those impossibly amusing Paris farces, on the borderland of all convention but so intensely comic that none could help their mirth, and Tristram shook with laughter and forgot for the time that he was a most miserable young man. And even Zara laughed. But it did not melt things between them. Tristram's feelings had been too wounded for any ordinary circumstances to cause him to relent.

"Do you care for some supper?" he said coldly when they came out. But she answered. "No," so he took her back, and as far as the lift where he left her, politely saying "Good night," and she saw him disappear towards the door, and knew he had again gone out.

And going on to the sitting-room alone, she found the English mail had come in, and there were the letters on the table, at least a dozen for Tristram, as she sorted them out--a number in women's handwriting--and but two for herself. One was from her uncle, full of agreeable congratulations subtly expressed; and the other, forwarded from Park Lane, from Mirko, as yet ignorant of her change of state, a small, funny, pathetic letter that touched her heart. He was better, and again able to go out, and in a fortnight Agatha, the little daughter of the Morleys, would be returning, and he could play with her. That might be a joy--girls were not so tiresome and did not make so much noise as boys.

Zara turned to the piano, which she had not yet opened, and sat down and comforted herself with the airs she loved; and the maid who listened, while she waited for her mistress to be undressed, turned up her eyes in wonder.

"Quel drole de couple!" she said.

And Tristram reencountered his friends and went off with them to sup.

Her ladyship was tired, he told them, and had gone to bed. And two of the Englishwomen who knew him quite well teased him and said how beautiful his bride was and how strange-looking, and what an iceberg he must be to be able to come out to supper and leave her alone! And they wondered why he then smiled cynically.

"For," said one to the other on their way home, "the new Lady Tancred is perfectly beautiful! Fancy, Gertrude, Tristram leaving her for a minute! And did you ever see such a face? It looks anything but cold."

Zara was wide-awake when, about two, he came in. She heard him in the sitting-room and suddenly became conscious that her thoughts had been with him ever since she went to bed, and not with Mirko and his letter.

She supposed he was now reading his pile of correspondence--he had such numbers of fond friends! And then she heard him shut the door, and go round into his room; but the carpets were very thick and she heard no more.

If she could have seen what happened beyond that closed door, would it have opened her eyes, or made her happy? Who can tell?

For Higgins, with methodical tidiness, had emptied the pockets of the coat his master had worn in the day, and there on top of a letter or two and a card-case was one tiny pink rose, a wee bud that had become detached from the torn bunch.

And when Tristram saw it his heart gave a great bound. So it had stayed behind, when he had returned the others, and was there now to hurt him with remembrance of what might have been! He was unable to control the violent emotion which shook him. He went to the window and opened it wide: the moon was rather over, but still blazed in the sky. Then he bent down and passionately kissed the little bud, while a scorching mist gathered in his eyes.

CHAPTER XX

So at last the Wednesday morning came--and they could go back to England. From that Saturday night until they left Paris Tristram's manner of icy, polite indifference to his bride never changed. She had no more quaking shocks nor any fear of too much ardor! He avoided every possible moment of her society he could, and when forced to be with her seemed aloof and bored.

And the freezing manner of Zara was caused no longer by haughty self-defense but because she was unconsciously numb at heart.

Unknown, undreamed-of emotion came over her, whenever she chanced to find him close, and during his long absences her thoughts followed him--sometimes with wonderment.

Just as they were going down to start for the train on the Wednesday morning a telegram was put into her hand. It was addressed "La Baronne de Tancred," and she guessed at once this would be Mimo's idea of her name. Tristram, who was already down the steps by the concierge's desk, turned and saw her open it, with a look of intense strain. He saw that as she read her eyes widened and stared out in front of them for a moment, and that her face grew pale.

For Mimo had wired, "Mirko not quite so well." She crumpled the blue paper in her hand, and followed her husband through the bowing personnel of the hotel into the automobile. She controlled herself and was even able to give one of her rare smiles in farewell, but when they started she leaned back, and again her face went white. Tristram was moved. Whom was her telegram from? She did not tell him and he would not ask, but the feeling that there were in her life, things and interests of which he knew nothing did not please him. And this particular thing--what was it? Was it from a man? It had caused her some deep emotion--he could plainly see that. He longed to ask her but was far too proud, and their terms had grown so distant he hardly liked to express even solicitude, which, however, he did.

"I hope you have not had any bad news?"

Then she turned her eyes upon him, and he saw that she had hardly heard him; they looked blank.

"What?" she asked vaguely; and then, recollecting herself confusedly, she went on, "No--not exactly--but something about which I must think."

So he was shut out of her confidence. He felt that, and carefully avoided taking any further notice of her.

When they got to the station he suddenly perceived she was not following him as he made way for her in the crowd, but had gone over to the telegraph office by herself.

He waited and fumed. It was evidently something about which she wished no one to see what she wrote, for she could perfectly well have given the telegram to Higgins to take, who would be waiting by the saloon door.

She returned in a few moments, and she saw that Tristram's face was very stern. It did not strike her that he was jealous about the mystery of the telegram; she thought he was annoyed at her for not coming on in case they should be late, so she said hurriedly, "There is plenty of time."

"Naturally," he answered stiffly as they walked along, "but it is quite unnecessary for Lady Tancred to struggle through this rabble and take telegrams herself. Higgins could have done it when we were settled in the train."

And with unexpected meekness all she said was, "I am very sorry."

So the incident ended there--but not the uneasy impression it left.

Tristram did not even make a pretense of reading the papers when the train moved on; he sat there staring in front of him, with his handsome face shadowed by a moody frown. And any close observer who knew him would have seen that there was a change in his whole expression, since the same time the last week.

The impossible disappointment of everything! What kind of a nature could his wife have, to be so absolutely mute and unresponsive as she had been? He felt glad he had not given her the chance to snub him again. These last days he had been able to keep to his determination, and at all events did not feel himself humiliated. How long would it be before he should cease to care for her? He hoped to God--soon, because the strain of crushing his passionate desires was one which no man could stand long.

The little, mutinous face, with its alluring, velvet, white skin, her slightly full lips, all curved and red, and tempting, and anything but cold in shape, and the extraordinary magnetic attraction of her whole personality, made her a most dangerous thing; and then his thoughts turned to the vision of her hair undone that he had had on that first evening at Dover. He had said once to Francis Markrute, he remembered, that these great passions were "storybook stuff." Good God! Well, in those days he had not known.

He thought, as he returned from his honeymoon this day, that he could not be more frightfully unhappy, but he was really only beginning the anguish of the churning of his soul--if he had known.

And Zara sat in her armchair, and pretended to read; but when he glanced at her he saw that it was a farce and that her expressive eyes were again quite blank.

And finally, after the uncomfortable hours, they arrived at Calais and went to the boat.

Here Zara seemed to grow anxious again and on the alert, and, stepping forward, asked Higgins to inquire if there was a telegram for her, addressed to the ship. But there was not, and she subsided once more quietly and sat in their cabin.

Tristram did not even attempt to play the part of the returning bridegroom beyond the ordinary seeing to her comfort about which he had never failed; he left her immediately and remained for all the voyage on deck.

And when they reached Dover Zara's expectancy showed again, but it was not until they were just leaving the station that a telegram was thrust through the window and he took it from the boy, while he could not help noticing the foreign form of address. And a certainty grew in his brain that it was "that same cursed man!"

He watched her face as she read it, and noticed the look of relief as, quite unconscious of his presence, his bride absently spread the paper out. And although deliberately to try and see what was written was not what he would ever have done, his eyes caught the signature, "Mimo," before he was aware of it.

Mimo--that was the brute's name!

And what could he say or do? They were not really husband and wife, and as long as she did nothing to disgrace the Tancred honor he had no valid reason for questions or complaints.

But he burnt with suspicion, and jealousy, and pain.

Then he thought over what Francis Markrute had said the first evening, when he had agreed to the marriage. He remembered how he had not felt it would be chivalrous or honorable to ask any questions, once he had blindly gone the whole length and settled she should be his; but how Francis had gratuitously informed him that she had been an immaculate wife until a year ago, and married to an unspeakable brute.

He knew the financier very well, and knew that he was, with all his subtle cleverness, a man of spotless honor. Evidently, then, if there was anything underneath he was unaware of it. But was there anything? Even though he was angry and suspicious he realized that the bearing of his wife was not guilty or degraded. She was a magnificently proud and noble-looking creature, but perhaps even the noblest women could stoop to trick from--love! And this thought caused him to jump up suddenly--much to Zara's astonishment. And she saw the veins show on the left side of his temple as in a knot, a peculiarity, like the horseshoe of the Redgauntlets, which ran in the Tancred race.

Then he felt how foolish he was, causing himself suffering over an imaginary thing; and here this piece of white marble sat opposite him in cold silence, while his being was wrung! He suddenly understood something which he had never done before, when he read of such things in the papers--how, passionately loving, a man could yet kill the thing he loved.

And Zara, comforted by the telegram, "Much better again to-day," had leisure to return to the subject which had lately begun unconsciously to absorb her--the subject of her lord!

She wondered what made him look so stern. His nobly-cut face was as though it were carved in stone. Just from an abstract, artistic point of view, she told herself, she honestly admired him and his type. It was finer than any other race could produce and she was glad she was half English, too. The lines were so slender and yet so strong; and every bone balanced--and the look of superb health and athletic strength.

Such must have been the young Greeks who ran in the Gymnasium at Athens, she thought.

And then, suddenly, an intense quiver of unknown emotion rushed over her.

And if at that moment he had clasped her and kissed her, instead of sitting there glaring into space, the rest of this story need never have been written!

But the moment passed, and she crushed whatever it was she felt of the dawning of love, and he dominated the uneasy suspicions of her fidelity; and they got out of the train at Charing Cross--after their remarkable wedding journey.

CHAPTER XXI

Francis Markrute's moral antennae upon which he prided himself informed him that all was not as it should be between this young bride and bridegroom. Zara seemed to have acquired in this short week even an extra air of regal dignity, aided by her perfect clothes; and Tristram looked stern, and less joyous and more haughty than he had done. And they were both so deadly cold, and certainly constrained! It was not one of the financier's habits ever to doubt himself or his deductions. They were based upon far too sound reasoning. No, if something had gone wrong or had not yet evolutionized it was only for the moment and need cause no philosophical **deus ex machina** any uneasiness.

For it was morally and physically impossible that such a perfectly developed pair of the genus human being could live together in the bonds of marriage, and not learn to love.

Meanwhile, it was his business as the friend and uncle of the two to be genial and make things go on greased wheels.

So he exerted himself to talk at dinner--their dinner *a trois*--. He told them all the news that had happened during the week--Was it only a week--Zara and Tristram both thought!

How there were rumors that in the coming spring there might be a general election, and that the Radicals were making fresh plots to ruin the country; but there was to be no autumn session, and, as usual, the party to which they all had the honor to belong was half asleep.

And then the two men grew deep in a political discussion, so as soon as Zara had eaten her peach she said she would leave them to their talk, and say "Good night," as she was tired out.

"Yes, my niece," said her uncle who had risen. And he did what he had not done since she was a child, he stooped and kissed her white forehead. "Yes, indeed, you must go and rest. We both want you to do us justice to-morrow, don't we, Tristram? We must have our special lady looking her best."

And she smiled a faint smile as she passed from the room.

"By George! my dear boy," the financier went on, "I don't believe I ever realized what a gorgeously beautiful creature my niece is. She is like some wonderful exotic blossom--a mass of snow and flame!"

And Tristram said with unconscious cynicism,

"Certainly snow--but where is the flame?"

Francis Markrute looked at him out of the corners of his clever eyes. She had been icy to him in Paris, then! But his was not the temperament to interfere. It was only a question of time. After all, a week was not long to grow accustomed to a perfect stranger.

Then they went back to the library, and smoked for an hour or so and continued their political chat; and at last Markrute said to his new nephew-in-law blandly,

"In a year or so, when you and Zara have a son, I will give you, my dear boy, some papers to read which will interest you as showing the mother's side of his lineage. It will be a fit balance, as far as actual blood goes, to your own."

In a year or so, when Zara should have a son!

Of all the aspects of the case, which her pride and disdain had robbed him of, this, Tristram felt, was perhaps--though it had not before presented itself to him-- the most cruel. He would have no son!

He got up suddenly and threw his unfinished cigar into the grate--that old habit of his when he was moved--and he said in a voice that the financier knew was strained,

"That is awfully good of you. I shall have to have it inserted in the family tree--some day. But now I think I shall turn in. I want to have my eye rested, and be as fit as a fiddle for the shoot. I have had a tiring week."

And Francis Markrute came out with him into the passage and up to the first floor, and when they got so far they heard the notes of the *Chanson Triste* being played again from Zara's sitting-room. She had not gone to bed, then, it seemed!

"Good God!" said Tristram. "I don't know why, but I wish to heaven she would not play that tune."

And the two men looked at one another with some uneasy wonder in their eyes.

"Go on and take her to bed," the financier suggested. "Perhaps she does not like being left so long alone."

Tristram went upstairs with a bitter laugh to himself.

He did not go near the sitting-room; he went straight into the room which had been allotted to himself: and a savage sense of humiliation and impotent rage convulsed him.

The next day, the express which would stop for them at Tylling Green, the little station for Montfitchet, started at two o'clock, and the financier had given orders to have an early lunch at twelve before they left. He, himself, went off to the City for half an hour to read his letters, at ten o'clock, and was surprised when he asked Turner if Lord and Lady Tancred had break-fasted to hear that her ladyship had gone out at half-past nine o'clock and that his lordship had given orders to his valet not to disturb him, in his lordship's room--and here Turner coughed--until half-past ten.

"See that they have everything they want," his master said, and then went out. But when he was in his electric brougham, gliding eastwards, he frowned to himself.

"The proud, little minx! So she has insisted upon keeping to the business bargain up till now, has she!" he thought. "If it goes on we shall have to make her jealous. That would be an infallible remedy for her caprice."

But Zara was not concerned with such things at all for the moment. She was waiting anxiously for Mimo at their trysting-place, the mausoleum of Halicarnassus in the British Museum, and he was late. He would have the last news of Mirko. No reply had awaited her to her telegram to Mrs. Morley from Paris, and it had been too late to wire again last night. And Mrs. Morley must have got the telegram, because Mimo had got his.

Some day, she hoped--when she could grow perhaps more friendly with her husband--she would get her uncle to let her tell him about Mirko. It would make everything so much more simple as regards seeing him, and why, since the paper was all signed and nothing could be altered, should there be any mystery now? Only, her uncle had said the day before the wedding,

"I beg of you not to mention the family disgrace of your mother to your husband nor speak to him of the man Sykypri for a good long time--if you ever need."

And she had acquiesced.

"For," Francis Markrute had reasoned to himself, "if the boy dies, as Morley thinks there is every likelihood that he will, why should Tristram ever know?"

The disgrace of his adored sister always made him wince.

Mimo came at last, looking anxious and haggard, and not his debonair self. Yes, he had had a telegram that morning. He had sent one, as he was obliged to do, in her name, and hence the confusion in the answer. Mrs. Morley had replied to the Neville Street address, and Zara wondered if she knew London very well and would see how impossible such a locality would be for the Lady Tancred!

But Mirko was better--decidedly better--the attack had again been very short. So she felt reassured for the moment, and was preparing to go when she remembered that one of the things she had come for was to give Mimo some money in notes which she had prepared for him; but, knowing the poor gentleman's character, she was going to do it delicately by buying the "Apache!" For she was quite aware that just money, for him to live, now that it was not a question of the welfare of Mirko, he would never accept from her. In such unpractical, sentimental ways does breeding show itself in some weak natures!

Mimo was almost suspicious of the transaction, and she was obliged to soothe and flatter him by saying that he must surely always have understood how intensely she had admired that work; and now she was rich it would be an everlasting pleasure to her to own it for her very own. So poor Mimo *was* comforted, and they parted after a while, all arrangements having been made that the telegrams--should any more come--were to go first, addressed to her at Neville Street, so that the poor father should see them and then send them on.

And as it was now past eleven o'clock Zara returned quickly back to Park Lane and was coming in at the door just as her husband was descending the stairs.

"You are up very early, Milady," he said casually, and because of the servants in the hall she felt it would look better to follow him into the library.

Tristram was surprised at this and he longed to ask her where she had been, but she did not tell him; she just said,

"What time do we arrive at your uncle's? Is it five or six?"

"It only takes three hours. We shall be in about five. And, Zara, I want you to wear the sable coat. I think it suits you better than the chinchilla you had when we left."

A little pink came into her cheeks. This was the first time he had ever spoken of her clothes; and to hide the sudden strange emotion she felt, she said coldly.

"Yes, I intended to. I shall always hate that chinchilla coat."

And he turned away to the window, stung again by her words which she had said unconsciously. The chinchilla had been her conventional "going away" bridal finery. That was, of course, why she hated the remembrance of it.

As soon as she had said the words she felt sorry. What on earth made her so often wound him? She did not know it was part of the same instinct of self-defense which had had to make up her whole attitude towards life. Only this time it was unconsciously to hide and so defend the new emotion which was creeping into her heart.

He stayed with his back turned, looking out of the window; so, after waiting a moment, she went from the room.

At the station they found Jimmy Danvers, and a Mr. and Mrs. Harcourt with the latter's sister, Miss Opie, and several men. The rest of the party, including Emily and Mary, Jimmy told them, had gone down by the eleven o'clock train.

Both Mrs. Harcourt and her sister and, indeed, the whole company were Tristram's old and intimate friends and they were so delighted to see him, and chaffed and were gay, and Zara watched, and saw that her uncle entered into the spirit of the fun in the saloon, and only she was a stranger and out in the cold.

As for Tristram, he seemed to become a different person to the stern, constrained creature of the past week, and he sat in a corner with Mrs. Harcourt, and bent over her and chaffed and whispered in her ear, and she--Zara--was left primly in one of the armchairs, a little aloof. But such a provoking looking type of beauty as hers did not long leave the men of the party cold to her charms; and soon Jimmy Danvers joined her and a Colonel Lowerby, commonly known as "the Crow," and she held a little court. But to relax and be genial and unregal was so difficult for her, with the whole contrary training of all her miserable life.

Hitherto men and, indeed, often women were things to be kept at a distance, as in one way or another they were sure to bite!

And after a while the party adjusted itself, some for bridge and some for sleep; and Jimmy Danvers and Colonel Lowerby went into the small compartment to smoke.

"Well, Crow," said Jimmy, "what do you think of Tristram's new lady? Isn't she a wonder? But, Jehoshaphat! doesn't she freeze you to death!"

"Very curious type," growled the Crow. "Bit of Vesuvius underneath, I expect."

"Yes, that is what a fellow'd think to look at her," Jimmy said, puffing at his cigarette. "But she keeps the crust on the top all the time; the bloomin' volcano don't get a chance!"

"She doesn't look stupid," continued the Crow. "She looks stormy--expect it's pretty well worth while, though, when she melts."

"Poor old Tristram don't look as if he had had a taste of paradise with his houri, for his week, does he? Before we'd heartened him up on the platform a bit--give you my word--he looked as mum as an owl," Jimmy said. "And she looked like an iceberg, as she's done all the time. I've never seen her once warm up."

"He's awfully in love with her," grunted the Crow.

"I believe that is about the measure, though I can't see how you've guessed it. You had not got back for the wedding, Crow, and it don't show now."

The Crow laughed--one of his chuckling, cynical laughs which to his dear friend Lady Anningford meant so much that was in his mind.

"Oh, doesn't it!" he said.

"Well, tell me, what do you really think of her?" Jimmy went on. "You see, I was best man at the wedding, and I feel kind of responsible if she is going to make the poor, old boy awfully unhappy."

"She's unhappy herself," said the Crow. "It's because she is unhappy she's so cold. She reminds me of a rough terrier I bought once, when I was a lad, from a particularly brutal bargeman. It snarled at every one who came near it, before they could show if they were going to kick or not, just from force of habit."

"Well?" questioned Jimmy, who, as before has been stated, was rather thick.

"Well, after I had had it for a year it was the most faithful and the gentlest dog I ever owned. That sort of creature wants oceans of kindness. Expect Tristram's pulled the curb--doesn't understand as yet."

"Why, how could a person who must always have had heaps of cash--Markrute's niece, you know--and a fine position be like your dog, Crow? You *are* drawing it!"

"Well, you need not mind what I say, Jimmy," Colonel Lowerby went on. "Judge for yourself. You asked my opinion, and as I am an old friend of the family I've given it, and time will show."

"Lady Highford's going to be at Montfitchet," Jimmy announced after a pause. "She won't make things easy for any one, will she!"

"How did that happen?" asked the Crow in an astonished voice.

"Ethelrida had asked her in the season, when every one supposed the affair was still on, and I expect she would not let them put her off--" And then both men looked up at the door, for Tristram peeped in.

"We shall be arriving in five minutes, you fellows," he said.

And soon they drew up at the little Tylling Green station, and the saloon was switched off, while the express flew on to King's Lynn.

There were motor cars and an omnibus to meet them, and Lady Ethelrida's own comfortable coupe for the bridal pair. They might just want to say a few words together alone before arriving, she had kindly thought. And so, though neither of the two were very eager for this tete-a-tete, they got in and started off. The little coupe had very powerful engines and flew along, so they were well ahead of the rest of the party and would get to the house first, which was what the hostess had calculated upon. Then Tristram could have the pleasure of presenting his bride to the assembled company at tea, without the interruptions of the greetings of the other folk. Zara felt excited. She was beginning to realize that these English people were all of her dead father's class, not creatures whom one must beware of until one knew whether or not they were gamblers or rogues. And it made her breathe more freely, and the black panther's look died out of her eyes. She did not feel nervous, as she well might have done--only excited and highly worked up. Tristram, for his part, wished to heaven Ethelrida had not arranged to send the coupe for them. It was such a terrible temptation for him to resist for five miles, sitting so near her all alone in the dusk of the afternoon! He clenched his hands under the rug, and drew as far away from her as he could; and she glanced at him and wondered, almost timidly, why he looked so stern.

"I hope you will tell me, if there is anything special you wish me to do, please?"

she said. "Because, you see, I have never been in the English country before, and my uncle has given me to understand the customs are different to those abroad."

He felt he could not look at her; the unusual gentleness in her voice was so alluring, and he had not forgotten the hurt of the chinchilla coat. If he relented in his attitude at all she would certainly snub him again; so he continued staring in front of him, and answered ordinarily,

"I expect you will do everything perfectly right, and every one will only want to be kind to you, and make you have a good time; and my uncle will certainly make love to you but you must not mind that."

And Zara allowed herself to smile as she answered,

"No, I shall not in the least object to that!"

He knew she was smiling--out of the corner of his eye--and the temptation to clasp her to him was so overpowering that he said rather hoarsely, "Do you mind if I put the window down?"

He must have some air; he was choking. She wondered more and more what was the matter with him, and they both fell into a constrained silence which lasted until they turned into the park gates; and Zara peered out into the ghostly trees, with their autumn leaves nearly off, and tried to guess from the lodge what the house would be like.

It was very enormous and stately, she found when they reached it, and, she walking with her empress air and Tristram following her, they at last came to the picture gallery where the rest of the party, who had arrived earlier, were all assembled in the center, by one of the big fireplaces, with their host and hostess having tea.

The Duke and Lady Ethelrida came forward, down the very long, narrow room (they had quite sixty feet to walk before they met them), and then, when they did, they both kissed Zara--their beautiful new relation!--and Lady Ethelrida taking her arm drew her towards the party, while she whispered,

"You dear, lovely thing! Ever so many welcomes to the family and Montfitchet!"

And Zara suddenly felt a lump in her throat. How she had misjudged them all in her hurt ignorance! And determining to repair her injustice she advanced with a smile and was presented to the group.

CHAPTER XXII

There was a good deal of running into each other's rooms before dressing for dinner among the ladies at Montfitchet, that night. They had, they felt, to exchange views about the new bride! And the opinions were favorable, on the whole; unanimous, as to her beauty and magnetic attraction; divided, as to her character; but fiercely and venomously antagonistic in one mean, little heart.

Emily and Mary and Lady Betty Burns clustered together in the latter's room. "We think she is perfectly lovely, Betty," Emily said, "but we don't know her as yet. She is rather stiff, and frightens us just a little. Perhaps she is shy. What do you think?"

"She looks just like the heroines in some of the books that Mamma does not let me read and I am obliged to take up to bed with me. Don't you know, Mary--especially the one I lent you--deeply, mysteriously tragic. You remember the one who killed her husband and then went off with the Italian Count; and then with some one else. It was frightfully exciting."

"Good gracious! Betty," exclaimed Emily. "How dreadful! You don't think our sister-in-law looks like that?"

"I really don't know," said Lady Betty, who was nineteen and wrote lurid melo-dramas--to the waste of much paper and the despair of her mother. "I don't know. I made one of my heroines in my last play have just those passionate eyes--and she stabbed the villain in the second act!"

"Yes, but," said Mary, who felt she must defend Tristram's wife, "Zara isn't in a play and there is no villain, and--why, Betty, no one has tragedies in real life!"

Lady Betty tossed her flaxen head, while she announced a prophecy, with an air of deep wisdom which positively frightened the other two girls.

"You mark my words, both of you, Emily and Mary--they will have some trag-edy before the year is out! And I shall put it all in my next play."

And with this fearful threat ringing in their ears Tristram's two sisters walked in a scared fashion to their room.

"Betty is wonderful, isn't she, darling?" Mary said. "But, Em, you don't think there is any truth in it, do you? Mother would be so horribly shocked if there was anything like one of Betty's plays in the family, wouldn't she? And Tristram would never allow it either!"

"Of course not, you goosie," answered Emily. "But Betty is right in one way--Zara has got a mysterious face, and--and, Mary--Tristram seemed somehow changed, I thought; rather sarcastic once or twice."

And then their maid came in and put a stop to their confidences.

*   *   *   *   *

"She is the most wonderful person I have ever met, Ethelrida," Lady Anning-ford was just then saying, as she and the hostess stopped at her door and let Lady Thornby and the young Countess of Melton go on.--"She is wickedly beautiful and attractive, and there is something odd about her, too, and it touches me; and I don't believe she is really wicked a bit. Her eyes are like storm clouds. I have heard her first husband was a brute. I can't think who told me but it came from some one at one of the Embassies."

"We don't know much about her, any of us," Lady Ethelrida said, "but Aunt Jane asked us all in the beginning to trust Tristram's judgment: he is awfully proud, you know. And besides, her uncle, Mr. Markrute, is so nice. But, Anne--" and Lady Ethelrida paused.

"Well, what, dear? Tristram is awfully in love with her, isn't he?" Lady An-ningford asked.

"Yes," said Lady Ethelrida, "but, Anne, do you really think Tristram looks hap-py? I thought when he was not speaking his face seemed rather sad."

"The Crow came down in the train with them," Lady Anningford announced. "I'll hear the whole exact impression of them after dinner and tell you. The Crow is always right."

"She is so very attractive, I am sure, to every man who sees her, Anne. I hope Lord Elterton won't begin and make Tristram jealous. I wish I had not asked him. And then there is Laura--It was awful taste, I think, her insisting upon coming, don't you?--Anne, if she seems as if she were going to be horrid you will help me to protect Zara, won't you?--And now we really must dress."

*   *   *   *   *

In another room Mrs. Harcourt was chatting with her sister and Lady Highford.

"She is perfectly lovely, Laura," Miss Opie said. "Her hair must reach down to the ground and looks as if it would not come off, and her skin isn't even powdered--I examined it, on purpose, in a side light. And those eyes! Je-hoshaphat! as Jimmy Danvers says."

"Poor, darling Tristram!" Laura sighed sentimentally while she inwardly registered her intense dislike of "the Opie girl." "He looks melancholy enough--for a bridegroom; don't you think so, Kate?" and she lowered her eyes, with a glance of would-be meaning, as though she could say more, if she wished. "But no wonder, poor dear boy! He loathed the marriage; it was so fearfully sudden. I suppose the Markrute man had got him in his power."

"You don't say so!" Mrs. Harcourt gasped. She was a much simpler person than her sister. "Jimmy assured me that Lord Tancred was violently in love with her, and that was it."

"Jimmy always was a fool," Lady Highford said, and as they went on to their rooms Lily Opie whispered,

"Kate, Laura Highford is an odious cat, and I don't believe a word about Mr. Markrute and the getting Lord Tancred into his power. That is only to make a salve for herself. The Duke would never have Mr. Markrute here if there was anything fishy about him. Why, ducky, you know it is the only house left in England, almost, where they have only US!"

*   *   *   *   *

Tristram was ready for dinner in good time but he hesitated about knocking at his wife's door. If she did not let him know she was ready he would send Higgins to ask for her maid.

His eyes were shining with the pride he felt in her. She had indeed come up to the scratch. He had not believed it possible that she could have been so gracious, and he had not even guessed that she would condescend to speak so much. And all his old friends had been so awfully nice about her and honestly admiring; except Arthur Elterton--he had admired rather too much!

And then this exaltation somewhat died down. It was after all but a very poor, outside show, when, in reality, he could not even knock at her door!

He wished now he had never let his pride hurl forth that ultimatum on the wedding night, because he would have to stick to it! He could not make the slightest advance, and it did not look as if she meant to do so. Tristram in an ordinary case when his deep feelings were not concerned would have known how to display a thousand little tricks for the allurement of a woman, would have known exactly how to cajole her, to give her a flower, and hesitate when he spoke her name--and a number of useful things--but he was too terribly in earnest to be anything but a real, natural man; that is, hurt from her coldness and diffident of himself, and iron-bound with pride.

And Zara at the other side of the door felt almost happy. It was the first evening in her life she had ever dressed without some heavy burden of care. Her self-protective, watchful instincts could rest for a while; these new relations were truly, not only seemingly, so kind. The only person she immediately and instinctively disliked was Lady Highford who had gushed and said one or two bitter-sweet things which she had not clearly nor literally understood, but which, she felt, were meant to be hostile.

And her husband, Tristram! It was plain to be seen every one loved him-- from the old Duke, to the old setter by the fire. And how was it possible for them all to love a man, when--and then her thoughts unconsciously turned to *if*--he were capable of so base a thing as his marriage with her had been? Was it possible there could be any mistake? On the first opportunity she would question her uncle; and although she knew that gentleman would only tell her exactly as much as he wished her to know, that much would be the truth.

Dinner was to be at half-past eight. She ought to be punctual, she knew; but it was all so wonderful, and refined, and old-world, in her charming room, she felt inclined to dawdle and look around.

It was a room as big as her mother's had been, in the gloomy castle near Prague, but it was full of cozy touches--beyond the great gilt state bed, which she admired immensely--and with which she instinctively felt only the English--and only such English--know how to endow their apartments.

Then she roused herself. She **must** dress. Fortunately her hair did not take any time to twist up.

"Miladi is a dream!" Henriette exclaimed when at last she was ready. "Milor will be proud!"

And he was.

She sent Henriette to knock at his door--his door in the passage--not the one between their rooms!--just on the stroke of half-past eight. He was at that moment going to send Higgins on a like errand! and his sense of humor at the grotesqueness of the situation made him laugh a bitter laugh.

The two servants as the messengers!--when he ought to have been in there himself, helping to fix on her jewels, and playing with her hair, and perhaps kissing exquisite bits of her shoulders when the maid was not looking, or fastening her dress!

Well, the whole thing was a ghastly farce that must be got through; he would take up politics, and be a wonderful landlord to the people at Wrayth; and somehow, he would get through with it, and no one should ever know, from him, of his awful mistake.

He hardly allowed himself to tell her she looked very beautiful as they walked along the great corridor. She was all in deep sapphire-blue gauze, with no jewels on at all but the Duke's splendid brooch.

That was exquisite of her, he appreciated that fine touch. Indeed, he appreciated everything about her--if she had known.

People were always more or less on time in this house, and after the silent hush of admiration caused by the bride's entrance they all began talking and laughing, and none but Lady Highford and another woman were late.

And as Zara walked along the white drawing-room, on the old Duke's arm, she felt that somehow she had got back to a familiar atmosphere, where she was at rest after long years of strife.

Lady Ethelrida had gone in with the bridegroom--to-night everything was done with strict etiquette--and on her left hand she had placed the bride's uncle. The new relations were to receive every honor, it seemed. And Francis Markrute, as he looked round the table, with the perfection of its taste, and saw how everything was going on beautifully, felt he had been justified in his schemes.

Lady Anningford sat beyond Tristram, and often these two talked, so Lady Ethelrida had plenty of time, without neglecting him, to converse with her other interesting guest.

"I am so glad you like our old home, Mr. Markrute," she said. "To-morrow I will show you a number of my favorite haunts. It seems sad, does it not, as so many people assert, that the times are trending to take all these dear, old things away from us, and divide them up?"

"It will be a very bad day for England when that time comes," the financier said. "If only the people could study evolution and the meaning of things there would not be any of this nonsensical class hatred. The immutable law is that no one long retains any position unless he, or she, is suitable for it. Nothing endures that is not harmonious. It is because England is now out of harmony, that this seething is going on. You and your race have been fitted for what you have held for hundreds of years; that is why you have stayed: and your influence, and such as you, have made England great."

"Then how do you account for the whole thing being now out of joint?" Lady Ethelrida asked. "As my father and I and, as far as I know, numbers of us have remained just the same, and have tried as well as we can to do our duty to every one."

"Have you ever studied the Laws of Lycurgus, Lady Ethelrida?" he asked. And she shook her sleek, fine head. "Well, they are worth glancing at, when you have time," he went on. "An immense value was placed upon discipline, and as long as it lasted in its iron simplicity the Spartans were the wonder of the then known world. But after their conquest of Athens, when luxury poured in and every general wanted something for himself and forgot the good of the state, then their discipline went to pieces, and, so--the whole thing. And that, applied in a modern way, is what is happening to England. All classes are forgetting their discipline, and, without fitting themselves for what they aspire to, they are trying to snatch from some other class. And the whole thing is rotten with mawkish sentimentality, and false prudery, and abeyance of common sense."

"Yes," said Lady Ethelrida, much interested.

"Lycurgus went to the root of things," the financier continued, "and made the people morally and physically healthy, and ruthlessly expunged the unfit--not like our modern nonsense, which encourages science to keep, among the prospective parents for the future generation, all the most diseased. Moral and physical balance and proportion were the ideas of the Spartans. They would not have even been allowed to compete in the games, if they were misshapen. And the analogy is, no one unfitted for a part ought to aspire to it, for the public good. Any one has a right to scream, if he does not obtain it when he is fitted for it."

"Yes, I see," said Lady Ethelrida. "Then what do you mean when you say every class is trying to snatch something from some other class? Do you mean from the class above it? Or what? Because unless we, for instance--technically speaking--snatched from the King from whom could we snatch?"

The financier smiled.

"I said purposely, 'some other class,' instead of 'some class above it,' for this reason: it is because a certain and ever-increasing number of your class, if I may say so, are snatching--not, indeed, from the King--but from all classes **beneath them**, manners and morals, and absence of tenue, and absence of pride--things for which their class was not fitted. They had their own vices formerly, which only hurt each individual and not the order, as a stain will spoil the look of a bit of machinery but will not upset its working powers like a piece of grit. What they put into the machine now is grit. And the middle classes are snatching what they think is gentility, and ridiculous pretenses to birth and breeding; and the lower classes are snatching everything they can get from the pitiful fall of the other two, and shouting that all men are equal, when, if you come down to the practical thing, the foreman of some ironworks, say--where the opinions were purely socialistic, in the abstract--would give the last joined stoker a sound trouncing for aspirations in his actual work above his capabilities; because he would know that if the stoker were then made foreman the machinery could not work. The stokers of life should first fit themselves to be foremen before they shout."

Then, as Lady Ethelrida looked very grave, and Francis Markrute was really a whimsical person, and seldom talked so seriously to women, he went on, smiling,

"The only really perfect governments in the world are those of the Bees, and Ants, because they are both ruled with ruthless discipline and no sentiment, and every individual knows his place!"

"I read once, somewhere, that it has been discovered," said Lady Ethelrida gently--she never laid down the law--"that the reason why the wonderful Greeks came to an end was not really because their system of government was not a good one, but because the mosquitoes came and gave them malaria, and enervated them and made them feeble, and so they could not stand against the stronger peoples of the North. Perhaps," she went on, "England has got some moral malarial mosquitoes and the scientists have not yet discovered the proper means for their annihilation."

Here Tristram who overheard this interrupted:

"And it would not be difficult to give the noisome insects their English names, would it, Francis? Some of them are in the cabinet."

And the three laughed. But Lady Ethelrida wanted to hear something more from her left-hand neighbor, so she said,

"Then the inference to be drawn from what you have said is--we should aim at making conditions so that it is possible for every individual to have the chance to make himself practically--not theoretically--fit for anything his soul aspires to. Is that it?"

"Absolutely in a nutshell, dear lady," Francis Markrute said, and for a minute he looked into her eyes with such respectful, intense admiration that Lady Ethelrida looked away.

CHAPTER XXIII

In the white drawing-room, afterwards, Lady Highford was particularly gushing to the new bride. She came with a group of other women to surround her, and was so playful and charming to all her friends! She must be allowed to sit next to Zara, because, she said, "Your husband and I are such very dear, old friends. And how lovely it is to think that now he will be able to reopen Wrayth! Dear Lady Tancred is so glad," she purred.

Zara just looked at her politely. What a done-up ferret woman! she thought. She had met many of her tribe. At the rooms at Monte Carlo, and in another class and another race, they were the kind who played in the smallest stakes themselves, and often snatched the other people's money.

"I have never heard my husband speak of you," she said presently, when she had silently borne a good deal of vitriolic gush. "You have perhaps been out of England for some time?"

And Lady Anningford whispered to Ethelrida, "We need not worry to be ready to defend her, pet! She can hold her own!" So they moved on to the group of the girls.

But at the end of their conversation, though Zara had used her method of silence in a considerable degree and made it as difficult as she could for Lady Highford, still, that artist in petty spite had been able to leave behind her some rankling stings. She was a mistress of innuendo. So that when the men came in, and Tristram, from the sense of "not funking things" which was in him, deliberately found Laura and sat down upon a distant sofa with her, Zara suddenly felt some unpleasant feeling about her heart. She found that she desired to watch them, and that, in spite of what any one said to her, her attention wandered back to the distant sofa in some unconscious speculation and unrest.

And Laura was being exceedingly clever. She scented with the cunning of her species that Tristram was really unhappy, whether he was in love with his hatefully beautiful wife or not. Now was her chance; not by reproaches, but by sympathy, and, if possible, by planting some venom towards his wife in his heart.

"Tristram, dear boy, why did you not tell me? Did you not know I would have been delighted at anything--if it pleased you?" And she looked down, and sighed. "I always made it my pleasure to understand you, and to promote whatever seemed for your good."

And in his astonishment at this attitude Tristram forgot to recall the constant scenes and reproaches, and the paltry little selfishnesses of which he had been the victim during the year their--friendship--had lasted. He felt somehow soothed. Here was some one who was devoted to him, even if his wife were not!

"You are a dear, Laura," he said.

"And now you must tell me if you are really happy--Tristram." She lingered over his name. "She is so lovely--your wife--but looks very cold. And I know, dear" (another hesitation over the word), "I know you don't like women to be cold."

"We will not discuss my wife," he said. "Tell me what you have been doing, Laura. Let me see, when did I see you last--in June?"

And the venom came to boiling-point in Laura's adder gland. He could not even remember when he had said good-by to her! It was in July, after the Eton and Harrow match!

"Yes, in June," she said sadly, turning her eyes down. "And you might have told me, Tristram. It came as such a sudden shock. It made me seriously ill. You must have known, and were probably engaged--even then."

Tristram sat mute; for how could he announce the truth?

"Oh, don't let us talk of these things, Laura. Let us forget those old times and begin again--differently. You will be a dear friend to me always, I am sure. You always were--" and then he stopped abruptly. He felt this was too much lying! and he hated doing such things.

"Of course I will, dar--Tristram," Laura said, and appeared much moved.

And from where Zara was trying to talk to the Duke she saw the woman shiver and look down provokingly and her husband stretch his long limbs out; and a sudden, unknown sensation of blinding rage came over her, and she did not hear a syllable of the Duke's speech.

Meanwhile Lady Anningford had retired to a seat in a window with the Crow.

"Is it all right, Crow?" she asked, and one of his peculiarities was to understand her--as Lady Ethelrida understood the Duke--and and not ask "What?"

"Will be--some day--I expect--unless they get drowned in the current first."

"Isn't she mysterious, Crow? I am sure she has some tragic history. Have you heard anything?"

"Husband murdered by another man in a row at Monte Carlo."

"Over her?"

"I don't know for a fact, but I gather--not. You may be certain, Queen Anne, that when a woman is as quiet and haughty as Lady Tancred looks, and her manners are as cold and perfectly sure of herself as hers are, she has not done anything she is ashamed of, or regrets."

"Then what can be the cause of the coolness between them? Look at Tristram now! I think it is horrid of him--sitting like that talking to Laura, don't you?"

"A viper, Laura," growled the Crow. "She's trying to get him again in the rebound."

"I cannot imagine why women cannot leave other women's husbands alone. They are hateful creatures, most of them."

"Natural instinct of the chase," said Colonel Lowerby.

But Lady Anningford flashed.

"You are a cynic, Crow."

*   *   *   *   *

"And you will really show me your favorite haunts to-morrow, Lady Ethelrida?" Francis Markrute was saying to his hostess. He had contrived insidiously to detach her conversation from a group to himself, and drew her unconsciously towards a seat where they would be uninterrupted. "One judges so of people by their tastes in haunts."

Lady Ethelrida never spoke of herself as a rule. She was not in the habit of getting into those--abstract to begin with, and personal to go on with--thrilling conversations with men, which most of the modern young women delight in, and which were the peculiar joy of Lily Opie.

It was because for some unacknowledged reason the financier personally pleased her that she now drifted where he wished.

"Mine are very simple, I fear, nothing for you to investigate," she said gently.

"So I should have thought--" and he again as he had done at dinner permitted himself to look into her eyes, and going on after an imperceptible pause he said softly, "simple, and pure, and sweet ...I always think of you, Lady Ethelrida, as the embodiment of sane things, balanced things--perfection." And his last word was almost a caress.

"I am most ordinary," she said; and she wondered why she was not angry with him, which she quite well could have been.

"It is only perfect balance in all things, if we but know it, which appeals to the sane eye," he went on, pulling himself up. "All weariness and satiety are caused in emotion; in pleasure in persons, places, or things; by the want of proportion in them somewhere which, like all simple things, is the hardest to find."

"Do you make theories about everything, Mr. Markrute?" she asked, and there was a smile in her eye.

"It is a wise thing to do sometimes; it keeps one from losing one's head."

Lady Ethelrida did not answer. She felt deliciously moved. She had often said to her friend, Anne Anningford, when they had been talking, that she did not like elderly men; she disliked to see their hair getting thin, and their chins getting fat, and their little habits and mannerisms growing pronounced. But here she found herself tremendously interested in one who, from all accounts, must be quite forty-five if not older, though it was true his brown colorless hair was excessively thick, and he was slight of build everywhere.

Now she felt she must turn the conversation to less personal things, so:

"Zara looks very lovely to-night," she said.

"Yes," replied the financier, with an air of detaching himself unwillingly from a thrilling topic, which was, indeed, what he felt. "Yes, and I hope some day they will be exceedingly happy."

"Why do you say some day?" Lady Ethelrida asked quickly. "I hoped they were happy now."

"Not very, I am afraid," he said. "But you remember our compact at dinner? They will be ideally so if they are left alone," and he glanced casually at Tristram and Laura.

Ethelrida looked, too, following his eyes.

"Yes," she said. "I wish I had not asked her--" and then she stopped abruptly, and grew a deep pink. She realized what the inference in her speech was, and if Mr. Markrute had never heard anything about the silly affair between her cousin and Lady Highford what would he think! What might she not have done!

"That won't matter," he said, with his fine smile. "It will be good for my niece. I meant something quite different."

But what he meant, he would not say.

And so the evening passed smoothly. The girls, and all the young men and the Crow, and Young Billy, and giddy, irresponsible people like that, had gathered at one end of the room; they were arranging some especial picnic for the morrow, as only some of them were going to shoot. And into their picnic plans they drew Zara, and barred Tristram out, with chaff.

"You are only an old, married man now, Tristram," they teased him with. "But Lady Tancred is young and comes with us!"

"And I will take care of her," announced Lord Elterton, looking sentimental-- much to Tristram's disgust.

Ethelrida seemed to have collected a lot of rotters, he thought to himself, although it was the same party he had so enjoyed last year!

"Lady Thornby and Lady Melton and Lily Opie and her sister are going out to the shooters' lunch," Laura said sweetly. "As you are going to be deprived of your lovely wife, Tristram, I will come, too."

And so, finally good nights were said and the ladies retired to their rooms; and Zara could not think why she no longer found the atmosphere of hers peaceful and delightful, as she had done before she went down.

For the first time in her life she felt she hated a woman.

And Tristram, her husband, when he came up an hour or so later, wondered if she were asleep. Laura had been perfectly sweet, and he felt greatly soothed. Poor old Laura! He supposed she had really cared for him rather, and perhaps he had behaved casually, even though she had been impossible, in the past. But how had he ever even for five minutes fancied himself in love with her? Why, she looked quite old to-night! and he had never remarked before how thin and fluffed out her hair was. Women ought certainly to have beautifully thick hair.

And then all the pretenses of any healing of his aches fell from him, and he went and stood by the door that separated him from his loved one, and he stretched out his arms and said aloud, "Darling, if only you could understand how happy I would make you--if you would let me! But I can't even break down this hateful door as I want to, because of my vow."

And then for most of the rest of the night he tossed restlessly in his bed.

CHAPTER XXIV

The next day did not look at all promising as regards the weather, but still the shooters, Tristram among them, started early for their sport. And after the merriest breakfast at little tables in the great dining-room the intending picnickers met in conclave to decide as to what they should do.

"It is perfectly sure to rain," Jimmy Danvers said. "There is no use attempting to go to Lynton Heights. Why don't we take the lunch to Montfitchet Tower and eat it in the big hall? There we wouldn't get wet."

"Quite right, Jimmy," agreed the Crow, who, with Lady Anningford, was to chaperon the young folk. "I'm all for not getting wet, with my rheumatic shoulder, and I hear you and Young Billy are a couple of firstclass cooks."

"Then," interrupted Lady Betty enthusiastically, "we can cook our own lunch! Oh, how delightful! We will make a fire in the big chimney. Uncle Crow, you are a pet!"

"I will go and give orders for everything at once," Lady Ethelrida agreed delightedly. "Jimmy, what a bright boy to have thought of the plan!"

And by twelve o'clock all was arranged. Now, it had been settled the night before that Mr. Markrute should shoot with the Duke and the rest of the more serious men; but early in the morning that astute financier had sent a note to His Grace's room, saying, if it were not putting out the guns dreadfully, he would crave to be excused as he was expecting a telegram of the gravest importance concerning the new Turkish loan, which he would be obliged to answer by a special letter, and he was uncertain at what time the wire would come. He was extremely sorry, but, he added whimsically, the Duke must remember he was only a poor, business-man!

At which His Grace had smiled, as he thought of his guest's vast millions, in comparison to his own.

Thus it was that just before twelve o'clock when the young party were ready to start for their picnic. Mr. Markrute, having written his letter and despatched it by express to London, chanced upon Lady Ethelrida in a place where he felt sure he should find her, and, expressing his surprise that they were not already gone, he begged to be allowed to come with them. He, too, was an excellent cook, he assured her, and would be really of use. And they all laughingly started.

And if she could have seen the important letter concerning the new Turkish loan, she would have found it contained a pressing reminder to Bumpus to send down that night certain exquisitely bound books!

*   *   *   *   *

Above all, the young ladies had demanded they should have no servants at their picnic--everything, even the fire, was to be made by themselves. Jimmy was to drive the donkey-cart, with Lady Betty, to take all the food. The only thing they permitted was that the pots and pans and the wood for the fire might be sent on.

And they were all so gay and looked so charming and suitably clad, in their rough, short, tweed frocks.

Zara, who walked demurely by Lord Elterton, had never seen anything of the sort. She felt like a strange, little child at its first party.

Before he had started in the morning Tristram had sent her a note (he could not stand the maid and valet as verbal messengers--it made him laugh too bitterly), it was just a few lines:

"You asked me to tell you anything special about our customs, so this is to say, just put on some thick, short, ordinary suit, and mind you have a pair of thick boots."

And it was signed "Tancred"--not "Tristram."

She gave a little quiver as she read it, and then asked and found his lordship had already gone down. She was to breakfast later with the non-shooters. She would not see him, then, for the entire day. And that odious woman with whom he was so friendly would have him all to herself!

These thoughts flashed into her mind before she was aware of it, and then she crushed them out--furious with herself. For of what possible matter could her husband's doings be to her? And yet, as she started, she found herself hoping it would rain, so that the five ladies who intended joining the guns in the farmhouse, for luncheon at two, would be unable to go. For just as she had come into the saloon where some of the party were writing letters that morning she had heard Lady Highford say to Mrs. Harcourt, in her high voice, "Yes, indeed, we mean to finish the discussion this afternoon after luncheon.--Dear Tristram! There is a long wait at the Fulton beat; we shall have plenty of time alone." And then she had turned round, and seemed confused at seeing her--Zara--and gushed more than the night before.

But she did not get the satisfaction of perceiving the bride turn a hair, though as Zara walked on to the end of the room she angrily found herself wondering who was this woman, and what had she been to Tristram? What was she *now*?

Lord Elterton had already fallen in love. He was a true *cavalier* servant; he knew, like the financier, as a fine art, how to manipulate the temperaments of most women. He prided himself upon it. Indeed, he spent the greater part of his life doing nothing else. Exquisite gentleness and sympathy was his method. There were such heaps of rough, rude brutes about that one would always have a chance by being the contrast; and husbands, he reasoned, were nearly always brutes--after a while--in the opinion of their wives! He had hardly ever known this plan to fail with the most devoted wife. So although Lady Tancred had only been married a week he hoped to render her not quite indifferent to himself in some way. He had seen at once that she and Tristram were not on terms of passionate love, and there was something so piquant about flirting with a bride! He divided women as a band into about four divisions. The quite impossible, the recalcitrant, the timid, and the bold. For the impossible he did not waste powder and shot. For the recalcitrant he used insidious methods of tickling their fancies, as he would tickle a trout. For the timid he was tender and protective; and for the bold subtly indifferent: but always gentle and nice!

He was not sure yet in which of the four divisions he should have to place his new attraction--probably the second--but he frankly admitted he had never before had any experience with one of her type. Her strange eyes thrilled him: he felt, when she turned the deep slate, melting disks upon him, his heart went "down into his bloomin' boots," as Jimmy Danvers would have described the sensation. So he began with extreme gentleness and care.

"You have not been long in this country, Lady Tancred, have you? One can see it--you are so exquisitely *chic*. And how perfectly you speak English! Not the slightest accent. It is delicious. Did you learn it when very young?"

"My father was an Englishman," said Zara, disarmed from her usual chilling reserve by the sympathy in his voice. "I always spoke it until I was thirteen, and since then, too. It is a nice, honest language, I think."

"You speak numbers of others, probably?" Lord Elterton went on, admiringly.

"Yes, about four or five. It is very easy when one is moving in the countries, and certain languages are very much alike. Russian is the most difficult."

"How clever you are!"

"No, I am not a bit. But I have had time to read a good deal--" and then Zara stopped. It was so against her habit to give personal information to any one like this.

Lord Elterton saw the little check, and went on another tack. "I have been an idle fellow and am not at all learned," he said. "Tristram and I were at Eton together in the same house, and we were both dunces; but he did rather well at Oxford, and I went straight into the Guards."

Zara longed to ask about Tristram. She had not even heard before that he had been to Oxford! And it struck her suddenly how ridiculous the whole thing was. She had sold herself for a bargain; she had asked no questions of any one; she had intended to despise the whole family and remain entirely aloof; and now she found every one of her intentions being gradually upset. But as yet she did not admit for a second to herself that she was falling in love. It would be such a perfectly impossible thing to do in any case, when now he was absolutely indifferent to her and showed it in every way. It made the whole thing all the more revolting--to have pretended he loved her on that first night! Yes, with certain modifications of classes and races men were all perfectly untrustworthy, if not brutes, and a woman, if she could relax her vigilance, as regards the defense of her person and virtue, could not afford to unbend a fraction as to her emotions!

And all the time she was thinking this out she was silent, and Lord Elterton watched her, thrilled with the attraction of the unobtainable. He saw plainly she had forgotten his very presence, and, though piqued, he grew the more eager.

"I would love to know what you were thinking of," he said softly; and then with great care he pulled a bramble aside so that it should not touch her. They had turned into a lane beyond the kitchen garden and the park.

Zara started. She had, indeed, been far away!

"I was thinking--" she said, and then she paused for a suitable lie but none came, so she grew confused, and stopped, and hesitated, and then she blurted out, "I was thinking was it possible there could ever be any one whom one could believe?"

Lord Elterton looked at her. What a strange woman!

"Yes," he said simply, "you can believe me when I tell you I have never been so attracted by any one in my life."

"Oh! for that!" she answered contemptuously. *"Mon Dieu!* how often I have heard of that!"

This was not what he had expected. There was no empty boast about the speech, as there would have been if Laura Highford had uttered it--she was fond of demonstrating her conquests and power in words. There was only a weariness as of something banal and tiring. He must be more careful.

"Yes, I quite understand," he said sympathetically. "You must be bored with the love of men."

"I have never seen any love of men. Do men know love?" she asked, not with any bitterness--only as a question of fact. What had Tristram been about? Lord Elterton thought. Here he had been married to this divine creature for a whole week, and she was plainly asking the question from her heart. And Tristram was no fool in a general way, he knew. There was some mystery here, but whatever it was there was the more chance for him! So he went on very tactfully, trying insidiously to soothe her, so that at last when they had arrived Zara had enjoyed her walk.

Montfitchet Tower was all that remained of the old castle destroyed by Cromwell's Ironsides. It was just one large, square room, a sort of great hall. It had stood roofless for many years and then been covered in by the old Duke's father, and contained a splendid stone chimney piece of colossal proportions. It had also been floored, and had the raised place still, where the family had eaten "above the salt." The rest of the old castle was a complete ruin, and at the Restoration the new one had been rebuilt about a mile further up the park.

Lady Ethelrida had collected several pieces of rough oak furniture to put into this great room which in height reached three stories up, and the supports of the mantelpieces of the upper floors could be seen on the blackened stone walls. It was here she gave her school treats and tenants' summer dances, because there was a great stretch of green, turfy lawn beyond, down to the river, where they could play their games. And on a wet day it was an ideal picnic place.

A bright wood fire was already blazing on top of the ashes that for many years had never been cleared out, and a big jack swung in front of it--for appearance sake! What fun every one seemed to be having, Zara thought, as from an oak bench she watched them all busy as bees over their preparations for the repast. She had helped to make a salad, and now sat with the Crow, and surveyed the rest.

Jimmy Danvers had turned up his sleeves and was thoroughly in earnest over his part; and he and Young Billy had gathered some brown bracken, and put it sprouting from a ham, to represent, they said, the peacock. For, they explained, a banquet in a baronial hall had to have a peacock, as well as a boar's head, and an ox roasted whole!

And suddenly Zara thought of her last picnic, with Mimo and Mirko in the Neville Street attic, when the poor little one had worn the paper cap, and had taken such pleasure in the new rosy cups. And the Crow who was watching her closely, wondered why this gay scene should make the lovely bride look so pitifully sad. "How *Maman* would have loved all this!" she was thinking, "with her gay, tender soul, and her delight in make-believe and joyous picnics." And her father--he had known all these sorts of people; they were his own class, and yet he had come to live in the great, gloomy castle, out of his own land, and expected his exquisite, young wife to stay there alone, most of the time. The hideous cruelty of men!

And there was her Uncle Francis, in quite a new character!--helping Lady Ethelrida to lay the table, as happily as a boy. Would she herself ever be happy, she wondered, ever have a time free from some agonizing strain or care? And then, from sorrow her expression changed to one of strange slumberous resentment at fate.

"Queen Anne," said the Crow, as they sat down to luncheon, "there is some tragedy hanging over that young woman. She has been suffering like the devil for at least ten minutes, and forgot I was even beside her and pretending to talk. You and Lady Ethelrida have two not altogether unkind hearts. Can't you find out what it is, and comfort her?"

CHAPTER XXV

A fter luncheon, which had been carried through with all the proper ceremonies of the olden time according to Jimmy Danvers and Young Billy's
interpretation of them, it came on to pour with rain; so these masters of
the revels said that now the medieval dances should begin, and accord-
ingly they turned on the gramophone that stood in the corner to amuse the children
at the school treats. And Mary and her admirer, Lord Henry Burns, and Emily and
a Captain Hume, and Lady Betty and Jimmy Danvers, gayly took the floor, while
Young Billy offered himself to the bride, as he said he as the representative of the
Lord of the Castle had a right to the loveliest lady; and, with his young, stolid self-
confidence, he pushed Lord Elterton aside.

Zara had not danced for a very long time--four years at least--and she had not
an idea of the two-steps and barn-dances and other sorts of whirling capers that
they invented; but she did her best, and gradually something of the excitement of
the gay young spirits spread to her, and she forgot her sorrows and began to enjoy
herself.

"You don't ever dance, I suppose, Mr. Markrute?" Lady Ethelrida asked, as she
stopped, with the gallant old Crow, flushed and smiling by the dais, where the financier and Lady Anningford sat. "If you ever do, I, as the Lady of the Castle, ask
you to 'tread a measure' with me!"

"No one could resist such, an invitation," he answered, and put his arm around
her for a valse.

"I do love dancing," she said, as they went along very well. She was so surprised
that this "grave and reverend signor," as she called him, should be able to valse!

"So do I," said Francis Markrute--"under certain circumstances. This is one of
them." And then he suddenly held her rather tight, and laughed. "Think of it all!"

he went on. "Here we are, in thick boots and country clothes capering about like savages round their fire, and, for all sorts of reasons, we all love it!"

"It is just the delicious exercise with me," said Lady Ethelrida.

"And it has nothing at all to do with that reason with me," returned her partner.

And Lady Ethelrida quivered with some sort of pleasure and did not ask him what his reason was. She thought she knew, and her eyes sparkled. They were the same height, and he saw her look; and as they went on, he whispered:

"I have brought you down the book we spoke of, you know, and you will take it from me, won't you? Just as a remembrance of this day and how you made me young for an hour!"

They stopped by one of the benches at the side and sat down, and Lady Ethelrida answered softly,

"Yes, if--you wish me to--"

Lord Elterton had now dislodged Young Billy and was waltzing with Zara himself: his whole bearing was one of intense devotion, and she was actually laughing and looking up in his face, still affected by the general hilarity, when the door of the wooden porch that had been built on as an entrance opened noiselessly, and some of the shooters peeped into the room. It had been too impossibly wet to go on, and they had sent the ladies back in the motors and had come across the park on their way home, and, hearing the sound of music, had glanced in. Tristram was in front of the intruders and just chanced to catch his bride's look at her partner, before either of them saw they were observed.

He felt frightfully jealous. He had never before seen her so smiling, to begin with, and never at all at himself. He longed to kick Arthur Elterton! Confounded impertinence!--And what tommyrot--dancing like this, in the afternoon with boots on! And when they all stopped and greeted the shooters, and crowded round the fire, he said, in a tone of rasping sarcasm--in reply to Jimmy Danvers' announcement that they were back in the real life of a castle in the Middle Ages:

"Any one can see that! You have even got My Lady's fool. Look at Arthur--with mud on his boots--jumping about!"

And Lord Elterton felt very flattered. He knew his old friend was jealous, and if he were jealous then the charming, cold lady must have been unbelievingly nice to him, and that meant he was getting on!

"You are jealous because your lovely bride prefers me, Young Lochinvar," and he laughed as he quoted:

"'For so faithful in love and so dauntless in war-- There ne'er was a gallant like Young Lochinvar!'"

And Zara saw that Tristram's eyes flashed blue steel, and that he did not like the chaff at all. So, just out of some contrariness--he had been with Lady Highford all day so why should she not amuse herself, too; indeed, why should either of them care what the other did--so just out of contrariness she smiled again at Lord Elterton and said:

"'Then tread we a measure, my Lord Lochinvar.'"

And off they went.

And Tristram, with his face more set than the Crusader ancestor's in Wrayth Church, said to his uncle, Lord Charles, "We are all wet through: let us come along."

And he turned round and went out.

And as he walked, he wondered to himself how much she must know of English poetry to have been able to answer Arthur like that. If only they could be friends and talk of the books he, too, loved! And then he realized more strongly than ever the impossibility of the situation--he, who had been willing to undertake it with the joyous self-confidence with which he had started upon a lion hunt!

He felt he was getting to the end of his tether; it could not go on. Her words that night at Dover, had closed down all the possible sources he could have used for her melting.

And a man cannot in a week break through a thousand years of inherited pride.

Before the Canada scheme had presented itself he had rather thought of joining with a friend for another trip to the Soudan: it might not be too late still, when they had got over the Wrayth ordeal, the tenants' dinners, and the speeches, and the cruel mockery of it all. He would see--perhaps--what could be done, but to go on living in this daily torture he would not submit to, for the "loving her less" had not yet begun!

And when he had left, although she would not own it to herself, Zara's joy in the day was gone.

The motors came to fetch them presently, and they all went back to the Castle to dress and have tea.

Tristram's face was still stony and he had sat down in a sofa by Laura, when a footman brought a telegram to Zara. He watched her open it, with concentrated interest. Whom were these mysterious telegrams from? He saw her face change as it had done in Paris, only not so seriously; and then she crushed up the paper into a ball and threw it in the fire. The telegram had been: "Very slightly feverish again," and signed "Mimo."

"Now I remember where I have seen your wife before," said Laura. And Tristram said absently,

"Where?"

"In the waiting-room at Waterloo station--and yet--no, it could not have been she, because she was quite ordinarily dressed, and she was talking very interestedly to a foreign man." She watched Tristram's face and saw she had hit home for some reason; so she went on, enchanted: "Of course it could not have been she, naturally; but the type is so peculiar that any other like it would remind one, would it not?"

"I expect so," he said. "It could not have been Zara, though, because she was in Paris until just before the wedding."

"I remember the occasion quite well. It was the day after the engagement was announced, because I had been up for Flora's wedding, and was going down into the country."

Then in a flash it came to him that that was the very day he himself had seen Zara in Whitehall, the day when she had not gone to Paris. And rankling, uncomfortable suspicions overcame him again.

Laura felt delighted. She did not know why he should be moved at her announcement; but he certainly was, so it was worth while rubbing it in.

"Has she a sister, perhaps? Because--now I come to think of it--the resemblance is extraordinary. I remember I was rather interested at the time because the man was so awfully handsome and as you know, dear boy, I always had a passion for handsome men!"

"My wife was an only child," Tristram answered. What was Laura driving at?

"Well, she has a double then," she laughed. "I watched them for quite ten minutes, so I am sure. I was waiting for my maid, who was to meet me, and I could not leave for fear of missing her."

"How interesting!" said Tristram coldly. He would not permit himself to demand a description of the man.

"Perhaps after all it was she, before she went to Paris, and I may be mistaken about the date," Laura went on. "It might have been her brother--he was certainly foreign--but no, it could not have been a brother." And she looked down and smiled knowingly.

Tristram felt gradually wild with the stings her words were planting, and then his anger rebounded upon herself. Little natures always miscalculate the effect of their actions, as factors in their desires, for their ultimate ends.

Laura only longed--after hurting Tristram as a punishment--to get him back again; but she was not clever enough to know that to make him mad with jealousy about his wife was not the way.

"I don't understand what you wish to insinuate, Laura," he said in a contemptuous voice; "but whatever it is, it is having no effect upon me. I absolutely adore my wife, and know everything she does or does not do."

"Oh! the poor, angry darling, there, there!" she laughed, spitefully, "and was It jealous! Well, It shan't be teased. But what a clever husband, to know all about his wife! He should be put in a glass case in a museum!" And she got up and left him alone.

Tristram would like to have killed some one--he did not know whom--this foreign man, "Mimo," most likely: he had not forgotten the name!

If his pride had permitted him he would have gone up to Zara, who had now retired to her room, and asked straight out for an explanation. He would if he had been sensible have simply said he was unhappy, and he would have asked her to reassure him. It would all have been perfectly simple and soon ended if treated with common sense. But he was too obstinate, and too hurt, and too passionately in love. The bogey of his insulted Tancred pride haunted him always, and, like all foolish things, caused him more suffering than if it had been a crime.

So once more the pair dressed to go down to the ducal dinner, with deeper estrangement in their hearts. And when Tristram was ready to-night, he went out into the corridor and pretended to look at the pictures. He would have no more servants' messages!--and there he was, with a bitter smile on his face, when Lady Anningford, coming from her room beyond, stopped to talk. She wondered at his being there--a very different state of things to her own with her dear old man, she remembered, who, after the wedding day, for weeks and weeks would hardly let her out of his sight!

Then Henriette peeped out of the door and saw that the message she was being sent upon was in vain, and went back; and immediately Zara appeared.

Her dress was pale gray to-night--with her uncle's pearls--and both Lady Anningford and Tristram noticed that her eyes were slumberous and had in them that smoldering fierceness of pain. And remembering the Crow's appeal Lady Anningford slipped her hand within her arm, and was very gentle and friendly as they went down to the saloon.

CHAPTER XXVI

Now if the evening passed with pain and unrest for the bride and bridegroom, it had quite another aspect for Francis Markrute and Lady Ethelrida! He was not placed by his hostess to-night at dinner, but when the power of manipulating circumstances with skill is in a man, and the desire to make things easy to be manipulated is in a woman, they can spend agreeable and numerous moments together.

So it fell about that without any apparent or pointed detachment from her other guests Lady Ethelrida was able to sit in one of the embrasures of the windows in, the picture gallery, whither the party had migrated to-night, and talk to her interesting new friend--for that he was growing into a friend she felt. He seemed so wonderfully understanding, and was so quiet and subtle and undemonstrative, and, underneath, you could feel his power and strength.

It had been his insidious suggestion, spread among the company, which had caused them to be in the picture gallery to-night, instead of in one of the great drawing-rooms. For in a very long narrow room it was much easier to separate people, he felt.

"Of course this was not built at the time the house was, in about 1670," Lady Ethelrida said. "It was added by the second Duke, who was Ambassador to Versailles in the time of Louis XV, and who thought he would like a 'galerie des glaces' in imitation of the one there. And then, when the walls were up, he died, and it was not decorated until thirty-five years later, in the Regent's time, and it was turned into a picture gallery then."

"People's brands of individuality in their houses are so interesting," Francis Markrute said. "I believe Wrayth is a series of human fancies, from the Norman Castle upwards, is it not? I have never been there."

"Oh! Wrayth is much more interesting than this," she answered. "Parts of it are so wonderfully old; there are stone floors in the upper rooms in one of the inner courtyards. They did not suffer, you see, from the hateful Puritans, because the then Tancred was only an infant when the civil war began; and his mother was a Frenchwoman, and they stayed in France all the time, and only came back when Charles II returned. He married a Frenchwoman, too. She was a wonderful person and improved many things. Wrayth has two long galleries and a chapel of Henry the Seventh's time, and numbers of staircases in unexpected places, and then a fine suite of state rooms, built on by Adam, and then the most awful Early-Victorian imitation Gothic wing and porch which one of those dreadful people, who spoilt such numbers of places, added in 1850."

"It sounds wonderful," said the financier.

"Lots of it is very shabby, of course, because Tristram's father was always very hard up; and nothing much had been done either in the grandfather's time--except the horrible wing. But with enough money to get it right again, I cannot imagine anything more lovely than it could be."

"It will be a great amusement to them in the coming year to do it all, then. Zara has the most beautiful taste, Lady Ethelrida. When you know her better I think you will like my niece."

"But I do now," she exclaimed. "Only I do wish she did not look so sad. May I ask it because of our bargain? "--and she paused with gentle timidity--"Will you tell me?--do you know of any special reason to-day to make her unhappy? I saw her face at dinner to-night, and all the while she talked there was an anxious, haunted look in her eyes."

Francis Markrute frowned for a moment; he had been too absorbed in his own interests to have taken in anything special about his niece. If there were something of the sort in her eyes it could only have one source--anxiety about the health of the boy Mirko. He himself had not heard anything. Then his lightning calculations decided him to tell Lady Ethelrida nothing of this. Zara's anxiety would mean the child's illness, and illness, Doctor Morley had warned him, could have only one end. He wished the poor little fellow no harm, but, on the other hand, he had no sentiment about him. If he were going to die then the disgrace would be wiped away and need never be spoken about. So he answered slowly:

"There is something which troubles her now and then. It will pass presently. Take no notice of it."

So Lady Ethelrida, as mystified as ever, turned the conversation.

"May I give you the book to-morrow morning before we go to shoot?" the financier asked after a moment. "It is your birthday, I believe, and all your guests on that occasion are privileged to lay some offering at your feet. I wanted to do so this afternoon after tea, but I was detained playing bridge with your father. I have several books coming to-morrow that I do so want you to have."

"It is very kind of you. I would like to show you my sitting-room, in the south wing. Then you could see that they would have a comfortable home!"

"When may I come?"

This was direct, and Lady Ethelrida felt a piquant sensation of interest. She had never in her life made an assignation with a man. She thought a moment.

"They will start only at eleven to-morrow, because the first covert is at a corner of the park, quite near, and if it is fine we are all coming out with you until luncheon which we have in the house; then you go to the far coverts in the motors. When, I wonder, would be best?"--It seemed so nice to leave it to him.

"You breakfast downstairs at half-past nine, like this morning?"

"Yes, I always do, and the girls will and almost every one, because it is my birthday."

"Then if I come exactly at half-past ten will you be there?"

"I will try. But how will you know the way?"

"I have a bump of locality which is rather strong, and I know the windows from the outside. You remember you showed them to me to-day as we walked to the tower."

Lady Ethelrida experienced a distinct feeling of excitement over this innocent rendezvous.

"There is a staircase--but no!"--and she laughed--"I shall tell you no more. It will be a proof of your sagacity to find the clue to the labyrinth."

"I shall be there," he said, and once again he looked into her sweet, gray eyes; and she rose with a slightly faster movement than usual and drew him to where there were more of her guests.

Meanwhile Lord Elterton was losing no time in his pursuit of Zara. He had been among the first to leave the dining-room, several paces in front of Tristram and the others, and instantly came to her and suggested a tour of the pictures. He quite agreed with the financier--these long, narrow rooms were most useful!

And Zara, thankful to divert her mind, went with him willingly, and soon found herself standing in front of an immense canvas given by the Regent, of himself, to the Duke's grandfather, one of his great friends.

"I have been watching you all through dinner," Lord Elterton said, "and you looked like a beautiful storm: your dress the gray clouds, and your eyes the thunder ones--threatening."

"One feels like a storm sometimes," said Zara.

"People are so tiresome, as a rule; you can see through them in half an hour. But no one could ever guess about what you were thinking."

"No one would want to--if they knew."

"Is it so terrible as that?" And he smiled--she must be diverted. "I wish I had met you long ago, because, of course, I cannot tell you all the things I now want to--Tristram would be so confoundedly jealous--like he was this afternoon. It is the way of husbands."

Zara did not reply. She quite agreed to this, for of the jealousy of husbands she had experience!

"Now if I were married," Lord Elterton went on, "I would try to make my wife so happy, and would love her so much she would never give me cause to be jealous."

"Love!" said Zara. "How you talk of love--and what does it mean? Gratification to oneself, or to the loved person?"

"Both," said Lord Elterton, and looked down so devotedly into her eyes that the old Duke, who was near, with Laura, thought it was quite time the young man's innings should be over!

So he joined them.

"Come with me, Zara, while I show you some of Tristram's ancestors on his mother's side."

And he placed her arm in his gallantly, and led her away to the most interesting pictures.

"Well, 'pon my soul!" he said, as they went along. "Things are vastly changed since my young days. Here, Tristram--" and he beckoned to his nephew who was with Lady Anningford--"come here and help me to show your wife some of your forbears." And then he went on with his original speech. "Yes, as I was saying, things are vastly changed since I brought Ethelrida's dear mother back here, after our honeymoon!--a month in those days! I would have punched any other young blood's head, who had even looked at her! And you philander off with that fluffy, little empty-pate, Laura, and Arthur Elterton makes love to your bride! A pretty state of things, 'pon my soul!" And he laughed reprovingly.

Tristram smiled with bitter sarcasm as he answered, "You were absurdly old-fashioned, Uncle. But perhaps Aunt Corisande was different to the modern woman."

Zara did not speak. The black panther's look, on its rare day of slumberous indifference when it condescends to come to the front of the cage, grew in her eyes, but the slightest touch could make her snarl.

"Oh! you must not ever blame the women," the Duke--this *preux chevalier*--said. "If they are different it is the fault of the men. I took care that my duchess wanted me! Why, my dear boy, I was jealous of even her maid, for at least a year!"

And Tristram thought to himself that he went further than that and was jealous of even the air Zara breathed!

"You must have been awfully happy, Uncle," he said with a sigh.

But Zara spoke never a word. And the Duke saw that there was something too deeply strained between them, for his kindly meant *persiflage* to do any good; so he turned to the pictures, and drew them into lighter things; and the moment he could, Tristram rejoined Lady Anningford by one of the great fires.

Laura Highford, left alone with Lord Elterton up at the end of the long picture gallery, felt she must throw off some steam. She could not keep from the subject which was devouring her; she knew now she had made an irreparable mistake in what she had said to Tristram in the afternoon, and how to repair it she did not know at present, but she must talk to some one.

"You will have lots of chance before a year is out, Arthur," she said with a bitter smile. "You need not be in such a hurry! That marriage won't last more than a few months--they hate each other already."

"You don't say so!" said Lord Elterton, feigning innocence. "I thought they were a most devoted couple!"--Laura would be a safe draw, and although he would not believe half he should hear, out of the bundle of chaff he possibly could collect some grains of wheat which might come in useful.

"Devoted couple!" she laughed. "Tristram is by no means the first with her. There is a very handsome foreign gentleman, looking like Romeo, or Rizzio--"

"Or any other 'O,'" put in Lord Elterton.

"Exactly--in whom she is much more interested. Poor Tristram! He has plenty to discover, I fear."

"How do you come to know about it? You are a wonder, Lady Highford--always so full of interesting information!"

"I happened to see them at Waterloo together--evidently just arrived from somewhere--and Tristram thought she was safe in Paris! Poor dear!"

"You have told him about it, of course?"--anxiously.

"I did just give him a hint."

"That was wise." And Lord Elterton smiled blandly and she did not see the twinkle in his eye. "He was naturally grateful?" he asked sympathetically.

"Not now, perhaps, but some day he will be!"

Laura's light hazel eyes flashed, and Lord Elterton laughed again as he answered lightly,

"There certainly is a poor spirit in the old boy if he doesn't feel under a lifelong obligation to you for your goodness. I should, if it were me.--Look, though, we shall have to go now; they are beginning to say good night."

And as they found the others he thought to himself, "Well, men may be poachers like I am, but I am hanged if they are such weasels as women!"

Lady Anningford joined Lady Ethelrida that night in her room, after they had seen Zara to hers, and they began at once upon the topic which was thrilling them all.

"There is something the matter, Ethelrida, darling," Lady Anningford said. "I have talked to Tristram for a long time to-night, and, although he was bravely trying to hide it, he was bitterly miserable; spoke recklessly of life one minute, and resignedly the next; and then asked me, with an air as if in an abstract discussion, whether Hector and Theodora were really happy--because she had been a widow. And when I said, 'Yes, ideally so,' and that they never want to be dragged away from Bracondale, he said, so awfully sadly, 'Oh, I dare-say; but then they have chil-dren.' It is too pitiful to hear him, after only a week! What can it be? What can have happened in the time?"

"It is not since, Anne," Ethelrida said, beginning to unfasten her dress. "It was always like that. She had just the look in her eyes the night we all first met her, at Mr. Markrute's at dinner--that strange, angry, pained, sorrowful look, as though she were a furnace of resentment against some fate. I remember an old colored pic-ture we had on a screen--it is now in the housekeeper's room--it was one of those badly-drawn, lurid scenes of prisoners being dragged off to Siberia in the snow, and there was a woman in it who had just been separated from her husband and baby and who had exactly the same expression. It used to haunt me as a child, and Mamma had it taken out of the old nursery. And Zara's eyes haunt me now in the same way."

"She never had any children, I suppose?" asked Lady Anningford.

"Never that I heard of--and she is so young; only twenty-three now."

"Well, it is too tragic! And what is to be done? Can't you ask the uncle? He must know."

"I did, to-night, Anne--and he answered, so strangely, that 'yes, there was something which at times troubled her, but it would pass.'"

"Good gracious!" said Anne. "It can't be a hallucination. She is not crazy, is she? That would be worse than anything."

"Oh, no!" cried Ethelrida, aghast. "It is not that in the least, thank goodness!"

"Then perhaps there are some terrible scenes, connected with her first hus-band's murder, which she can't forget. The Crow told me Count Shulski was shot at Monte Carlo, in a fray of some sort."

"That must be it, of course!" said Ethelrida, much relieved. "Then she will get over it in time. And surely Tristram will be able to make her love him, and forget them. I do feel better about it now, Anne, and shall be able to sleep in peace."

So they said good night, and separated--comforted.

But the object of their solicitude did not attempt to get into her bed when she had dismissed her maid. She sat down in one of the big gilt William-and-Mary arm-chairs, and clasped her hands tightly, and tried to think.

Things were coming to a crisis with her. Destiny had given her another cross to bear, for suddenly this evening, as the Duke spoke of his wife, she had become conscious of the truth about herself: she was in love with her husband. And she herself had made it impossible that he could ever come back to her. For, indeed, the tables were turned, with one of those ironical twists of Fate.

And she questioned herself--Why did she love him? She had reproached him on her wedding night, when he had told her he loved her, because in her ignorance she felt then it could only be a question of sense. She had called him an animal! she remembered; and now she had become an animal herself! For she could prove no loftier motive for her emotion towards him than he had had for her then: they knew one another no better. It had not been possible for her passion to have arisen from the reasons she remembered having hurled at him as the only ones from which true love could spring, namely, knowledge, and tenderness, and devotion. It was all untrue; she understood it now. Love--deep and tender--could leap into being from the glance of an eye.

They were strangers to each other still, and yet this cruel, terrible thing called love had broken down all the barriers in her heart, melted the disdainful ice, and turned it to fire. She felt she wanted to caress him, and take away the stern, hard look from his face. She wanted to be gentle, and soft, and loving--to feel that she belonged to him. And she passionately longed for him to kiss her and clasp her to his heart. Whether he had consented originally to marry her for her uncle's money or not, was a matter, now, of no further importance. He had loved her after he had seen her, at all events, and she had thrown it all away. Nothing but a man's natural jealousy of his possessions remained.

"Oh, why did I not know what I was doing!" she moaned to herself, as she rocked in the chair. "I must have been very wicked in some former life, to be so tortured in this!"

But it was too late now. She had burnt her ships, and nothing remained to her but her pride. Since she had thrown away joy she could at least keep that and never let him see how she was being punished.

And to-night it was her turn to look in anguish at the closed door, and to toss in restless pain of soul, on her bed.

CHAPTER XXVII

A bombshell, in the shape of Lady Betty Burns, burst into the bedroom of Emily and Mary next morning, while the two girls were sitting up in their great bed at about eight o'clock, reading their letters and sipping their tea.

"May I come in, darlings?" a voice full of purpose said, and a flaxen head peeped in.

"Why, Betty, of course!" both girls answered and, in a blue silk dressing-gown and a long fair plait of hair hanging down, Lady Betty stalked in.

None of the Council of Three, going to deliver secret sentence, could have advanced with more dignity or consciousness of the solemnity of the occasion. Emily and Mary were thrilled.

"Be prepared!" she said dramatically, while she climbed to the foot of the bed and sat down. "It is just what I told you. She's been the heroine of a murder--if she did not do it herself!"

"Heavens! Betty, who?" almost screamed the girls.

"Your sister-in-law! I had to come at once to tell you, darlings. Last night, Aunt Muriel (the young Lady Melton was her uncle's second wife and chaperoning her to the party) would drag me into her room, and I could not get to you. You would have been asleep when I at last escaped, so I determined to come the first thing this morning and tell you my news."

Four round eyes of excited horror fixed themselves upon her, so with deep importance of voice and manner, Lady Betty went on:

"I sat with Captain Hume in the picture gallery, just before we went to bed. Believe me, I have not been able to sleep all night from it, dears! Well, we had been speaking of that fighting scene by Teniers in a beer house, you know, the one which hangs by the big Snuyders. The moon--no, it could not have been the moon. It must have been the arc light over the entrance which shines in from the angle. Anyway, it felt as if it were the moon, when I drew aside the blind; and it struck my heart with a cold foreboding, as he said such things, fights, happened now sometimes, and he was at Monte Carlo when Count Shulski was shot; and, though it was hushed up by the authorities and no one hardly heard of it much, still it made a stir. And," continued Lady Betty, now rising majestically and pointing an accusing forefinger at Emily and Mary, "Countess Shulski was your sister-in-law's name!"

"Oh, hush, Betty!" said Emily, almost angrily. "You must not say such things. There might have been a lot of Count Shulskis. Foreigners are all counts."

But Lady Betty shook her head with tragic sorrow and dignity, much at variance with her sweet little childish turned-up nose.

"Alas, darlings, far be it from me to bring the terrible conviction home to you!" Great occasions like this required a fine style, she felt. "Far be it from me! But Captain Hume went on to say, that, of course, was the reason of Lady Tancred's dreadfully mysterious and remorseful look."

"It is perfectly impossible, Betty," Mary cried excitedly. "But even if her husband were shot, it does not prove she had anything to do with it."

"Of course it does!" said Lady Betty, forgetting for a moment her style. "There's always a scene of jealousy, in which the husband stabs the other man, and then falls dead himself. Unless," and this new bright thought came to her, "she were a political spy!"

"Oh, Betty!" they both exclaimed at once. And then Emily said gravely,

"Please do tell us exactly what Captain Hume really said. Remember, it is our brother's wife you are speaking of, not one of the heroines in your plays!"

Thus admonished, Lady Betty got back on to the bed, and gradually came down to facts, which were meager enough. For Captain Hume had instantly pulled himself up, it appeared; and he had merely said that, as her first husband had been killed in a row, Lady Tancred had cause to have tragedy imprinted upon her face.

"Betty, dearest," Emily then said, "please, please don't tell anything of your exciting story to any one else, will you? Because people are so unkind."

At this, Lady Betty bounced off again offendedly.

"You are an ungrateful pair," she flashed. "Before I brave meeting Jimmy Danvers in the passage again, in my dressing-gown, to come and tell you delicious things, I'll be hanged!"

And it was with difficulty that Emily and Mary mollified her, and got her to re-seat herself on the bed and have a bit of their bread-and-butter. She had fled to announce her thrilling news before her own tea had come.

"I do think men look perfectly horrid with their hair unbrushed in the morning, don't you, Em?" she said, presently, as she munched, while Mary poured her out some tea into the emptied sugar-basin and handed it to her. "Henry's fortunate, because his is curly"--Here Mary blushed--"and I believe Jimmy Danvers gets his valet to glue his down before he goes to bed. But you should see what Aunt Muriel has to put up with, when Uncle Aubrey comes in to talk to her, while I am there. The front, anyhow, and a lock sticking up in the back! There is one thing I am determined about. Before I'm married, I shall insist upon knowing how my husband stands the morning light."

"I thought you said just now Jimmy's was quite decent and glued down," Emily retorted slyly.

"Pouff!" said Lady Betty, with superb calm. "I have not made up my mind at all about Jimmy. He is dying to ask me, I know; but there is Bobby Harland, too. However, this morning--"

"You've seen Jimmy this morning, Betty!" Mary exclaimed.

"Well, how could I help it, girls?" Lady Betty went on, feeling that she was now a heroine. "I had to come to you. It was my bounden duty; and it's miles away, for Aunt Muriel always will have me in the dressing-room next her, when she takes me to stay out, and Uncle Aubrey across the passage; and it makes him so cross. But that's not it. I mean, it is not my fault, if the Duke has only arranged three new bathrooms down the bachelors' wing, and people are obliged to be waiting about for their turn, and I had to pass the entrance to that passage, and it happened to be Jimmy's, and he was just going in, when he saw me and rushed along, and said 'Good morning,' not a bit put out! I thought it would look silly to run, so I said 'Good morning,' too; and then we both giggled, and I came on. But I am rather glad after all, because now I've seen him; and he looks better--like that--than I am sure Bobby would have done, so perhaps, after all, I'll marry him! And you will be my bridesmaids, darlings, and now I must run!"

Upon such slender threads--the brushing of his hair--how often does the fate of man hang! If he but knew!

Almost every one was punctual for breakfast. They all came in with their gifts for Lady Ethelrida; and there was much chaffing and joking, and delightful little shrieks of surprise, as the parcels were opened.

Every soul loved Lady Ethelrida, from the lordly Groom of the Chambers to the humblest pantry boy and scullery maid; and it was their delight every year to present her, from them all, with a huge trophy of flowers, while the post brought countless messages and gifts of remembrance from absent friends. No one could have been more sweet and gracious than her ladyship was; and underneath, her gentle heart was beating with an extra excitement, when she thought of her rendezvous at half-past ten o'clock. Would he--she no longer thought of him as Mr. Markrute--would he be able to find the way?

"I must go and give some orders now," she said, about a quarter past ten, to the group which surrounded her, when they had all got up and were standing beside the fire. "And we all assemble in the hall at eleven." And so she slipped away.

Francis Markrute, she noticed, had retired some moments before.

"Heinrich," he had said to his Austrian valet, the previous evening, as he was helping him on with his coat for dinner, "I may want to know the locality of the Lady Ethelrida's sitting-room early to-morrow. Make it your business to become friendly with her ladyship's maid, so that I can have a parcel of books, which will arrive in the morning, placed safely there at any moment I want to, unobserved. Unpack the books, leaving their tissue papers still upon them, and bring them in when you call me. I will give you further orders then for their disposal. You understand?"

It was as well to be prepared for anything, he thought, which was most fortunate, as it afterwards turned out. He had meant to make her ask him to her sitting-room in any case, and his happiness was augmented, as they had talked in the picture gallery, when she did it of her own accord.

Lady Ethelrida stood looking out of her window, in her fresh, white-paneled, lilac-chintzed bower. Her heart was actually thumping now. She had not noticed the books, which were carefully placed in a pile down beside her writing table. Would he ever get away from her father, who seemed to have taken to having endless political discussions with him? Would he ever be able to come in time to talk for a moment, before they must both go down? She had taken the precaution to make herself quite ready to start--short skirt, soft felt hat, thick boots and all.

Would he? But as half-past ten chimed from the Dresden clock on the mantel-piece, there was a gentle tap at the door, and Francis Markrute came in.

He knew in an instant, experienced fowler that he was, that his bird was flut-tered with expectancy, and it gave him an exquisite thrill. He was perfectly cog-nizant of the value of investing simple circumstances with delightful mystery, at times; and he knew, to the Lady Ethelrida, this trysting with him had become a momentous thing.

"You see, I found the way," he said softly, and he allowed something of the joy and tenderness he felt to come into his voice.

And Lady Ethelrida answered a little nervously that she was glad, and then continued quickly that she must show him her bookcases, because there was so little time.

"Only one short half-hour--if you will let me stay so long," he pleaded.

In his hand he carried the original volume he had spoken about, a very old edition of Shakespeare's Sonnets, from which he had carefully had one or two re-moved. It was exquisitely bound and tooled, and had her monogram worked into a beautiful little medallion--a work of art. He handed it to her first.

"This I ventured to have ordered for you long ago," he said. "Six weeks it is nearly, and I so feared until yesterday that you would not let me give it to you. It does not mean for your birthday: it is our original bond of acquaintance."

"It is too beautiful," said Lady Ethelrida, looking down.

"And over there by your writing table"--he had carefully ascertained this local-ity from Heinrich--"you will find the books that are my birthday gift, if you will give me the delight of accepting them."

She went forward with a little cry of surprise and pleasure, while, instanta-neously, the wonder of how he should know where they would be presented itself to her mind.

They were about six volumes. A Heine, a couple of de Musset's, and then three volumes of selected poems, from numbers of the English poets. Lady Ethelrida picked them up delightedly. They, too, were works of art, in their soft mauve morocco bindings, *chiffre*, with her monogram like the other, and tooled with gold.

"How enchanting!" she said. "And look! They match my room. How could you have guessed--?" And then she broke off and again looked down.

"You told me, the night I dined with you at Glastonbury House, that you loved mauve as a color and that violets were your favorite flower. How could I forget?" And he permitted himself to come a step nearer to her.

She did not move away. She turned over the leaves of the English volume rather hurriedly. The paper was superlatively fine and the print a gem of art. And then she looked up, surprised.

"I have never seen this collection before," she said wonderingly. "All the things one loves under the same cover!" And then she turned to the title-page to see which edition it was; and she found that, as far as information went, it was blank. Simply,

"To The Lady Ethelrida Montfitchet
from
"F.M."

was inscribed upon it in gold. A deep pink flush grew on her delicate face, and she dared not raise her eyes.

It would be too soon yet to tell her everything that was in his heart, he reasoned. All could be lost by one false step. So, with his masterly self-control, he resisted all temptation to fold her in his arms, and said gently:

"I thought it would be nice to have, as you say, 'all the bits one loves' put together; and I have a very intelligent friend at my book-binder's, who, when I had selected them, had them all arranged and printed for me, and bound as I thought you might wish. It will gratify me greatly, if it has pleased you."

"Pleased me!" she said, and now she looked up; for the sudden conviction came to her, that to have this done took time and a great deal of money; and except once or twice before, casually, she had never met him until the evening, when, among a number of her father's political friends, he had dined at their London house. When could he have given the order and what could this mean? He read her thoughts.

"Yes," he said simply. "From the very first moment I ever saw you, Lady Ethelrida, to me you seemed all that was true and beautiful, the embodiment of my ideal of womanhood. I planned these books then, two days after I dined with you at Glastonbury House; and, if you had refused them, it would have caused me pain."

Ethelrida was so moved by some new, sudden and exquisite emotion that she could not reply for a moment. He watched her with growing and passionate delight, but he said nothing. He must give her time.

"It is too, too nice of you," she said softly, and there was a little catch in her breath. "No one has ever thought of anything so exquisite for me before, although, as you saw this morning, every one is so very kind. How shall I thank you, Mr. Markrute? I do not know."

"You must not thank me at all, you gracious lady," he said. "And now I must tell you that the half-hour is nearly up, and we must go down. But--may I--will you let me come again, perhaps to-morrow afternoon? I want to tell you, if it would interest you, the history of a man."

Ethelrida had turned to look at the clock, also, and had collected herself. She was too single-minded to fence now, or to push this new, strange joy out of her life, so she said,

"When the others go out for a walk, then, after lunch, yes, you may come."

And without anything further, they left the room. At the turn in the corridor to the other part of the house, he bent suddenly; and with deep homage kissed her hand, then let her pass on, while he turned to the right and disappeared towards the wing, where was his room.

CHAPTER XXVIII

Zara had, at first, thought she would not go out with the shooters. She felt numb, as if she could not pluck up enough courage to make conversation with any one. She had received a letter from Mimo, by the second post, with all details of what he had heard of Mirko. Little Agatha, the Morleys' child, was to return home the following day; and Mirko himself had written an excited little letter to announce this event, which Mimo enclosed. He seemed perfectly well then, only at the end, as she would see, he had said he was dreaming of *Maman* every night; and Mimo knew that this must mean he was a little feverish again, so he had felt it wiser to telegraph. Mirko had written out the score of the air which *Maman* always came and taught him, and he was longing to play it to his dear Papa and his Cherisette, the letter ended with.

And the pathos of it all caused Zara a sharp pain. She did not dare to look ahead, as far as her little brother was concerned. Indeed, to look ahead, in any case, meant nothing very happy.

She was just going up the great staircase at about a quarter to eleven, with the letter in her hand, when she met Tristram coming from his room, with his shooting boots on, ready to start. He stopped and said coldly--they had not spoken a word yet that day--

"You had better be quick putting your things on. My uncle always starts punctually."

Then his eye caught the foreign writing on the letter, and he turned brusquely away, although, as he reasoned with himself a moment afterwards, it was ridiculous of him to be so moved, because she would naturally have a number of foreign correspondents. She saw him turn away, and it angered her in spite of her new mood. He need not show his dislike so plainly, she thought. So she answered haughtily,

"I had not intended to come. I am tired; and I do not know this sport, or whether it will please me. I should feel for the poor birds, I expect."

"I am sorry you are tired," he answered, contrite in an instant. "Of course, you must not come if you are. They will be awfully disappointed. But never mind. I will tell Ethelrida."

"It is nothing--my fatigue, I mean. If you think your cousin will mind, I will come." And she turned, without waiting for him to answer, and went on to her room.

And Tristram, after going back to his for something he had forgotten, presently went on down the stairs, a bitter smile on his face, and at the bottom met--Laura Highford.

She looked up into his eyes, and allowed tears to gather in hers. She had always plenty at her command.

"Tristram," she said with extreme gentleness, "you were cross with me yesterday afternoon, because you thought I was saying something about your wife. But don't you know, can't you understand, what it is to me to see you devoted to another woman? You may be changed, but I am always the same, and I--I--" And here she buried her face in her hands and went into a flood of tears.

Tristram was overcome with confusion and horror. He loathed scenes. Good heavens! If any one should come along!

"Laura, for goodness' sake! My dear girl, don't cry!" he exclaimed. He felt he would say anything to comfort her, and get over the chance of some one seeing this hateful exhibition.

But she continued to sob. She had caught sight of Zara's figure on the landing above, and her vengeful spirit desired to cause trouble, even at a cost to herself. Zara had been perfectly ready, all but her hat, and had hurried exceedingly to be in time, and thus had not been five minutes after her husband.

"Tristram!" wailed Laura, and, putting up her hands, placed them on his shoulders. "Darling, just kiss me once--quickly--to say good-bye."

And it was at this stage that Zara came full upon them, from a turn in the stairs. She heard Tristram say disgustedly, "No, I won't," and saw Lady Highford drop her arms; and in the three steps that separated them, her wonderful iron self-control, the inheritance of all her years of suffering, enabled her to stop as if she had seen nothing, and in an ordinary voice ask if they were to go to the great hall.

"The woman," as she called Laura, should not have the satisfaction of seeing a trace of emotion in her, or Tristram either. He had answered immediately, "Yes," and had walked on by her side, in an absolutely raging temper.

How dare Laura drag him into a disgraceful and ridiculous scene like this! He could have wrung her neck. What must Zara think? That he was simply a cad! He could not offer a single explanation, either; indeed, she had demanded none. He did blurt out, after a moment,

"Lady Highford was very much upset about something. She is hysterical."

"Poor thing!" said Zara indifferently, and walked on.

But when they got into the hall, where most of the company were, she suddenly felt her knees giving way under her, and hurriedly sank down on an oak chair.

She felt sick with jealous pain, even though she had plainly seen that Tristram was no willing victim. But upon what terms could they be, or have been, for Lady Highford so to lose all sense of shame?

Tristram was watching her anxiously. She must have seen the humiliating exhibition. It followed, then, she was perfectly indifferent, or she would have been annoyed. He wished that she had reproached him, or said something--anything--but to remain completely unmoved was too maddening.

Then the whole company, who were coming out, appeared, and they started. Some of the men were drawing lots to see if they should shoot in the morning or in the afternoon. The party was primarily for Lady Ethelrida's birthday, and the shoot merely an accessory.

Zara walked by the Crow, who was not shooting at all. She was wearied with Lord Elterton; wearied with every one. The Crow was sententious and amused her, and did not expect her to talk.

"You have never seen your husband shoot yet, I expect, Lady Tancred, have you?" he asked her; and when she said, "No," he went on, "Because you must watch him. He is a very fine shot."

She did not know anything about shooting, only that Tristram looked particularly attractive in his shooting clothes, and that English sportsmen were natural, unceremonious creatures, whom she was beginning to like very much. She wished she could open her heart to this quaint, kind old man, and ask him to explain things to her; but she could not, and presently they got to a safe place and watched.

Tristram happened to be fairly near them; and, yes, he was a good shot--she could see that. But, at first, the thud of the beautiful pheasants falling to the ground caused her to wince--she, who had looked upon the shattered face of Ladislaus, her husband, with only a quiver of disgust! But these creatures were in the glory of their beauty and the joy of life, and had preyed upon the souls of no one.

Her wonderful face, which interested Colonel Lowerby so, was again abstract-ed. Something had brought back that hateful moment to her memory; she could hear Feto, the dancer's shrieks, and see the blood; and she shivered suddenly and clasped her hands.

"Do you mind seeing the birds come down?" the Crow asked kindly.

"I do not know," she said. "I was thinking of some other shooting."

"Because," the Crow went on, "the women who rage against sport forget one thing,--the birds would not exist at all, if it were not for preserving them for this very reason. They would gradually be trapped and snared and exterminated; where-as, now they have a royal time, of food and courtship and mating, and they have no knowledge of their coming fate, and so live a life of splendor up to the last mo-ment."

"How much better! Yes, indeed, I will never be foolish about them again. I will think of that." Then she exclaimed, "Oh, that was wonderful!" for Tristram got two rocketters at right and left, and then another with his second gun. His temper had not affected his eye, it seemed.

"Tristram is one of the best all-round sportsmen I know," the Crow announced, "and he has one of the kindest hearts. I have known him since he was a toddler. His mother was one of the beauties, when I first put on a cuirass."

Zara tried to control her interest, and merely said, "Yes?"

"Are you looking forward to the reception at Wrayth on Monday? I always wonder how a person unaccustomed to England would view all the speeches and dinners, the bonfire, and triumphal arches, and those things of a home-coming. Rather an ordeal, I expect."

Zara's eyes rounded, and she faltered,

"And shall I have to go through all that?"

The Crow was nonplussed. Had not her husband, then, told her, what every one else knew? Upon what terms could they possibly be? And before he was aware of it, he had blurted out, "Good Lord!"

Then, recollecting himself, he said,

"Why, yes. Tristram will say I have been frightening you. It is not so very bad, after all--only to smile and look gracious and shake hands. They will be all ready to think you perfect, if you do that. Even though there are a lot of beastly radicals about, Old England still bows down to a beautiful woman!"

Zara did not answer. She had heard about her beauty in most European languages, since she was sixteen. It was the last thing which mattered, she thought.

Then the Crow turned the conversation, as they walked on to the next stand.

Did she know that Lady Ethelrida had commanded that all the ladies were to get up impromptu fancy dresses for to-night, her birthday dinner, and all the men would be in hunt coats? he asked. Large parties were coming from the only two other big houses near, and they would dance afterward in the picture gallery. "A wonderful new band that came out in London this season is coming down," he ended with; and, then, as she replied she had heard, he asked her what she intended to be. "It must be something with your hair down--you must give us the treat of that."

"I have left it all to Lady Ethelrida and my sisters-in-law," she said. "We are going to contrive things the whole afternoon, after lunch."

Tristram came up behind them then, and the Crow stopped.

"I was telling your wife she must give us the pleasure of seeing her hair down, to-night, for the Tomfools' dinner, but I can't get a promise from her. We will have to appeal to you to exert your lordly authority. Can't be deprived of a treat like that!"

"I am afraid I have no influence or authority," Tristram answered shortly, for with a sudden pang he thought of the only time he had seen the glorious beauty of it, her hair, spread like a cloak around her, as she had turned and ordered him out of her room at Dover. She remembered the circumstance, too, and it hurt her equally, so that they walked along silently, staring in front of them, and each suffering pain; when, if they had had a grain of sense, they would have looked into each other's eyes, read the truth, and soon been in each other's arms. But they had not yet "dree'd their weird." And Fate, who mocks at fools, would not yet let them be.

So the clouds gathered overhead, as in their hearts, and it came on to pour with rain; and the ladies made a hurried rush to the house.

The hostess did not stand near Francis Markrute during the shooting. Some shy pleasure made her avoid him for the moment. She wanted to hug the remembrance of her great joy of the morning, and the knowledge that to-morrow, Sunday, after lunch, would bring her a like pleasure. And for the time being there was the delight of thinking over what he had said, the subtlety of his gift, and the manner of its giving. Nothing so goes to the head of a woman of refined sensibilities as the intoxicating flattery of thought-out action in a man, when it is to lay homage at her feet, and the man is a grave and serious person, who is no worshiper of women.

Ethelrida trod on air, and looked unusually sweet and gracious.

And Francis Markrute watched her quietly, with great tenderness in his heart, and not the faintest misgiving. "Slow and sure" was his motto, and thus he drew always the current of success and contentment.

His only crumpled roseleaf was the face of his niece, which rather haunted him. There seemed no improvement in the relations of the pair, in spite of Zara having had ample cause to feel jealous about Lady Highford since their arrival. Elinka, too, had had strange and unreasonable turns in her nature, that is what had made her so attractive. What if Zara and this really fine young Englishman, with whom he had mated her, should never get on? Then he laughed, when he thought of the impossibility of his calculations finally miscarrying. It was, of course, only a question of time. However, he would tell her before she left for her "home-coming" at Wrayth on Monday, what he thought it was now safe and advisable that she should know, namely, that on her husband's side the marriage had been one of headlong desire for herself, after having refused the bargain before he had seen her. That would give her some bad moments of humiliation, he admitted, which perhaps she had not deserved, though it would certainly bring her to her knees and so, to Tristram's arms.

But for once, being really quite preoccupied with his own affairs and a little unbalanced by love as well, he miscalculated the force of a woman's pride. Zara's one idea now was to hide from Tristram the state of her feelings, believing, poor, bruised, wounded thing, that he no longer cared for her, believing that she herself had extinguished the torch of love.

CHAPTER XXIX

There was an air of restrained excitement, importance and mystery among the ladies at luncheon. They had got back to the house in time to have their conclave before that meal, and everything was satisfactorily settled. Lady Anningford, who had not accompanied them out shooting, had thought out a whole scheme, and announced it upon their return amidst acclamations.

They would represent as many characters as they could from the "Idylls of the King," because the style would be such loose, hanging kinds of garments, the maids could run up the long straight seams in no time. And it would be so much more delightful, all to carry out one idea, than the usual powdered heads and non-descript things people chose for such impromptu occasions. It only remained to finally decide the characters. She considered that Ethelrida should undoubtedly be *Guinevere*; but, above all, Zara must be *Isolt*!

"Of course, of course!" they all cried unanimously, while Zara's eyes went black. "Tristram and *Isolt*! How splendid!"

"And I shall be *Brangaine*, and give the love potion," Lady Anningford went on. "Although it does not come into the 'Idylls of the King,' it should do so. It is just because Tennyson was so fearfully, respectably Early Victorian! I have been looking all the real thing up in the 'Morte d' Arthur' in the library, and in the beautiful edition of 'Tristram and Yseult' in Ethelrida's room."

"How perfectly enchanting!" cried Lady Betty. "I must be the *Lady of the Lake*--it is much the most dramatic part. And let us get the big sword out of the armory for *Excalibur*! I can have it, and brandish it as I enter the room."

"Oh, nonsense, Betty darling!" Ethelrida said. "You are the very picture of *Lynette*, with your enchanting nose 'tiptilted like the tender petal of a flower,' and your shameful treatment of poor Jimmy!"

And Lady Betty, after bridling a little, consented.

Then the other parts were cast. Emily should be *Enid* and Mary, *Elaine*, while Lady Melton, Lady Thornby and Mrs. Harcourt should be the *Three Fair Queens*.

"I shall be *Ettarre*," said Lily Opie. "The others are all good and dull; and I prefer her, because I am sure she wasn't! And certainly Lady Highford must be *Vivien*! She is exactly the type, in one of her tea gowns!"

Laura rather liked the idea of *Vivien*. It had *cachet*, she thought. She was very fond of posing as a mysterious enchantress, the mystic touch pleased her vanity.

So, of the whole party, only Zara did not feel content. Tristram might think she had chosen this herself, as an advance towards him.

Then the discussion, as to the garments to be worn, began. Numbers of ornaments and bits of tea-gowns would do. But with her usual practical forethought, Lady Anningford had already taken time by the forelock, and asked that one of the motors, going in to Tilling Green on a message, should bring back all the bales of bright and light-colored merinos and nunscloths the one large general shop boasted of.

And, amidst screams of delighted excitement from the girls, the immense parcel was presently unpacked.

It contained marvels of white and creams, and one which was declared the exact thing for *Isolt*. It was a merino of that brilliant violent shade of azure, the tone which is advertised as "Rickett's Paris blue" for washing clothes. It had been in the shop for years, and was unearthed for this occasion--a perfect relic of later Victorian aniline dye.

"It will be simply too gorgeously wonderful, with just a fillet of gold round her head, and all her adorable red hair hanging down," Lady Anningford said to Ethelrida.

"We shan't have to wear a stitch underneath," Lady Betty announced decidedly, while she pirouetted before a cheval glass--they were all in Lady Anningford's room--with some stuff draped round her childish form. "The gowns must have the right look, just long, straight things, with hanging sleeves and perhaps a girdle. I shall have cream, and you, Mary, as *Elaine*, must have white; but Emily had better have that mauve for *Enid*, as she was married."

"Why must *Enid* have mauve because she is married?" asked Emily, who did not like the color.

"I don't know why," Lady Betty answered, "except that, if you are married, you can't possibly have white, like Mary and me, who aren't. People are quite different--after, and mauve is very respectable for them," she went on. Grammar never troubled her little ladyship, when giving her valuable opinion upon things and life.

"I think *Enid* was a goose," said Emily, pouting.

"Not half as much as *Elaine*," said Mary. "She had secured her *Geraint*, whereas *Elaine* made a perfect donkey of herself over *Lancelot*, who did not care for her."

"I like our parts much the best, Lily's and mine," said Lady Betty. "I do give my Jim--Gareth?--a lively time, at all events! Just what I should do, if it were in real life."

"What you do do, you mean, not what you would do, Minx!" said her aunt, laughing.

And at this stage the shooters were seen advancing across the park, and the band of ladies, full of importance, descended to luncheon.

Lady Anningford sat next the Crow and told him what they had decided, in strict confidence, of course.

"We shall have the most delightful fun, Crow. I have thought it all out. At dessert I am going to hand one of the gold cups in which we are going to put a glass of some of the Duke's original old Chartreuse, to the bridal pair, as if to drink their health; and then, when they have drunk it, I am going to be overcome at the mistake of having given them a love-potion, just as in the real story! You can't tell--it may bring them together."

"Queen Anne, you wonder!" said the Crow.

"It is such a deliciously incongruous idea, you see," Lady Anningford went on. "All of us in long pre-mediaeval garments, with floating hair, and all of you in modern hunt coats! I should like to have seen Tristram in gold chain armor."

The Crow grunted approval.

"Ethelrida is going to arrange that they go in to dinner together. She is going to say it will be their last chance before they get to *King Mark*. Won't it all be perfect?"

"Well, I suppose you know best," the Crow said, with his wise old head on one side. "But they are at a ticklish pass in their careers, I tell you. The balance might go either way. Don't make it too hard for them, out of mistaken kindness."

"You are tiresome, Crow!" retorted Lady Anningford. "I never can do a thing I think right without your warning me over it. Do leave it to me."

So, thus admonished, Colonel Lowerby went on with his luncheon.

Zara's eyes looked more stormy than ever, when her husband chanced to see them. He was sitting nearly opposite her, and he wondered what on earth she was thinking about. He was filled with a concentrated bitterness from the events of the morning. Her utter indifference over the Laura incident had galled him unbearably, although he told himself, as he had done before, the unconscionable fool he was to allow himself to go on being freshly wounded by each continued proof of her disdain of him. Why, when he knew a thing, should he not be prepared for it? He had a strong will; he *would* overcome his emotion for her. He could, at least, make himself treat her, outwardly with the same apparent insolent indifference, as she treated him.

He made a firm resolve once again, he would not speak to her at all, any more than he had done the last three days in Paris. He would accept the position until the Wrayth rejoicings were over, and then he would certainly make arrangements to go and shoot lions, or travel, or something. There should be no further "perhaps" about it. Life, with the agonizing longing for her, seeing her daily and being denied, was more than could be borne.

There was something about Zara's type, the white, exquisite beauty of her skin, her slenderly voluptuous shape, the stormy suggestion of hidden passion in her slumberous eyes, which had always aroused absolutely mad emotions in men. Tristram, who was a normal Englishman, self-contained and reserved, and too completely healthy to be highly-strung, felt undreamed-of sensations rise in him when he looked at her, which was as rarely as possible. He understood now what was meant by an obsession--all the states of love he had read of in French novels and dismissed as "tommyrot." She did not only affect him with a thrilling physical passion. It was an obsession of the mind as well. He suffered acutely; as each day passed it seemed as if he could not bear any more, and the next always brought some further pain.

They had actually only been married for ten days! and it seemed an eternity of anguish to both of them, for different reasons.

Zara's nature was trying to break through the iron bands of her life training. Once she had admitted to herself that she loved her husband, her suffering was as deep as his, only that she was more practiced in the art of suppressing all emotion. But it was no wonder that they both looked pale and stern, and quite unbridal.

The sportsmen started immediately after lunch again, and the ladies returned to their delightful work; and, when they all assembled for tea, everything was almost completed. Zara had been unable to resist the current of light-hearted gayety which was in the air, and now felt considerably better; so she allowed Lord Elterton to sit beside her after tea and pour homage at her feet, with the expression of an empress listening to an address of loyalty from some distant colony; and the Crow leant back in his chair and chuckled to himself, much to Lady Anningford's annoyance.

"What in the world is it, Crow?" she said. "When you laugh like that, I always know some diabolically cynical idea is floating in your head, and it is not good for you. Tell me at once what you mean!"

But Colonel Lowerby refused to be drawn, and presently took Tristram off into the billiard-room.

It was arranged that all the men, even the husbands, were to go down into the great white drawing-room first, so that the ladies might have the pleasure of making an entrance *en bande*, to the delight of every one. And when this group of Englishmen, so smart in their scarlet hunt coats, were assembled at the end, by the fireplace, footmen opened the big double doors, and the groom of the chambers announced,

"Her Majesty, *Queen Guinevere*, and the Ladies of her Court."

And Ethelrida advanced, her fair hair in two long plaits, with her mother's all-round diamond crown upon her head, and clothed in some white brocade garment, arranged with a blue merino cloak, trimmed with ermine and silver. She looked perfectly regal, and as nearly beautiful as she had ever done; and to the admiring eyes of Francis Markrute, she seemed to outshine all the rest.

Then, their names called as they entered, came Enid and Elaine, each fair and sweet; and Vivien and Ettarre; then Lynette walking alone, with her saucy nose in the air and her flaxen curls spread out over her cream robe, a most bewitching sight.

Several paces behind her came the ***Three Fair Queens***, all in wonderfully contrived garments, and misty, floating veils; and lastly, quite ten paces in the rear, walked ***Isolt***, followed by her ***Brangaine***. And when the group by the fireplace caught sight of her, they one and all drew in their breath.

For Zara had surpassed all expectations. The intense and blatant blue of her long clinging robe, which would have killed the charms of nine women out of ten, seemed to enhance the beauty of her pure white skin and marvelous hair. It fell like a red shining cloak all round her, kept in only by a thin fillet of gold, while her dark eyes gleamed with a new excitement. She had relaxed her dominion of herself, and was allowing the natural triumphant woman in her to have its day. For once in her life she forgot everything of sorrow and care, and permitted herself to rejoice in her own beauty and its effect upon the world before her.

"Jee-hoshaphat!" was the first articulate word that the company heard, from the hush which had fallen upon them; and then there was a chorus of general admiration, in which all the ladies had their share. And only the Crow happened to glance at Tristram, and saw that his face was white as death.

Then the two parties, about twenty people in all, began to arrive from the other houses, and delighted exclamations of surprise at the splendor of the impromptu fancy garments were heard all over the room, and soon dinner was announced, and they went in.

"My Lord Tristram," Ethelrida had said to her cousin, "I beg of you to conduct to my festal board your own most beautiful ***Lady Isolt***. Remember, on Monday you leave us for the realm of ***King Mark***, so make the most of your time!" And she turned and led forward Zara, and placed her hand in his; she, and they all, were too preoccupied with excitement and joy to see the look of deep pain in his eyes.

He held his wife's hand, until the procession started, and neither of them spoke a word. Zara, still exalted with the spirit of the night, felt only a wild excitement. She was glad he could see her beauty and her hair, and she raised her head and shook it back, as they started, with a provoking air.

But Tristram never spoke; and by the time they had reached the banqueting-hall, some of her exaltation died down, and she felt a chill.

Her hair was so very long and thick that she had to push it aside, to sit down, and in doing so a mesh flew out and touched his face; and the Crow, who was watching the whole drama intently, noticed that he shivered and, if possible, grew more pale. So he turned to his own servant, behind his chair, who with some of the other valets, was helping to wait, and whispered to him, "Go and see that Lord Tancred is handed brandy, at once, before the soup."

And so the feast began.

On Zara's other hand sat the Duke, and on Tristram's, Brangaine--for so she and Ethelrida had arranged for their later plan; and after the brandy, which Tristram dimly wondered why he should have been handed, he pulled himself together, and tried to talk; and Zara busied herself with the Duke. She quite came out of her usual silence, and laughed, and looked so divinely attractive that the splendid old gentleman felt it all going to his head; and his thoughts wondered bluntly, how soon, if he were his nephew, he would take her away after dinner and make love to her all to himself! But these modern young fellows had not half the mettle that he had had!

So at last dessert-time came, with its toasts for the **Queen Guinevere**. And the bridal pair had spoken together never a word; and Lady Anningford, who was watching them, began to fear for the success of her plan. However, there was no use turning back now. So, amidst jests of all sorts in keeping with the spirit of Camelot and the Table Round, at last **Brangaine** rose and, taking the gold cup in front of her, said,

"I, **Brangaine**, commissioned by her Lady Mother, to conduct the **Lady Isolt** safely to **King Mark**, under the knightly protection of the **Lord Tristram**, do now propose to drink their health, and ye must all do likewise, Lords and Ladies of Arthur's court." And she sipped her own glass, while she handed the gold cup to the Duke, who passed it on to the pair; and Tristram, because all eyes were upon him, forced himself to continue the jest. So he rose and, taking Zara's hand, while he bowed to the company, gave her the cup to drink, and then took it himself, while he drained the measure. And every one cried, amidst great excitement, "The health and happiness of **Tristram** and **Isolt**!"

Then, when the tumult had subsided a little, **Brangaine** gave a pretended shriek.

"Mercy me! I am undone!" she cried. "They have quaffed of the wrong cup! That gold goblet contained a love-potion distilled from rare plants by the Queen, and destined for the wedding wine of **Isolt** and **King Mark**! And now the **Lord**

Tristram and she have drunk it together, by misadventure, and can never be parted more! Oh, misery me! What have I done!"

And amidst shouts of delighted laughter led by the Crow--in frozen silence, Tristram held his wife's hand.

But after a second, the breeding in them both, as on their wedding evening before the waiters, again enabled them to continue the comedy; and they, too, laughed, and, with the Duke's assistance, got through the rest of dinner, until they all rose and went out, two and two, the men leading their ladies by the hand, as they had come in.

And if the cup had indeed contained a potion distilled by the Irish sorceress Queen, the two victims could not have felt more passionately in love.

But Tristram's pride won the day for him, for this one time, and not by a glance or a turn of his head did he let his bride see how wildly her superlative attraction had kindled the fire in his blood. And when the dancing began, he danced with every other lady first, and then went off into the smoking-room, and only just returned in time to be made to lead out his "Isolt" in a final quadrille--not a valse. No powers would have made him endure the temptation of a valse!

And even this much, the taking of her hand, her nearness, the sight of the exquisite curves of her slender figure, and her floating hair, caused him an anguish unspeakable, so that when the rest of the company had gone, and good nights were said, he went up to his room, changed his coat, and strode away alone, out into the night.

CHAPTER XXX

Every one was so sleepy and tired on Sunday morning, after their night at Arthur's Court, that only Lady Ethelrida and Laura Highford, who had a pose of extreme piety always ready at hand, started with the Duke and Young Billy for church. Francis Markrute watched them go from his window, which looked upon the entrance, and he thought how stately and noble his fair lady looked; and he admired her disciplined attitude, no carousal being allowed to interfere with her duties. She was a rare and perfect specimen of her class.

His lady fair! For he had determined, if fate plainly gave him the indication, to risk asking her to-day to be his fair lady indeed. A man must know when to strike, if the iron is hot.

He had carefully prepared all the avenues; and had made himself of great importance to the Duke, allowing his masterly brain to be seen in glimpses, and convincing His Grace of his possible great usefulness to the party to which he belonged. He did not look for continued opposition in that quarter, once he should have assured himself that Lady Ethelrida loved him. That he loved her, with all the force of his self-contained nature, was beyond any doubt. Love, as a rule, recks little of the suitability of the object, when it attacks a heart; but in some few cases--that is the peculiar charm--Francis Markrute had waited until he was forty-six years old, firmly keeping to his ideal, until he found her, in a measure of perfection, of which even he had not dared to dream. His theory, which he had proved in his whole life, was that nothing is beyond the grasp of a man who is master of himself and his emotions. But even his iron nerves felt the tension of excitement, as luncheon drew to an end, and he knew in half an hour, when most of the company were safely disposed of, he should again find his way to his lady's shrine.

Ethelrida did not look at him. She was her usual, charmingly-gracious self to her neighbors, solicitous of Tristram's headache. He had only just appeared, and looked what he felt--a wreck. She was interested in some news in the Sunday papers, which had arrived; and in short, not a soul guessed how her gentle being was uplifted, and her tender heart beating with this, the first real emotion she had ever experienced.

Even the Crow, so thrilled with his interest in the bridal pair, had not scented anything unusual in his hostess's attitude towards one of her guests.

"I think Mr. Markrute is awfully attractive, don't you, Crow?" said Lady Anningford, as they started for their walk. To go to Lynton Heights after lunch on Sunday was almost an invariable custom at Montfitchet. "I can't say what it is, but it is something subtle and extraordinary, like that in his niece--what do you think?"

Colonel Lowerby paused, struck from her words by the fact that he had been too preoccupied to have noticed this really interesting man.

"Why, 'pon my soul--I haven't thought!" he said, "but now you speak of it, I do think he is a remarkable chap."

"He is so very quiet," Lady Anningford went on, "and, whenever he speaks, it is something worth listening to; and if you get on any subject of books, he is a perfect encyclopaedia. He gives me the impression of all the forces of power and will, concentrated in a man. I wonder who he really is? Not that it matters a bit in these days. Do you think there is any Jew in him? It does not show in his type, but when foreigners are very rich there generally is."

"Sure to be, as he is so intelligent," the Crow growled. "If you notice, numbers of the English families who show brains have a touch of it in the background. So long as the touch is far enough away, I have no objection to it myself--prefer folks not to be fools."

"I believe I have no prejudices at all," said Lady Anningford. "If I like people, I don't care what is in their blood."

"It is all right till you scratch 'em. Then it comes out; but if, as I say, it is far enough back, the Jew will do the future Tancred race a power of good, to get the commercial common sense of it into them--knew Maurice Grey, her father, years ago, and he was just as indifferent to money and material things, as Tristram is himself. So the good will come from the Markrute side, we will hope."

"I rather wonder, Crow--if there ever will be any more of the Tancred race.

I thought last night we had a great failure, and that nothing will make that affair prosper. I don't believe they ever see one another from one day to the next! It is extremely sad."

"I told you they had come to a ticklish point in their careers," the Crow permitted himself to remind his friend, "and, 'pon my soul, I could not bet you one way or another how it will go. 'I hae me doots,' as the Scotchman said."

Meanwhile, Ethelrida, on the plea of letters to write, had retired to her room; and there, as the clock struck a quarter past three, she awaited--what? She would not own to herself that it was her fate. She threw dust in her own eyes, and called it a pleasant talk!

She looked absurdly young for her twenty-six years, just a dainty slip of a patrician girl, as she sat there on her chintz sofa, with its fresh pattern of lilacs and tender green. Everything was in harmony, even to her soft violet cloth dress trimmed with fur.

And again as the hour for the trysting chimed, her lover that was to be, entered the room.

"This is perfectly divine," he said, as he came in, while the roguish twinkle of a schoolboy, who has outwitted his mates sparkled in his fine eyes. "All those good people tramping for miles in the cold and damp, while we two sensible ones are going to enjoy a nice fire and a friendly chat."

Thus he disarmed her nervousness, and gave her time.

"May I sit by you, my Lady Ethelrida?" he said; and as she smiled, he took his seat, but not too near her--nothing must be the least hurried or out of place.

So for about a quarter of an hour they talked of books--their favorites--hers, all so simple and chaste, his, of all kinds, so long as they showed style, and were masterpieces of taste and balance. Then, as a great piece of wood fell in the open grate and made a volley of sparks, he leaned forward a little and asked her if he might tell her that for which he had come, the history of a man.

The daylight was drawing in, and they had an hour before them.

"Yes," said Ethelrida, "only let us make up the fire first, and only turn on that one soft light," and she pointed to a big gray china owl who carried a simple shade of white painted with lilacs on his back. "Then we need not move again, because I want extremely to hear it--the history of a man."

He obeyed her commands, and also drew the silk blinds.

"Now, indeed, we are happy; at least, I am," he said.

Lady Ethelrida leant back on her muslin embroidered cushion and prepared herself to listen with a rapt face.

Francis Markrute stood by the fire for a while, and began from there:

"You must go right back with me to early days, Sweet Lady," he said, "to a palace in a gloomy city and to an artiste--a ballet-dancer--but at the same time a great *musicienne* and a good and beautiful woman, a woman with red, splendid hair, like my niece. There she lived in a palace in this city, away from the world with her two children; an Emperor was her lover and her children's father; and they all four were happy as the day was long. The children were a boy and a girl, and presently they began to grow up, and the boy began to think about life and to reason things out with himself. He had, perhaps, inherited this faculty from his grandfather, on his mother's side, who was a celebrated poet and philosopher and a Spanish Jew. So his mother, the beautiful dancer, was half Jewess, and, from her mother again, half Spanish noble; for this philosopher had eloped with the daughter of a Spanish grandee, and she was erased from the roll. I go back this far not to weary you, but that you may understand what forces in race had to do with the boy's character. The daughter again of this pair became an artist and a dancer, and being a highly educated, as well as a superbly beautiful woman--a woman with all Zara's charm and infinitely more chiseled features--she won the devoted love of the Emperor of the country in which they lived. I will not go into the moral aspect of the affair. A great love recks not of moral aspects. Sufficient to say, they were ideally happy while the beautiful dancer lived. She died when the boy was about fifteen, to his great and abiding grief. His sister, who was a year or two younger than he, was then all he had to love, because political and social reasons in that country made it very difficult, about this time, for him often to see his father, the Emperor.

"The boy was very carefully educated, and began early, as I have told you, to think for himself and to dream. He dreamed of things which might have been, had he been the heir and son of the Empress, instead of the child of her who seemed to him so much the greater lady and queen, his own mother, the dancer; and he came to see that dreams that are based upon regrets are useless and only a factor in the degradation, not the uplifting of a man. The boy grew to understand that from that sweet mother, even though the world called her an immoral woman, he had inherited something much more valuable to himself than the Imperial crown--the faculty of perception and balance, physical and moral, to which the family of the Emperor, his father, could lay no claim. From them, both he and his sister had inherited a stubborn, indomitable pride. You can see it, and have already remarked it, in Zara--that sister's child.

"So when the boy grew to be about twenty, he determined to carve out a career for himself, to create a great fortune, and so make his own little kingdom, which should not be bound by any country or race. He had an English tutor--he had always had one--and in his studies of countries and peoples and their attributes, the English seemed to him to be much the finest race. They were saner, more understanding, more full of the sense of the fitness of things, and of the knowledge of life and how to live it wisely.

"So the boy, with no country, and no ingrained patriotism for the place of his birth, determined he, being free and of no nation, should, when he had made this fortune, migrate there, and endeavor to obtain a place among those proud people, whom he so admired in his heart. That was his goal, in all his years of hard work, during which time he grew to understand the value of individual character, regardless of nation or of creed; and so, when finally he did come to this country, it was not to seek, but to command." And here Francis Markrute, master of vast wealth and the destinies of almost as many human souls as his father, the Emperor, had been, raised his head. And Lady Ethelrida, daughter of a hundred noble lords, knew her father, the Duke, was no prouder than he, the Spanish dancer's son. And something in her fine spirit went out to him; and she, there in the firelight with the soft owl lamp silvering her hair, stretched out her hand to him; and he held it and kissed it tenderly, as he took his seat by her side.

"My sweet and holy one," he said. "And so you understand!"

"Yes, yes!" said Ethelrida. "Oh, please go on"--and she leaned back against her pillow, but she did not seek to draw away her hand.

"There came a great grief, then, in the life of the boy who was now a grown man. His sister brought disgrace upon herself, and died under extremely distressful circumstances, into which I need not enter here; and for a while these things darkened and embittered his life." He paused a moment, and gazed into the fire, a look of deep sorrow and regret on his sharply-cut face, and Ethelrida unconsciously allowed her slim fingers to tighten in his grasp. And when he felt this gentle sympathy, he stroked her hand.

"The man was very hard then, sweet lady," he went on. "He regrets it now, deeply. The pure angel, who at this day rules his life, with her soft eyes of divine mercy and gentleness, has taught him many lessons; and it will be his everlasting regret that he was hard then. But it was a great deep wound to his pride, that quality which he had inherited from his father, and had not then completely checked and got in hand. Pride should be a factor for noble actions and a great spirit, but not for overbearance toward the failings of others. He knows that now. If this lady, whom he worships, should ever wish to learn the whole details of this time, he will tell her even at any cost to his pride, but for the moment let me get on to pleasanter things."

And Ethelrida whispered, "Yes, yes," so he continued:

"All his life from a boy's to a man's, this person we are speaking of had kept his ideal of the woman he should love. She must be fine and shapely, and noble and free; she must be tender and devoted, and gracious and good. But he passed all his early manhood and grew to middle age, before he even saw her shadow across his path. He looked up one night, eighteen months ago, at a court ball, and she passed him on the arm of a royal duke, and unconsciously brushed his coat with her soft dove's wing; and he knew that it was she, after all those years, so he waited and planned, and met her once or twice; but fate did not let him advance very far, and so a scheme entered his head. His niece, the daughter of his dead sister, had also had a very unhappy life; and he thought she, too, should come among these English people, and find happiness with their level ways. She was beautiful and proud and good, so he planned the marriage between his niece and the cousin of the lady he worshiped, knowing by that he should be drawn nearer his star, and also pay the debt to his dead sister, by securing the happiness of her child; but primarily it was his desire to be nearer his own worshiped star, and thus it has all come about." He paused, and looked full at her face, and saw that her sweet eyes were moist with some tender, happy tears. So he leaned forward, took her other hand, and kissed them both, placing the soft palms against his mouth for a second; then he whispered hoarsely, his voice at last trembling with the passionate emotion he felt:

"Ethelrida--darling--I love you with my soul--tell me, my sweet lady, will you be my wife?"

And the Lady Ethelrida did not answer, but allowed herself to be drawn into his arms.

And so in the firelight, with the watchful gray owl, the two rested blissfully content.

CHAPTER XXXI

When Lady Ethelrida came down to tea, her sweet face was prettily flushed, for she was quite unused to caresses and the kisses of a man. Her soft gray eyes were shining with a happiness of which she had not dreamed, and above all things, she was filled with the exquisite emotion of having a secret!--a secret of which even her dear friend Anne was ignorant--a blessed secret, just shared between her lover and herself. And Lady Anningford, who had no idea that she had spent the afternoon with the financier, but believed she had religiously written letters alone, wondered to herself what on earth made Ethelrida look so joyous and not the least fatigued, as most of the others were. She really got prettier, she thought, as she grew older, and was always the greatest dear in the whole world. But, to look as happy as that and have a face so flushed, was quite mysterious and required the opinion of the Crow!

So she dragged Colonel Lowerby off to a sofa, and began at once:

"Crow, do look at Ethelrida's face! Did you ever see one so idiotically blissful, except when she has been kissed by the person she loves?"

"Well, how do you know that is not the case with our dear Ethelrida?" grunted the Crow. "She did not come out for a walk. You had better count up, and see who else stayed at home!"

So Lady Anningford began laughingly. The idea was too impossible, but she must reason it out.

"There was Lord Melton but Lady Melton stayed behind, too, and the Thornbys--all impossible. There was no one else except Tristram, who I know was in the smoking-room, with a fearful headache, and Mr. Markrute, who was with the Duke."

"Was he with the Duke?" queried the Crow.

"Crow!" almost gasped Lady Anningford. "Do you mean to tell me that you think Ethelrida would have her face looking like that about a foreigner! My dear friend, you must have taken leave of your seven senses--" and then she paused, for several trifles came back to her recollection, connected with these two, which, now that the Crow had implanted a suspicion in her breast, began to assume considerable proportions.

Ethelrida had talked of most irrelevant matters always during their good-night chats, unless the subject happened to be Zara, and she had never once mentioned Mr. Markrute personally or given any opinion about him; and yet, as Anne had seen, they had often talked. There must be something in it, but that was not enough to account for Ethelrida's face. A pale, rather purely colorless complexion like hers did not suddenly change to bright scarlet cheeks, without some practical means! And, as Anne very well knew, kisses were a very practical means! But her friend Ethelrida would never allow any man to kiss her, unless she had promised to marry him. Now, if it had been Lily Opie, she could not have been so sure, though she hoped she could be sure of any nice girl; but about Ethelrida she could take her oath. It followed, as Ethelrida had been quite pale at lunch and was not a person who went to sleep over fires, something extraordinary must have happened--but what?

"Crow, dear, I have never been so thrilled in my life," she said, after her thoughts had come to this stage. "The lurid tragedy of the honeymoon pair cannot compare in interest to anything connected with my sweet Ethelrida, for me, so it is your duty to put that horribly wise, cynical brain of yours to work and unravel me this mystery. Look, here is Mr. Markrute coming in--let us watch his face!"

But, although they subjected the financier to the keenest good-natured scrutiny, he did not show a sign or give them any clue. He sat down quietly, and began talking casually to the group by the tea-table, while he methodically spread his bread and butter with blackberry jam. Such delicious schoolroom teas the company indulged in, at the hospitable tea-table of Montfitchet! He did not seem to be even addressing Ethelrida. What could it be?

"I believe we have made a mistake after all, Crow," Lady Anningford said disappointedly. "Look--he is quite unmoved."

The Crow gave one of his chuckles, while he answered slowly, between his sips of tea:

"A man doesn't handle millions in the year, and twist and turn about half the governments of Europe, if he can't keep his face from showing what he doesn't mean you to see! Bless your dear heart, Mr. Francis Markrute is no infant!" and the chuckle went on.

"You may think yourself very wise, Crow, and so you are," Lady Anningford retorted severely, "but you don't know anything about love. When a man is in love, even if he were Machiavelli himself, it would be bound to show in his eye--if one looked long enough."

"Then your plan, my dear Queen Anne, is to look," the Crow said, smiling. "For my part, I want to see how the other pair have got on. They are my pets; and I don't consider they have spent at all a suitable honeymoon Sunday afternoon--Tristram, with a headache in the smoking-room, and the bride, taking a walk and being made love to by Arthur Elterton, and Young Billy, alternately. The kid is as wild about her as Tristram himself, I believe!"

"Then you still think Tristram is in love with her, do you, Crow?" asked Anne, once more interested in her original thrill. "He did not show the smallest signs of it last night then, if so; and how he did not seize her in his arms and devour her there and then, with all that lovely hair down and her exquisite shape showing the out-line so in that dress--I can't think! He must be as cold as a stone, and I never thought him so before, did you?"

"No, and he isn't either, I tell you what, my dear girl, there is something pretty grim keeping those two apart, I am sure. She is the kind of woman who arouses the fiercest passions; and Tristram is in the state that, if something were really to set alight his jealousy, he might kill her some day."

"Crow--how terrible!" gasped Anne, and then seeing that her friend's face was serious, and not chaffing, she, too, looked grave. "Then what on earth is to be done?" she asked.

"I don't know, I have been thinking it over ever since I came in. I found him in the smoking-room, staring in front of him, not even pretending to read, and look-ing pretty white about the gills; and when he saw it was only me, and I asked him if his head were worse, and whether he had not better have a brandy and soda, he simply said: 'No, thanks, the whole thing is a d---- rotten show.' I've known him since he was a blessed baby you know, so he didn't mind me for a minute. Then he recollected himself, and said, yes, he would have a drink; and when he poured it out, he only sipped it, and then forgot about it, jumped up, and blurted out he had some letters to write, so I left him. I am awfully sorry for the poor chap, I can tell you. If it is not fate, but some caprice of hers, she deserves a jolly good beating, for making him suffer like that."

"Couldn't you say something to her, Crow, dear? We are all so awfully fond of Tristram, and there does seem some tragedy hanging over them that ought to be stopped at once. Couldn't you, Crow?"

But Colonel Lowerby shook his head.

"It is too confoundedly ticklish," he grunted. "It might do some good, and it might just do the other thing. It is too dangerous to interfere."

"Well, you have made me thoroughly uncomfortable," Lady Anningford said. "I shall get hold of him to-night, and see what I can do."

"Then, mind you are careful, Queen Anne--that is all that I can say," and at that moment, the Duke joining them, the tete-a-tete broke up.

Zara had not appeared at tea. She said she was very tired, and would rest until dinner. If she had been there, her uncle had meant to take her aside into one of the smaller sitting-rooms, and tell her the piece of information he deemed it now advisable for her to know; but as she did not appear, or Tristram, either, he thought after all they might be together, and his interference would be unnecessary. But he decided, if he saw the same frigid state of things at dinner, he would certainly speak to her after it; and relieved from duty, he went once more to find his lady love in her sitting-room.

"Francis!" she whispered, as he held her next his heart for a moment. "You must not stay ten minutes, for Lady Anningford or Lady Melton is sure to come in--Anne, especially, who has been looking at me with such reproachful eyes, for having neglected her all this, our last afternoon."

"I care not for a thousand Annes, Ethelrida mine!" he said softly, as he kissed her. "If she does come, will it matter? Would you rather she did not guess anything yet, my dearest?"

"Yes--" said Ethelrida, "--I don't want any one to know, until you have told my father,--will you do so to-night--or wait until to-morrow? I--I can't--I feel so shy--and he will be so surprised." She did not add her secret fear that her parent might be very angry.

They had sat down upon the sofa now, under the light of their kindly gray owl; and Francis Markrute contented himself with caressing his lady's hair, as he answered:

"I thought of asking the Duke, if I might stay until the afternoon train, as I had something important to discuss with him, and then wait and see him quietly, when all the others have gone, if that is what you would wish, my sweet. I will do exactly as you desire about all things. I want you to understand that. You are to have your own way in everything in life."

"You know very well that I should never want it, if it differed from yours, Francis." What music he found in his name! "You are so very wise, it will be divine to let you guide me!" Which tender speech showed that the gentle Ethelrida had none of the attitude of the modern bride.

And thus it was arranged. The middle-aged, but boyishly-in-love, fiance was to tackle his future father-in-law in the morning's light; and to-night, let the household sleep in peace!

So, after a blissful interlude, as he saw in spite of the joy they found together, his Ethelrida was still slightly nervous of Lady Anningford's entrance, he got up to say good night, as alas! this would probably be the last chance they would have alone before he left.

"And you will not make me wait too long, my darling," he implored, "will you? You see, every moment away from you, will now be wasted. I do not know how I have borne all these years alone!"

And she promised everything he wished, for Francis Markrute, at forty-six, had far more allurements than an impetuous young lover. Not a tenderness, a subtlety of flattery and homage, those things so dear to a woman's heart, were forgotten by him. He really worshiped Ethelrida and his fashion of showing his feeling was in all ways to think first of what she would wish; which proved that if her attitude were unmodern, as far as women were concerned, his was even more so, among men!

Tristram had gone out for another walk alone, after the Crow had left him. He wanted to realize the details of the coming week, and settle with himself how best to get through with them.

He and Zara were to start in their own motor at about eleven for Wrayth, which was only forty miles across the border into Suffolk. They would reach it inside of two hours easily, and arrive at the first triumphal arch of the park before one; and so go on through the shouting villagers to the house, where in the great banqueting hall, which still remained, a relic of Henry IV's time, joined on to the Norman keep, they would have to assist at a great luncheon to the principal tenants, while the lesser fry feasted in a huge tent in the outer courtyard.

Here, endless speeches would have to be made and listened to, and joy simulated, and a general air of hilarity kept up; and the old housekeeper would have prepared the large rooms in the Adam wing for their reception; and they would not be free to separate, until late at night, for there would be the servants' and employes' ball, after a tete-a-tete dinner in state, where their every action would be watched and commented upon by many curious eyes. Yes, it was a terrible ordeal to go through, under the circumstances; and no wonder he wanted the cold, frosty evening air to brace him up!

At the end of his troubled thoughts he had come to the conclusion that there was only one thing to be done--he must speak to her to-night, tell her what to expect, and ask her to play her part. "She is fortunately game, even if cold as stone," he said to himself, "and if I appeal to her pride, she will help me out." So he came back into the house, and went straight up to her room. He had been through too much suffering and anguish of heart, all night and all day, to be fearful of temptation. He felt numb, as he knocked at the door and an indifferent voice called out, "Come in!"

He opened it a few inches and said: "It is I--Tristram--I have something I must say to you--May I come in?--or would you prefer to come down to one of the sitting-rooms? I dare say we could find one empty, so as to be alone."

"Please come in," her voice said, and she was conscious that she was trembling from head to foot.

So he obeyed her, shutting the door firmly after him and advancing to the fireplace. She had been lying upon the sofa wrapped in a soft blue tea-gown, and her hair hung in the two long plaits, which she always unwound when she could to take its weight from her head. She rose from her reclining position and sat in the corner; and after glancing at her for a second, Tristram turned his eyes away, and leaning on the mantelpiece, began in a cold grave voice:

"I have to ask you to do me a favor. It is to help me through to-morrow and the few days after, as best you can, by conforming to our ways. It has been always the custom in the family, when a Tancred brought home his bride, to have all sorts of silly rejoicings. There will be triumphal arches in the park, and collections of village people, a lunch for the principal tenants, speeches, and all sorts of boring things. Then we shall have to dine alone in the state dining-room, with all the servants watching us, and go to the household and tenants' ball in the great hall. It will all be ghastly, as you can see." He paused a moment, but he did not change the set tone in his voice when he spoke again, nor did he look at her. He had now come to the hardest part of his task.

"All these people--who are my people," he went on, "think a great deal of these things, and of us--that is--myself, as their landlord, and you as my wife. We have always been friends, the country folk at Wrayth and my family, and they adored my mother. They are looking forward to our coming back and opening the house again--and--and--all that--and--" here he paused a second time, it seemed as if his throat were dry, for suddenly the remembrance of his dreams as he looked at Tristram Guiscard's armor, which he had worn at Agincourt, came back to him--his dreams in his old oak-paneled room--of their home-coming to Wrayth; and the mockery of the reality hit him in the face.

Zara clasped her hands, and if he had glanced at her again, he would have seen all the love and anguish which was convulsing her shining in her sad eyes.

He mastered the emotion which had hoarsened his voice, and went on in an even tone: "What I have to ask is that you will do your share--wear some beautiful clothes, and smile, and look as if you cared; and if I feel that it will be necessary to take your hand or even kiss you, do not frown at me, or think I am doing it from choice--I ask you, because I believe you are as proud as I am,--I ask you, please, to play the game."

And now he looked up at her, but the terrible emotion she was suffering had made her droop her head. He would not kiss her or take her hand--from choice-- that was the main thing her woman's heart had grasped, the main thing, which cut her like a knife.

"You can count upon me," she said, so low he could hardly hear her; and then she raised her head proudly, and looked straight in front of her, but not at him, while she repeated more firmly: "I will do in every way what you wish--what your mother would have done. I am no weakling, you know, and as you said, I am as proud as yourself."

He dared not look at her, now the bargain was made, so he took a step towards the door, and then turned and said:

"I thank you--I shall be grateful to you. Whatever may occur, please believe that nothing that may look as if it was my wish to throw us together, as though we were really husband and wife, will be my fault; and you can count upon my making the thing as easy for you as I can--and when the mockery of the rejoicings are over--then we can discuss our future plans."

And though Zara was longing to cry aloud in passionate pain, "I love you! I love you! Come back and beat me, if you will, only do not go coldly like that!" she spoke never a word. The strange iron habit of her life held her, and he went sadly from the room.

And when he had gone, she could control herself no longer and, forgetful of coming maid and approaching dinner, she groveled on the white bearskin rug before the fire, and gave way to passionate tears--only to recollect in a moment the position of things. Then she got up and shook with passion against fate, and civilization, and custom--against the whole of life. She could not even cry in peace. No! She must play the game! So her eyes had to be bathed, the window opened, and the icy air breathed in, and at last she had quieted herself down to the look of a person with a headache, when the dressing-gong sounded, and her maid came into the room.

CHAPTER XXXII

This, the last dinner at Montfitchet, passed more quietly than the rest. The company were perhaps subdued, from their revels of the night before; and every one hates the thought of breaking up a delightful party and separating on the morrow, even when it has only been a merry gathering like this.

And two people were divinely happy, and two people supremely sad, and one mean little heart was full of bitterness and malice unassuaged. So after dinner was over, and they were all once more in the white drawing-room, the different elements assorted themselves.

Lady Anningford took Tristram aside and began, with great tact and much feeling, to see if he could be cajoled into a better mood; and finally got severely snubbed for her trouble, which hurt her more because she realized how deep must be his pain than from any offense to herself. Then Laura caught him and implanted her last sting:

"You are going away to-morrow, Tristram,--into your new life--and when you have found out all about your wife--and her handsome friend--you may remember that there was one woman who loved you truly--" and then she moved on and left him sitting there, too raging to move.

After this, his uncle had joined him, had talked politics, and just at the end, for the hearty old gentleman could not believe a man could really be cold or indifferent to as beautiful a piece of flesh and blood as his new niece, he had said:

"Tristram, my dear boy,--I don't know whether it is the modern spirit--or not--but, if I were you, I'd be hanged if I would let that divine creature, your wife, out of my sight day or night!--When you get her alone at Wrayth, just kiss her until she can't breathe--and you'll find it is all right!"

With which absolutely sensible advice, he had slapped his nephew on the back, fixed in his eyeglass, and walked off; and Tristram had stood there, his blue eyes hollow with pain, and had laughed a bitter laugh, and gone to play bridge, which he loathed, with the Meltons and Mrs. Harcourt. So for him, the evening had passed.

And Francis Markrute had taken his niece aside to give her his bit of salutary information. He wished to get it over as quickly as possible, and had drawn her to a sofa rather behind a screen, where they were not too much observed.

"We have all had a most delightful visit, I am sure, Zara," he had said, "but you and Tristram seem not to be yet as good friends as I could wish."

He paused a moment, but as usual she did not speak, so he went on:

"There is one thing you might as well know, I believe you have not realized it yet, unless Tristram has told you of it himself."

She looked up now, startled--of what was she ignorant then?

"You may remember the afternoon I made the bargain with you about the marriage," Francis Markrute went on. "Well, that afternoon Tristram, your husband, had refused my offer of you and your fortune with scorn. He would never wed a rich woman he said, or a woman he did not know or love, for any material gain; but I knew he would think differently when he had seen how beautiful and attractive you were, so I continued to make my plans. You know my methods, my dear niece."

Zara's blazing and yet pitiful eyes were all his answer.

"Well, I calculated rightly. He came to dinner that night, and fell madly in love with you, and at once asked to marry you himself, while he insisted upon your fortune being tied up entirely upon you, and any children that you might have, only allowing me to pay off the mortgages on Wrayth for himself. It would be impossible for a man to have behaved more like a gentleman. I thought now, in case you had not grasped all this, you had better know." And then he said anxiously, "Zara--my dear child--what is the matter?" for her proud head had fallen forward on her breast, with a sudden deadly faintness. This, indeed, was the filling of her cup.

His voice pulled her together, and she sat up; and to the end of his life, Francis Markrute will never like to remember the look in her eyes.

"And you let me go on and marry him, playing this cheat? You let me go on and spoil both our lives! What had I ever done to you, my uncle, that you should be so cruel to me? Or is it to be revenged upon my mother for the hurt she brought to your pride?"

If she had reproached him, stormed at him, anything, he could have borne it better; but the utter lifeless calm of her voice, the hopeless look in her beautiful white face, touched his heart--that heart but newly unwrapped and humanized from its mummifying encasements by the omnipotent God of Love. Had he, after all, been too coldly calculating about this human creature of his own flesh and blood? Was there some insurmountable barrier grown up from his action? For the first moment in his life he was filled with doubt and fear.

"Zara," he said, anxiously, "tell me, dear child, what you mean? I let you go on in the 'cheat,' as you call it, because I knew you never would consent to the bargain, unless you thought it was equal on both sides. I know your sense of honor, dear, but I calculated, and I thought rightly, that, Tristram being so in love with you, he would soon undeceive you, directly you were alone. I never believed a woman could be so cold as to resist his wonderful charm--Zara--what has happened?--'Won't you tell me, child?"

But she sat there turned to stone. She had no thought to reproach him. Her heart and her spirit seemed broken, that was all.

"Zara--would you like me to do anything? Can I explain anything to him? Can I help you to be happy? I assure you it hurts me awfully, if this will not turn out all right--Zara," for she had risen a little unsteadily from her seat beside him. "You cannot be indifferent to him for ever--he is too splendid a man. Cannot I do anything for you, my niece?"

Then she looked at him, and her eyes in their deep tragedy seemed to burn out of her deadly white face.

"No, thank you, my uncle,--there is nothing to be done--everything is now too late." Then she added in the same monotonous voice, "I am very tired, I think I will wish you a good night." And with immense dignity, she left him; and making her excuses with gentle grace to the Duke and Lady Ethelrida, she glided from the room.

And Francis Markrute, as he watched her, felt his whole being wrung with emotion and pain.

"My God!" he said to himself. "She is a glorious woman, and it will--it must--

come right--even yet."

And then he set his brain to calculate how he could assist them, and finally his reasoning powers came back to him, and he comforted himself with the deductions he made.

She was going away alone with this most desirable young man into the romantic environment of Wrayth. Human physical passion, to say the least of it, was too strong to keep them apart for ever, so he could safely leave the adjusting of this puzzle to the discretion of fate.

And Zara, freed at last from eye of friend or maid, collapsed on to the white bearskin in front of the fire again, and tried to think. So she had been offered as a chattel and been refused! Here her spirit burnt with humiliation. Her uncle, she knew, always had used her merely as a pawn in some game--what game? He was not a snob; the position of uncle to Tristram would not have tempted him alone; he never did anything without a motive and a deep one. Could it be that he himself was in love with Lady Ethelrida? She had been too preoccupied with her own affairs to be struck with those of others, but now as she looked back, he had shown an interest which was not in his general attitude towards women. How her mother had loved him, this wonderful brother! It was her abiding grief always, his unforgiveness,-- and perhaps, although it seemed impossible to her, Lady Ethelrida was attracted by him, too. Yes, that must be it. It was to be connected with the family, to make his position stronger in the Duke's eyes, that he had done this cruel thing. But, would it have been cruel if she herself had been human and different? He had called her from struggling and poverty, had given her this splendid young husband, and riches and place,--no, there was nothing cruel in it, as a calculated action. It should have given her her heart's desire. It was she, herself, who had brought about things as they were, because of her ignorance, that was the cruelty, to have let her go away with Tristram, in ignorance.

Then the aspect of the case that she had been offered to him and refused! scourged her again; then the remembrance that he had taken her, for love. And what motive could he imagine she had had? This struck her for the first time--how infinitely more generous he had been--for he had not allowed, what he must have thought was pure mercenariness and desire for position on her part to interfere with his desire for her personally. He had never turned upon her, as she saw now he very well could have done, and thrown this in her teeth. And then she fell to bitter sobbing, and so at last to sleep.

And when the fire had died out, towards the gray dawn, she woke again shivering and in mortal fright, for she had dreamed of Mirko, and that he was being torn from her, while he played the ***Chanson Triste***. Then she grew fully awake and remembered that this was the beginning of the new day--the day she should go to her husband's home; and she had accused him of all the base things a man could do, and he had behaved like a gentleman; and it was she who was base, and had sold herself for her brother's life, sold what should never be bartered for any life, but only for love.

Well, there was nothing to be done, only to "play the game"--the hackneyed phrase came back to her; he had used it, so it was sacred. Yes, all she could do for him now was, to "play the game"--everything else was--too late.

CHAPTER XXXIII

People left by all sorts of trains and motors in the morning; but there were still one or two remaining, when the bride and bridegroom made their departure, in their beautiful new car with its smart servants, which had come to fetch them, and take them to Wrayth.

And, just as the Dover young ladies on the pier had admired their embarkation, with its *apanages* of position and its romantic look, so every one who saw them leave Montfitchet was alike elated. They were certainly an ideal pair.

Zara had taken the greatest pains to dress herself in her best. She remembered Tristram had admired her the first evening they had arrived for this visit, when she had worn sapphire blue, so now she put on the same colored velvet and the sable coat--yes, he liked that best, too, and she clasped some of his sapphire jewels in her ears and at her throat. No bride ever looked more beautiful or distinguished, with her gardenia complexion and red burnished hair, all set off by the velvet and dark fur.

But Tristram, after the first glance, when she came down, never looked at her--he dared not. So they said their farewells quietly; but there was an extra warmth and tenderness in Ethelrida's kiss, as, indeed, there was every reason that there should be. If Zara had known! But the happy secret was still locked in the lovers' breasts.

"Of course it must come all right, they look so beautiful!" Ethelrida exclaimed unconsciously, waving her last wave on the steps, as the motor glided away.

"Yes, it must indeed," whispered Francis, who was beside her, and she turned and looked into his face.

"In twenty minutes, all the rest will be gone except the Crow, and Emily, and Mary, and Lady Anningford, who are staying on; and oh, Francis, how shall I get through the morning, knowing you are with Papa!"

"I will come to your sitting-room just before luncheon time, my dearest," he whispered back reassuringly. "Do not distress yourself--it will be all right."

And so they all went back into the house, and Lady Anningford, who now began to have grave suspicions, whispered to the Crow:

"I believe you are perfectly right, Crow. I am certain Ethelrida is in love with Mr. Markrute! But surely the Duke would never permit such a thing! A foreigner whom nobody knows anything of!"

"I never heard that there was any objection raised to Tristram marrying his niece. The Duke seemed to welcome it, and some foreigners are very good chaps," the Crow answered sententiously, "especially Austrians and Russians; and he must be one of something of that sort. He has no apparent touch of the Latin race. It's Latins I don't like."

"Well, I shall probably hear all about it from Ethelrida herself, now that we are alone. I am so glad I decided to stay with the dear girl until Wednesday, and you will have to wait till then, too, Crow."

"As ever, I am at your orders," he grunted, and lighting a cigar, he subsided into a great chair to read the papers, while Lady Anningford went on to the saloon. And presently, when all the departing guests were gone, Ethelrida linked her arm in that of her dear friend, and drew her with her up to her sitting-room.

"I have heaps to tell you, Anne!" she said, while she pushed her gently into a big low chair, and herself sank into the corner of her sofa. Ethelrida was not a person who curled up among pillows, or sat on rugs, or little stools. All her movements, even in her most intimate moments of affection with her friend, were dignified and reserved.

"Darling, I am thrilled," Lady Anningford responded, "and I guess it is all about Mr. Markrute--and oh, Ethelrida, when did it begin?"

"He has been thinking of me for a long time, Anne--quite eighteen months--but I--" she looked down, while a tender light grew in her face, "I only began to be interested the night we dined with him--it is a little more than a fortnight ago--the dinner for Tristram's engagement. He said a number of things not like any one else, then, and he made me think of him afterwards--and I saw him again at the wedding--and since he has been here--and do you know, Anne, I have never loved any one before in my life!"

"Ethelrida, you darling, I know you haven't!" and Anne bounded up and gave her a hug. "And I knew you were perfectly happy, and had had a blissful afternoon when you came down to tea yesterday. Your whole face was changed, you pet!"

"Did I look so like a fool, Anne?" Ethelrida cried.

Then Lady Anningford laughed happily, as she answered with a roguish eye,

"It was not exactly that, darling, but your dear cheeks were scarlet, as though they had been exquisitely kissed!"

"Oh!" gasped Ethelrida, flaming pink, as she laughed and covered her face with her hands.

"Perhaps he knows how to make love nicely--I am no judge of such things--in any case, he makes me thrill. Anne, tell me, is that--that curious sensation as though one were rather limp and yet quivering--is that just how every one feels when they are in love?"

"Ethelrida, you sweet thing!" gurgled Anne.

Then Ethelrida told her friend about the present of books, and showed them to her, and of all the subtlety of his ways, and how they appealed to her.

"And oh, Anne, he makes me perfectly happy and sure of everything; and I feel that I need never decide anything for myself again in my life!"

Which, taking it all round, was a rather suitable and fortunate conviction for a man to have implanted in his lady love's breast, and held out the prospect of much happiness in their future existence together.

"I think he is very nice looking," said Anne, "and he has the most perfect clothes. I do like a man to have that groomed look, which I must say most Englishmen have, but Tristram has it, especially, and Mr. Markrute, too. If you knew the despair my old man is to me with his indifference about his appearance. It is my only crumpled rose leaf, with the dear old thing."

"Yes," agreed Ethelrida, "I like them to be smart--and above all, they must have thick hair. Anne, have you noticed Francis' hair? It is so nice, it grows on his forehead just as Zara's does. If he had been bald like Papa, I could not have fallen in love with him!"

So once more the fate of a man was decided by his hair!

And during this exchange of confidences, while Emily and Mary took a brisk walk with the Crow and young Billy, Francis Markrute faced his lady's ducal father in the library.

He had begun without any preamble, and with perfect calm; and the Duke, who was above all a courteous gentleman, had listened, first with silent consternation and resentment, and then with growing interest.

Francis Markrute had manipulated infinitely more difficult situations, when the balance of some of the powers of Europe depended upon his nerve; but he knew, as he talked to this gallant old Englishman, that he had never had so much at stake, and it stimulated him to do his best.

He briefly stated his history, which Ethelrida already knew; he made no apology for his bar sinister; indeed, he felt none was needed. He knew, and the Duke knew, that when a man has won out as he had done, such things fade into space. And then with wonderful taste and discretion he had but just alluded to his vast wealth, and that it would be so perfectly administered through Lady Ethelrida's hands, for the good of her order and of mankind.

And the Duke, accustomed to debate and the watching of methods in men, could not help admiring the masterly reserve and force of this man.

And, finally, when the financier had finished speaking, the Duke rose and stood before the fire, while he fixed his eyeglass in his eye.

"You have stated the case admirably, my dear Markrute," he said, in his distinguished old voice. "You leave me without argument and with merely my prejudices, which I dare say are unjust, but I confess they are strongly in favor of my own countrymen and strongly against this union--though, on the other hand, my daughter and her happiness are my first consideration in this world. Ethelrida was twenty-six yesterday, and she is a young woman of strong and steady character, unlikely to be influenced by any foolish emotion. Therefore, if you have been fortunate enough to find favor in her eyes--if the girl loves you, in short, my dear fellow, then I have nothing to say.--Let us ring and have a glass of port!"

And presently the two men, now with the warmest friendship in their hearts for one another, mounted the staircase to Lady Ethelrida's room, and there found her still talking to Anne.

Her sweet eyes widened with a question as the two appeared at the door, and then she rushed into her father's arms and buried her face in his coat; and with his eyeglass very moist, the old Duke kissed her fondly--as he muttered.

"Why, Ethelrida, my little one. This is news! If you are happy, darling, that is all I want!"

So the whole dreaded moment passed off with rejoicing, and presently Lady Anningford and the fond father made their exit, and left the lovers alone.

"Oh, Francis, isn't the world lovely!" murmured Ethelrida from the shelter of his arms. "Papa and I have always been so happy together, and now we shall be three, because you understand him, too, and you won't make me stay away from him for very long times, will you, dear?"

"Never, my sweet. I thought of asking the Duke, if you would wish it, to let me take the place from him in this county, which eventually comes to you, and I will keep on Thorpmoor, my house in Lincolnshire, merely for the shooting. Then you would feel you were always in your own home, and perhaps the Duke would spend much time with us, and we could come to him here, in an hour; but all this is merely a suggestion--everything shall be as you wish."

"Francis, you are good to me," she said.

"Darling," he whispered, as he kissed her hair, "it took me forty-six years to find my pearl of price."

Then they settled all kinds of other details: how he would give Zara, for her own, the house in Park Lane, which would not be big enough now for them; and he would purchase one of those historic mansions, looking on The Green Park, which he knew was soon to be in the market. Ethelrida, if she left the ducal roof for the sake of his love, should find a palace worthy of her acceptance waiting for her.

He had completely recovered his balance, upset a little the night before by the uncomfortable momentary fear about his niece.

She and Tristram had arranged to come up to Park Lane for two nights again at the end of the week, to say good-bye to the Dowager Lady Tancred, who was starting with her daughters for Cannes. If he should see then that things were still amiss, he would tell Tristram the whole history of what Zara had thought of him. Perhaps that might throw some light on her conduct towards him, and so things could be cleared up. But he pinned his whole faith on youth and propinquity to arrange matters before then, and dismissed it from his mind.

Meanwhile, the pair in question were speeding along to Wrayth.

Of all the ordeals of the hours which Tristram had had to endure since his wedding, these occasions, upon which he had to sit close beside her in a motor, were the worst. An ordinary young man, not in love with her, would have found something intoxicating in her atmosphere--and how much more this poor Tristram, who was passionately obsessed.

Fortunately, she liked plenty of window open and did not object to smoke; but with the new air of meekness which was on her face and the adorably attractive personal scent of the creature, nearly two hours with her, under a sable rug, was no laughing matter.

At the end of the first half hour of silence and nearness, her husband found he was obliged to concentrate his mind by counting sheep jumping over imaginary stiles to prevent himself from clasping her in his arms.

It was the same old story, which has been chronicled over and over again. Two young, human, natural, normal people fighting against iron bars. For Zara felt the same as he, and she had the extra anguish of knowing she had been unjust, and that the present impossible situation was entirely her own doing.

And how to approach the subject and confess her fault? She did not know. Her sense of honor made her feel she must, but the queer silent habit of her life was still holding her enchained. And so, until they got into his own country, the strained speechlessness continued, and then he looked out and said:

"We must have the car opened now--please smile and bow as we go through the villages when any of the old people curtsey to you; the young ones won't do it, I expect, but my mother's old friends may."

So Zara leaned forward, when the footman had opened the landaulette top, and tried to look radiant.

And the first act of this pitiful comedy began.

CHAPTER XXXIV

Every sort of emotion convulsed the new Lady Tancred's heart, as they began to get near the park, with the village nestling close to its gates on the far side. So this was the home of her love and her lord; and they ought to be holding hands, and approaching it and the thought of their fond life together there with full hearts,--well, her heart was full enough, but only of anguish and pain. For Tristram, afraid of the smallest unbending, maintained a freezing attitude of contemptuous disdain, which she could not yet pluck up enough courage to break through to tell him she knew how unjust and unkind she had been.

And presently they came through cheering yokels to the South Lodge, the furthest away from the village, and so under a triumphant arch of evergreens, with banners floating and mottoes of "God Bless the Bride and Bridegroom" and "Health and Long Life to Lord and Lady Tancred." And now Tristram did take her hand and, indeed, put his arm round her as they both stood up for a moment in the car, while raising his hat and waving it gayly he answered graciously:

"My friends, Lady Tancred and I thank you so heartily for your kind wishes and welcome home."

Then they sat down, and the car went on, and his face became rigid again, as he let go her hand.

And at the next arch by the bridge, the same thing, only more elaborately carried out, began again, for here were all the farmers of the hunt, of which Tristram was a great supporter, on horseback; and the cheering and waving knew no end. The cavalcade of mounted men followed them round outside the Norman tower and to the great gates in the smaller one, where the portcullis had been.

Here all the village children were, and the old women from the almshouse, in their scarlet frieze cloaks and charming black bonnets; and every sort of wish for their happiness was shouted out. "Bless the beautiful bride and bring her many little lords and ladies, too," one old body quavered shrilly, above the din, and this pleasantry was greeted with shouts of delight. And for that second Tristram dropped his lady's hand as though it had burnt him, and then, recollecting himself, picked it up again. They were both pale with excitement and emotion, when they finally reached the hall-door in the ugly, modern Gothic wing and were again greeted by all the household servants in rows, two of them old and gray-haired, who had stayed on to care for things when the house had been shut up. There was Michelham back at his master's old home, only promoted to be groom of the chambers, now, with a smart younger butler under him.

Tristram was a magnificent orderer, and knew exactly how things ought to be done.

And the stately housekeeper, in her black silk, stepped forward, and in the name of herself and her subordinates, bade the new mistress welcome, and hoping she was not fatigued, presented her with a bouquet of white roses. "Because his lordship told us all, when he was here making the arrangements, that your ladyship was as beautiful as a white rose!"

And tears welled up in Zara's eyes and her voice trembled, as she thanked them and tried to smile.

"She was quite overcome, the lovely young lady," they told one another afterwards, "and no wonder. Any woman would be mad after his lordship. It is quite to be understood."

How they all loved him, the poor bride thought, and he had told them she was a beautiful white rose. He felt like that about her then, and she had thrown it all away. Now he looked upon her with loathing and disdain, and no wonder either--there was nothing to be done.

Presently, he took her hand again and placed it on his arm, as they walked through the long corridor, to the splendid hall, built by the brothers Adam, with its stately staircase to the gallery above.

"I have prepared the state rooms for your ladyship, pending your ladyship's choice of your own," Mrs. Anglin said. "Here is the boudoir, the bedroom, the bathroom, and his lordship's dressing-room--all en suite--and I hope your ladyship will find them as handsome, as we old servants of the family think they are!"

And Zara came up to the scratch and made a charming little speech.

When they got to the enormous bedroom, with its windows looking out on the French garden and park, all in exquisite taste, furnished and decorated by the Adams themselves, Tristram gallantly bent and kissed her hand, as he said:

"I will wait for you in the boudoir, while you take off your coat. Mrs. Anglin will show you the toilet-service of gold, which was given by Louis XIV to a French grandmother and which the Ladies Tancred always use, when they are at Wrayth. I hope you won't find the brushes too hard," and he laughed and went out.

And Zara, overcome with the state and beauty and tradition of it all, sat down upon the sofa for a moment to try to control her pain. She was throbbing with rage and contempt at herself, at the remembrance that she, in her ignorance, her ridiculous ignorance, had insulted this man--this noble gentleman, who owned all these things--and had taunted him with taking her for her uncle's wealth.

How he must have loved her in the beginning to have been willing to give her all this, after seeing her for only one night. She writhed with anguish. There is no bitterness as great as the bitterness of loss caused by oneself.

Tristram was standing by the window of the delicious boudoir when she went in. Zara, who as yet knew very little of English things, admired the Adam style; and when Mrs. Anglin left them discreetly for a moment, she told him so, timidly, for something to say.

"Yes, it is rather nice," he said stiffly, and then went on: "We shall have to go down now to this fearful lunch, but you had better take your sable boa with you. The great hall is so enormous and all of stone, it may be cold. I will get it for you," and he went back and found it lying by her coat on the chair, and brought it, and wrapped it round her casually, as if she had been a stone, and then held the door for her to go out. And Zara's pride was stung, even though she knew he was doing exactly as she herself would have done, so that instead of the meek attitude she had unconsciously assumed, for a moment now she walked beside him with her old mien of head in the air, to the admiration of Mrs. Anglin, who watched them descend the stairs.

"She is as haughty-looking as our own ladyship," she thought to herself. "I wonder how his lordship likes that!"

The great hall was a survival of the time of Henry IV with its dais to eat above the salt, and a magnificent stone fireplace, and an oak screen and gallery of a couple of centuries later. The tables were laid down each side, as in the olden time, and across the dais; and here, in the carved oak "Lord" and "Lady" chairs, the bride and bridegroom sat with a principal tenant and his wife on either side of them, while the powdered footmen served them with lunch.

And all the time, when one or two comic incidents happened, she longed to look at Tristram and laugh; but he maintained his attitude of cold reserve, only making some genial stereotyped remark, when it was necessary for the public effect.

And presently the speeches began, and this was the most trying moment of all. For the land-steward, who proposed their healths, said such nice things; and Zara realized how they all loved her lord, and her anger at herself grew and grew. In each speech from different tenants there was some intimate friendly allusion about herself, too, linking her always with Tristram; and these parts hurt her particularly.

Then Tristram rose to answer them in his name and hers. He made a splendid speech, telling them that he had come back to live among them and had brought them a beautiful new Lady--and here he turned to her a moment and took and kissed her hand--and how he would always think of all their interests in every way; and that he looked upon them as his dear old friends; and that he and Lady Tancred would always endeavor to promote their welfare, as long as the radicals--here he laughed, for they were all true blue to a man--would let them! And when voices shouted, "We want none of them rats here," he was gay and chaffed them; and finally sat down amidst yells of applause.

Then an old apple-cheeked farmer got up from far down the table and made a long rambling harangue, about having been there, man and boy, and his forbears before him, for a matter of two hundred years; but he'd take his oath they had none of them ever seen such a beautiful bride brought to Wrayth as they were welcoming now; and he drank to her ladyship's health, and hoped it would not be long before they would have another and as great a feast for the rejoicings over the son and heir!

At this deplorable bit of bucolic wit and hearty taste, Tristram's face went stern as death; and he bit his lips, while his bride became the color of the red roses on the table in front of her.

Thus the luncheon passed. And amidst countless hand-shakes of affection, accelerated by port wine and champagne, the bride and bridegroom, followed by the land-steward and a chosen few, went to receive and return the same sort of speeches among the lesser people in the tent. Here the allusions to marital felicity were even more glaring, and Zara saw that each time Tristram heard them, an instantaneous gleam of bitter sarcasm would steal into his eyes. So, worn out at last with the heat in the tent and the emotions of the day, at about five, the bridegroom was allowed to conduct his bride to tea in the boudoir of the state rooms. Thus they were alone, and now was Zara's time to make her confession, if it ever should come.

Tristram's resolve had held him, nothing could have been more gallingly cold and disdainful than had been his treatment of her, so perfect, in its acting for 'the game,' and, so bitter, in the humiliation of the between times. She would tell him of her mistake. That was all. She must guard herself against showing any emotion over it.

They each sank down into chairs beside the fire with sighs of relief.

"Good Lord!" he said, as he put his hand to his forehead. "What a hideous mockery the whole thing is, and not half over yet! I am afraid you must be tired. You ought to go and rest until dinner--when, please be very magnificent and wear some of the jewels--part of them have come down from London on purpose, I think, beyond those you had at Montfitchet."

"Yes, I will," she answered, listlessly, and began to pour out the tea, while he sat quite still staring into the fire, a look of utter weariness and discouragement upon his handsome face.

Everything about the whole thing was hurting him so, all the pleasure he had taken in the improvements and the things he had done, hoping to please her; and now, as he saw them about, each one stabbed him afresh.

She gave him his cup without a word. She had remembered from Paris his tastes in cream and sugar; and then as the icy silence continued, she could bear it no longer.

"Tristram," she said, in as level a voice as she could. At the sound of his name he looked at her startled. It was the first time she had ever used it!

She lowered her head and, clasping her hands, she went on constrainedly, so overcome with emotion she dared not let herself go. "I want to tell you something, and ask you to forgive me. I have learned the truth, that you did not marry me just for my uncle's money. I know exactly what really happened now. I am ashamed, humiliated, to remember what I said to you. But I understood you had agreed to the bargain before you had ever seen me. The whole thing seemed so awful to me--so revolting--I am sorry for what I taunted you with. I know now that you are really a great gentleman."

His face, if she had looked up and seen it, had first all lightened with hope and love; but as she went on coldly, the warmth died out of it, and a greater pain than ever filled his heart. So she knew now, and yet she did not love him. There was no word of regret for the rest of her taunts, that he had been an animal, and the blow in his face! The recollection of this suddenly lashed him again, and made him rise to his feet, all the pride of his race flooding his being once more.

He put down his tea-cup on the mantelpiece untasted, and then said hoarsely:

"I married you because I loved you, and no man has ever regretted a thing more."

Then he turned round, and walked slowly from the room.

And Zara, left alone, felt that the end had come.

CHAPTER XXXV

A pale and most unhappy bride awaited her bridegroom in the boudoir at a few minutes to eight o'clock. She felt perfectly lifeless, as though she had hardly enough will left even to act her part. The white satin of her dress was not whiter than her face. The head gardener had sent up some splendid gardenias for her to wear and the sight of them pained her, for were not these the flowers that Tristram had brought her that evening of her wedding day, not a fortnight ago, and that she had then thrown into the grate. She pinned some in mechanically, and then let the maid clasp the diamonds round her throat and a band of them in her hair. They were so very beautiful, and she had not seen them before; she could not thank him for them even--all conversation except before people was now at an end. Then, for her further unhappiness, she remembered he had said: "When the mockery of the rejoicings is over then we can discuss our future plans." What did that mean? That he wished to separate from her, she supposed. How could circumstance be so cruel to her! What had she done? Then she sat down for a moment while she waited, and clenched her hands. And all the passionate resentment her deep nature was capable of surged up against fate, so that she looked more like the black panther than ever, and her mood had only dwindled into a sullen smoldering rage--while she still sat in the peculiar, concentrated attitude of an animal waiting to spring--when Tristram opened the door, and came in.

The sight of her thus, looking so unEnglish, so barbaric, suddenly filled him with the wild excitement of the lion hunt again. Could anything be more diabolically attractive? he thought, and for a second, the idea flashed across him that he would seize her to-night and treat her as if she were the panther she looked, conquer her by force, beat her if necessary, and then kiss her to death! Which plan, if he had carried it out, in this case, would have been very sensible, but the training of hundreds of years of chivalry toward women and things weaker than himself was still in his blood. For Tristram, twenty-fourth Baron Tancred, was no brute or sensualist, but a very fine specimen of his fine, old race.

So, his heart beating with some uncontrollable excitement, and her heart filled with smoldering rage, they descended the staircase, arm in arm, to the admiration of peeping housemaids and the pride of her own maid. And the female servants all rushed to the balustrade to get a better view of the delightful scene which, they had heard whispered among them, was a custom of generations in the family--that when the Lord of Wrayth first led his lady into the state dining-room for their first dinner alone he should kiss her before whoever was there, and bid her welcome to her new home. And to see his lordship, whom they all thought the handsomest young gentleman they had ever seen, kiss her ladyship, would be a thrill of the most agreeable kind!

What would their surprise have been, could they have heard him say icily to his bride as he descended the stairs:

"There is a stupid custom that I must kiss you as we go into the dining-room, and give you this little golden key--a sort of ridiculous emblem of the endowment of all the worldly goods business. The servants are, of course, looking at us, so please don't start." Then he glanced up and saw the rows of interested, excited faces; and that devil-may-care, rollicking boyishness which made him so adored came over him, and he laughed up at them, and waved his hand: and Zara's rage turned to wild excitement, too. There would be the walk across the hall of sixty paces, and then he would kiss her. What would it be like? In those sixty paces her face grew more purely white, while he came to the resolve that for this one second he would yield to temptation and not only brush her forehead with his lips, as had been his intention, but for once--just for this once--he would kiss her mouth. He was past caring about the footmen seeing. It was his only chance.

So when they came to the threshold of the big, double doors he bent down and drew her to him, and gave her the golden key. And then he pressed his warm, young, passionate lips to hers. Oh! the mad joy of it! And even if it were only from duty and to play the game, she had not resisted him as upon that other occasion. He felt suddenly, absolutely intoxicated, as he had done on the wedding night. Why, why must this ghastly barrier be between them? Was there nothing to be done?

Then he looked at his bride as they advanced to the table, and he saw that she was so deadly white that he thought she was going to faint. For intoxication, affects people in different ways; for her, the kiss had seemed the sweetness of death.

"Give her ladyship some champagne immediately," he ordered the butler, and, still with shining eyes, he looked at her, and said gently, "for we must drink our own healths."

But Zara never raised her lids, only he saw that her little nostrils were quivering, and by the rise and fall of her beautiful bosom he knew that her heart must be beating as madly as was his own--and a wild triumph filled him. Whatever the emotion she was experiencing, whether it was anger, or disdain, or one he did not dare to hope for, it was a considerably strong one; she was, then, not so icily cold! How he wished there were some more ridiculous customs in his family! How he wished he might order the servants out of the room, and begin to make love to her all alone. And just out of the devilment which was now in his blood he took the greatest pleasure in "playing the game," and while the solemn footmen's watchful eyes were upon them, he let himself go and was charming to her; and then, each instant they were alone he made himself freeze again, so that she could not say he was not keeping to the bargain. Thus in wild excitement for them both the dinner passed. With her it was alternate torture and pleasure as well, but with him, for the first time since his wedding, there was not any pain. For he felt he was affecting her, even if she were only "playing the game." And gradually, as the time went on and dessert was almost come, the conviction grew in Zara's brain that he was torturing her on purpose, overdoing the part when the servants were looking; for had he not told her but three hours before that he *had* loved her--using the past tense--and no man regretted a thing more! Perhaps--was it possible--he had seen when he kissed her that she loved him! And he was just punishing her, and laughing at his dominion over her in his heart; so her pride took fire at once. Well, she would not be played with! He would see she could keep to a bargain; and be icy, too, when the play was over. So when at last the servants had left the room, before coffee was brought, she immediately stiffened and fell into silence; and the two stared in front of them, and back over him crept the chill. Yes, there was no use deceiving himself. He had had his one moment of bliss, and now his purgatory would begin again.

Thus the comedy went on. Soon they had to go and open the ball, and they both won golden opinions from their first partners--hers, the stalwart bailiff, and his, the bailiff's wife.

"Although she is a foreigner, Agnes," Mr. Burrs said to his life's partner when they got home, "you'd hardly know it, and a lovelier lady I have never seen."

"She couldn't be too lovely for his lordship," his wife retorted. "Why, William, he made me feel young again!"

The second dance the bridal pair were supposed to dance together; and then when they should see the fun in full swing they were supposed to slip away, because it was considered quite natural that they might wish to be alone.

"You will have to dance with me now, I am afraid, Zara," Tristram said, and, without waiting for her answer, he placed his arm round her and began the valse. And the mad intoxication grew again in both of them, and they went on, never stopping, in a wild whirl of delight--unreasoning, passionate delight--until the music ceased.

Then Zara who, by long years of suffering, was the more controlled, pulled herself together first, and, with that ingrained instinct to defend herself and her secret love, and to save his possible true construction of her attitude, said stiffly:

"I suppose we can go now. I trust you think that I have 'played the game.'"

"Too terribly well," he said--stung back to reality. "It shows me what we have irreparably lost." And he gave her his arm and, passed down the lane of admiring and affectionate guests to their part of the house; and at the door of the boudoir he left her without a word.

So, with the bride in lonely anguish in the great state bed, the night of the home-coming passed, and the morrow dawned.

For thus the God of Pride makes fools of his worshipers.

*   *   *   *   *

It poured with rain the next day, but the same kind of thing went on for the different grades of those who lived under the wing of the Tancred name, and neither bride nor bridegroom failed in their roles, and the icy coldness between them increased. They had drawn upon themselves an atmosphere of absolute restraint and it seemed impossible to exchange even ordinary conversation; so that at this, their second dinner, they hardly even kept up a semblance before the household servants, and, being free from feasting, Zara retired almost immediately the coffee had come. One of the things Tristram had said to her before she left the room was:

"To-morrow if it is fine you had better see the gardens and really go over the house, if you wish. The housekeeper and the gardeners will think it odd if you don't! How awful it is to have to conform to convention!" he went on. "It would be good to be a savage again. Well, perhaps I shall be, some day soon."

Then as she paused in her starting for the door to hear what he had further to say, he continued:

"They let us have a day off to-morrow; they think, quite naturally, we require a rest. So if you will be ready about eleven I will show you the gardens and the parts my mother loved--it all looks pretty dreary this time of the year, but it can't be helped."

"I will be ready," Zara said.

"Then there is the Address from the townspeople at Wrayth, on Thursday," he continued, while he walked toward the door to open it for her, "and on Friday we go up to London to say good-bye to my mother. I hope you have not found it all too impossibly difficult, but it will soon be over now."

"The whole of life is difficult," she answered, "and one never knows what it is for, or why?" And then without anything further she went out of the door, and so upstairs and through all the lonely corridors to the boudoir. And here she opened the piano for the first time, and tried it; and finding it good she sat a long time playing her favorite airs--but not the **Chanson Triste**--she felt she could not bear that.

The music talked to her: what was her life going to be? What if, in the end, she could not control her love? What if it should break down her pride, and let him see that she regretted her past action and only longed to be in his arms. For her admiration and respect for him were growing each hour, as she discovered new traits in him, individually, and began to understand what he meant to all these people whose lord he was. How little she had known of England, her own father's country! How ridiculously little she had really known of men, counting them all brutes like Ladislaus and his friends, or feckless fools like poor Mimo! What an impossible attitude was this one she had worn always of arrogant ignorance! Something should have told her that these people were not like that. Something should have warned her, when she first saw him, that Tristram was a million miles above anything in the way of his sex that she had yet known. Then she stopped playing, and deliberately went over and looked in the glass. Yes, she was certainly beautiful, and quite young. She might live until she were seventy or eighty, in the natural course of events, and the whole of life would be one long, dreary waste if she might not have her Love. After all, pride was not worth so very much. Suppose she were very gentle to him, and tried to please him in just a friendly way, that would not be undignified nor seem to be throwing herself at his head. She would begin to-morrow, if she could. Then she remembered Lady Ethelrida's words at the dinner party--was it possible that was only three weeks ago this very night--the words that she had spoken so unconsciously, when she had showed so plainly the family feeling about Tristram and Cyril being the last in the male line of Tancred of Wrayth. She remembered how she had been angered and up in arms then, and now a whole education had passed over her, and she fully understood and sympathized with their point of view.

And at this stage of her meditations her eyes grew misty as they gazed into distance, and all soft; and the divine expression of the Sistine Madonna grew in them, as it grew always when she held Mirko in her arms.

Yes, there were things in life which mattered far, far more than pride. And so, comforted by her resolutions, she at last went to bed.

And Tristram sat alone by the fire in his own sitting-room, and stared at that other Tristram Guiscard's armor. And he, too, came to a resolution, but not of the same kind. He would speak to Francis Markrute when they arrived on Friday night and he could get him quietly alone. He would tell him that the whole thing was a ghastly failure, but as he had only himself to blame for entering into it he did not intend to reproach any one. Only, he would frankly ask him to use his clever brain and invent some plan that he and Zara could separate, without scandal, until such time as he should grow indifferent, and so could come back and casually live in the house with her. He was only a human man, he admitted, and the present arrangement was impossible to bear. He was past the anguish of the mockery of everything to-night--he was simply numb. Then some waiting fiend made him think of Laura and her last words. What if there were some truth in them after all? He had himself seen the man twice, under the most suspicious circumstances. What if he were her lover? How could Francis Markrute know of all her existence, when he had said she had been an immaculate wife? And gradually, on top of his other miseries, trifles light as air came and tortured him until presently he had worked up a whole chain of evidence, proving the lover theory to be correct!

Then he shook in his chair with rage, and muttered between his teeth: "If I find this is true then I will kill him, and kill her, also!"

So near to savages are all human beings, when certain passions are aroused. And neither bride nor bridegroom guessed that fate would soon take things out of their hands and make their resolutions null and void.

CHAPTER XXXVI

The gardens at Wrayth were famous. The natural beauty of their position and the endless care of generations of loving mistresses had left them a monument of what nature can be trained into by human skill. They had also in the eighteenth century by some happy chance escaped the hand of Capability Brown. And instead of pulling about and altering the taste of the predecessor the successive owners had used fresh ground for their fancies. Thus the English rose-garden and the Dutch-clipped yews of William-and-Mary's time were as intact as the Italian parterre.

But November is not the time to judge of gardens, and Tristram wished the sun would come out. He waited for his bride at the foot of the Adam staircase, and, at eleven, she came down. He watched her as she put one slender foot before the other in her descent, he had not noticed before how ridiculously inadequate they were--just little bits of baby feet, even in her thick walking-boots. She certainly knew how to dress--and adapt herself to the customs of a country. Her short, serge frock and astrakhan coat and cap were just the things for the occasion; and she looked so attractive and chic, with her hands in her monster muff, he began to have that pain again of longing for her, so he said icily:

"The sky is gray and horrid. You must not judge of things as you will see them to-day; it is all really rather nice in the summer."

"I am sure it is," she answered meekly, and then could not think of anything else to say, so they walked on in silence through the courtyard and round under a deep, arched doorway in the Norman wall to the southern side of the Adam erection, with its pillars making the centerpiece. The beautiful garden stretched in front of them. This particular part was said to have been laid out from plans of Le Notre, brought there by that French Lady Tancred who had been the friend of Louis XIV.

There were traces of her all over the house--Zara found afterwards. It was a most splendid and stately scene even in the dull November gloom, with the groups of statuary, and the ***tapis vert***, and the general look of Versailles. The vista was immense. She could see far beyond, down an incline, through a long clearing in the park, far away to the tower of Wrayth church.

"How beautiful it all is!" she said, with bated breath, and clasped her hands in her muff. "And how wonderful to have the knowledge that your family has been here always, and these splendid things are their creation. I understand that you must be a very proud man."

This was almost the longest speech he had ever heard her make, in ordinary conversation--the first one that contained any of her thoughts. He looked at her startled for a moment, but his resolutions of the night before and his mood of suspicion caused him to remain unmoved. He was numb with the pain of being melted one moment with hope and frozen again the next; it had come to a pass now that he would not let himself respond. She could almost have been as gracious as she pleased, out in this cold, damp air, and he would have remained aloof.

"Yes, I suppose I am a proud man," he said, "but it is not much good to me; one becomes a cynic, as one grows older."

Then with casual indifference he began to explain to her all about the gardens and their dates, as they walked along, just as though he were rather bored but acting cicerone to an ordinary guest, and Zara's heart sank lower and lower, and she could not keep up her little plan to be gentle and sympathetic; she could not do more than say just "Yes," and "No." Presently they came through a door to the hothouses, and she had to be introduced to the head gardener, a Scotchman, and express her admiration of everything, and eat some wonderful grapes; and here Tristram again "played the game," and chaffed, and was gay. And so they went out, and through a clipped, covered walk to another door in a wall, which opened on the west side--the very old part of the house--and suddenly she saw the Italian parterre. Each view as she came upon it she tried to identify with what she had seen in the pictures in ***Country Life***, but things look so different in reality, with the atmospheric effects, to the cold gray of a print. Only there was no mistake about this--the Italian parterre; and a sudden tightness grew round her heart, and she thought of Mirko and the day she had last seen him. And Tristram was startled into looking at her by a sudden catching of her breath, and to his amazement he perceived that her face was full of pain, as though she had revisited some scene connected with sorrowful memories. There was even a slight drawing back in her attitude, as if she feared to go on, and meet some ghost. What could it be? Then the malevolent sprite who was near him just now whispered: "It is an Italian garden, she has seen such before in other lands; perhaps the man is an Italian--he looks dark enough." So instead of feeling solicitous and gentle with whatever caused her pain--for his manners were usually extremely courteous, however cold--he said almost roughly:

"This seems to make you think of something! Well, let us get on and get it over, and then you can go in!"

He would be no sympathetic companion for her sentimental musings--over another man!

Her lips quivered for a moment, and he saw that he had struck home, and was glad, and grew more furious as he strode along. He would like to hurt her again if he could, for jealousy can turn an angel into a cruel fiend. They walked on in silence, and a look almost of fear crept into her tragic eyes. She dreaded so to come upon Pan and his pipes. Yes, as they descended the stone steps, there he was in the far distance with his back to them, forever playing his weird music for the delight of all growing things.

She forgot Tristram, forgot she was passionately preoccupied with him and passionately in love, forgot even that she was not alone. She saw the firelight again, and the pitiful, little figure of her poor, little brother as he poured over the picture, pointing with his sensitive forefinger to Pan's shape. She could hear his high, child-ish voice say: "See, Cherisette, he, too, is not made as other people are! Look, and he plays music, also. When I am with **Maman** and you walk there you must remember that this is me!"

And Tristram, watching her, knew not what to think. For her face had become more purely white than usual, and her dark eyes were swimming with tears.

God! how she must have loved this man! In wild rage he stalked beside her until they came quite close to the statue in the center of the star, surrounded by its pergola of pillars, which in the summer were gay with climbing roses.

Then he stepped forward, with a sharp exclamation of annoyance, for the pipes of Pan had been broken and lay there on the ground.

Who had done this thing?

When Zara saw the mutilation she gave a piteous cry; to her, to the mystic part of her strange nature, this was an omen. Pan's music was gone, and Mirko, too, would play no more.

With a wail like a wounded animal's she slipped down on the stone bench, and, burying her face in her muff, the tension of soul of all these days broke down, and she wept bitter, anguishing tears.

Tristram was dumbfounded. He knew not what to do. Whatever was the cause, it now hurt him horribly to see her weep--weep like this--as if with broken heart.

For her suffering was caused by remembrance--remembrance that, absorbed in her own concerns and heart-burnings over her love, she had forgotten the little one lately; and he was far away and might now be ill, and even dead.

She sobbed and sobbed and clasped her hands, and Tristram could not bear it any longer.

"Zara!" he said, distractedly. "For God's sake do not cry like this! What is it? Can I not help you--Zara?" And he sat down beside her and put his arm round her, and tried to draw her to him--he must comfort her whatever caused her pain.

But she started up and ran from him; he was the cause of her forgetfulness.

"Do not!" she cried passionately, that southern dramatic part of her nature coming out, here in her abandon of self-control. "Is it not enough for me to know that it is you and thoughts of you which have caused me to forget him!--Go! I must be alone!"--and like a fawn she fled down one of the paths, and beyond a great yew hedge, and so disappeared from view.

And Tristram sat on the stone bench, too stunned to move.

This was a confession from her, then--he realized, when his power came back to him. It was no longer surmise and suspicion--there was some one else. Some one to whom she owed--love. And he had caused her to forget him! And this thought made him stop his chain of reasoning abruptly. For what did that mean? Had he then, after all, somehow made her feel--made her think of him? Was this the secret in her strange mysterious face that drew him and puzzled him always? Was there some war going on in her heart?

But the comforting idea which he had momentarily obtained from that inference of her words went from him as he pondered, for nothing proved that her thoughts of him had been of love.

So, alternately trying to reason the thing out, and growing wild with passion and suspicion and pain, he at last went back to the house expecting he would have to go through the ordeal of luncheon alone; but as the silver gong sounded she came slowly down the stairs.

And except that she was very pale and blue circles surrounded her heavy eyes, her face wore a mask, and she was perfectly calm.

She made no apology, nor allusion to her outburst; she treated the incident as though it had never been! She held a letter in her hand, which had come by the second post while they were out. It was written by her uncle from London, the night before, and contained his joyous news.

Tristram looked at her and was again dumbfounded. She was certainly a most extraordinary woman. And some of his rage died down and he decided he would not, after all, demand an explanation of her now; he would let the whole, hideous rejoicings be finished first and then, in London, he would sternly investigate the truth. And not the least part of his pain was the haunting uncertainty as to what her words could mean, as regarded himself. If by some wonderful chance it were some passion in the past and she now loved him, he feared he could forgive her--he feared even his pride would not hold out over the mad happiness it would be to feel her unresisting and loving, lying in his arms!

So with stormy eyes and forced smiles the pair sat down to luncheon, and Zara handed him the epistle she carried in her hand. It ran:

"MY DEAR NIECE:

"I have to inform you of a piece of news that is a great gratification to myself, and I trust will cause you, too, some pleasure.

"Lady Ethelrida Montfitchet has done me the honor to accept my proposal for her hand, and the Duke, her father, has kindly given his hearty consent to my marriage with his daughter, which is to take place as soon as things can be arranged with suitability. I hope you and Tristram will arrive in time to accompany me to dinner at Glastonbury House on Friday evening, when you can congratulate my beloved fiance, who holds you in affectionate regard.

"I am, my dear niece, always your devoted uncle,

"FRANCIS MARKRUTE."

When Tristram finished reading he exclaimed:

"Good Lord!" For, quite absorbed in his own affairs, he had never even noticed the financier's peregrinations! Then as he looked at the letter again he said meditatively:

"I expect they will be awfully happy--Ethelrida is such an unselfish, sensible, darling girl--"

And it hurt Zara even in her present mood, for she felt the contrast to herself in his unconscious tone.

"My uncle never does anything without having calculated it will turn out perfectly," she said bitterly--"only sometimes it can happen that he plays with the wrong pawns."

And Tristram wondered what she meant. He and she had certainly been pawns in one of the Markrute games, and now he began to see this object, just as Zara had done. Then the thought came to him.--Why should he not now ask her straight out--why she had married him? It was not from any desire for himself, nor his position, he knew that: but for what?

So, the moment the servants went out of the room to get the coffee--after a desultory conversation about the engagement until then, he said coldly:

"You told me on Monday that you now know the reason I had married you: may I ask you why did you marry me?"

She clasped her hands convulsively. This brought it all back--her poor little brother--and she was not free yet from her promise to her uncle: she never failed to keep her word.

A look of deep, tragic earnestness grew in her pools of ink, and she said to him, with a strange sob in her voice:

"Believe me I had a strong reason, but I cannot tell it to you now."

And the servants reentered the room at the moment, so he could not ask her why: it broke the current.

But what an unexpected inference she always put into affairs! What was the mystery? He was thrilled with suspicious, terrible interest. But of one thing he felt sure--Francis Markrute did not really know.

And in spite of his chain of reasoning about this probable lover some doubt about it haunted him always; her air was so pure--her mien so proud.

And while the servants were handing the coffee and still there Zara rose, and, making the excuse that she must write to her uncle at once, left the room to avoid further questioning. Then Tristram leant his head upon his hands and tried to think.

He was in a maze--and there seemed no way out. If he went to her now and demanded to have everything explained he might have some awful confirmation of his suspicions, and then how could they go through to-morrow--and the town's address? Of all things he had no right--just because of his wild passion in marrying this foreign woman--he had no right to bring disgrace and scandal upon his untarnished name: "noblesse oblige" was the motto graven on his soul. No, he must bear it until Friday night after the Glastonbury House dinner. Then he would face her and demand the truth.

And Zara under the wing of Mrs. Anglin made a thorough tour of the beautiful, old house. She saw its ancient arras hangings, and panellings of carved oak, and heard all the traditions, and looked at the portraits--many so wonderfully like Tristram, for they were a strong, virile race--and her heart ached, and swelled with pride, alternately. And, last of all, she stood under the portrait that had been painted by Sargent, of her husband at his coming of age, and that master of art had given him, on the canvas, his very soul. There he stood, in a scarlet hunt-coat--debonair, and strong, and true--with all the promise of a noble, useful life in his dear, blue eyes. And suddenly this proud woman put her hand to her throat to check the sob that rose there; and then, again, out of the mist of her tears she saw Pan and his broken pipes.

CHAPTER XXXVII

Tristram passed the afternoon outdoors, inspecting the stables, and among his own favorite haunts, and then rushed in, too late for tea and only just in time to catch the post. He wrote a letter to Ethelrida, and his uncle-in-law that was to be. How ridiculous that sounded! He would be his uncle and Zara's cousin now, by marriage! Then, when he thought of this dear Ethelrida whom he had loved more than his own young sisters, he hurriedly wrote out, as well, a telegram of affection and congratulation which he handed to Michelham as he came in to get the letters--and the old man left the room. Then Tristram remembered that he had addressed the telegram to Montfitchet, and Ethelrida would, of course, he now recollected, be at Glastonbury House, as she was coming up that day--so he went to the door and called out:

"Michelham, bring me back the telegram."

And the grave servant, who was collecting all the other letters from the post-box in the hall, returned and placed beside his master on the table a blue envelope. There were always big blue envelopes, for the sending of telegrams, on all the writing tables at Wrayth.

Tristram hurriedly wrote out another and handed it, and the servant finally left the room. Then he absently pulled out his original one and glanced at it before tearing it up; and before he realized what he did his eye caught: "To Count Mimo Sykypri"--he did not read the address--"Immediately, to-morrow, wire me your news. Cherisette."

And ere his rage burst in a terrible oath he noticed that stamps were enclosed. Then he threw the paper with violence into the fire!

There was not any more doubt nor speculation; a woman did not sign herself "Cherisette"--"little darling"--except to a lover! Cherisette! He was so mad with rage that if she had come into the room at that moment he would have strangled her, there and then.

He forgot that it was time to dress for dinner--forgot everything but his over-mastering fury. He paced up and down the room, and then after a while, as ever, his balance returned. The law could give him no redress yet: she certainly had not been unfaithful to him in their brief married life, and the law recks little of sins committed before the tie. Nothing could come now of going to her and reproaching her--only a public scandal and disgrace. No, he must play his part until he could consult with Francis Markrute, learn all the truth, and then concoct some plan. Out of all the awful ruin of his life he could at least save his name. And after some concentrated moments of agony he mastered himself at last sufficiently to go to his room and dress for dinner.

But Count Mimo Sykypri would get no telegram that night!

The idea that there could be any scandalous interpretations put upon any of her actions or words never even entered Zara's brain; so innocently unconscious was she of herself and her doings that that possible aspect of the case never struck her. She was the last type of person to make a mystery or in any way play a part. The small subtly-created situations and hidden darknesses and mysterious appearances which delighted the puny soul of Laura Highford were miles beneath her feet. If she had even faintly dreamed that some doubts were troubling Tristram she would have plainly told him the whole story and chanced her uncle's wrath. But she had not the slightest idea of it. She only knew that Tristram was stern and cold, and showed his disdain of her, and that even though she had made up her mind to be gentle and try to win him back with friendship, it was almost impossible. She looked upon his increased, icy contempt of her at dinner as a protest at her outburst of tears during the day.

So the meal was got through, and the moment the coffee was brought he gulped it down, and then rose: he could not stand being alone with her for a moment.

She was looking so beautiful, and so meek, and so tragic, he could not contain the mixed emotions he felt. He only knew if he had to bear them another minute he should go mad. So, hardly with sufficient politeness he said:

"I have some important documents to look over; I will wish you good night." And he hurried her from the room and went on to his own sitting-room in the other part of the house. And Zara, quite crushed with her anxiety and sorrow about Mirko, and passionately unhappy at Tristram's treatment of her, once more returned to her lonely room. And here she dismissed her maid, and remained looking out on the night. The mist had gone and some pure, fair stars shone out.

Was that where *Maman* was--up there? And was Mirko going to her soon, away out of this cruel world of sorrow and pain? As he had once said, surely there, there would be room for them both.

But Zara was no morbidly sentimental person, the strong blood ran in her veins, and she knew she must face her life and be true to herself, whatever else might betide. So after a while the night airs soothed her, and she said her prayers and went to bed.

But Tristram, her lord, paced the floor of his room until almost dawn.

*   *   *   *   *

The next day passed in the same kind of way, only, it was nearly all in public, with local festivities again; and both of the pair played their parts well, as they were now experienced actors, and only one incident marked the pain of this Thursday out from the pains of the other days. It was in the schoolhouse at Wrayth, where the buxom girl who had been assistant mistress, and had married, a year before, brought her first-born son to show the lord and lady--as he had been born on their wedding day, just a fortnight ago! She was pale and wan, but so ecstatically proud and happy looking; and Tristram at once said, they--he and Zara--must be the god-parents of her boy; and Zara held the crimson, crumpled atom for a moment, and then looked up and met her husband's eyes, and saw that they had filled with tears. And she returned the creature to its mother--but she could not speak, for a moment.

And finally they had come home again--home to Wrayth--and no more unhappy pair of young, healthy people lived on earth.

Zara could hardly contain her impatience to see if a telegram for her from Mimo had come in her absence. Tristram saw her look of anxiety and strain, and smiled grimly to himself. She would get no answering telegram from her lover that day!

And, worn out with the whole thing, Zara turned to him and asked if it would matter or look unusual if she said--what was true--that she was so fatigued she would like to go to bed and not have to come down to dinner.

"I will not do so, if it would not be in the game," she said.

And he answered, shortly:

"The game is over, to-night: do as you please."

So she went off sadly, and did not see him again until they were ready to start in the morning--the Friday morning, which Tristram called the beginning of the end!

He had arranged that they should go by train, and not motor up, as he usually did because he loved motoring; but the misery of being so close to her, even now when he hoped he loathed and despised her, was too great to chance. So, early after lunch, they started, and would be at Park Lane after five. No telegram had come for Zara--Mimo must be away--but, in any case, it indicated nothing unusual was happening, unless he had been called to Bournemouth by Mirko himself and had left hurriedly. This idea so tortured her that by the time she got to London she could not bear it, and felt she must go to Neville Street and see. But how to get away?

Francis Markrute was waiting for them in the library, and seemed so full of the exuberance of happiness that she could not rush off until she had poured out and pretended to enjoy a lengthy tea.

And the change in the reserved man struck them both. He seemed years younger, and full of the milk of human kindness. And Tristram thought of himself on the day he had gone to Victoria to meet Zara, when she had come from Paris, and he had given a beggar half a sovereign, from sheer joy of life.

For happiness and wine open men's hearts. He would not attempt to speak about his own troubles until the morning: it was only fair to leave the elderly lover without cares until after the dinner at Glastonbury House.

At last Zara was able to creep away. She watched her chance, and, with the cunning of desperation, finding the hall momentarily empty, stealthily stole out of the front door. But it was after half-past six o'clock, and they were dining at Glastonbury House, St. James's Square, at eight.

She got into a taxi quickly, finding one in Grosvenor Street because she was afraid to wait to look in Park Lane, in case, by chance, she should be observed; and at last she reached the Neville Street lodging, and rang the noisy bell.

The slatternly little servant said that the gentleman was "hout," but would the lady come in and wait? He would not be long, as he had said "as how he was only going to take a telegram."

Zara entered at once. A telegram!--perhaps for her--Yes, surely for her. Mimo had no one else, she knew, to telegraph to. She went up to the dingy attic studio. The fire was almost out, and the little maid lit one candle and placed it upon a table. It was very cold on this damp November day. The place struck her as piteously poor, after the grandeur from which she had come. Dear, foolish, generous Mimo! She must do something for him--and would plan how. The room had the air of scrupulous cleanness which his things always wore, and there was the "Apache" picture waiting for her to take, in a new gold frame; and the "London Fog" seemed to be advanced, too; he had evidently worked at it late, because his palette and brushes, still wet, were on a box beside it, and on a chair near was his violin. He was no born musician like Mirko, but played very well. The palette and brushes showed he must have put them hurriedly down. What for? Why? Had some message come for him? Had he heard news? And a chill feeling gripped her heart. She looked about to see if Mirko had written a letter, or one of his funny little postcards? No, there was nothing--nothing she had not seen except, yes, just this one on a picture of the town. Only a few words: "Thank Cherisette for her letter, Agatha is *tres jolie*, but does not understand the violin, and wants to play it herself. And heavens! the noise!" How he managed to post these cards was always a mystery; they were marked with the mark of doubling up twice, so it showed he concealed them somewhere and perhaps popped them into a pillar-box, when out for a walk. This one was dated two days ago. Could anything have happened since? She burned with impatience for Mimo to come in.

A cheap, little clock struck seven. Where could he be? The minutes seemed to drag into an eternity. All sorts of possibilities struck her, and then she controlled herself and became calm.

There was a large photograph of her mother, which Mimo had colored really well. It was in a silver frame upon the mantelpiece, and she gazed and gazed at that, and whispered aloud in the gloomy room:

"Maman, adoree! Take care of your little one now, even if he must come to you soon."

And beside this there was another, of Mimo, taken at the same time, when Zara and her mother had gone to the Emperor's palace in that far land. How wonderfully handsome he was then, and even still!--and how the air of *insouciance* suited him, in that splendid white and gold uniform. But Mimo looked always a gentleman, even in his shabbiest coat.

And now that she knew what the passion of love meant herself, she better understood how her mother had loved. She had never judged her mother, it was not in her nature to judge any one; underneath the case of steel which her bitter life had wrought her, Zara's heart was as tender as an angel's.

Then she thought of the words in the Second Commandment: "And the sins of the fathers shall be visited upon the children." Had they sinned, then? And if so how terribly cruel such Commandments were--to make the innocent children suffer. Mirko and she were certainly paying some price. But the God that *Maman* had gone to and loved and told her children of, was not really cruel, and some day perhaps she--Zara--would come into peace on earth. And Mirko? Mirko would be up there, happy and safe with *Maman*.

The cheap clock showed nearly half-past seven. She could not wait another moment, and also she reasoned if Mimo were sending her a telegram it would be to Park Lane. He knew she was coming up; she would get it there on her return, so she scribbled a line to Count Sykypri, and told him she had been--and why--and that she must hear at once, and then she left and hurried back to her uncle's house. And when she got there it was twenty minutes to eight.

Her maid had been dreadfully worried, as she had given no orders as to what she would wear--but Henriette, being a person of intelligence, had put out what she thought best,--only she could not prevent her anxiety and impatience from causing her to go on to the landing, and hang over the stairs at every noise; and Tristram, coming out of his room already dressed, found her there--and asked her what she was doing.

"I wait for *Miladi*, *Milor*, she have not come in," Henriette said. "And I so fear *Miladi* will be late."

Tristram felt his heart stop beating for a second--strong man as he was. *Miladi* had not come in!--But as they spoke, he perceived her on the landing below, hurrying up--she had not waited to get the lift--and he went down to meet her, while Henriette returned to her room.

"Where have you been?" he demanded, with a pale, stern face. He was too angry and suspicious to let her pass in silence, and he noticed her cheeks were flushed with nervous excitement and that she was out of breath; and no wonder, for she had run up the stairs.

"I cannot wait to tell you now," she panted. "And what right have you to speak to me so? Let me pass, or I shall be late."

"I do not care if you are late, or no. You shall answer me!" he said furiously, barring the way. "You bear my name, at all events, and I have a right because of that to know."

"Your name?" she said, vaguely, and then for the first time she grasped that there was some insulting doubt of her in his words.

She cast upon him a look of withering scorn, and, with the air of an empress commanding an insubordinate guard, she flashed:

"Let me pass at once!"

But Tristram did not move, and for a second they glared at one another, and she took a step forward as if to force her way. Then he angrily seized her in his arms. But at that moment Francis Markrute came out of his room and Tristram let her go--panting. He could not make a scene, and she went on, with her head set haughtily, to her room.

"I see you have been quarreling again," her uncle said, rather irritably: and then he laughed as he went down.

"I expect she will be late," he continued; "well, if she is not in the hall at five minutes to eight, I shall go on."

And Tristram sat down upon the deep sofa on the broad landing outside her room, and waited: the concentrated essence of all the rage and pain he had yet suffered seemed to be now in his heart.

But what had it meant--that look of superb scorn? She had no mien of a guilty person.

At six minutes to eight she opened the door, and came out. She had simply flown into her clothes, in ten minutes! Her eyes were still black as night with resentment, and her bosom rose and fell, while in her white cheeks two scarlet spots flamed.

"I am ready," she said, haughtily, "let us go," and not waiting for her husband she swept on down the stairs, exactly as her uncle opened the library door.

"Well done, my punctual niece!" he cried genially. "You are a woman of your word."

"In all things," she answered, fiercely, and went towards the door, where the electric brougham waited.

And both men as they followed her wondered what she could mean.

CHAPTER XXXVIII

The dinner for Ethelrida's betrothal resembled in no way the one for Zara and Tristram; for, except in those two hearts there was no bitter strain, and the fiances in this case were radiantly happy, which they could not conceal, and did not try to.

The Dowager Lady Tancred arrived a few minutes after the party of three, and Zara heard her mother-in-law gasp, as she said, "Tristram, my dear boy!" and then she controlled the astonishment in her voice, and went on more ordinarily, but still a little anxiously, "I hope you are very well?"

So he was changed then--to the eye of one who had not seen him since the wedding--and Zara glanced at him critically, and saw that--yes, he was, indeed, changed. His face was perfectly set and stern, and he looked older. It was no wonder his mother should be surprised.

Then Lady Tancred turned to Zara and kissed her. "Welcome back, my dear daughter," she said. And Zara tried to answer something pleasant: above all things, this proud lady who had so tenderly given her son's happiness into her keeping must not guess how much there was amiss.

But Lady Tancred was no simpleton--she saw immediately that her son must have gone through much suffering and strain. What was the matter? It tore her heart, but she knew him too well to say anything to him about it.

So she continued to talk agreeably to them, and Tristram made a great effort, and chaffed her, and became gay. And soon they went in to dinner. And Lady Tancred sat on Francis Markrute's other side, and tried to overcome her prejudice against him. If Ethelrida loved him so much he must be really nice. And Zara sat on one side of the old Duke, and Lady Anningford on the other, and on her other side was Young Billy who was now in an idiotic state of calf love for her--to the amusement of every one. So, with much gayety and chaff the repast came to an end, and the ladies, who were all old friends--no strangers now among them--disposed themselves in happy groups about one of the drawing-rooms, while they sipped their coffee.

Ethelrida drew Zara aside to talk to her alone.

"Zara," she said, taking her soft, white hand, "I am so awfully happy with my dear love that I want you to be so, too. Dearest Zara, won't you be friends with me, now--real friends?"

And Zara, won by her gentleness, pressed Ethelrida's hand with her other hand.

"I am so glad, nothing my uncle could have done would have given me so much pleasure," she said, with a break in her voice. "Yes, indeed, I will be friends with you, dear Ethelrida. I am so glad--and touched--that you should care to have me as your friend." Then Ethelrida bent forward and kissed her. "When one is as happy as I am," she said, "it makes one feel good, as if one wanted to do all the kind things and take away all sorrow out of the world. I have thought sometimes, Zara dear, that you did not look as happy as--as--I would like you to look."

Happy! the mockery of the word!

"Ethelrida," Zara whispered hurriedly--"don't--don't ask me anything about it, please, dear. No one can help me. I must come through with it alone--but you of Tristram's own family, and especially you whom he loves so much, I don't want you ever to misjudge me. You think perhaps I have made him unhappy. Oh, if you only knew it all!--Yes, I have. And I did not know, nor understand. I would die for him now, if I could, but it is too late; we can only play the game!"

"Zara, do not say this!" said Ethelrida, much distressed. "What can it be that should come between such beautiful people as you? And Tristram adores you, Zara dear."

"He did love me--once," Zara answered sadly, "but not now. He would like never to have to see me again. Please do not let us talk of it; please--I can't bear any more."

And Ethelrida, watching her face anxiously, saw that it wore a hopeless, hunted look, as though some agonizing trouble and anxiety brooded over her. And poor Zara could say nothing of her other anxiety, for now that Ethelrida was engaged to her uncle her lips, about her own sorrow concerning her little brother, must be more than ever sealed. Perhaps--she did not know much of the English point of view yet--perhaps if the Duke knew that there was some disgrace in the background of the family he might forbid the marriage, and then she would be spoiling this sweet Ethelrida's life.

And Ethelrida's fine senses told her there was no use pressing the matter further, whatever the trouble was this was not the moment to interfere; so she turned the conversation to lighter things, and, finally, talked about her own wedding, and so the time passed.

The Dowager Lady Tancred was too proud to ask any one any questions, although she talked alone with Lady Anningford and could easily have done so: the only person she mentioned her anxiety to was her brother, the Duke, when, later, she spoke a few words with him alone.

"Tristram looks haggard and very unhappy, Glastonbury," she said simply, "have you anything to tell me about it?"

"My dear Jane," replied the Duke, "it is the greatest puzzle in the world; no one can account for it. I gave him some sound advice at Montfitchet, when I saw things were so strained, and I don't believe he has taken it, by the look of them to-night. These young, modern people are so unnaturally cold, though I did hear they had got through the rejoicings, in fine style."

"It troubles me very much, Glastonbury--to go abroad and leave him looking like that. Is it her fault? Or what--do you think?"

"'Pon my soul, I can't say--even the Crow could not unravel the mystery. Laura Highford was at Montfitchet--confound her--would come; can she have had anything to do with it, I wonder?"

Then they were interrupted and no more could be said, and finally the party broke up, with the poor mother's feeling of anxiety unassuaged. Tristram and Zara were to lunch with her to-morrow, to say good-bye, and then she was going to Paris--by the afternoon train.

And Francis Markrute staying on to smoke a cigar with the Duke, and, presumably, to say a snatched good night to his fiance, Tristram was left to take Zara home alone.

Now would come the moment of the explanation! But she outwitted him, for they no sooner got into the brougham and he had just begun to speak than she leaned back and interrupted him:

"You insinuated something on the stairs this evening, the vileness of which I hardly understood at first; I warn you I will hear no more upon the subject!" and then her voice broke suddenly and she said, passionately and yet with a pitiful note, "Ah! I am suffering so to-night, please--please don't speak to me--leave me alone."

And Tristram was silenced. Whatever it was that soon she must explain, he could not torture her to-night, and, in spite of his anger and suspicions and pain, it hurt him to see her, when the lights flashed in upon them, huddled up in the corner--her eyes like a wounded deer's.

"Zara!" he said at last--quite gently, "what is this, awful shadow that is hanging over you?--If you will only tell me--" But at that moment they arrived at the door, which was immediately opened, and she walked in and then to the lift without answering, and entering, closed the door. For what could she say?

She could bear things no longer. Tristram evidently saw she had some secret trouble, she would get her uncle to release her from her promise, as far as her husband was concerned at least,--she hated mysteries, and if it had annoyed him for her to be out late she would tell him the truth--and about Mirko, and everything.

Evidently he had been very much annoyed at that, but this was the first time he had even suggested he had noticed she was troubled about anything, except that day in the garden at Wrayth. Her motives were so perfectly innocent that not the faintest idea even yet dawned upon her that anything she had ever done could even look suspicious. Tristram was angry with her because she was late, and had insinuated something out of jealousy; men were always jealous, she knew, even if they were perfectly indifferent to a woman. What really troubled her terribly to-night Was the telegram she found in her room. She had told the maid to put it there when it came. It was from Mimo, saying Mirko was feverish again--really ill, he feared, this time.

So poor Zara spent a night of anguish and prayer, little knowing what the morrow was to bring.

And Tristram went out again to the Turf, and tried to divert his mind away from his troubles. There was no use in speculating any further, he must wait for an explanation which he would not consent to put off beyond the next morning.

So at last the day of a pitiful tragedy dawned.

Zara got up and dressed early. She must be ready to go out to try and see Mimo, the moment she could slip away after breakfast, so she came down with her hat on: she wanted to speak to her uncle alone, and Tristram, she thought, would not be there so early--only nine o'clock.

"This is energetic, my niece!" Francis Markrute said, but she hardly answered him, and as soon as Turner and the footman had left the room she began at once:

"Tristram was very angry with me last night because I was out late. I had gone to obtain news of Mirko, I am very anxious about him and I could give Tristram no explanation. I ask you to relieve me from my promise not to tell him--about things."

The financier frowned. This was a most unfortunate moment to revive the family skeleton, but he was a very just man and he saw, directly, that suspicion of any sort was too serious a thing to arouse in Tristram's mind.

"Very well," he said, "tell him what you think best. He looks desperately unhappy--you both do--are you keeping him at arm's length all this time, Zara? Because if so, my child, you will lose him, I warn you. You cannot treat a man of his spirit like that; he will leave you if you do."

"I do not want to keep him at arm's length; he is there of his own will. I told you at Montfitchet everything is too late--"

Then the butler entered the room: "Some one wishes to speak to your ladyship on the telephone, immediately," he said.

And Zara forgot her usual dignity as she almost rushed across the hall to the library, to talk:--it was Mimo, of course, so her presence of mind came to her and as the butler held the door for her she said, "Call a taxi at once."

She took the receiver up, and it was, indeed, Mimo's voice--and in terrible distress.

It appeared from his almost incoherent utterances that little Agatha had teased Mirko and finally broken his violin. And that this had so excited him, in his feverish state, that it had driven him almost mad, and he had waited until all the household, including the nurse, were asleep, and, with superhuman cunning, crept from his bed and dressed himself, and had taken the money which his Cherisette had given him for an emergency that day in the Park, and which he had always kept hidden in his desk; and he had then stolen out and gone to the station--all in the night, alone, the poor, poor lamb!--and there he had waited until the Weymouth night mail had come through, and had bought a ticket, and got in, and come to London to find his father--with the broken violin wrapped in its green baize cover. And all the while coughing--coughing enough to kill him! And he had arrived with just enough money to pay a cab, and had come at about five o'clock and could hardly wake the house to be let in; and he, Mimo, had heard the noise and come down, and there found the little angel, and brought him in, and warmed him in his bed. And he had waited to boil him some hot milk before he could come to the public telephone near, to call her up. Oh! but he was very ill--very, very ill--and could she come at once--but oh!--at once!

And Tristram, entering the room at that moment, saw her agonized face and heard her say, "Yes, yes, dear Mimo, I will come now!" and before he could realize what she was doing she brushed past him and rushed from the room, and across the hall and down to the waiting taxicab into which she sprang, and told the man where to go, with her head out of the window, as he turned into Grosvenor Street.

The name "Mimo" drove Tristram mad again. He stood for a moment, deciding what to do, then he seized his coat and hat and rushed out after her, to the amazement of the dignified servants. Here he hailed another taxi, but hers was just out of sight down to Park Street, when he got into his.

"Follow that taxi!" he said to the driver, "that green one in front of you--I will give you a sovereign if you never lose sight of it."

So the chase began! He must see where she would go! "Mimo!" the "Count Sykypri" she had telegraphed to--and she had the effrontery to talk to her lover, in her uncle's house! Tristram was so beside himself with rage he knew if he found them meeting at the end he would kill her. His taxi followed the green one, keeping it always in view, right on to Oxford Street, then Regent Street, then Mortimer Street. Was she going to Euston Station? Another of those meetings perhaps in a waiting-room, that Laura had already described! Unutterable disgust as well as blind fury filled him. He was too overcome with passion to reason with himself even. No, it was not Euston--they were turning into the Tottenham Court Road-- and so into a side street. And here a back tire on his taxi went, with a loud report, and the driver came to a stop. And, almost foaming with rage, Tristram saw the green taxi disappear round the further corner of a mean street, and he knew it would be lost to view before he could overtake it: there was none other in sight. He flung the man some money and almost ran down the road--and, yes, when he turned the corner he could see the green taxi in the far distance; it was stopping at a door. He had caught her then, after all! He could afford to go slowly now. She had entered the house some five or ten minutes before he got there. He began making up his mind.

It was evidently a most disreputable neighborhood. A sickening, nauseating revulsion crept over him: Zara--the beautiful, refined Zara--to be willing to meet a lover here! The brute was probably ill, and that was why she had looked so distressed. He walked up and down rapidly twice, and then he crossed the road and rang the bell; the taxi was still at the door. It was opened almost immediately by the little, dirty maid--very dirty in the early morning like this.

He controlled his voice and asked politely to be taken to the lady who had just gone in. With a snivel of tears Jenny asked him to follow her, and, while she was mounting in front of him, she turned and said: "It ain't no good, doctor, I ken tell yer; my mother was took just like that, and after she'd once broke the vessel she didn't live a hour." And by this time they had reached the attic door which, without knocking Jenny opened a little, and, with another snivel, announced, "The doctor, missis."

And Tristram entered the room.

CHAPTER XXXIX

And this is what he saw.

The poor, mean room, with its scrupulous neatness slightly disturbed by the evidences of the boiling of milk and the warming of flannel, and Zara, kneeling by the low, iron bed where lay the little body of a child. For Mirko had dwindled, these last weeks of his constant fever, so that his poor, small frame, undersized for his age at any time, looked now no more than that of a boy of six years old. He was evidently dying. Zara held his tiny hand, and the divine love and sorrowful agony in her face wrung her husband's soul. A towel soaked with blood had fallen to the floor, and lay there, a ghastly evidence of the "broken vessel" Jenny had spoken of. Mimo, with his tall, military figure shaking with dry sobs, stood on the other side, and Zara murmured in a tender voice of anguish: "My little one! My Mirko!" She was oblivious in her grief of any other presence--and the dying child opened his eyes and called faintly, "Maman!"

Then Mimo saw Tristram by the door, and advanced with his finger on his quivering lips to meet him.

"Ah, sir," he said. "Alas! you have come too late. My child is going to God!"

And all the manhood in Tristram's heart rose up in pity. Here was a tragedy too deep for human judgment, too deep for thoughts of vengeance, and without a word he turned and stole from the room. And as he stumbled down the dark, narrow stairs he heard the sound of a violin as it wailed out the beginning notes of the **Chanson Triste**, and he shivered, as if with cold.

For Mirko had opened his piteous eyes again, and whispered in little gasps:

"Papa--play to me the air **Mamam** loved. I can see her blue gauze wings!" And in a moment, as his face filled with the radiance of his vision he fell back, dead, into Zara's arms.

When Tristram reached the street he looked about him for a minute like a blinded man; and then, as his senses came back to him, his first thought was what he could do for her--that poor mother upstairs, with her dying child. For that the boy was Zara's child he never doubted. Her child--and her lover's--had he not called her "Maman." So this was the awful tragedy in her life. He analyzed nothing as yet; his whole being was paralyzed with the shock and the agony of things: the only clear thought he had was that he must help her in whatever way he could.

The green taxi was still there, but he would not take it, in case she should want it. He walked on down the street and found a cab for himself, and got driven to his old rooms in St. James's Street: he must be alone to think.

The hall-porter was surprised to see him. Nothing was ready for his lordship--but his wife would come up--?

But his lordship required nothing, he wished to find something alone.

He did not even notice that there was no fire in the grate, and that the room was icy cold--the agony of pain in his mind and soul made him unconscious of lesser ills. He pulled one of the holland sheets off his own big chair, and sat down in it.

Poor Zara, poor, unhappy Zara!--were his first thoughts--then he stiffened suddenly. This man must have been her lover before even her first marriage!--for Francis Markrute had told him she had married very soon. She was twenty-three years old now, and the child could not have been less than six; he must have been born when she was only seventeen. What devilish passion in a man could have made him tempt a girl so young! Of course this was her secret, and Francis Markrute knew nothing of it. For one frightful moment the thought came that her husband was not really dead and that this was he: but no, her husband's name had been Ladislaus, and this man she had called "Mimo," and if the boy were the child of her marriage there need then have been no secret about his existence. There was no other solution--this Count Sykypri had been her lover when she was a mere child, and probably the concealment had gone through all her first married life. And no doubt her reason for marrying him, which she admitted was a very strong one, had been that she might have money to give to the child--and its father.

The sickening--sickening, squalid tragedy of it all!

And she, Zara, had seemed so proud and so pure! Her look of scorn, only the night before, at his jealous accusation, came back to him. He could not remember a single movement nor action of hers that had not been that of an untarnished queen. What horrible actresses women were! His whole belief had crumbled to the dust.

And the most terrible part of it all to him was the knowledge that in spite of everything he still loved her--loved her with a consuming, almighty passion that he knew nothing now could kill. It had been put to the bitterest proof. Whatever she had done he could love no other woman.

Then he realized that his life was over. The future a blank, unutterable, hopeless gray which must go on for years and years. For he could never come back to her again, nor even live in the house with her, under the semblance of things.

Then an agonizing bitterness came to him, the hideous malevolence of fate, not to have let him meet this woman first before this other man; think of the faithfulness of her nature, with all its cruel actions to himself! She had been absolutely faithful to her lover, and had defended herself from his--Tristram's--caresses, even of her finger-tips. What a love worth having, what a strong, true character--worth dying for--in a woman!

And now, he must never see her again; or, if once more, only for a business meeting, to settle things without scandal to either of them.

He would not go back to Park Lane, yet--not for a week; he would give her time to see to the funeral, without the extra pain of his presence.

The man had taken him for the doctor, and she had not even been aware of his entrance: he would go back to Wrayth, alone, and there try to think out some plan. So he searched among the covered-up furniture for his writing table, and found some paper, and sat down and wrote two notes, one to his mother. He could not face her to-day--she must go without seeing him--but he knew his mother loved him, and, in all deep moments, never questioned his will even if she did not understand it.

The note to her was very short, merely saying something was troubling him greatly for the time, so neither he nor Zara would come to luncheon; and she was to trust him and not speak of this to any one until he himself told her more. He might come and see her in Cannes, the following week.

Then he wrote to Zara, and these were his words:

"I know everything. I understand now, and however I blame you for your deception of me you have my deep sympathy in your grief. I am going away for a week, so you will not be distressed by seeing me. Then I must ask you to meet me, here or at your uncle's house, to arrange for our future separation.

"Yours,

"Tancred."

Then he rang for a messenger boy, and gave him both notes, and, picking up the telephone, called up his valet and told him to pack and bring his things here to his old rooms, and, if her ladyship came in, to see that she immediately got the note he was sending round to her. Francis Markrute would have gone to the City by now and was going to lunch with Ethelrida, so he telephoned to one of his clerks there--finding he was out for the moment--just to say he was called away for a week and would write later.

She should have the first words with her uncle. Whether she would tell him or no she must decide, he would not do anything to make her existence more difficult than it must naturally be.

And then when all this was done the passionate jealousy of a man overcame him again, and when he thought of Mimo he once more longed to kill.

CHAPTER XL

It was late in the afternoon when Zara got back to her uncle's house. She had been too distracted with grief to know or care about time, or what they would be thinking of her absence.

Just after the poor little one was dead frantic telegrams had come from the Morleys, in consternation at his disappearance, and Mimo, quite prostrate in his sorrow, as he had been at her mother's death, had left all practical things to Zara.

No doctor turned up, either. Mimo had not coherently given the address, on the telephone. Thus they passed the day alone with their dead, in anguish; and at last thought came back to Zara. She would go to her uncle, and let him help to settle things; she could count upon him to do that.

Francis Markrute, anxious and disturbed by Tristram's message and her absence, met her as she came in and drew her into the library.

The butler had handed her her husband's note, but she held it listlessly in her hand, without opening it. She was still too numb with sorrow to take notice of ordinary things. Her uncle saw immediately that something terrible had happened.

"Zara, dear child," he said, and folded her in his arms with affectionate kindness, "tell me everything."

She was past tears now, but her voice sounded strange with the tragedy in it.

"Mirko is dead, Uncle Francis," was all she said. "He ran away from Bournemouth because Agatha, the Morleys' child, broke his violin. He loved it, you know *Maman* had given it to him. He came in the night, all alone, ill with fever, to find his father, and he broke a blood vessel this morning, and died in my arms--there, in the poor lodging."

Francis Markrute had drawn her to the sofa now, and stroked her hands. He was deeply moved.

"My poor, dear child! My poor Zara!" he said.

Then, with most pathetic entreaty she went on,

"Oh, Uncle Francis, can't you forgive poor Mimo, now? *Maman* is dead and Mirko is dead, and if you ever, some day, have a child yourself, you may know what this poor father is suffering. Won't you help us? He is foolish always--unpractical--and he is distracted with grief. You are so strong--won't you see about the funeral for my little love?"

"Of course I will, dear girl," he answered. "You must have no more distresses. Leave everything to me." And he bent and kissed her white cheek, while he tenderly began to remove the pins from her fur toque.

"Thank you," she said gently, as she took the hat from his hand, and laid it beside her. "I grieve because I loved him--my dear little brother. His soul was all music, and there was no room for him here. And oh! I loved *Maman* so! But I know that it is better as it is; he is safe there, with her now, far away from all his pain. He saw her when he was dying." Then after a pause she went on: "Uncle Francis, you love Ethelrida very much, don't you? Try to look back and think how *Maman* loved Mimo, and he loved her. Think of all the sorrow of her life, and the great, great price she paid for her love; and then, when you see him--poor Mimo--try to be merciful."

And Francis Markrute suddenly felt a lump in his throat. The whole pitiful memory of his beloved sister stabbed him, and extinguished the last remnant of rancor towards her lover, which had smoldered always in his proud heart.

There was a moisture in his clever eyes, and a tremulous note in his cold voice as he answered his niece:

"Dear child, we will forget and forgive everything. My one thought about it all now, is to do whatever will bring you comfort."

"There is one thing--yes," she said, and there was the first look of life in her face. "Mirko, when I saw him last at Bournemouth, played to me a wonderful air; he said *Maman* always came back to him in his dreams when he was ill--feverish, you know--and that she had taught it to him. It talks of the woods where she is, and beautiful butterflies; there is a blue one for her, and a little white one for him. He wrote out the score--it is so joyous--and I have it. Will you send it to Vienna or Paris, to some great artist, and get it really arranged, and then when I play it we shall always be able to see *Maman*."

And the moisture gathered again in Francis Markrute's eyes.

"Oh, my dear!" he said. "Will you forgive me some day for my hardness, for my arrogance to you both? I never knew, I never understood--until lately--what love could mean in a life. And you, Zara, yourself, dear child, can nothing be done for you and Tristram?"

At the mention of her husband's name Zara looked up, startled; and then a deeper tragedy than ever gathered in her eyes, as she rose.

"Let us speak of that no more, my uncle," she said. "Nothing can be done, because his love for me is dead. I killed it myself, in my ignorance. Nothing you or I can do is of any avail now--it is all too late."

And Francis Markrute could not speak. Her ignorance had been his fault, his only mistake in calculation, because he had played with souls as pawns in those days before love had softened him. And she made him no reproaches, when that past action of his had caused the finish of her life's happiness! Verily, his niece was a noble woman, and, with deepest homage, as he led her to the door he bent down and kissed her forehead; and no one in the world who knew him would have believed that she felt it wet with tears.

When she got to her room she remembered she still carried some note, and she at last looked at the superscription. It was in Tristram's writing. In spite of her grief and her numbness to other things it gave her a sharp emotion. She opened it quickly and read its few cold words. Then it seemed as if her knees gave way under her, as at Montfitchet that day when Laura Highford had made her jealous. She could not think clearly, nor fully understand their meaning; only one point stood out distinctly. He must see her to arrange for their separation. He had grown to hate her so much, then, that he could not any longer even live in the house with her, and all her grief of the day seemed less than this thought. Then she read it again. He knew all? Who could have told him? Her Uncle Francis? No, he did not himself know that Mirko was dead until she had told him. This was a mystery, but it was unimportant. Her numb brain could not grasp it yet. The main thing was that he was very angry with her for her deception of him: that, perhaps, was what was causing him finally to part from her. How strange it was that she was always punished for keeping her word and acting up to her principles! She did not think this bitterly, only with utter hopelessness. There was no use in her trying any longer; happiness was evidently not meant for her. She must just accept things--and life, or death, as it came. But how hard men were--she could never be so stern to any one for such a little fault, for *any* fault--stern and unforgiving as that strange God who wrote the Commandments.

And then she felt her cheeks suddenly burn, and yet she shivered; and when her maid came to her, presently, she saw that her mistress was not only deeply grieved, but ill, too. So she put her quickly to bed, and then went down to see Mr. Markrute.

"I think we must have a doctor, monsieur," she said. "Miladi is not at all well."

And Francis Markrute, deeply distressed, telephoned at once for his physician.

His betrothed had gone back to the country after luncheon, so he could not even have the consolation of her sympathy, and where Tristram was he did not know.

For the four following days Zara lay in her bed, seriously ill. She had caught a touch of influenza the eminent physician said, and had evidently had a most severe shock as well. But she was naturally so splendidly healthy that, in spite of grief and hopelessness, the following Thursday she was able to get up again. Francis Markrute thought her illness had been merciful in a way because the funeral had all been got over while she was confined to her room. Zara had accepted everything without protest. She had not desired even to see Mirko once more. She had no morbid fancies; it was his soul she loved and remembered, not the poor little suffering body.

It came to her as a comfort that her uncle and Mimo had met and shaken hands in forgiveness, and now poor Mimo was coming to say good-bye to her that afternoon.

He was leaving England at once, and would return to his own country and his people. In his great grief, and with no further ties, he hoped they would receive him. He had only one object now in life--to get through with it and join those he loved in some happier sphere.

This was the substance of what he said to Zara when he came; and they kissed and blessed one another, and parted, perhaps for ever. The "Apache" and the "London Fog," which would never be finished now he feared--the pain would be too great--would be sent to her to keep as a remembrance of their years of life together and the deep ties that bound them by the memory of those two graves.

And Zara in her weakness had cried for a long time after he had left.

And then she realized that all that part of her life was over now, and the outlook of what was to come held out no hope.

Francis Markrute had telegraphed to Wrayth, to try and find Tristram, but he was not there. He had not gone there at all. At the last moment he could not face it, he felt; he must go somewhere away alone--by the sea. A great storm was coming on--it suited his mood--so he had left even his servant in London and had gone off to a wild place on the Dorsetshire coast that he knew of, and there heard no news of any one. He would go back on the Friday, and see Zara the next day, as he had said he would do. Meanwhile he must fight his ghosts alone. And what ghosts they were!

Now on this Saturday morning Francis Markrute was obliged to leave his niece. His vast schemes required his attention in Berlin and he would be gone for a week, and then was going down to Montfitchet. Ethelrida had written Zara the kindest letters. Her fiance had told her all the pitiful story, and now she understood the tragedy in Zara's eyes, and loved her the more for her silence and her honor.

But all these thoughts seemed to be things of naught to the sad recipient of her letters, since the one and only person who mattered now in her life knew, also, and held different ones. He was aware of all, and had no sympathy or pity--only blame--for her. And now that her health was better and she was able to think, this ceaseless question worried her; how could Tristram possibly have known all? Had he followed her? As soon as she would be allowed to go out she would go and see Jenny, and question her.

And Tristram, by the wild sea--the storm like his mood had lasted all the time--came eventually to some conclusions. He would return and see his wife and tell her that now they must part, that he knew of her past and he would trouble her no more. He would not make her any reproaches, for of what use? And, besides, she had suffered enough. He would go abroad at once, and see his mother for a day at Cannes, and tell her his arrangements, and that Zara and he had agreed to part-- he would give her no further explanations--and then he would go on to India and

Japan. And, after this, his plans were vague. It seemed as if life were too impossible to look ahead, but not until he could think of Zara with calmness would he return to England.

And if Zara's week of separation from him had been grief and suffering, his had been hell.

On the Saturday morning, after her uncle had started for Dover, a note, sent by hand, was brought to Zara. It was again only a few words, merely to say if it was convenient to her, he--Tristram--would come at two o'clock, as he was motoring down to Wrayth at three, and was leaving England on Monday night.

Her hand trembled too much to write an answer.

"Tell the messenger I will be here," she said; and she sat then for a long time, staring in front of her.

Then a thought came to her. Whether she were well enough or no she must go and question Jenny. So, to the despair of her maid, she wrapped herself in furs and started. She felt extremely faint when she got into the air, but her will pulled her through, and when she got there the little servant put her doubts at rest.

Yes, a very tall, handsome gentleman had come a few minutes after herself, and she had taken him up, thinking he was the doctor.

"Why, missus," she said, "he couldn't have stayed a minute. He come away while the Count was playin' his fiddle."

So this was how it was! Her thoughts were all in a maze: she could not reason. And when she got back to the Park Lane house she felt too feeble to go any further, even to the lift.

Her maid came and took her furs from her, and she lay on the library sofa, after Henriette had persuaded her to have a little chicken broth; and then she fell into a doze, and was awakened only by the sound of the electric bell. She knew it was her husband coming, and sat up, with a wildly beating heart. Her trembling limbs would not support her as she rose for his entrance, and she held on by the back of a chair.

And, grave and pale with the torture he had been through, Tristram came into the room.

CHAPTER XLI

He stopped dead short when he saw her so white and fragile looking. Then he exclaimed, "Zara--you have been ill!"

"Yes," she faltered.

"Why did they not tell me?" he said hurriedly, and then recollected himself. How could they? No one, not even his servant, knew where he had been.

She dropped back unsteadily on the sofa.

"Uncle Francis did telegraph to you, to Wrayth, but you were not there," she said.

He bit his lips--he was so very moved. How was he to tell her all the things he had come to say so coldly, with her looking so pitiful, so gentle? His one longing was to take her to his heart and comfort her, and make her forget all pain.

And she was so afraid of her own weakness, she felt she could not bear to hear her death-knell, yet. If she could only gain a little time! It was characteristic of her that she never dreamed of defending herself. She still had not the slightest idea that he suspected Mimo of being her lover. Tristram's anger with her was just because he was an Englishman--very straight and simple--who could brook no deception! that is what she thought.

If she had not been so lately and so seriously ill--if all her fine faculties had been in their full vigor--perhaps some idea might have come to her; but her soul was so completely pure it did not naturally grasp such things, so even that is doubtful.

"Tristram--" she said, and there was the most piteous appeal in her tones, which almost brought the tears to his eyes. "Please--I know you are angry with me for not telling you about Mirko and Mimo, but I had promised not to, and the poor, little one is dead. I will tell you everything presently, if you wish, but don't ask me to now. Oh! if you must go from me soon--you know best--I will not keep you, but-

-but please won't you take me with you to-day--back to Wrayth--just until I get quite well? My uncle is away, and I am so lonely, and I have not any one else on earth."

Her eyes had a pleading, frightened look, like a child's who is afraid to be left alone in the dark.

He could not resist her. And, after all, her sin was of long ago--she could have done nothing since she had been his wife--why should she not come to Wrayth? She could stay there if she wished, for a while after he had gone. Only one thing he must know.

"Where is Count Sykypri?" he asked hoarsely.

"Mimo has gone away, back to his own country," she said simply, wondering at his tone. "Alas! I shall perhaps never see him again."

A petrifying sensation of astonishment crept over Tristram. With all her meek gentleness she had still the attitude of a perfectly innocent person. It must be because she was only half English, and foreigners perhaps had different points of reasoning on all such questions.

The man had gone, then--out of her life. Yes, he would take her back to Wrayth if it would be any comfort to her.

"Will you get ready now?" he said, controlling his voice into a note of sternness which he was far from feeling. "Because I am sure you ought not to be out late in the damp air. I was going in the open car, and to drive myself, and it takes four hours. The closed one is not in London, as you know." And then he saw she was not fit for this, so he said anxiously, "But are you sure you ought to travel to-day at all? You look so awfully pale."

For there was a great difference in her present transparent, snowy whiteness, with the blue-circled eyes, to her habitual gardenia hue; even her lips were less red.

"Yes, yes, I am quite able to go," she said, rising to show him she was all right. "I will be ready in ten minutes. Henriette can come by train with my things." And she walked towards the door, which he held open for her. And here she paused, and then went on to the lift. He followed her quickly.

"Are you sure you can go up alone?" he asked anxiously. "Or may I come?"

"Indeed, I am quite well," she answered, with a little pathetic smile. "I will not trouble you. Wait, I shall not be long." And so she went up.

And when she came down again, all wrapped in her furs, she found Tristram had port wine ready for her, poured out.

"You must drink this--a big glass of it," he said; and she took it without a word.

Then when they got to the door she found instead of his own open motor he had ordered one of her uncle's closed ones, which with footwarmer and cushions was waiting, so that she should be comfortable and not catch further cold.

"Thank you--that is kind of you," she said.

He helped her in, and the butler tucked the fur rug over them, while Tristram settled the cushions. Then she leaned back for a second and closed her eyes--everything was going round.

He was very troubled about her. She must have been very ill, even in the short time--and then her grief,--for, even though she had been so much separated from it, a mother always loves her child. Then this thought hurt him again. He hated to remember about the child.

She lay there back against the pillows until they had got quite out of London, without speaking a word. The wine in her weak state made her sleepy, and she gradually fell into a doze, and her head slipped sideways and rested against Tristram's shoulder, and it gave him a tremendous thrill--her beautiful, proud head with its thick waves of hair showing under her cap.

He was going to leave her so soon, and she would not know it--she was asleep--he must just hold her to him a little; she would be more comfortable like that. So, with cautious care not to wake her, he slipped his arm under the cushion, and very gently and gradually drew her into his embrace, so that her unconscious head rested upon his breast.

And thus more than two hours of the journey were accomplished.

And what thoughts coursed through his brain as they went!

He loved her so madly. What did it matter how she had sinned? She was ill and lonely, and must stay in his arms--just for to-day. But he could never really take her to his heart--the past was too terrible for that. And, besides, she did not love him; this gentleness was only because she was weak and crushed, for the time. But how terribly, bitterly sweet it was, all the same! He had the most overpowering temptation to kiss her, but he resisted it; and presently, when they came to a level crossing and a train gave a wild whistle, she woke with a start. It was quite dark now, and she said, in a frightened voice, "Where am I? Where have I been?"

Tristram slipped his arm from round her instantly, and turned on the light.

"You are in the motor, going to Wrayth," he said. "And I am glad to say you have been asleep. It will do you good."

She rubbed her eyes.

"Ah! I was dreaming. And Mirko was there, too, with *Maman*, and we were so happy!" she said, as if to herself.

Tristram winced.

"Are we near home--I mean, Wrayth?" she asked.

"Not quite yet," he answered. "There will be another hour and a half."

"Need we have the light on?" she questioned. "It hurts my eyes."

He put it out, and there they sat in the growing darkness, and did not speak any more for some time; and, bending over her, he saw that she had dozed off again. How very weak she must have been!

He longed to take her into his arms once more, but did not like to disturb her--she seemed to have fallen into a comfortable position among the pillows--so he watched over her tenderly, and presently they came to the lodge gates of Wrayth, and the stoppage caused her to wake and sit up.

"It seems I had not slept for so long," she said, "and now I feel better. It is good of you to let me come with you. We are in the park, are we not?"

"Yes, we shall be at the door in a minute."

And then she cried suddenly,

"Oh! look at the deer!" For a bold and valiant buck, startled and indignant at the motor lights, was seen, for an instant, glaring at them as they flashed past.

"You must go to bed as soon as you have had some tea," Tristram said, "after this long drive. It is half-past six. I telegraphed to have a room prepared for you. Not that big state apartment you had before, but one in the other part of the house, where we live when we are alone; and I thought you would like your maid next you, as you have been ill."

"Thank you," she whispered quite low.

How kind and thoughtful he was being to her! She was glad she had been ill!

Then they arrived at the door, and this time they turned to the left before they got to the Adam's hall, and went down a corridor to the old paneled rooms, and into his own sitting-room where it was all warm and cozy, and the tea-things were laid out. She already looked better for her sleep; some of the bluish transparency seemed to have left her face.

She had not been into this room on her inspection of the house. She liked it best of all, with its scent of burning logs and good cigars. And Jake snorted by the fire with pleasure to see his master, and she bent and patted his head.

But everything she did was filling Tristram with fresh bitterness and pain. To be so sweet and gentle now when it was all too late!

He began opening his letters until the tea came. There were the telegrams from Francis Markrute, sent a week before to say Zara was ill, and many epistles from friends. And at the end of the pile he found a short note from Francis Markrute, as well. It was written the day before, and said that he supposed he, Tristram, would get it eventually; that Zara had had a very sad bereavement which he felt sure she would rather tell him about herself, and that he trusted, seeing how very sad and ill she had been, that Tristram would be particularly kind to her. So her uncle knew, then! This was incredible: but perhaps Zara had told him, in her first grief.

He glanced up at her; she was lying back in a great leather chair now, looking so fragile and weary, he could not say what he intended. Then Jake rose leisurely and put his two fat forepaws up on her knees and snorted as was his habit when he approved of any one. And she bent down and kissed his broad wrinkles.

It all looked so homelike and peaceful! Suddenly scorching tears came into Tristram's eyes and he rose abruptly, and walked to the window. And at that moment the servants brought the teapot and the hot scones.

She poured the tea out silently, and then she spoke a little to Jake, just a few silly, gentle words about his preference for cakes or toast. She was being perfectly adorable, Tristram thought, with her air of pensive, subdued sorrow, and her clinging black dress.

He wished she would suggest going to her room. He could not bear it much longer.

She wondered why he was so restless. And he certainly was changed; he looked haggard and unhappy, more so even than before. And then she remembered how radiantly strong and splendid he had appeared, at dinner on their wedding night, and a lump rose in her throat.

"Henriette will have arrived by now," she said in a few minutes. "If you will tell me where it is I will go to my room."

He got up, and she followed him.

"I expect you will find it is the blue, Chinese damask one just at the top of these little stairs." Then he strode on in front of her quickly, and called out from the top, "Yes, it is, and your maid is here."

And as she came up the low, short steps, they met on the turn, and stopped.

"Good night," he said. "I will have some soup and suitable things for an invalid sent up to you; and then you must sleep well, and not get up in the morning. I shall be very busy to-morrow. I have a great many things to do before I go on Monday. I am going away for a long time."

She held on to the banisters for a minute, but the shadows were so deceiving, with all the black oak, that he was not sure what her expression said. Her words were a very low "Thank you--I will try to sleep. Good night."

And she went up to her room, and Tristram went on, downstairs--a deeper ache than ever in his heart.

CHAPTER XLII

It was not until luncheon time that Zara came down, next day. She felt he did not wish to see her, and she lay there in her pretty, old, quaint room, and thought of many things, and the wreck of their lives, above all. And she thought of Mirko and her mother, and the tears came to her eyes. But that grief was past, in its bitterness; she knew it was much better so.

The thought of Tristram's going tore her very soul, and swallowed up all other grief.

"I cannot, cannot bear it!" she moaned to herself.

He was sitting gazing into the fire, when she timidly came into his sitting-room. She had been too unhappy to sleep much and was again looking very pale.

He seemed to speak to her like one in a dream. He was numb with his growing misery and the struggle in his mind: he must leave her--the situation was unendurable--he could not stay, because in her present softened mood it was possible that if he lost control of himself and caressed her she might yield to him; and, then, he knew no resolutions on earth could hold him from taking her to his heart. And she must never really be his wife. The bliss of it might be all that was divine at first, but there would be always the hideous skeleton beneath, ready to peep out and mock at them: and then if they should have children? They were both so young that would be sure to happen; and this thought, which had once, in that very room, in his happy musings, given him so much joy, now caused him to quiver with extra pain. For a woman with such a background should not be the mother of a Tancred of Wrayth.

Tristram was no Puritan, but the ingrained pride in his old name he could not eliminate from his blood. So he kept himself with an iron reserve. He never once looked at her, and spoke as coldly as ice; and they got through luncheon. And Zara said, suddenly, she would like to go to church.

It was at three o'clock, so he ordered the motor without a word. She was not well enough to walk there through the park.

He could not let her go alone, so he changed his plans and went with her. They did not speak, all the way.

She had never been into the church before, and was struck with the fine windows, and the monuments of the Guiscards, and the famous tomb of the Crusader in the wall of the chancel pew where they sat; and all through the service she gazed at his carven face, so exactly like Tristram's, with the same, stern look.

And a wild, miserable rebellion filled her heart, and then a cold fear; and she passionately prayed to God to protect him. For what if he should go on some dangerous hunting expedition, and something should happen, and she should never see him again! And then, as she stood while they sang the final hymn, she stopped and caught her breath with a sob. And Tristram glanced at her in apprehension, and he wondered if he should have to suffer anything further, or if his misery were at its height.

The whole congregation were so interested to see the young pair, and they had to do some handshakings, as they came out. What would all these good people think, Tristram wondered with bitter humor, when they heard that he had gone away on a long tour, leaving his beautiful bride alone, not a month after their marriage? But he was past caring what they thought, one way or another, now.

Zara went to her room when they got back to the house, and when she came down to tea he was not there, and she had hers alone with Jake.

She felt almost afraid to go to dinner. It was so evident he was avoiding her. And while she stood undecided her maid brought in a note:

"I ask you not to come down--I cannot bear it. I will see you to-morrow morning, before I go, if you will come to my sitting-room at twelve."

That was all.

And, more passionately wretched than she had ever been in her life, she went to bed.

She used the whole strength of her will to control herself next morning. She must not show any emotion, no matter how she should feel. It was not that she had any pride left, or would not have willingly fallen into his arms; but she felt no woman could do so, unsolicited and when a man plainly showed her he held her in disdain.

So it was, with both their hearts breaking, they met in the sitting-room.

"I have only ten minutes," he said constrainedly. "The motor is at the door. I have to go round by Bury St. Edmunds; it is an hour out of my way, and I must be in London at five o'clock, as I leave for Paris by the night mail. Will you sit down, please, and I will be as brief as I can."

She fell, rather than sank, into a chair. She felt a singing in her ears; she must not faint--she was so very weak from her recent illness.

"I have arranged that you stay here at Wrayth until you care to make fresh arrangements for yourself," he began, averting his eyes, and speaking in a cold, passionless voice. "But if I can help it, after I leave here to-day I will never see you again. There need be no public scandal; it is unnecessary that people should be told anything; they can think what they like. I will explain to my mother that the marriage was a mistake and we have agreed to part--that is all. And you can live as you please and I will do the same. I do not reproach you for the ruin you have brought upon my life. It was my own fault for marrying you so heedlessly. But I loved you so--!" And then his voice broke suddenly with a sob, and he stretched out his arms wildly.

"My God!" he cried, "I am punished! The agony of it is that I love you still, with all my soul--even though I saw them with my own eyes--your lover and--your child!"

Here Zara gave a stifled shriek, and, as he strode from the room not daring to look at her for fear of breaking his resolution, she rose unsteadily to her feet and tried to call him. But she gasped and no words would come. Then she fell back unconscious in the chair.

He did not turn round, and soon he was in the motor and gliding away as though the hounds of hell were after him, as, indeed, they were, from the mad pain in his heart.

And when Zara came to herself it was half an hour later, and he was many miles away.

She sat up and found Jake licking her hands.

Then remembrance came back. He was gone--and he loved her even though he thought her--that!

She started to her feet. The blood rushed back to her brain. She must act.

She stared around, dazed for a moment, and then she saw the time tables--the Bradshaw and the A.B.C. She turned over the leaves of the latter with feverish haste. Yes, there was a train which left at 2:30 and got to London at half-past five; it was a slow one--the express which started at 3:30, did not get in until nearly six. That might be too late--both might be too late, but she must try. Then she put her hand to her head in agony. She did not know where he had gone. Would he go to his mother's, or to his old rooms in St. James's Street? She did not know their number.

She rang the bell and asked that Michelham should come to her.

The old servant saw her ghastly face, and knew from Higgins that his master intended going to Paris that night. He guessed some tragedy had happened between them, and longed to help.

"Michelham," she said, "his lordship has gone to London. Do you know to what address? I must follow him--it is a matter of life and death that I see him before he starts for Paris. Order my motor for the 2:30 train--it is quicker than to go by car all the way."

"Yes, my lady," Michelham said. "Everything will be ready. His lordship has gone to his rooms, 460 St. James's Street. May I accompany your ladyship? His lordship would not like your ladyship to travel alone."

"Very well," she said. "There is no place anywhere, within driving distance that I could catch a train that got in before, is there?"

"No, my lady; that will be the soonest," he said. "And will your ladyship please to eat some luncheon? There is an hour before the motor will be round. I know your ladyship's own footman, James, should go with your ladyship, but if it is something serious, as an old servant, and, if I may say so, a humble and devoted friend of his lordship's, I would beg to accompany your ladyship instead."

"Yes, yes, Michelham," said Zara, and hurried from the room.

She sent a telegram when at last she reached the station--to the St. James's Street rooms.

"What you thought was not true. Do not leave until I come and explain. I am your own Zara."

Then the journey began--three hours of agony, with the constant stoppages, and the one thought going over and over in her brain. He believed she had a lover and a child, and yet he loved her! Oh, God! That was love, indeed!--and she might not be in time.

But at last they arrived--Michelham and she--and drove to Tristram's rooms.

Yes, his lordship had been expected at five, but had not arrived yet; he was late. And Michelham explained that Lady Tancred had come, and would wait, while he himself went round to Park Lane to see if Lord Tancred had been there.

He made up a splendid fire in the sitting-room, and, telling Higgins not to go in and disturb her even with tea, the kind old man started on his quest--much anxiety in his mind.

Ten minutes passed, and Zara felt she could hardly bear the suspense. The mad excitement had kept her up until now. What if he were so late that he went straight to the train? But then she remembered it went at nine--and it was only six. Yes, he would surely come.

She did not stir from her chair, but her senses began to take in the room. How comfortable it was, and what good taste, even with the evidences of coming departure about! She had seen two or three telegrams lying on the little hall table, waiting for him, as she came in--hers among the number, she supposed. A motor stopped, surely!--Ah! if it should be he! But there were hundreds of such noises in St. James's Street, and it was too dark and foggy to see. She sat still, her heart beating in her throat. Yes, there was the sound of a latch key turning in the lock! And, after stopping to pick up his telegrams, Tristram, all unexpecting to see any one, entered the room.

She rose unsteadily to meet him, as he gave an exclamation of surprise and--yes--pain.

"Tristram!" she faltered. It seemed as if her voice had gone again, and the words would make no sound. But she gathered her strength, and, with pitiful pleading, stretched out her arms.

"Tristram--I have come to tell you--I have never had a lover: Mimo was at last married to *Maman*. He was her lover, and Mirko was their child--my little brother. My uncle did not wish me to tell you this for a time, because it was the family disgrace." Then, as he made a step forward to her, with passionate joy in his face, she went on:

"Tristram! You said, that night--before you would ever ask me to be your wife again, I must go down upon my knees--See--I do!--for Oh!--I love you!" And suddenly she bent and knelt before him, and bowed her proud head.

But she did not stay in this position a second, for he clasped her in his arms, and rained mad, triumphant kisses upon her beautiful, curved lips, while he murmured,

"At last--my Love--my own!"

*   *   *   *   *

Then when the delirium of joy had subsided a little,--with what tenderness he took off her hat and furs, and drew her into his arms, on the sofa before the fire.--The superlative happiness to feel her resting there, unresisting, safe in his fond embrace, with those eyes, which had been so stormy and resentful, now melting upon him in softest passion.

It seemed heaven to them both. They could not speak coherent sentences for a while--just over and over again they told each other that they loved.--It seemed as if he could not hear her sweet confession often enough--or quench the thirst of his parched soul upon her lips.

Then the masterfulness in him which Zara now adored asserted itself. He must play with her hair! He must undo it, and caress its waves, to blot out all remembrance of how its forbidden beauty had tortured him.--And she just lay there in his arms, in one of her silences, only her eyes were slumberous with love.

But at last she said, nestling closer,

"Tristram, won't you listen to the story that I must tell you? I want there never to be any more mysteries between us again--"

And, to content her, he brought himself back to earth--

"Only I warn you, my darling," he said, "all such things are side issues for me now that at last we have obtained the only thing which really matters in life--we know that we love each other, and are not going to be so foolish as to part again for a single hour--if we can help it--for the rest of time."

And then his whole face lit up with radiant joy, and he suddenly buried it in her hair. "See," he inurmured, "I am to be allowed to play with this exquisite net to ensnare my heart; and you are not to be allowed to spend hours in state rooms--alone! Oh! darling! How can I listen to anything but the music of your whispers, when you tell me you love me and are my very own!"

Zara did, however, finally get him to understand the whole history from beginning to end. And when he heard of her unhappy life, and her mother's tragic story, and her sorrow and poverty, and her final reason for agreeing to the marriage, and how she thought of men, and then of him, and all her gradual awakening into this great love, there grew in him a reverent tenderness.

"Oh! my sweet--my sweet!" he said. "And I dared to be suspicious of you and doubt you, it seems incredible now!"

Then he had to tell his story--of how reasonable his suspicions looked, and, in spite of them, of his increasing love. And so an hour passed with complete clearing up of all shadows, and they could tenderly smile together over the misunderstandings which had nearly caused them to ruin both their lives.

"And to think, Tristram," said Zara, "a little common sense would have made it all smooth!"

"No, it was not that," he answered fondly, with a whimsical smile in his eyes, "the troubles would never have happened at all if I had only not paid the least attention to your haughty words in Paris, nor even at Dover, but had just continued making love to you; all would have been well!--However," he added joyously, "we will forget dark things, because to-morrow I shall take you back to Wrayth, and we shall have our real honeymoon there in perfect peace."

And, as her lips met his, Zara whispered softly once more,

"Tu sais que je t'aime!"

*   *   *   *   *

Oh! the glorious joy of that second home-coming for the bridal pair! To walk to all Tristram's favorite haunts, to wander in the old rooms, and plan out their improvements, and in the late afternoons to sit in the firelight in his own sitting-room, and make pictures of their future joys together. Then he would tell her of his dreams, which once had seemed as if they must turn to Dead Sea fruit, but were now all bright and glowing with glad promise of fulfillment.

His passionate delight in her seemed as if it could not find enough expression, as he grew to know the cultivation of her mind and the pure thoughts of her soul.--And her tenderness to him was all the sweeter in its exquisite submission, because her general mien was so proud.

They realized they had found the greatest happiness in this world, and with the knowledge that they had achieved their desires, after anguish and pain, they held it next their hearts as heaven's gift.

And when they went to Montfitchet again, to spend that Christmas, the old Duke was satisfied!

*   *   *   *   *

Now, all this happened two years ago. And on the second anniversary of the Tancred wedding Mr. Francis and Lady Ethelrida Markrute dined with their nephew and niece.

And when they came to drinking healths, bowing to Zara her uncle raised his glass and said,

"I propose a toast, that I prophesied I would, to you, my very dear niece--the toast of four supremely happy people!"

And as they drank, the four joined hands.

The Codes Of Hammurabi And Moses
W. W. Davies

QTY

The discovery of the Hammurabi Code is one of the greatest achievements of archaeology, and is of paramount interest, not only to the student of the Bible, but also to all those interested in ancient history...

Religion   **ISBN:** *1-59462-338-4*

Pages:132
MSRP $12.95

The Theory of Moral Sentiments
Adam Smith

QTY

This work from 1749. contains original theories of conscience amd moral judgment and it is the foundation for systemof morals.

Philosophy   ISBN: *1-59462-777-0*

Pages:536
MSRP $19.95

Jessica's First Prayer
Hesba Stretton

QTY

In a screened and secluded corner of one of the many railway-bridges which span the streets of London there could be seen a few years ago, from five o'clock every morning until half past eight, a tidily set-out coffee-stall, consisting of a trestle and board, upon which stood two large tin cans, with a small fire of charcoal burning under each so as to keep the coffee boiling during the early hours of the morning when the work-people were thronging into the city on their way to their daily toil...

Pages:84

Childrens   ISBN: *1-59462-373-2*   *MSRP $9.95*

My Life and Work
Henry Ford

QTY

Henry Ford revolutionized the world with his implementation of mass production for the Model T automobile. Gain valuable business insight into his life and work with his own auto-biography... "We have only started on our development of our country we have not as yet, with all our talk of wonderful progress, done more than scratch the surface. The progress has been wonderful enough but..."

Pages:300

Biographies/   ISBN: *1-59462-198-5*   *MSRP $21.95*

The Art of Cross-Examination
Francis Wellman

QTY

I presume it is the experience of every author, after his first book is published upon an important subject, to be almost overwhelmed with a wealth of ideas and illustrations which could readily have been included in his book, and which to his own mind, at least, seem to make a second edition inevitable. Such certainly was the case with me; and when the first edition had reached its sixth impression in five months, I rejoiced to learn that it seemed to my publishers that the book had met with a sufficiently favorable reception to justify a second and considerably enlarged edition. ...

Reference   **ISBN:** *1-59462-647-2*

Pages:412
MSRP $19.95

On the Duty of Civil Disobedience
Henry David Thoreau

QTY

Thoreau wrote his famous essay, On the Duty of Civil Disobedience, as a protest against an unjust but popular war and the immoral but popular institution of slave-owning. He did more than write—he declined to pay his taxes, and was hauled off to gaol in consequence. Who can say how much this refusal of his hastened the end of the war and of slavery ?

Law   **ISBN:** *1-59462-747-9*

Pages:48
MSRP $7.45

Dream Psychology Psychoanalysis for Beginners
Sigmund Freud

QTY

Sigmund Freud, born Sigismund Schlomo Freud (May 6, 1856 - September 23, 1939), was a Jewish-Austrian neurologist and psychiatrist who co-founded the psychoanalytic school of psychology. Freud is best known for his theories of the unconscious mind, especially involving the mechanism of repression; his redefinition of sexual desire as mobile and directed towards a wide variety of objects; and his therapeutic techniques, especially his understanding of transference in the therapeutic relationship and the presumed value of dreams as sources of insight into unconscious desires.

Psychology   **ISBN:** *1-59462-905-6*

Pages:196
MSRP $15.45

The Miracle of Right Thought
Orison Swett Marden

QTY

Believe with all of your heart that you will do what you were made to do. When the mind has once formed the habit of holding cheerful, happy, prosperous pictures, it will not be easy to form the opposite habit. It does not matter how improbable or how far away this realization may see, or how dark the prospects may be, if we visualize them as best we can, as vividly as possible, hold tenaciously to them and vigorously struggle to attain them, they will gradually become actualized, realized in the life. But a desire, a longing without endeavor, a yearning abandoned or held indifferently will vanish without realization.

Self Help   **ISBN:** *1-59462-644-8*

Pages:360
MSRP $25.45

QTY

☐ **The Rosicrucian Cosmo-Conception Mystic Christianity** *by Max Heindel* ISBN: *1-59462-188-8* **$38.95**
The Rosicrucian Cosmo-conception is not dogmatic, neither does it appeal to any other authority than the reason of the student. It is: not controversial, but is: sent forth in the, hope that it may help to clear...
New Age/Religion Pages 646

☐ **Abandonment To Divine Providence** *by Jean-Pierre de Caussade* ISBN: *1-59462-228-0* **$25.95**
"The Rev. Jean Pierre de Caussade was one of the most remarkable spiritual writers of the Society of Jesus in France in the 18th Century. His death took place at Toulouse in 1751. His works have gone through many editions and have been republished...
Inspirational/Religion Pages 400

☐ **Mental Chemistry** *by Charles Haanel* ISBN: *1-59462-192-6* **$23.95**
Mental Chemistry allows the change of material conditions by combining and appropriately utilizing the power of the mind. Much like applied chemistry creates something new and unique out of careful combinations of chemicals the mastery of mental chemistry...
New Age Pages 354

☐ **The Letters of Robert Browning and Elizabeth Barret Barrett 1845-1846 vol II** ISBN: *1-59462-193-4* **$35.95**
by Robert Browning and Elizabeth Barrett
Biographies Pages 596

☐ **Gleanings In Genesis (volume I)** *by Arthur W. Pink* ISBN: *1-59462-130-6* **$27.45**
Appropriately has Genesis been termed "the seed plot of the Bible" for in it we have, in germ form, almost all of the great doctrines which are afterwards fully developed in the books of Scripture which follow...
Religion/Inspirational Pages 420

☐ **The Master Key** *by L. W. de Laurence* ISBN: *1-59462-001-6* **$30.95**
In no branch of human knowledge has there been a more lively increase of the spirit of research during the past few years than in the study of Psychology, Concentration and Mental Discipline. The requests for authentic lessons in Thought Control, Mental Discipline and... New Age/Business Pages 422

☐ **The Lesser Key Of Solomon Goetia** *by L. W. de Laurence* ISBN: *1-59462-092-X* **$9.95**
This translation of the first book of the "Lernegton" which is now for the first time made accessible to students of Talismanic Magic was done, after careful collation and edition, from numerous Ancient Manuscripts in Hebrew, Latin, and French...
New Age/Occult Pages 92

☐ **Rubaiyat Of Omar Khayyam** *by Edward Fitzgerald* ISBN:*1-59462-332-5* **$13.95**
Edward Fitzgerald, whom the world has already learned, in spite of his own efforts to remain within the shadow of anonymity, to look upon as one of the rarest poets of the century, was born at Bredfield, in Suffolk, on the 31st of March, 1809. He was the third son of John Purcell... Music Pages 172

☐ **Ancient Law** *by Henry Maine* ISBN: *1-59462-128-4* **$29.95**
The chief object of the following pages is to indicate some of the earliest ideas of mankind, as they are reflected in Ancient Law, and to point out the relation of those ideas to modern thought.
Religiom/History Pages 452

☐ **Far-Away Stories** *by William J. Locke* ISBN: *1-59462-129-2* **$19.45**
"Good wine needs no bush, but a collection of mixed vintages does. And this book is just such a collection. Some of the stories I do not want to remain buried for ever in the museum files of dead magazine-numbers an author's not unpardonable vanity..." Fiction Pages 272

☐ **Life of David Crockett** *by David Crockett* ISBN: *1-59462-250-7* **$27.45**
"Colonel David Crockett was one of the most remarkable men of the times in which he lived. Born in humble life, but gifted with a strong will, an indomitable courage, and unremitting perseverance...
Biographies/New Age Pages 424

☐ **Lip-Reading** *by Edward Nitchie* ISBN: *1-59462-206-X* **$25.95**
Edward B. Nitchie, founder of the New York School for the Hard of Hearing, now the Nitchie School of Lip-Reading, Inc, wrote "LIP-READING Principles and Practice". The development and perfecting of this meritorious work on lip-reading was an undertaking... How-to Pages 400

☐ **A Handbook of Suggestive Therapeutics, Applied Hypnotism, Psychic Science** ISBN: *1-59462-214-0* **$24.95**
by Henry Munro
Health/New Age/Health/Self-help Pages 376

☐ **A Doll's House: and Two Other Plays** *by Henrik Ibsen* ISBN: *1-59462-112-8* **$19.95**
Henrik Ibsen created this classic when in revolutionary 1848 Rome. Introducing some striking concepts in playwriting for the realist genre, this play has been studied the world over.
Fiction/Classics/Plays 308

☐ **The Light of Asia** *by sir Edwin Arnold* ISBN: *1-59462-204-3* **$13.95**
In this poetic masterpiece, Edwin Arnold describes the life and teachings of Buddha. The man who was to become known as Buddha to the world was born as Prince Gautama of India but he rejected the worldly riches and abandoned the reigns of power when... Religion/History/Biographies Pages 170

☐ **The Complete Works of Guy de Maupassant** *by Guy de Maupassant* ISBN: *1-59462-157-8* **$16.95**
"For days and days, nights and nights, I had dreamed of that first kiss which was to consecrate our engagement, and I knew not on what spot I should put my lips..."
Fiction/Classics Pages 240

☐ **The Art of Cross-Examination** *by Francis L. Wellman* ISBN: *1-59462-309-0* **$26.95**
Written by a renowned trial lawyer, Wellman imparts his experience and uses case studies to explain how to use psychology to extract desired information through questioning.
How-to/Science/Reference Pages 408

☐ **Answered or Unanswered?** *by Louisa Vaughan* ISBN: *1-59462-248-5* **$10.95**
Miracles of Faith in China
Religion Pages 112

☐ **The Edinburgh Lectures on Mental Science (1909)** *by Thomas* ISBN: *1-59462-008-3* **$11.95**
This book contains the substance of a course of lectures recently given by the writer in the Queen Street Hail, Edinburgh. Its purpose is to indicate the Natural Principles governing the relation between Mental Action and Material Conditions... New Age/Psychology Pages 148

☐ **Ayesha** *by H. Rider Haggard* ISBN: *1-59462-301-5* **$24.95**
Verily and indeed it is the unexpected that happens! Probably if there was one person upon the earth from whom the Editor of this, and of a certain previous history, did not expect to hear again...
Classics Pages 380

☐ **Ayala's Angel** *by Anthony Trollope* ISBN: *1-59462-352-X* **$29.95**
The two girls were both pretty, but Lucy who was twenty-one who supposed to be simple and comparatively unattractive, whereas Ayala was credited, as her Bombwhat romantic name might show, with poetic charm and a taste for romance. Ayala when her father died was nineteen... Fiction Pages 484

☐ **The American Commonwealth** *by James Bryce* ISBN: *1-59462-286-8* **$34.45**
An interpretation of American democratic political theory. It examines political mechanics and society from the perspective of Scotsman James Bryce
Politics Pages 572

☐ **Stories of the Pilgrims** *by Margaret P. Pumphrey* ISBN: *1-59462-116-0* **$17.95**
This book explores pilgrims religious oppression in England as well as their escape to Holland and eventual crossing to America on the Mayflower, and their early days in New England...
History Pages 268

QTY

The Fasting Cure *by Sinclair Upton*   ISBN: *1-59462-222-1*   **$13.95**
In the Cosmopolitan Magazine for May, 1910, and in the Contemporary Review (London) for April, 1910, I published an article dealing with my experiences in fasting. I have written a great many magazine articles, but never one which attracted so much attention... New Age/Self Help/Health Pages 164

Hebrew Astrology *by Sepharial*   ISBN: *1-59462-308-2*   **$13.45**
In these days of advanced thinking it is a matter of common observation that we have left many of the old landmarks behind and that we are now pressing forward to greater heights and to a wider horizon than that which represented the mind-content of our progenitors... Astrology Pages 144

Thought Vibration or The Law of Attraction in the Thought World   ISBN: *1-59462-127-6*   **$12.95**

by William Walker Atkinson   Psychology/Religion Pages 144

Optimism *by Helen Keller*   ISBN: *1-59462-108-X*   **$15.95**
Helen Keller was blind, deaf, and mute since 19 months old, yet famously learned how to overcome these handicaps, communicate with the world, and spread her lectures promoting optimism. An inspiring read for everyone... Biographies/Inspirational Pages 84

Sara Crewe *by Frances Burnett*   ISBN: *1-59462-360-0*   **$9.45**
In the first place, Miss Minchin lived in London. Her home was a large, dull, tall one, in a large, dull square, where all the houses were alike, and all the sparrows were alike, and where all the door-knockers made the same heavy sound... Childrens/Classic Pages 88

The Autobiography of Benjamin Franklin *by Benjamin Franklin*   ISBN: *1-59462-135-7*   **$24.95**
The Autobiography of Benjamin Franklin has probably been more extensively read than any other American historical work, and no other book of its kind has had such ups and downs of fortune. Franklin lived for many years in England, where he was agent... Biographies/History Pages 332

Name	
Email	
Telephone	
Address	
City, State ZIP	

☐ **Credit Card**   ☐ **Check / Money Order**

Credit Card Number	
Expiration Date	
Signature	

Please Mail to: Book Jungle
PO Box 2226
Champaign, IL 61825
or Fax to: *630-214-0564*

ORDERING INFORMATION

web: *www.bookjungle.com*
email: *sales@bookjungle.com*
fax: *630-214-0564*
mail: *Book Jungle PO Box 2226 Champaign, IL 61825*
or PayPal *to sales@bookjungle.com*

Please contact us for bulk discounts

DIRECT-ORDER TERMS

**20% Discount if You Order
Two or More Books**
Free Domestic Shipping!
Accepted: Master Card, Visa,
Discover, American Express

www.ingramcontent.com/pod-product-compliance
Lightning Source LLC
Chambersburg PA
CBHW080953020726
47505CB00009B/2189